The
Herringbone
Harbor Mystery

The Herringbone Harbor Mystery

Sally Goldenbaum

KENSINGTON PUBLISHING CORP.

kensingtonbooks.com

KENSINGTON BOOKS are published by

Kensington Publishing Corp.
900 Third Ave.
New York, NY 10022

All Kensington titles, imprints, and distributed lines are available at special quantity discounts for bulk purchases for sales promotion, premiums, fund-raising, educational, or institutional use. Special book excerpts or customized printings can also be created to fit specific needs. For details, write or phone the office of the Kensington Special Sales Manager: Attn. Special Sales Department, Kensington Publishing Corp., 900 Third Ave., New York, NY 10022. Phone: 1-800-221-2647.

Library of Congress Control Number: 2024940938

ISBN: 978-1-4967-4718-1
First Kensington Hardcover Edition: December 2024

ISBN: 978-1-4967-4720-4 (ebook)

10 9 8 7 6 5 4 3 2 1

Printed in the United States of America

For Don,
With love always

Cast for The Herringbone Harbor Mystery

The Seaside Knitters

Birdie Favazza (Bernadette): Sea Harbor's wealthy and wise octogenarian; widow of Sonny Favazza

Cass Halloran Brandley (Catherine): Co-owner of the Halloran Lobster Company; married to Danny Brandley; toddler son, Joey

Izzy Chambers Perry (Iz): Owner of the Sea Harbor Yarn Studio; married to Sam, award-winning photographer; their daughter, Abigail (Abby)

Nell Endicott: Retired nonprofit director; Izzy Perry's aunt; married to Ben Endicott, retired lawyer and family business owner

Friends and Townsfolk

Alex Arcado: Fire chief

Alphonso Santos: Wealthy Sea Harbor business owner; married to Liz Palazola Santos

Annabelle Palazola: Owner of the Sweet Petunia Restaurant; Liz Santos's mother

Archie and Harriet Brandley: Owners of Sea Harbor bookstore; Danny's parents

Beatrice Scaglia: Mayor of Sea Harbor

Bobby Palazola: Chef at the Lazy Lobster and Soup Café; twin sister, Bella

Daisy Danvers: Teenage dog walker; friends with Gabby

Ella and Harold Sampson: Birdie Favazza's housekeeper and groundskeeper

Elena Costa: Mother, and wife of Marco Costa

Elizabeth Hartley: Former school headmistress

Gabby (Gabrielle) Marietti: Birdie's teenage granddaughter
Gracie Santos: Owner of Lazy Lobster and Soup Café
Harry and Margaret Garozzo: Owners of Garozzo's Deli
Isabella (Bella) Palazola: Meteorologist; Bobby Palazola's twin sister
Jake Risso: Owner of the Gull Tavern
Jane and Ham Brewster: Founders of Canary Cove Art Colony
Jerry Thompson: Police chief
Liz Palazola Santos: Manager of the Sea Harbor Yacht Club
Lucky (Luigi) Bianchi: Birdie's godson; owner of Lucky's Place bar
MJ Arcado: Owner of MJ's Salon
Mae Anderson: Shop manager at Sea Harbor Yarn Studio
Marco Costa: Fisherman; married to Elena
Merry Jackson: Owner of the Artist's Palate Bar & Grill
Nick Cabot: Business owner
Pete Halloran: Cass's younger brother; co-owner of the Halloran Lobster Company
Tommy Porter: Police detective

Chapter 1

A week of rain had turned Sea Harbor into a garden of green. Even the bricks lining the streets in the neighborhood known to the locals as Fishermen's Village held a sheen of new life.

Nick Cabot felt the pleasant vibe as he stepped out on his deck. The morning was balmy, the sun a rosy haze over the water. Early summer or late spring. He wasn't sure. It was perfect.

From his deck, he could see the whole harbor, the huge houses along the eastern point on one end, the backs of taverns and restaurants and shops along Harbor Road on the other. The tops of small houses that cradled the cove shoreline, where mothers would soon be taking their young kids to swim.

And the place where he lived—Fishermen's Village, his birthplace and that of other Cabots before him—was where the history of Sea Harbor began to have roots.

It wasn't a real village, but it felt like it was to the fishermen families who lived in the neighborhood. Nick Cabot loved every inch of it.

Most of the homes in the neighborhood were small, but age

had finally taken its toll on the Cabots' small frame house, where Nick, his sister, and his dad, before them, were born. It was one of Nick Senior's final wishes that if the house was someday beyond repair, his son would keep the land, at least, and build something new. He'd done that, he thought.

He'd kept the spirit of the old: the old wooden table he and Nancy had carved names and hearts and comic figures into. The old milk box from his grandmother's days was fixed into a new kitchen wall. The sleeping porch had become a den, with eight panes in the bow window that looked over all his pop's favorite fishing spots. And his mom's candleholder collection? Candles and holders collected from the area's amazing artists had a home. *Finally. A home, at last.* Shelves built right into the wall with a glass door to keep them dust free. The whole house was wood and glass, open and airy. With a dock that he could still see his pop sitting on. It stretched out far into the waters, into the deep. Deep enough that his sailboat could anchor at the very end.

Noise below brought Nick's attention back to the beach. Two retired fishermen were lumbering along the narrow rocky span of beach between Nick's deck and the water. It was part of Cabot property, but that didn't seem to matter to anyone, least of all Nick.

One of the men spotted Nick and hollered up to him. "Hey, Nicko, whatta you doing, spying on us?"

"Spying on *you*? What's there to see, Wally?" Nick called back. "Couple old geezers, that's all I see."

Wally laughed, his belly moving beneath his stained POND ICE tee. "Hey, is it true what I've been hearing?"

"Probably not, Wally."

"Just heard a couple words yesterday in one of our fine establishments." He held up one arm and wagged a finger back and forth.

Nick laughed. "What fine place was that? The Pickled Plover?"

"Well, okay, yah, young man. Also down at the state pier. People talk."

"Well, you know what they say, Wally. All fishermen are liars."

Wally guffawed, too loudly, and Nick wondered how many neighbors were out on their decks, listening. He hoped Wally and his buddy Sly would hold back on the cusswords. Fishermen wives got up early.

"Anyway," Wally said, "*Mayor Cabot*. Those were the words, and I'm like, like, liking the sound of it, ya know? You'd be just like your granddad. Finest mayor we've ever had, I'd swear to it. It'd be great to have things come full circle like that. Nice and neat. I like things that way. Think about it, Nicko. It'd make your old man proud."

Nick laughed and looked at the other man, obviously the quieter of the two. "Hey, Sly, has this guy been drinking at this hour of the day? You need to take better care of him."

"Ah, none of that, Nicky. He's dry as a bone."

Nick laughed. "Just kidding you, Sly. But he's now all yours. You take this guy and his mouth out of my backyard, will you? He's going to wake the dead."

"You got it, Nicky boy. Matter of fact, we were just about to mosey along." He bent his arm and poked an elbow into Wally's side, nearly knocking him off balance. "This fool talks too much."

They both laughed and gave a wave. Nick waved back, watching the two men move on. He loved these old guys. And if he could bet on it, he'd bet they wouldn't go far.

He watched.

A few more yards took them to the step onto Nick's wide dock. They took the step, then ambled to the very end of the long dock, side by side.

He kept watching them—as good a way as any to start the day.

He knew exactly how it would play out. First they'd put their poles down on the deck floor. Next they'd arrange a couple of coolers side by side beside their rods, the smaller cooler filled with bait, and the other chilling an ample supply of Sam Adams, with maybe a couple of sardine sandwiches squeezed in between the cans. Finally they'd pull out two of Nick's short-legged folding chairs from a wooden chest, and they'd arrange their bodies in them, rocking side by side until they were comfortable. Then Nick would hear them sigh, maybe pull out a smoke, or sometimes not. And finally they'd get serious, throwing out their lines and hoping they'd catch a few. Maybe go home at the end of the day with a catch of striped bass or gray trout, enough for a decent dinner.

Often, when Nick and his dog came back from a morning run, they'd go over and talk to the old guys, listening to their exaggerated fish tales that seemed to gain weight and substance with each telling. Some of the stories included Nick's own father and grandfather—which maybe explained why they felt privy to Nick's property. His dad would have been down there with them—that was Nick's memory—a fisherman to the core.

A bark at the large glass door told him his dog had seen the fishermen. The goofy dog loved the old guys as much as he did.

He went over and opened the glass door, letting the dog out. "But you can't go down there, buddy. Your charming dog walkers will be here soon. Those old guys can't hold a candle to Daisy and Gabby."

As if he'd understood every word, Squid thumped his tail on the deck, then jumped up on a chaise lounge and settled down.

Nick carried his coffee mug over and sat on the chaise next to his dog, not sure which one of them was in charge.

His bare legs were hot from the sun, but cooled by the breeze. Nick watched the tide coming in, the shore disappearing, as mesmerizing as watching a fire. His morning meditation.

He picked up his phone and checked the calendar. Today: He'd head to the office in Ipswich and catch up on things. Then touch base with his friend Gracie Santos to help her with a couple tricky work issues that she was having at her Lazy Lobster and Soup Café. Hiring the wrong people can mess up a kitchen. It might be an easy fix.

A quick dinner at the Sea Harbor Yacht Club, to see his longtime friend Liz and her husband, Alphonso. And a trip to the Y to sweat out the idea of running for mayor. He was surprised it was already riding the gossip train. When approached by a few guys on the council, asking if he'd ever thought about running for mayor, he'd been honest. *No, never,* he'd said. But once the thought was in there, it had stayed.

The thought of having to convince people you were better, smarter, more qualified than someone else appealed to him about as much as eating octopus (about which he'd read many books and now abstained).

But in one ear, he could hear his pop saying, *Old Wally is wiser than he looks, Nicky. I'd be damn proud of you, son.*

Nicholas Cabot Senior had forgiven his son on many fronts: for not following the family tradition of going into fishing. At least, not exactly. Instead, he'd started a fishing supply company that was now all over the state, supplying hundreds of jobs. And he'd excused his son for not giving him grandbabies and carrying on the family name. At least, sort of.

He had lots of friends who were women. Sometimes who were more than just friends. But it was always comfortable. Until recently.

He pushed aside the thought that both parents might have known more than he did. But it refused to disappear completely.

Maybe it was his birthday. Some of his friends were moved by that landmark to get fancy cars or season tickets to the Celtics. But that wasn't what Nick was feeling. This was different. Unexpected. And he liked it. Love? He wondered, wishing his mom were alive to help him sort through his feelings. A partner for life?

A sudden bark broke through the morning quiet and scattered Nick's thoughts. He glanced at his watch, then swung his legs to the deck floor, pulling himself off the chaise. "Good dog," he said, realizing he hadn't needed a doorbell since the day he'd found the shaggy dog. The two had bonded like peanut butter and jelly, and Nick was secretly happy his honest pursuits to find the dog's owner failed. He was crazy about Squid, the name the dog had accepted politely when Nick pinned it on him.

"That will be your amazing dog walkers, pal," Nick said.

Squid barked, thumping his tail against the chaise, his gentle way of telling Nick to *move it.*

"Yeah, I know. You're one lucky mutt, you know that? Those two teens are making you the talk of the park—the whole neighborhood, in fact. If your luck holds out, you may even get to have more overnights with Gabby soon. I got the feeling your short stay over there was as comfortable as my time away was."

The dog followed Nick through the light-filled living area, with a fireplace filling one wall, and to the entryway. He got ready to leap as Nick opened the front door. But when the door opened, Nick's subdued greeting caused the dog's tail to still.

A man of average height and a muscular build stood on the doorstep. He wore running shorts and a Red Sox hat with a smiley face. The cap sat crookedly on a head of thick damp hair. The man's face was contorted in anger, turning his handsome looks into dangerous ones.

It was clearly not the vision Squid was expecting to see. The dog sat stiffly beside Nick.

"Hey, man, what's up?" Nick asked, surprised. "Want to come—"

"You scumbag," the man yelled, cutting off Nick's words, his face twisted in anger as he punctuated his insult with a clenched fist pounding the air. "What are you trying to do? Kill me? Kill her? Kill the restaurant? Can you sink any lower? You should be shot."

"Ouch," Nick said, grimacing. "Hey, bud, give it a rest. You're acting crazy."

His comment was met with a string of expletives, so loud they drowned out a lawn mower down the street.

Squid's body froze, his ears back. A low growl escaped from deep in his throat.

Nick took a step back as the man's closed fist moved closer to his face. It was then he noticed movement on the sidewalk: two sixteen-year-olds, standing next to his mailbox at the curb. They held water bottles and wore T-shirts declaring it was A PAWFECT DAY. A finely groomed poodle and another unidentifiable, but friendly-looking, dog sat beside them, the dogs' leashes dangling from the girls' hands.

One of the girls was standing with her mouth open, her eyes wide as she stared at the two men. The other seemed to be looking at a lawn mower racket down the street.

Nick took a deep breath, then waved to the dog walkers. *All was okay,* his wave assured them.

He looked back at the man in front of him and lowered his voice. "What the hell is going on with you, pal? Calm down. I don't have a clue what you're talking about. But whatever it is, you got it all wrong. She's fine. The place is fine. Or it will be. It'll all work out. I give my help to friends when it's needed. You know that as well as anyone. You'll both figure this out—"

"*Figure it out?* Figure *me* out, you mean. Once you ruin me and my reputation and succeed in driving me out of town? Is that how it'll be figured out? You're a liar and a sleazeball, Cabot."

Nick's attempt to quiet the man failed again. He gave up, waiting for the well to run dry. Soon, he hoped.

The man wasn't through. "You're trying to ruin my life, my work. Other people's lives. You with your easy life. You ever work, Cabot? Like real work? Things are always so easy for big Nick Cabot."

Nick stuck out one hand. "Hey, stop right there. Where'd all this come from? I don't get it. Come on inside if you want and we'll figure out whatever's turning you into a crazy man. You could use a glass of water. A beer?"

Seeming to get a second breath, the man's voice rumbled like an oncoming nor'easter.

"You're nothing but a jerk with a fancy house. Smoke and mirrors. You've fooled some in my family, but you'll never fool me. So here it is, pal. A warning. Stay away from me, and stay away from her, or I swear, I'll wring your ugly neck. Someone should have done away with you a long time ago."

Nick looked around, wondering if his neighbor was on the phone with the police yet. But in the next minute, the man turned and jogged down the walkway like he was on fire. He nearly bumped into Gabby Marietti and Daisy Danvers standing at the curb, their eyes wide and their hands gripping the leashed dogs.

After a muttered apology to the startled young women, the man jogged down the road, his muscular runner's calves propelling him around the corner and out of sight.

Chapter 2

A week or so later, on a quiet knitting night in the backroom of Izzy Perry's yarn shop, a shaggy-haired dog and teenage girl visited the four knitters, arriving just minutes before they were going to dish up Nell Endicott's new pasta casserole.

"Hi, guys," Gabby said, leaping down the three steps, her long, dark braid flying behind her.

A chorus of hellos greeted both of them.

From her place near the fireplace, Birdie put down her knitting, her small face breaking into a smile at the sight of her granddaughter.

"Where are the others?" she asked with some hesitation, her smile fading a bit.

"Others?" Nell said.

Izzy answered her aunt. "Dogs. Gabby and Daisy, Sea Harbor's Pawfect Day Dog Walkers, now have a fleet of five dogs."

"You're walking five dogs now?" Cass said. "Geesh, Gabs. You're going to need to grow more hands."

"Exactly what I told her," Birdie said.

Gabby's dog had already found his way to Birdie and was

pressing tightly against her knees. On her other side, Purl, Izzy's yarn shop cat, eyed the newcomer cautiously.

"Five is a lot, Gabby," Nell said. "What if they all head in different directions at the same time?"

Gabby laughed, then stood with one hand on the back of Nell's chair, leaning slightly forward. "Anyway, Squid is a great pup and truly loves people. We even had a sleepover one night a week or so ago. Squid, I mean, had a sleepover. His guy was in Boston for the weekend and it was too late for him to get someone to stay at the house with Squid. Anyway, Squid spent the night at our house. Well, Nonna's house."

"*Our* house," Birdie corrected.

Gabby went on. "And since I forgot to bring dog food for breakfast, Ella made him oatmeal. With some bananas and blueberries. She'd googled it somewhere. It's good for dogs, apparently. Squid thought he'd died and gone to heaven. But I think he loved Nonna even better than the breakfast. He even tried to sleep with her."

Gabby attempted to smother a laugh at the memory.

The others didn't even try. The thought of the shaggy dog bouncing onto Birdie's very high, imported bed brought out-right laughter from Nell, Cass, and Izzy—along with a bark from Squid, as if he were taking a bow.

Izzy walked around the low coffee table and crouched down, giving the dog a hug. "You're a very smart dog, with excellent taste in people and in food," she murmured. She pushed a thick swatch of dog hair away from the dog's eyes and looked up. "Do you know his breed, Gabby?"

"Nobody seems to know. He's just a plain old wonderful dog, that's what he is. Except the vet says he's not that old. He loves you, Iz."

"Of course he does," Izzy said. "I make homemade doggie treats for him and dish them out every time he and his pals walk by. Which is becoming more and more frequent. Squid's no dummy."

"That's true," Gabby said. "Your outside water bowl helps, too. It's always clean, unlike some other Harbor Road shop owners, whose names I won't mention."

Izzy sat back on her legs. "He may love us all, but right now Squid is focused on my aunt Nell's pasta salad."

Cass, seated on the other side of the low coffee table, immediately leaned forward and moved their Thursday-night dinner to the center of the yarn shop's coffee table. "Sorry, pal," she said to the dog.

"I think that's a sign that we should leave," Gabby said. "The only reason I'm interrupting your knitting night is to make sure you all had a chance to meet Squid."

"Which we loved," Nell said. "Thanks, Gabby."

"I also had a little time to spare before Daisy meets me. She's taking Hammer, Gus McGlucken's dog, home."

Birdie's eyes were still focused on the dog. She wove her fingers through his shaggy coat. "I think Squid thinks we're related. We both have plenty of gray and white going for us."

That drew smiles as they watched Birdie with Squid. They knew without a doubt that Birdie was so happy to have her granddaughter in Sea Harbor for the summer that Gabby could probably bring her whole canine entourage for a sleepover. Birdie would simply smile and make sure Ella had enough fruit and oats for breakfast.

"Are you sure you don't want some pasta salad, Gabby?" Nell asked. She leaned over and placed a basket of warm pita bread and a pot of butter on the table. "We always have more than enough."

"No thanks, Nell. But it looks fantastic. You guys go ahead. I don't want to slow anything down, and I can tell Cass is about to die of starvation."

"You're right about that," Cass said. "Where are you heading from here?"

"Oh, crazy, wild plans, Cass. Daisy and I'll walk Squid home."

"And then?" Cass asked. "What's the postwork plan? Where do you go? I'm not in the loop on what teens do these days."

"Right, you're ancient, Cass," Gabby said. "It must be hard to remember those Stone Age years. After we drop off Squid, we'll head to the beach for pizza. Did you know Angelo's delivers down there? Some kids may jump in the water. It's still too cold for me. Then we'll hang out. And eventually we'll find a ride home."

"Go in the water after dark?" Birdie's brows lifted, then lowered instantly. Gabby was a teenager. She'd be in college before Birdie blinked. She was no longer the young girl who had showed up unexpectedly in her life those years ago. But even then, when Gabby was living in a New York penthouse with her father most of the year, and recently, a year in a Switzerland school, had made her very independent. She'd grown tall and slender and older, something Birdie had to remind herself of frequently.

"I caught that look, Nonna," Gabby said. "We won't do anything stupid." She picked up Squid's leash and started to turn toward the steps.

"Wait one sec," Cass called out, stopping Gabby at the steps. "Did you say Squid lived in Fishermen's Village? Those are my people, you know. Most of my lobster crew live there."

Cass got up and looked at Squid, then knelt beside him and looked him in the eyes. "He looks familiar. But I may be thinking of my grandmother's rag rug—"

Gabby groaned and covered Squid's ears.

"His owner's a fisherman?" Nell asked.

"We don't say owner, Nell," Gabby said. "Partner is better. Or companion. Squid's companion is a good guy who rescued

Squid. And no, he doesn't fish. His dad did. His grandfather, too, I think."

"Does he have a name?" Cass asked.

"Nick. He's nice. Kind of old, but 'a looker,' as Daisy's mom put it. He's 'lovely,' as you would say, Nonna. Daisy says he has rizz."

"*Rizz?*" Cass laughed.

"Well, whatever it is you guys would call a man who looks a little like a Jonas Brother, but has some silvery streaks in his hair that weren't put there by MJ's Salon. He knows all you guys. Nick Ca—"

"Nick Cabot," Cass interrupted with a laugh. "Of course. And you described him to a T, Gabby, except for the 'old' part. Nick Cabot is just a few years older than I am. So watch your mouth, young lady."

"Now you know why Squid is such a wonderful dog," Gabby said. "Nick Cabot has rubbed off on him."

"Nick's dad and mine fished together," Cass said. "And you're right, the grandpa was a fisherman, too. Everyone thought Nick would follow in their tracks, because that's kind of what you do around here. But he went off to college somewhere. Then Harvard Business School, I think. We all figured he'd come back."

"To become a fisherman with an MBA from Harvard?" Izzy asked.

"Not to fish. He came back because he loves Sea Harbor, and to be close to family. His sister, Nancy, was in Gracie's and my class." Cass said. "Nick was always a brainy guy. He and Gracie Santos have been great friends forever. People sometimes think he's older, I think, because he's successful and has gone a little gray in the sideburn area."

"Cass, you're simply a treasure trove of information," Birdie said.

Cass laughed. "Yes, I am. My dad knew Nick's dad, who

knew Lord knows who. That's how it goes around here. Even though he doesn't fish, Nick knows everything about the industry from both sides, which is why his dad forgave him for not getting down and dirty on the boats."

Gabby started laughing. "You all sound like a fan club. But anyway, you're right about him doing good things for people. Like Daisy and me, for example."

"How's that?" Cass asked.

"He told us we weren't charging enough. Can you believe that?"

"And what did you and Daisy say?" Nell asked.

"Well, so, we didn't say anything. We kind of laughed. We assumed he was just giving us a compliment. But then when we left Squid off at the end of the first week, we looked at his check, and it was over three times what we'd asked for."

Gabby shook her head. "It's crazy, right? I mean, who does that? And you say he has a business degree, Cass? He must have skipped an accounting class along the way. Anyway, we thought about giving it back, but that didn't seem right, either. So here we are, the best-paid dog walkers on the North Shore. I may have enough to buy a car at the end of the summer."

Birdie looked up. "A car?"

"Well, yes. Anyway, in addition to all those other good things, Nick adores his dog. That says everything there is to say about him, in my humble opinion."

Gabby smiled at Squid as if he were listening and agreeing with her words. She started to turn again toward the stairs. Then turned around again.

"Oh, all this nice talk about Nick reminds me of a weird thing that happened. As much as you are all fans of Nick Cabot, he's not a saint. At least, not everyone thinks so."

"Well, none of us are, dear," Birdie said.

"Right. But anyway, a week or so ago, this guy came to Nick's house and—"

A racket at the front door broke into Gabby's sentence. She and Squid looked toward the archway as a voice called out Gabby's name.

"Sorry. That's Daisy. We're out of here," Gabby said.

"Someone came where? Did what?" Birdie asked, suddenly alert.

"Oh, it has nothing to do with Daisy and me, Nonna. No big deal. I'll fill you in later." With a quick hug for Birdie, and a wave to the others, Gabby and the shaggy dog took the three steps to the shop's main floor in a single leap. In the next second, the front door slammed shut and the shop was filled with quiet so big it filled the whole shop.

Chapter 3

They sat back in their chairs, quiet for a moment, looking at the empty space left by a lively teenager and a sweet dog. And feeling the life that was left in their wake.

Finally Birdie spoke, her eyes still on the now-vacant steps. "Goodness. What life she brings into the room."

"And to those *in* the room, too," Nell said.

Birdie chuckled and passed around a stack of napkins. "She's amazing, if I do say so myself."

"Yes, she is." Izzy leaned forward and filled four wineglasses.

Birdie held hers aloft. "Here's to Gabby and Squid, and to life. And to dear friends. How I love you all."

The others raised their glasses in unison. A gesture they'd made nearly every Thursday night for years as they settled into the yarn shop knitting room, wrapping themselves in friendship, food, and soft, comforting fibers. And tonight, in fondness for a sweet dog and deep love for a wonderful dog walker.

"And, not to diminish the additional nourishment," Cass said, "here's to the greatest chicken salad known to man." She set her wineglass down and immediately lifted a forkful of salad with her other, reciting the ingredients: "Arugula, spinach, roasted pine nuts, wine, and . . . and . . ." She struggled with one more ingredient.

Nell chuckled at Cass's amazing sense of taste and smell. Although the lobsterwoman wasn't known for making anything more complicated than grilled cheese and canned tomato soup, her taste buds and sense of smell were worthy of their own Michelin award. "You missed the—"

"Shush. I got it." Cass held up a hand, then said victoriously: "Ginger. Freshly grated."

"Simply amazing." Nell shook her head.

Izzy passed the basket of warm pita around, fiddled with an app on her phone, then sat down next to Cass. "Another night in paradise."

The quiet that followed was comfortable and satisfying and spoke of deep friendship.

It wasn't long before Cass helped herself to more salad, wineglasses were topped off, and the quiet gave way to murmurs of satisfaction.

Between bites, asked Nell. "Hey, how's Elizabeth Hartley doing, now that she's back in town?"

"Fine, I think. Ben and I had dinner with her not too long ago. It was one of those charity dinners and we were assigned to the same table. Ben and Nick had shuffled place cards so that we were able to hear each other. It ended up being far more enjoyable than those dinners sometimes are."

"She was with Nick Cabot?" Cass said.

"Yes. Strange that we were just talking about him. Anyway, she's on the board of the nonprofit that was sponsoring the dinner, and he was her guest. She looked exuberant that night. Lively and talkative."

"Are they a couple? I've seen them together a couple times," Izzy said. "She seemed older when she was a headmistress. She looks younger now."

"I agree. But she's only a couple years older than Nick."

"I think she made herself look older when she was head-mistress of the Sea Harbor Community Day School," Birdie said. "Maybe she thought she had to."

"I heard a rumor about Nick recently," Cass said. "Something about him running for mayor next election? It seems weird that someone just a few years older than I am could be mayor. But on the other hand, he'd be perfect. And he could afford to do it, since the smidget of pay our mayors get wouldn't be an issue to him."

"That came up at that dinner. Nick wants to talk to Ben about it."

"Well, that's probably a waste of time," Izzy said.

"Why?" Birdie said. "I think it's a fine idea. New blood."

"You know why, Birdie. Beatrice Scaglia would never allow it. *She's* the mayor, and she will be the next one, too. No questions asked. It's as simple as that."

They all laughed.

"Well, there is that," Nell said. "And our determined mayor is known to somehow get her way with things."

"Speaking of determination," Izzy said, "if everyone's finished eating, I'm determined we make progress on our afghan tonight."

"A lovely segue, Izzy," Birdie said.

Cass had finished the chicken salad, and in short order, they cleared the dishes and opened their yarn baskets.

"People seem excited about making things for the art auction," Birdie said. "I've seen some lovely works of fiber art being made." She looked over at Cass. "How are you doing on that herringbone pattern, Cass?"

"Don't look at me, Miz. Favazza. I am doing just fine," Cass said.

Which brought a round of laughter. They all knew that Cass's work would be dutifully monitored by her mystery-writer husband, Danny, whose knitting expertise far surpassed his wife's.

Birdie finished her row, putting her knitting out on the coffee table. The others leaned in to look. The narrow panel of stitches was now long enough that they could recognize the design. Lines of vertical stitches were clearly forming V's and inverted V's as the panel grew longer.

"Using those shades of blue was a masterful decision, Birdie," Izzy said, fingering the soft panel. "I think we should use this color to frame our blanket. It'll be a perfect border."

Birdie chuckled. "Dear Izzy, what you mean is that you'd like me to knit four pieces instead of one."

"Well, there's that . . ."

The four knitters had chosen the yarns, needle size, and colors that would work in sync with the others, creating a work of art worthy of their seaside environs. A herringbone-patterned afghan, with each person knitting a long panel that would finally be knit together to form a whole.

"It's all about togetherness," Birdie said.

"Right." Izzy traced the slanted lines of the herringbone design with her finger. "It's been a long time since we've worked on a project together. It's nice."

Togetherness. Yes. Nell looked over at Izzy. Having her niece living and working in Sea Harbor still brought unexpected pleasures like this. Being a Boston attorney turned out not to work out for Izzy. But she had never considered it lost time, something she assured both her parents, who had generously helped her with her degrees.

Nell and her sister—Izzy's mom, Caroline—had shared the whole experience with many hours on their cell phones.

Nell tuned back to the conversation as Izzy went on.

"Our afghan will be a great addition to the auction. Blankets are always a draw in Sea Harbor."

The others pulled out their wool panels in various degrees of completion. They lined the knit pieces up next to each other on the coffee table.

"Just beautiful," Nell said, her voice hushed.

The varied shades of blue and green and pale gold seemed to melt into one another like a wave, a palate of beauty.

They sat in silence for a short while, admiring what their mind's eye could see: a piece of art that they hoped would contribute nicely to Boston Children's Hospital.

A sudden noise from the main shop room was an assault to their quiet, admiring moment, although it was merely the front door closing and footsteps crossing the hardwood floor.

"Gabby?" Izzy called out. "What did you forget?"

They looked up, but instead of a dog and teenager, it was Mayor Beatrice Scaglia, framed in the archway as if posing for a portrait.

She was dressed in her usual silk suit, her hair perfectly coiffed, and a large black leather bag hanging from one arm. All that was missing was the perfect smile that Beatrice always put in place when voters were around.

The Sea Harbor mayor was clearly not happy.

"Geez," Cass said under her breath. For a brief second, they all felt like teenagers, wondering if she'd been listening to them.

"Beatrice," Izzy said. "Hi."

The mayor walked down the few steps as if expecting a guest, her narrow heels tapping lightly.

"I've just come from a dinner meeting. An unpleasant one, I might say."

"Would you like to sit?" Izzy asked, politeness overriding the desire to pick up her knitting needles or to ask the mayor to come by another day.

"No," Beatrice said. Then, "Yes."

She sat down on Izzy's vacated chair.

Izzy moved over to the fireplace hearth, her elbows on her knees. Waiting.

They all smiled politely. Beatrice never assumed she wouldn't be welcome wherever she went. It was a mayor's job, she often said.

"You should lock your door, Izzy," she said sternly. "Who knows who could walk in on you?"

"No worries," Cass chimed in. "Not with a super conscientious mayor who protects us from all evil."

Beatrice frowned at Cass.

Cass took a drink of wine. Although she and Beatrice occasionally sent comments back and forth that were sometimes wrapped in jest, sometimes in something else, Cass was good at sensing a mood and knowing when to back off.

Beatrice simply smiled. "Anyway, that's certainly true, Cass. And actually, that brings me to why I am here."

"To protect us?" Birdie asked nicely.

"A wonderful segue, Birdie," the mayor said, nodding her approval. "And in a way, it's true. I always want to protect my town. And I fully intend to continue to do so. But to achieve that, I may need your help."

"Of course," Birdie said.

"I'd make a good crossing guard," Cass said, raising her hand.

Beatrice closed her down with another *not now, Cass* looks, and went on to explain.

"Before I get to business, some news. Jane Brewster was at tonight's dinner meeting, and she mentioned that Elizabeth Hartley has agreed to be in charge of the art auction for the children's hospital."

"That's good news," Izzy said. "In fact, it's a relief. Sometimes those things get dropped in our laps."

"She's certainly used to overseeing things," Nell said. "And she's very smart. She accomplished some great things at the private day school."

"Yes, I know all that." Beatrice waved away any more comments. "I'm not here to talk about her. Although she may be helpful with another issue."

Now they were all confused. Nell wondered if the meeting Beatrice had attended involved cocktails. Several, perhaps.

"The meeting was both social and business. We met at Gracie's renovated restaurant. She has a little nook where small meetings can be held. It's nice. Not as nice as meeting at the yacht club, but pleasant."

"What kind of meeting? Why didn't you just meet at city hall?"

"I thought it would be nice to check out the meeting area. And the food."

"So, how did it go?" Cass asked.

"The meeting? It went well. It was the social part that didn't." Beatrice paused for effect.

When all she got were blank looks, she went on.

"You're all aware, of course, that my mayoral election will be held later this year."

My election, Nell thought, holding back a smile.

"I had heard inklings of this in past weeks, but I ignored them at first. It seems that several influential people in our town have approached Nick Cabot to run for my job."

They all looked at her, waiting.

Beatrice was silent.

Finally Birdie said, "Beatrice, you're not surprised, are you? There's always competition in the mayoral race. And you, Beatrice, have ended up victorious these past few years."

"People here enjoy elections," Nell said. "It's not bloodthirsty, like in cities. The rallies, the music, the congenial gatherings. *Sixty Minutes* should have a special about Sea Harbor elections."

"It's not fun, nor will it be," Beatrice snapped. Then she quickly apologized. "I'm sorry, Nell. The evening must have gotten to me. You're right. In the past, they've been decent. Even my own campaigns were not stressful. It was clear from the beginning that I would win. The men who ran almost did it as volunteers, I think. They had a good time. But this one won't be congenial, trust me. It will not be good for my town."

"Beatrice, this doesn't sound like you," Birdie said.

Beatrice went on as if Birdie hadn't spoken. "It's true that Nick Cabot knows everyone. He's good at supporting causes. But that's because he has the money to do it. It's easy for him. Those are his strong points. Oh, and I realized today from the plaque in city hall that his grandfather was once the mayor. But as far as I know, legacy should mean nothing when wanting the best person to lead our town into the future. In fact, it should be illegal."

"Beatrice, you know everyone, too. And you have experience. It would be a credit to our town if two such capable people were willing to serve in this way."

Again Beatrice turned a deaf ear to Birdie. She went on. "Knowing the needs of my town, and managing it, is simply not in Nick's repertoire. That being acknowledged, we need to be sure that he's discouraged from running. It needs to be nipped in the bud. That will be easier on everyone. And that's why I'm here tonight. I have a plan."

"Discourage Nick?" Izzy asked. "How?"

"And why?" Cass asked. "Competition isn't all bad, Beatrice—"

"Nick has far more money than I will ever have," Beatrice said. "He'd certainly be able to wage a vigorous campaign. But I am not through with what I want to achieve in Sea Harbor. Maybe in a couple years."

Nell saw a steely determination in Beatrice's eyes. Something she'd not seen there before. Although the mayor had been married once, she had never had children. And the realization came to Nell in that moment—Beatrice's elected position in Sea Harbor wasn't just a job for her, it was truly her life. It was not only her child; it was *who* she was, at least in her own mind. Losing that position and recognition and semblance of power would be losing her identity. In her own mind, she would be nothing.

"I don't know if Nick Cabot would be a good mayor or a bad mayor, Beatrice," Birdie said kindly. "I do know that you have been a fine mayor, but you've also worked tirelessly for years at that job. Perhaps you would find—"

"No, dear Birdie," Beatrice broke in. "You are wise and considerate, and I love you. But no, no. I am not ready to be put out to pasture. Not yet."

"It sounds like it's not even certain Nick will run, Beatrice," Nell said. "Maybe this is just talk. Perhaps your concern is a little premature."

"That's true," Izzy said. "Lots of people have opinions, but has Nick himself said he wants to run for mayor?"

"I don't know. But he will. Yes, he will run for mayor. And it simply can't happen. I have my sources and I know that support is forming for him, even if Nick himself hasn't announced anything. It will happen unless he can be talked out of it. Or has a good reason not to run."

Beatrice had helped herself to a glass of wine, taking sips while she talked. Now she paused, tilted her head back, and swallowed the remaining liquid. She set the empty glass down on the table, eyed the bottle, and then refrained from asking for a refill.

"What would that reason be?" Birdie asked.

"I suppose it could be many things."

"Nick is a thoughtful person," Nell said, "and very approachable. Maybe you should talk to him yourself. Explain the things you still would like to accomplish."

Beatrice was quiet, then took a deep breath, dismissing Nell's suggestion as if it hadn't been given. "Among the four of you, you know everyone in this town. I know you agree with me that it would be good for the town for me to have another term. People will listen to you. I mentioned it to Jane and Ham, too. They have influence."

The four women looked sympathetic, but also baffled.

Birdie glanced at Beatrice's empty wineglass. "Beatrice, I'm not sure what you are asking of us. Perhaps we might talk tomorrow?"

Without answering, the mayor went on. "Elizabeth Hartley is becoming known in our town also."

"And that's relevant, how?" Cass asked.

"I think it's obvious." She turned and looked over at Nell and Birdie. "You two were on a board with her those years back. You need to explain to her that this isn't Nick's time. Those two seem to be quite close. She could use her influence, in turn, to explain that to him. There are ways this can be done without hurting anyone. I think we need to approach this issue on all sides."

Nell looked at Cass, wondering if she was going to point out to Beatrice how offensive her comments were.

Cass caught Nell's look and acknowledged with a grimace that she'd behave.

"I would like you to form an election action committee for me."

Drops of perspiration had appeared on the mayor's upper lip as she talked, something they had never seen happen in all the years they'd known the impeccably dressed and carefully put-together mayor. All four of them looked at it, uncomfortable. Then quickly looked away. Waiting.

The room was quiet.

Beatrice delicately pulled a tissue from her pocket and dabbed at her upper lip.

After taking a moment to compose herself, she slipped her characteristic smile in place. Then, after brushing an imaginary crumb from her silk skirt, she smiled comfortably at each of the women. She started to stand, then glanced down at the knit panels stretched out on the coffee table. Her voice was calm and pleasant. "Oh, goodness," she said. "How absolutely beautiful, Birdie."

Surprised at the abrupt change in mood, but relieved that the puzzling conversation might be over, Birdie held it up for her to see.

"A scarf?"

"No. It will be an afghan, Beatrice. Each of us is working on a panel. Then we will bind them together into a larger piece. And contribute it to the art auction."

"Intriguing." Beatrice looked more closely at the panel as if interested in it. "It's a herringbone design?"

"Yes. An old pattern. The Roman builders constructed roads using this design," Birdie said. "They were more stable."

"Perhaps I will bid on this myself then. I may have to build my own stable Roman road soon. With help, of course."

She stood and picked up her black leather bag as if to leave.

"There's one more thing I meant to tell you," she said.

The four women visibly tensed.

"It's about Gracie's restaurant. I hadn't been there since Chef Bobby came on the scene, though I'd read the initial rave reviews."

"And?" Birdie asked.

"Something was missing," Beatrice said. "As one reviewer wrote so astutely, 'Something fishy is going on in those lobster pots.'"

"But you had your meeting there, anyway?" Cass asked. "It couldn't have been that bad."

"Of course I went. I don't believe reviewers, good or bad. I know Gracie is your good friend. I love her, too. But the food, namely one of the specials, simply wasn't that good."

"I don't get it," Cass said. "Gracie's put her heart and soul into that restaurant."

All the seaside knitters had helped with Gracie's dream. Going over at night, painting and polishing and decorating the small waterfront restaurant. It had left them all with a strong relationship to the little restaurant on the pier. Hearing it spoken ill of felt personal. And bad for their friend.

"I know, I know," the mayor said. "It has always been a wonderful addition to our town's restaurants. And then even better when Bobby moved back and helped Gracie expand the menu. Those specials are his original recipes, you know. But when I asked, a couple of those who had ordered them didn't give rave reviews."

Cass frowned, as if challenging Beatrice for proof. "Danny and I ate there a month or so ago, and it was great."

Beatrice took a deep breath and slipped her purse strap over her shoulder. "Yes. I hear that, too. Here's the truth: There isn't a home kitchen in Sea Harbor that hasn't produced a bland piece of cod once or twice, me included. But that isn't what you expect to get from a Bobby Palazola kitchen, which is how some people refer to it now. It's delicious now and then, but not consistently, I hear. Some are saying Gracie was better off before she brought him back to town."

"Sam had lunch there the other day and said it was good," Izzy said.

"Oh, Izzy," Beatrice said, frowning. "Sam Perry loves all food. How he stays so skinny, I'll never know. I've seen your husband eat cold mac and cheese. Of course he said it was good."

"It's probably just a bump in the road," Nell said. "Bobby has only been there a few months, and it's not unusual for new restaurants to have to feel their way around the town's tastes."

"Perhaps." She paused, then said, "I probably shouldn't tell you this, but the health department got a report from someone, and it's going to have to check out the kitchen."

Cass groaned.

Beatrice waved away the sound. "I'm sorry about that. But Gracie is a smart young woman. This will have a good end. Her restaurant has a place in our town. Tourists love it. I just want it healed quickly. There's a new restaurant coming to town that just got its liquor license. It's opening in the old bank around the corner from the museum. I saw a copy of the menu, and it will be competition for Bobby. Gracie needs to get her act together."

Nell watched the mayor as she spoke. She knew she cared about Gracie, but she loved what tourism did for her town, too. *Her* town, which was exactly what Beatrice Scaglia considered Sea Harbor to be. *Hers.* Not Nick Cabot's or anyone else's.

Beatrice glanced at her phone, flicking through emails. She looked up. "Well, ladies, I should leave you to your evening. And I have a heap of messages waiting for me."

They waited, knowing there was one more line to come from Beatrice, and in the next breath, she complied.

"As you know, a mayor's work is never done."

Chapter 4

Most Sea Harbor natives knew that Bobby Palazola wasn't your typical chef. Although, if asked, they wouldn't be able to tell you what atypical meant. Bobby had never been to Paris and had never been inside an elite culinary institute. Nor had he ever had a cooking show on TV, except for a local cable show when he was just starting out. But his gift for original, creative foods had earned him accolades in several cities. And then in New York. Culinary heaven. Decent accolades, but definitely good for a small-town kid.

But for Izzy, who wasn't a Sea Harbor native, he was a mystery man. And the fact that he might be causing a problem for her friend Gracie Santos was worth concern.

"What does he look like?" Izzy asked Cass, her voice coming in stops and starts as she slowed her early-morning run to a walk. She plucked her damp T-shirt away from her body and took a breath.

"Who?" Cass asked. They walked toward the stone steps leading up from the water to the parking lot of Gracie Santos's Lazy Lobster and Soup café. Gracie was always in at the crack of dawn, hours before she opened the door to customers, which was perfect for Izzy and Cass, who always needed a pit stop after their run. And no matter how sweaty they were, Gracie always let them in.

"Who? Bobby Palazola, of course, you dope. I've yet to meet the guy, even though Sam, Abby, and I are regulars at Gracie's place—a week without her lobster mac and cheese is more than Abby can handle. Does he hide in the kitchen? An introvert, maybe?"

"*Introvert?*" Cass released a snort. "Not on your life."

"Gracie says he's good-looking."

"Good-looking? Maybe."

"His twin, Bella, definitely is. She comes into my shop sometimes with Liz Santos."

"Right. They're cousins, too. When we were in high school, Liz and Bella were like goddesses. Everyone loved them. There was nothing they couldn't do."

"And Bobby?"

"Definitely not a goddess. He was a different kind of legend. In trouble a lot, but with a knack for charming his way out of it. He had this weird charm that made people love him no matter what he did. Even teachers."

"And you? Did his charm work on you?"

"Ha," Cass laughed. "He and Bella were both yacht club sailing instructors in the summer. They taught us younger kids. One thing I unfortunately remember is that Bobby always called me Hairy Halloran because my lovely black tresses were usually messy and flying around my face. At least, it wasn't my legs he was talking about. At least, I don't think he was. But I still hated it."

Izzy noticed Cass was smiling while she told the story. Clearly, she hadn't been damaged for life.

They walked up the windy path from the beach and turned toward the Lazy Lobster and Soup Café. It felt like home to them. It was a town favorite, from the lobsters served on newspapers on the back deck, to chowder and mac and cheese entrees, to the well-rubbed stone lobster that stood guard at the front door.

Izzy walked up and rubbed the lobster sculpture, adding to its very shiny head.

They peered through the window into the darkened eating space, then turned and saw Gracie Santos walking around the far corner of the restaurant, her eyes on her cell phone and a frown on her face. She carried a fistful of weeds in the other hand and walked as if the ground had done something awful to her. Finally she looked up, then shielded her eyes from the bright sun and looked more closely at the two women coming her way.

Her face lit up, and she dropped the weeds, rushing over to Izzy and Cass and wrapping them both in a single, tight hug.

Cass finally stepped back. "That was one big hug, Gracie. And an admirable one, since Iz and I both smell from our run."

Gracie leaned toward her again and sniffed, then stepped back, pushing a crooked smile to her face. "Yes, you do. But your smelly tees are now covered with my dirt, so at least we match."

"What's up?" Izzy asked. "Why the frown? We're here for our post run pit stop. Is the coffee ready?"

Gracie pushed a damp strand of ash-blonde hair away from her face. The blunt hairdo looked self-cut, yet surprisingly attractive; and on the petite restaurant owner, it only brought more attention to huge blue eyes that seemed to fill her whole face. "Coffee? Oh. No, sorry, guys. No coffee. We're not going to open today, so I didn't make any. Didn't you see the Closed sign on the front door?"

"Closed? Of course you're closed," Cass said. "It's still practically dawn. But it's never closed to us."

"You're right. But since the restaurant isn't going to open, I didn't start the coffee. Sorry."

"You're not open the whole day? Why? It's Friday," Izzy

said. A worry line formed on her forehead as she instantly thought the worst. They'd all worked hard at trying to ignore the rumors flying around about the restaurant's quality of food. But she'd felt a sudden twinge that maybe the rumors had some teeth to them.

"Oh, it's nothing to worry about," Gracie said, reading Izzy's face. "We're getting the new stove checked out later today and another minor inspection. Nothing to worry about. I have a meeting with my uncle today, too, and am meeting a friend later, so it all works out."

"So you had a chance to sleep in and passed it up. Shame on you," Cass said.

"I'd be here, anyway. There's always something to do. We've expanded the staff some—Bobby needed a little extra help in the kitchen. I need to keep track of them, make sure the schedule works out. All those silly things that I need to stay on top of. Oh, for the days when all I had to do was make lobster rolls and mac and cheese and have people swoon over them. Some days I yearn for that simple time. Just me, my lobsters, and a couple of teens handling the tables, a good guy at the bar. So simple. Remember those days?"

Izzy laughed. "Of course I do. But things grow, right? And this is all good. Exciting."

"Why do you need more kitchen help?" Cass asked.

"I don't know. But Bobby knows his needs in there. It's cleanup work, mainly. Except for one guy he hired some weeks ago to take over some of his job. He'd prefer to do it himself, but there's only one of him."

"Who did he find?"

"He didn't have to look. This guy just appeared out of nowhere. I wasn't here that day, but Bobby said he came to the back door looking for work. He was exactly what Bobby was looking for, so he hired him on the spot."

"What's his name? If he's into fishing, I probably know him."

"Marco Costa."

"Oh," Cass frowned.

"That was a telling 'oh.' Do you know him?"

"He used to work for Pete and me."

"Did you . . . did you fire him?"

"No, he quit."

"You're not bending over with praise for this guy. Bobby says he knows everything about fish—skin color, smells, freshness. All those things. So he's doing some of the buying. He also manages staples that we need, herbs and spices. The kind Bobby uses in his specials."

"He probably learned about herbs because he grew lots of pot in his yard until he got married and his wife made him pull it all up. She was afraid their toddler would get in it."

"Bobby wanted to hire him full-time, but the guy refused, which I was happy about. I guess he has other jobs."

"Do you know where?" Cass asked.

"I asked him that, which he didn't like. Nor does he like me. He said he wasn't working in any other kitchen, and that whatever else he does is his own business, and definitely not mine."

"That sounds like Costa," Cass said.

"Well, he's right that it's not my business, but the way he said it was almost scary. The truth is, I don't like him or trust him. Yet I'm torn. If he's making it easier for Bobby, maybe it's okay. As long as he doesn't plant hemp in my garden." Her smile was tired.

"Well, the guy truly does know fish, probably better than the fish know themselves. I think his dad took him fishing before he was born. But all he had to do for us was meet fishing quotas and he was good at that."

"That's Elena's husband, right?" Izzy said.

Cass nodded.

"Elena's husband," Gracie said. "Geesh. I didn't make the

connection. That was just a few years ago. You took that yoga class for pregnant mothers with her."

"Yes, I did. 'The young and the restless old,' as I called us. And so did everyone else in the class," Cass said. "Elena was what, twenty? I keep in touch with her because our toddlers are in a kids' music class together. A couple months ago, she told me that Marco had moved out, looking for greener pastures."

"Sorry to hear that," Izzy said. "I often see her on the beach near Rico's place with little James. Rico is always there, too. He's turned into a first-class grandpa."

"Yeah, old Rico Silva's becoming a softy," Cass said. "He never grumps at me anymore, even laughs if I joke with him. Not always. But sometimes."

Wealthy Rico Silva's discovery a few years before that he not only had a daughter he didn't know about, but a pregnant one, had transformed the old man's whole existence into an amazing and loving one. "A true miracle," as Rico himself called it. "Who gets a daughter and a grandson in one fell swoop?" he'd ask.

"Elena will be okay, no matter how it turns out with Marco," Cass said. "Old Rico won't allow anything less. He'll make sure she and little James are greatly loved and have a good life."

"Why did Marco quit? You'd think with a baby, he wouldn't just up and quit a decent job," Izzy said.

"He told my brother that he wants a different kind of life. Big house, big boat. He wants out of Fishermen's Village, too. He thinks the neighborhood isn't good enough for him, unlike Elena, who loves it there. She has lots of young mom friends, there's that great park they all play in. It's like a little commune. And she's very happy."

"So Marco just up and left?" Gracie asked. "What a jerk."

"It was more mutual than that. Elena didn't spell it out, but Pete said Marco was out a lot. Some gambling. Lots of booze. He's kind of a wheeler-dealer, trying to get the best of others to benefit himself. He's gotten into some messy things along the way."

"But he fell for Elena big-time," Izzy said. "I thought he had mellowed."

"Me too. But the routine of home life with a baby wasn't quite what he'd signed up for. Anyway, Elena says they're separated while Marco figures out his life and how to win the lottery."

Gracie managed a smile. "That's not going to happen here, I'm afraid."

Cass seemed unwilling to let the topic go. "Have you talked to Nick Cabot about him? He knows Marco even better than I do."

"It's ironic you mentioned Nick. We're getting together later today. Just to catch up." She looked over her shoulder, as if not wanting her conversation heard. "Nick's been helping me figure things out with all the changes in the restaurant. Listening to me moan, I guess. He sees everything so clearly. Anyway, he calms me down when I sometimes feel the roof is falling in on me. Bobby's not crazy about Nick, so I don't advertise our friendship."

"Oh, geesh. Still? That's been going on since high school, Gracie. You know that. Bobby just needs to get over it and grow up. You and Nick have been friends since forever."

"Right. And I hired Bobby to cook, not to pick my friends. Nick's friendship is important to me. He's like the two of you. I can say anything to you, and you will still love me. Nick too. Anyway, it's really good to see you guys."

Izzy took off her sunglasses and stepped close, noticing the small lines near Gracie's eyes. "Gracie, are you sure you're okay? You look a little . . . well, a little wan. Peaked, as my mother would say."

"I'm just tired, I guess."

"Gracie, you never get tired," Cass said.

"I know. First time ever. I don't like it, either, so it may be my last time." She forced a grin.

"What's with the gardener's outfit?" Cass pointed to Gracie's bib overalls. "You should be dressed to kill, being a famous restaurateur and all."

"Kill, ugh." Gracie frowned. "That's what I'd like to do to some people around this town."

Cass frowned. "I hope we're not on that list. You look fierce, lady."

Gracie shook her head. "Of course not. It's nothing. But anyway, come follow me. I will take you to my happy place. It makes everything right."

Chapter 5

Gracie's expression lightened as they followed her around the corner of the restaurant to a wide patch of lawn. It sat between Gracie's restaurant on one side and Lucky Bianchi's bar and grill, Lucky's Place, on the other.

"Voila," Gracie said, stretching her arms wide to frame the neat rows of garden beds, each one featuring rows of leafy greens and staked vines, some readying themselves to bear fruit, and others with sprigs of green peeking through the soil, showing early signs of life. A watering system sent a light spray over the gardens, creating rainbows in the early-morning light. A small half-moon bench sat in a grassy circle in the middle of the garden.

"Wow. This is beautiful, Gracie," Cass said. "Who knew you were a farmer at heart?"

Gracie planted her fists on her small hips, nodding proudly. Strands of golden hair swept across her face in the breeze. "We're not all about lobsters here, you know."

"Well, that's for sure," Izzy said. "This is terrific, Gracie. As is your new restaurant menu. I haven't seen you up close to tell you that, but Sam and I were blown away by the Scallops Crudo. It was perfecto."

Gracie's smile wasn't as full as expected. "The menu is coming along slower than we'd like, but every item is fussed over until it becomes exactly the way Bobby wants it to be. His own specials, which, by the way, he refuses to share with anyone, are taking longer than we'd hoped to be consistent. And sometimes, like when 'important people' seem to be dining with us—like reviewers, or the mayor last night—an entrée can flop. Bobby's going crazy trying to figure it out. I'm just happy we still serve plain old lobsters with melted butter out on the deck, and lobster mac and cheese. It makes me feel secure. You know—"

Gracie was interrupted by a door slamming near the back of the restaurant.

The three women turned toward the sound. An aproned man walked down the side deck steps and turned toward the harbor water.

Oblivious to the women watching him, he stood at the rocky edge, his feet planted apart and his hands stuck into pants pockets. He was still, staring out at the water that lapped against the shore.

"Is that our homegrown, famous chef?" Cass asked, craning to see the man's profile. But all that she could see were thick hunks of wavy black hair escaping from beneath a backward Red Sox hat with a smiley face on it.

"Yep, in the flesh," Gracie said. "Can you believe it, Cass? Our youth is coming back to us full force."

"He's been hiding in the kitchen every time Danny and I have been here. I was beginning to think you'd made him up."

"He's probably afraid of you, Cass. All those secrets from his life as Bobby Palazola could come raining down on him."

At the sound of their voices, the man turned around. He looked over at the women, then took off his sunglasses and looked again, frowning. A minute later, he slapped the side of his head and shouted, "Is that you, Halloran? I don't believe it. You finally found me."

Laughing, he walked toward the women.

Cass laughed. "Gads. What happened to you, Bobby? You're actually good-looking. How did that happen since last we met? Did you go under the knife?"

Izzy was smiling at the man, who looked nothing like the image she'd concocted from Cass's humorous jabs. She liked him immediately. Bobby Palazola was medium height, measuring about her own five-eight. He was well-built and handsome, with smoky eyes and a strong jaw, far from the tattooed kid she'd imagined.

"Ha," the man responded to Cass, wrapping her in a huge hug. "It's all about healthy living, would you believe it? No. Of course you wouldn't!"

"You've got that right, Bobby."

"Okay, okay, but tell me, Halloran, where've you been? I've been looking around for you. I've seen baby brother Pete over at Lucky's Place now and then, but I haven't seen hide or hair of you."

"What do you—"

"No, no, wait." Bobby shushed her with an outstretched palm. "Come to think of it, I think I heard that loud Irish laugh of yours floating into my kitchen a few times. It made one of my soufflés fall flat."

A full laugh escaped Izzy, and Bobby gave her a wide, smiling nod of appreciation.

"Ah, that adolescent humor lives on," Cass said, grinning.

Bobby laughed again, something that seemed to come easily to the chef. "Gracie confirmed that you hadn't run off with some traveling salesman. Danny Brandley's a good guy. It's good to see you, Cass."

Then the chef turned all his attention to Izzy. He squeezed

his thick, dark brows together, as if trying to come up with a name.

Gracie stepped in with introductions. "Sorry, Bobby. Izzy Perry is a good friend of Cass and mine, so you better behave. She's not a Sea Harbor native, but we love her, anyway."

"Ah, Izzy Perry. Sure. Sure." He slapped his head again. "I know you. Or the guy you live with, anyway. Sam Perry, right? He's a great photographer. I met Sam years ago. He did a photo shoot for me back in the day when I was starting out in New York. We got along great. He did a great job. He made my shack of a restaurant look great in our marketing materials. Me too."

"You? He's good at Photoshop," Cass said.

"Quiet, Halloran." Bobby feigned a scowl. "We're having a private conversation."

He turned back to Izzy. "So I've seen Sam around town. We had beers together one night. But I haven't seen you. So, why's that?"

"Maybe you should get out more, Bobby," Cass interjected. "Izzy gave up a big-deal law career to come to our remarkable town and open a shop. She and Sam have an amazing daughter, and Izzy offers yarn therapy to half the town. She's a wonder woman."

"It's all true, Bobby," Gracie said.

Izzy shushed them. "I've been in Lazy Lobster a few times for dinner, but you were busy in the kitchen making the amazing meals we enjoyed. Truly wonderful, Bobby."

"Well, okay, then." Bobby's whole face turned into a smile, and he spontaneously hugged Izzy.

Surprised, Izzy discreetly pulled away, trying to leave behind the pungent smells of garlic, onions, and coriander coming from his apron. "It's good to finally put a face to the food," she said. "Cass has told me lots about you."

Bobby looked over at Cass and pretended to moan. "I hope

she didn't tell you everything. My youthful antics seem to stick around in the annals of Sea Harbor, at least in the minds of some. But that's okay."

He moved closer to Gracie and put one arm around her shoulder. "Gracie here has looked the other way, at least long enough to hire me."

Bobby glanced at Gracie, as if she might disagree.

"Well, it was a tough call," Gracie said. "When an award-winning chef offers to transform your lobster shack into one of the best places to eat on the North Shore, does one say, 'Well, gosh, I'm just not sure. Maybe check back later?'"

"Anyway," Bobby said, clearly pleased with the answer, "I love this place, this town. I always knew I'd come back. My mom is here and not doing well, so it's good to be close to her. My sis is close by in Boston. We're close, too. And there are lots of old friends around, like these two here. It's all good."

"I see Bella on TV reporting the weather. She's talented. She's been in the shop a few times, too. Customers treat her like a celebrity."

"Well, she deserves it. She's amazing," Bobby said. "Much more than a pretty face. Bella's a true scientist. She really knows her stuff. Well, except maybe her choice in men sometimes."

"What?" Cass said. "Shame on you, Bobby."

"You're right. I should know better. I don't want to go anywhere near my sister's love life. I wish she wouldn't let me near it, either. Got a text today that she wants to see me this weekend while she's here. She wants to talk to me. That always makes me think she's about to do something rash."

"Bella? She's not the 'rash' type, Bobby," Cass said. "I doubt if she's ever done anything rash."

Bobby shook his head, looking slightly embarrassed. "You're right. But I have a suspicion she's in love. And I'm not sure how I'll handle that. Anyway, sorry I said that."

"Okay, back to you," Izzy said, detecting that his sister's

private life was clearly off limits and they should move on. "Welcome home. I can tell you have lots of good reasons to be back here."

"You got it. Lots of reasons. Lots of family, and I love to cook. And who could ask for a better partner in crime than Gracie here? I'm a heck of a lucky guy. That's how I see it."

"Well, that's true," Cass said. "You hit the jackpot working with Gracie. It's good to have you back, Bobby."

"Thanks. That's enough about me. Tell me what you two are doing over here on the dock at this hour. You come here to eat or look at Gracie's vegetables?" Bobby looked at Cass with a frown. "Most people don't show up at dawn for fine dining. We're not your twenty-four-hour diner, y'know."

"So glad you educated us, Bobby," Cass said. "I guess we'll have to head to Dunkin'."

Izzy laughed. "The truth is that this is our favorite pit stop on early-morning runs. Gracie's always here at the crack of dawn, and she makes great coffee."

"Ah. You come for the coffee?"

"And to catch up on lives."

"So girl talk," Bobby said. "Sure, I get that."

"That, and much, much more," Gracie said. "All hush-hush. Don't try eavesdropping or we'll have to kill you."

Her voice dropped off as the sound of a car broke through the air. Gracie turned and looked beyond Cass and Izzy toward the noise. A large, shiny vehicle pulled up in front of the Lazy Lobster and Soup Café.

Gracie took a step away from Bobby and apologized to her friends, her expression turning serious. "It looks like we'll have to do that catching up later. My uncle is here."

Izzy glanced at the car—a long black Mercedes SUV. She turned back to Gracie. And then looked at Bobby Palazola, whose smile was gone, but his warm, dark eyes were steady and focused on Gracie.

Gracie gave Izzy and Cass quick hugs, urging them to pick some baby spinach before they left, then hurried over to the man getting out of the car.

Alphonso Santos was a tall, imposing figure, the owner of a large North Shore construction company and several other businesses. He had become a more settled man after he married a much younger Liz Palazola Santos, with whom he had three little girls. Alphonso doted on his family, including niece Gracie.

Bobby looked at Cass and Izzy and managed a nod and a smile. "Sorry about the coffee. Come back and I'll treat you to my amazing bluefin tuna sushi to make up for it. Really good to see you." Then he pulled the baseball cap off his head, releasing a head of thick curly hair, and hurried over to the car, greeting Gracie's uncle with a firm handshake and a solemn expression on his face.

In the next minute, the threesome walked into the Lazy Lobster and Soup Café.

Izzy and Cass stood beside the garden watching them disappear through the wide, welcoming restaurant door, one that suddenly seemed less welcoming.

Izzy finally broke the silence.

"He's in love with her," she said.

"Who and who?"

"Who and *whom*," Izzy said. "Bobby Palazola. He's in love with Gracie."

Cass stared at her friend.

"He is, Cass. I'd bet my life on it. And I don't know if that's a good thing or a bad one."

Chapter 6

Once home, Cass stripped off her smelly running clothes and jumped into the shower. Thoughts of Bobby Palazola filled her head, along with Izzy's observation of his feelings for Gracie. Bobby was fun and likable and had grown up nicely. She and Gracie had enjoyed times with him over the years, but as buddies. Images of him and Gracie as a couple were difficult to hold on to. She knew Gracie inside out, and Bobby Palazola didn't seem to be her type. But then, Danny Brandley hadn't always seemed to be her type—this very smart, award-winning mystery writer—and yet she loved that man more than life. Maybe matters of the heart can't be seen.

When the water started to turn cold, she reluctantly stepped out of the shower and toweled off. She rubbed her hair especially hard, as if to put things in order before she had to face the rest of her day. Then she pulled on jeans and a light sweater and headed downstairs.

She paused at the door to Danny's den, looking at his back as he sat at his desk, typing on his laptop. And thinking about love, she walked in quietly, then hugged him from behind, causing his glasses to fall down his nose. Danny pushed them back up without missing a single keystroke.

Cass shook her head in amazement at his total absorption in figuring out a clue or a plot twist or a motive in the mystery he was writing.

"I love you," she whispered into his ear, then turned and walked away, hearing a reciprocal murmur from him as she headed out to her own job, one without the drama Danny managed to conjur up.

She drove down the hill through the Canary Cove Art Colony neighborhood and headed to her office, where a stack of paperwork and fishing reports would be waiting for her. Her least favorite part of running the Halloran Lobster Company. As she walked through the front door, the cell phone in her pocket began vibrating.

She put the phone on speaker as she shuffled through the mail.

"Hi, Gracie, what's up? How did the meeting with Uncle Alphonso go?"

"Oh, it's okay. But I need a favor."

"Sure. What is it?"

Gracie paused.

"You there, Gracie?" Cass asked.

"Sorry, I was reading a text from him."

"Who is 'him'?"

"Nick Cabot. He's at Lucky's Place. He said we should meet him there."

"*We?*"

"You and me."

"But, Gracie—"

"Sorry, Cass, I have another call. I'll meet you there in fifteen."

Gracie hung up.

Cass looked over at her assistant, dutifully preparing the

fishing schedule for the next few days. Her fingers moved as fast as Danny's on the keyboard, Cass thought, still holding her cell, as if waiting for it to call back.

"You're wondering if I still work here, aren't you, Ruthie?" Cass said.

Taking off her large orange glasses, Ruthie swiveled in her chair until she faced Cass.

"Hey, boss, here's what I think. When Gracie calls, you should go. She'd do it for you. Whatever 'it' is." She started to swing back to her desk, then turned back again. "Oh, one more thing. I'd like my burger medium rare and a side of truffle fries. Lucky's fries are the greatest. Please and thank you."

She swiveled back to her computer and started tapping the keys.

Cass parked in Gracie's lot, then jogged the short distance past the Lazy Lobster and Soup Café to Lucky's Place.

It was noisy when she walked in, with people ordering lunch, and groups of college kids reuniting with friends and enjoining their summer away from books. Their happy voices vied with Taylor Swift's, pouring from invisible speakers. In a large area behind the bar, a group of retired fishermen were beginning a serious game of pool, the balls breaking with a loud clack, and the *pinging* and *bleeping* of pinball machines forming a raucous background chorus.

Lucky Bianchi, the owner and Cass's good friend, was standing behind the bar. He waved at her, then pointed to a booth near the bar, where Gracie was already seated. It was the booth closest to the TV lounge area but made private by a grouping of three large rubber trees separating the areas and buffering the sound.

Cass mouthed a thank-you and headed to the booth.

"Okay, Gracie, why am I here?" She pushed a thick plant leaf aside and slid into the booth.

"Because I wanted you here. You suggested I talk to Nick about Marco Costa. I realized after you left that I had sugar-coated the way I feel about the guy. I don't trust him at all, zero. And the feeling grows every day. A couple days ago, after Bobby went out for something, I walked into the kitchen and saw Costa snooping around where maybe he sh—" She stopped, hearing her name called from across the way. Both women looked up as Nick walked toward them.

"Hi, you two," Nick said, leaning over to give Cass a hug, then sitting down beside Gracie. "No wonder Bianchi named this place after himself. It brings luck to everyone. Here I sit with two amazing ladies."

"Ever the gallant flirt," Gracie said.

"It's good to see you, Cass. I hope you're bringing your lit-tle man to our Fishermen Festival coming up."

"Joey wouldn't miss it for anything. Nor would I. Or Danny. He likes it better than Christmas."

"Great. Now tell me what's new in lobster land."

"Not much. Things are good. I'm more interested in learn-ing what's going on with you, Mister Maybe Mayor?"

Nick laughed. "Who knows? It's an intriguing thought. I need more information for sure. Some self-assessment, too, and talking to people wiser than I. Maybe I could bring some new ideas to the town, if there's a way to do it without upsetting anyone's apple cart."

"Upsetting apple carts shouldn't be a factor," Cass said. She thought about Beatrice Scaglia, upset and angry, but once she calmed down, she'd have to consider that her time might be up.

"Maybe, we'll see," Nick said. "There's plenty of time. This weekend, I'm putting it all out of my mind. Seeing all those col-lege kids in here reminded me of doing the same thing that first year we were all away at school, then came back for the sum-mer. In fact, our old group is getting together this weekend. Watching these kids, I can feel what they feel."

"Ah, then it's true. I heard that through the grapevine. That rowdy high-school gang that ruled the school is getting together," Cass said. "How long ago was that?"

Nick laughed. "Seems like yesterday. But Bella, Liz, Andy Risso, a couple others—we've all stayed close."

"You were our heroes," Gracie said back then.

"Ha. How misled you were. But longtime friendships—well, like the two of you have—are special. There's something about the history we share. We know each other so well that it makes a lot of questions unnecessary when we get together. You just jump right back into the friendship. Being with them may even help me see this election decision more clearly. Anyway, it's going to be a great weekend. One of the best. Memorable, even."

"Memorable?" Gracie said. "Hmm." She turned toward him, meeting his eyes and holding them.

Nick looked at Cass. "Does Gracie do this to you? She has this way of slowly needling her way into my thoughts, then looking around inside my head, searching for hidden things." He made movements with his fingers on the table, demonstrating Gracie's sneaky travels into his mind.

"Speaking of hidden things," Cass said, "you were the talk of our knitting group last night."

"That sounds dangerous," Nick said.

"Actually we were talking about Elizabeth Hartley. You, Nell, and Birdie all knew her when she was headmistress at the private day school?"

"Elizabeth? Yes, that's true. We crossed over briefly on the school's board. Birdie and Nell left the board before it got tough on Elizabeth. Those were ugly times for her."

"But she came back, so maybe she's forgotten all that," Cass said.

"Maybe. I was surprised she came back, but she seems to be settling in. Do Birdie and Nell agree?"

"I guess. They said that you've spent a lot of time helping that happen."

"I hope so. Jane Brewster has helped, too, introducing her to the art colony folks. Elizabeth had a rough time recovering from that job. Hopefully, Sea Harbor will prove to be a good move."

Esther, a longtime waitress, appeared at the edge of the booth, balancing a tray of burgers and fries. She looked at Cass and Gracie, nodding her head toward Nick. "The big guy here ordered for all of you before he sat down. He got it wrong, of course, so I'm bringing you what you really want." Esther had never completely accepted that the bar and grill was willed to Lucky when his parents died, and not to her.

"Thanks, Esther. We can always count on you. But I'll need one more," Cass said. "Ruthie's hungry. I'll pick it up at the bar when we're through."

"Got it." Esther held up a thumb. She turned away slowly, the same way Esther performed most things, and almost caught her apron on one of the rubber trees that Lucky refused to move, insisting they helped mute the lounge noise where the huge TV was usually showing some game. She swatted the leaf, then went on.

Nick picked up his burger in both hands and took a giant bite. A strand of melted cheese and juice dripped down on the plate. "Gads, these are good. I shouldn't be enjoying burgers so much, but sometimes Lucky's burgers are the only way to go."

"Can you listen and eat at the same time, Nick?" Gracie asked.

"Sure. Go ahead. Shoot."

"We hired a new guy a month or so ago at the restaurant. He's helping Bobby in the kitchen. Cass says he lives in your neighborhood, and you know him."

"Marco Costa," Cass said. She grabbed a fry, dipping it in Lucky's special sauce.

"Oh?" Nick said. He looked up from the burger.

"Is that an 'Oh yes, I know him' or an 'Oh no'?" Gracie asked.

"I know him. He and Elena live on my block. The neighborhood is a close one. Everyone knows everyone else's business, for better or for worse."

"So is Marco 'better' or 'worse'?"

Nick hesitated, his head moving back and forth, as if deciding which way to go.

Gracie stepped into the pause and explained why Bobby had hired Marco.

"Cass confirmed that the guy really does know a lot about fish and fishing," she added.

Nick looked across the table. "That's right. He worked for you and Pete."

"He did."

"Is he causing problems for you, Gracie?" Nick didn't look happy.

"Problems? I don't know. But the thing is, I don't trust him. Some days, I think that he's responsible for the problems we're having at the restaurant. Like he's a bad-luck charm."

She paused for a moment, then shook her head. "That's silly, right? And I probably feel that way because he doesn't like me. When I speak to him, it's as if I were a fly he'd like to swat away."

"It's not silly," Nick said. "This isn't even an issue. Just fire him. I wish you'd asked me before you hired him."

"I don't have a reason to fire him, Nick. I'm going on emotion. Bobby's got enough on his mind right now and this guy is a huge help to him. So maybe that should trump my feelings? And he's only part-time, anyway. But I wanted your opinion on the whole thing. You and Cass know me better than anyone."

"Where else does he work?"

"That's a mystery, too. He won't tell me. But wherever it is, they pay better."

"How do you know that?" Nick asked.

"It's only a guess. But recently he's been flaunting things. Like gold necklaces he never wore before. A fancy Rolex. New cell phone. That kind of thing."

Nick's noncommittal expression had given way to a deep frown as Gracie tried to talk herself out of hers, as if they were passing one person's worries onto the other.

"Does Bobby know what Marco's other job is? Most salaries in the fishing industry are average, not the kind that buys Rolex watches."

"No, Bobby didn't push him on it. He's just relieved to have someone helping with the extra things so he could work on figuring out his entrees. The only thing we know is that he's not working in another kitchen."

"I saw him recently at a restaurant," Nick said, frowning. Then he explained. "Jack Riley, a friend of mine, is part of the LLC group that owns that new place near the museum. He took Sam Perry and me over to see it. Costa was there, leaning up against the building, smoking."

"Maybe he lied to me," Gracie said. "Maybe he's trying to get a job there. But why would he lie? He can work anywhere he wants."

"Right, why would he?" Nick said. He finished off the remaining fries, wiped his mouth, and sat back against the back of the leather booth.

"Did you talk to him?" Cass asked.

"Just a nod, that's all." He pulled out his phone and typed a note into it. "Gracie, here's what I think we should do. I do know more about Marco Costa, more than I'd like. He's had some troubles over the years in the neighborhood. I've even pulled him out of a couple messes myself when he was younger. There wasn't a dad around and his mother had her own problems.

"Anyway, here's what I'm going to do. I'm going to check with my buddy Jack to see if he knows why Costa is hanging around the restaurant. Frankly, Gracie, I'd feel better about it if he's gone from your place. If it's a problem for Bobby, there're plenty of guys I could recommend. Costa could be trouble. But you're right, it'd be better if we had some concrete reason to fire him. I'll gather what we need. In the meantime, just give him the weekend off, with pay if you have to. Make up something."

Gracie sighed, then forced a smile. "Thanks, my friend. What would I do without you?"

"I'm glad you told me about this."

"Well, it just sort of happened. He walked in the kitchen door one day and asked for the job."

"That's odd, too," Nick said. "I won't be able to do anything about this for the next few days, but I'll make a call on Monday. And then we'll talk again and figure out the best way to go. It'll work out."

"That's scaring me a little, Nick."

"No, you'll be fine. And things will be okay. I promise." He finished his last bite of burger, wiped off his mouth, and waved to Esther to put the meal on his tab. "I'm off to do a little boat cleaning today. We might get a short sail in tomorrow if the wind cooperates. One of my buddies is a great sailor. A great person, in fact."

He stood and slipped some bills beneath his glass.

Gracie and Cass stood, too. "This was good, I think," Gracie said. "Thanks, Nick."

"I thank you, too," Cass said. "Gracie has enough on her mind without adding a kitchen dude who infects the atmosphere of her kitchen."

"Well said, Cass." Nick gave her a pat on the back.

"And have a great weekend with the old gang." Cass grinned. "And as for that great sailor friend, I think I took classes from her once upon a time."

Nick laughed. "She's good, right?"

"I'm heading for the bar to get Ruthie's lunch," Cass said. "You two, go on ahead." She hugged them both and walked over to an empty barstool, watching Nick and Gracie gathering their things.

She swiveled on the stool, looking over to the lounge area. The floor-to-ceiling TV screen was filled with soccer players, with a crowd of Lucky's customers hooting and hollering at intervals. She scanned the crowd, then frowned as she looked at the back edge of the group, her eyes focused on a lone figure not at all interested in the goals being made.

Marco Costa stood so still he could have been mistaken for the tall rubber trees he stood behind. The same tree Esther had swatted. Had she swatted harder, she might have hit a man clearly eavesdropping on the booth where Nell, Gracie, and herself had just enjoyed Lucky's burgers. Marco's back was to the soccer game, his eyes fixed on the backs of her two friends, now walking away from the booth and toward the exit. She wondered how long he'd been there. From the expression on his face, it had been long enough.

Cass felt someone near her and looked up at Lucky Bianchi. He was standing behind the bar, also watching Marco Costa. He turned toward Cass and shook his head. "Costa is trouble, Cass. If that guy's looks could kill," he said, "Nick and Gracie wouldn't have a chance."

Chapter 7

Nell grabbed her keys off the kitchen counter and walked to the den door. "Ben, don't forget—we're having dinner at Izzy and Sam's tonight. I'm off to pick up the wine and a dessert. Then off to run a few errands."

Ben nodded. Only then did Nell notice that Ben was on a call.

"Oops, sorry," she said, then gave a small wave and headed out to her car and to Harbor Road.

She'd barely seen Ben that day. He'd left the house early while she was in the shower, leaving a note that he was meeting a friend for coffee, then to a meeting at city hall with the planning committee, a run to the library, and back home for a couple of Zoom calls.

Nell drove down Harbor Road, smiling at thoughts of the retirement life they'd carved out in the not-always-sleepy seaside town. Even Saturdays were sometimes busy. But that was fine. Being involved on boards and town committees, volunteering, and enjoying friends and hobbies kept them both moving. It was a coveted retirement, in both their minds.

Nell pulled into the parking lot near the downtown harbor park, filled today with walkers and runners. Frisbee throwers and small, giggling bodies climbing on a green space filled with granite boulders, a nice playground that nature had provided.

Nell watched for a minute, then headed on.

The new bakery was on a side street, not too far from Harry Garozzo's place. A little too close, she thought, as she walked by her friend's deli and restaurant. She wondered if his Italian delicacies might be overshadowed by the wonderful pies and cakes the new place was advertising. But Harry didn't make key lime pie, hence her trek to the new bakery. Too Irish, he said, and when reminded that people usually connected key lime pie to Florida, he pooh-poohed that. Saying it didn't matter. It was still too green.

Nell turned at the next corner and walked down a narrow sidewalk. A large painted sign above the door read: BAKED TO PERFECTION BAKERY. A brightly colored WELCOME! was scrolled across the display window.

Nell walked in, finding herself at the end of a long line of customers. The air was redolent with the enticing aromas of freshly baked bread. The scent mingled in a mouthwatering way with the sweet and buttery scent of cakes and pies. From the looks of the crowd, the shop was off to a good start. She was happy Izzy had preordered the pie, or she might have had to leave empty-handed.

She found her place in the line and fidgeted in her purse for her phone, then pulled up the pie receipt. A dozen or so people stood in front of her. A good sign for the owners. The customers seemed relaxed, not rushed as they took in the ambiance of the new bakery with its fresh paint colors and framed photos of gorgeous wedding cakes.

A familiar voice made its way through the conversations going on in the waiting line. Nell took a step to the side and looked up the slowly moving row.

Beatrice Scaglia was walking down the line, greeting each person, most of them by name and adding a personal comment about a husband or wife's new job or new baby, a child's graduation, or the like.

Her deep blue suit was partially covered by a crisp, rainbow-colored apron with a wide pocket across the front. It reminded Nell of a vendor at Fenway selling peanuts, not at all the usual Beatrice attire. In the crook of one arm, she balanced an open, flat box.

As customers moved forward, Beatrice moved closer to her, and Nell noticed that the box in her arm held miniature cupcakes. Beatrice carefully handed one to each person, along with a brightly colored card that she'd slip out of her apron pocket. Nell glanced at one in a departing customer's hand. It featured a large colorful *THANK YOU* printed across the top.

When the mayor reached Nell, her eyes lit up, her greeting warm and welcoming, as if Nell had walked into the mayor's own home.

"I'd hug you, Nell," Beatrice said, "but it might cause me to drop my delicious samples."

"This is a surprise, Beatrice. Since when did our mayor get a side job?"

Beatrice's smile was tired. "Isn't this a lovely new bakery? I promised the owners that I would come by. Be sure you tell people about the bakery. They've opened just in time for summer."

No matter how exhausting Beatrice could be, she was open and honest. As Birdie had said once, "In spite of her intelligence, there's something naïve, kind, and entertaining about Beatrice." And "calculating," she'd added.

It appeared she was combining all of those today. Campaigning this far ahead of time, and disguising it by welcoming a new bakery in town, was clever indeed.

"I'm sure the shop appreciates your bringing attention to it. It's generous of you, Beatrice. And your cupcakes look delicious."

"Well, as you know well, Nell, I didn't make them. My baking skills match my knitting expertise. But for both, I only buy the very best products." She handed a cupcake to Nell, along with a small napkin and a card that she pulled from her apron pocket.

The printed card read:

THANK YOU
Thank you, my dear Sea Harbor family, for your
support, your kindness, and for your eternal goodwill
and support. I am here for you and for all your needs,
wanting to make your lives in Sea Harbor safe and
productive. I am grateful that you stand by me. Al-
ways.
*   I look forward to successful years ahead as we*
work together to meet all your needs.
*   With affection, your mayor—past, present, and fu-*
ture—and your good friend,
*   Blessings,*
*   Mayor Beatrice Scaglia*

On each tiny cupcake, the mayor's initials were sugar-scrolled into the frosting.

"Well, my friend, I must finish this up and head out," the mayor said. "There're a million things waiting for my attention." Beatrice managed a small wave, then slipped her smile in place and greeted the next person in line like a dear friend— who, of course, just happened to be a voter.

Nell turned back toward the counter. There'd been a steeliness in Beatrice's eyes today. It was something Nell had never noticed in her before. It reminded Nell of an athlete, willing to do anything to win at all cost. It didn't suit the mayor well, Nell decided.

While waiting for her pie to be boxed up, she looked in the

glass case at dozens of the miniature cupcakes and added a dozen to her order. Her grandniece, Abby, would love them.

Outside the bakery, a breeze came up from the water. Nell paused for a moment, taking in the view. The street wasn't long, with just a handful of shops lining each side, most with small apartments above and a view of the water at the far end. Stacks of lobster traps were piled in the small lot near the ocean and nearby, a whale-watching boat was moving out of the inner harbor, carrying a crowd toward Provincetown and hopefully families of whales. In the distance, several sailboats caught the breeze and skimmed across the water. Ben and Sam were making noises about taking their Hinckley sailboat, the *Dream Weaver* out soon.

She turned and started back up the narrow sidewalk toward Harbor Road, following several shoppers carrying white bakery boxes, some with Beatrice's card balanced on top.

One of her boxes started to slip, and she took a step toward the building, getting a better grip on it. Hearing a noise, she looked up the block, then recognized Beatrice's voice. She wondered briefly if she was hearing things. Scanning the parked cars along the street, she spotted Beatrice's YOUR MAYOR license plate. The driver's-side window of her car was down and the mayor's head was visible in the opening, with her hands waving, and her voice angry, aimed at a tall man standing on the sidewalk.

A few passersby stopped, stared at the car, then quickly walked on.

Nell wondered if Beatrice was aware of them. It wasn't a very good look for the mayor.

The man moved closer to the car, as if trying to hear her better. Or maybe so she'd lower her voice. He leaned down slightly. One large hand rested on the side of the mayor's car, his arm and shoulder blocking his face from view.

Nell stood still for a minute, not wanting to walk past a private conversation. But running quickly past them, carrying her packages, would definitely not look good, either, and could result in a smashed key lime pie on the sidewalk. She took a few steps back toward the bakery.

Beatrice's words floated up the sidewalk. "Don't even try."

And then, louder, "I promise you on my life and yours, Nick Cabot, it is not going to happen. Never. I will not allow you to tear my life apart. You have no right." The words were harsh, only slightly controlled. And then they suddenly stopped.

Before Nell could fully process what was going on, the mayor gunned the engine and pulled away from the curb, the tires screeching. She watched Nick step back. He stood quietly on the sidewalk for a minute, looking after the disappearing car. His head moved slightly, as if he wasn't sure what had just happened. Finally he turned and began walking in Nell's direction. His head was down, as if in thought, and Nell realized he'd soon bump into her on the narrow sidewalk if she didn't warn him that he wasn't alone.

"Hi, Nick," she called out.

He looked up suddenly. "Oh, Nell. Hi. I'm sorry, I didn't see you there. Daydreaming, I guess." He managed a semblance of a smile. Then he looked back toward the vacated parking spot. "I'm thinking you may have heard that?"

Nell nodded. "I was trying not to. Beatrice's voice seems to travel farther than she realizes."

"Practice from all those mayor talks when the microphone goes bad, I guess."

Nell chuckled. "Maybe."

Nick shook his head. "It sounds like I'm not our mayor's favorite person right now."

"Well, we all have our days, Nick, right?"

"True." He lifted one brow and said with a grin, "But who knows? She could be mad at your husband. Ben and I had coffee earlier today and Beatrice happened to walk by Coffee's. If looks could kill, we'd both be flat on Coffee's patio stones right now."

"Oh, my." Nell held back a smile, imagining the sight.

"I've always liked Beatrice. She's got spunk, and she's been a decent mayor. She and I have had coffee together a couple times. I once spent an hour in the bookstore with her, talking about a book we both loved. Archie finally kicked us out so he could lock up. And we both love this crazy little town. I consider her a friend. I hadn't considered the harsh side of all this election business."

"Beatrice is complicated," Nell said, unsure of how serious or open this mayoral consideration was. One of her boxes began to slip and she shifted, getting it back in place.

"Hey, sorry, Nell. You have a load there. Let me help."

Nell's balance returned. "No thanks, Nick. I got it."

Attempting to lighten the conversation, she said, "By the way, if you need something to sweeten that encounter, this bakery has amazing choices."

Nick glanced at the window display. It was filled with tiers of inviting items—wedding cake, croissants and pies, breads and tortes. He laughed. "Actually, that's an excellent idea. Even timely. I'm getting together with friends this weekend and sweets are always welcome. Especially for one of them. I'm hoping to make her weekend special. I'll do exactly that."

They said their good-byes and began to walk separate ways when Nick turned back and called to her. "Hey, Nell," he said. "D'you think I should drop a few sweets off on our mayor's doorstep?"

Nell looked back at him and laughed. "My advice, Nick, would be to wait a day or two."

Chapter 8

Izzy and Sam walked down Harbor Road with Abby between them. She had grabbed a hand of each parent and was swinging happily, her feet kicking up in the air.

A free Saturday afternoon with Sam and Abby was Izzy's idea of heaven, and she wondered if maybe she was even more excited than Abby about going to a puppet show.

"We're getting close," Sam said, looking down at his curly-haired daughter.

As they rounded the corner onto the museum street, Abby shrieked and let go of their hands. She pointed to the giant wooden puppet in front of the museum. The Pinocchio-like figure was nearly fifteen feet tall and hung from puppet strings attached to the museum canopy. One of its motorized hands was flapping merrily to a crowd of delighted children and parents, who were already lining up on the wide museum steps.

"We're early for once," Izzy laughed. "That's a first for the Perrys."

Sam checked the tickets to the puppet show. "You're right

on both accounts. It *is* amazing." He glanced at the crowded steps. "I have an idea. How about if we avoid the crowd and check out that new restaurant being worked on around the corner? We have plenty of time. It's an old bank, Abby, and they're turning it into a good-looking restaurant."

"For mac and cheese?" Abby asked, climbing up on a low granite wall. She stretched her arms out like a bird and started walking slowly along the surface.

"I doubt if they'll have mac and cheese, kiddo, but it doesn't matter. No one can beat our Gracie's special mac and cheese. They wouldn't dare try."

"So not my kinda place?" Abby asked, walking a little faster along the wall, her arms moving up and down.

Izzy and Sam laughed.

"Right," Izzy said. "A grown-up place. But Gracie's restaurant is both."

Satisfied, Abby continued her balancing act, moving ahead.

"I hope that's true," Nick said.

"What?"

"That Gracie's place stays family oriented. Bobby told me that after the initial raves, highlighting his special entrees, the Lazy Lobster's evening clientele became less family oriented and more couples. Probably because of expense. And now, even that crowd is shrinking."

"I think Gracie wants to keep it family oriented," Izzy said, speaking more to herself. She tucked the thought away to dig up later.

"You'll like this place. I went over with Nick Cabot the other day to see it."

"With Nick? Why?"

"A friend of his is one of the owners. Jack something. He was in town and interested in getting some photos of the place when it was finished. They invited me to tag along."

"He knows you do documentary photography, right?"

Sam nodded, his eyes on Abby, now yards ahead of them. "Nick thought I might be able to recommend someone who does more commercial work."

"And you were itching to get inside."

"That too." Sam chuckled and called out to his daughter, "Hey, slow the locomotive. That's our destination, Abby!"

Izzy hurried to reach Abby and redirect her to the building.

The old Sea Harbor Bank had been closed for years and was a major eyesore for the town. But some creative architects were bringing it back to life.

They walked closer to the building and stood on a narrow patch of grass in front of it.

The granite and brick structure still retained the look of the original bank, with intricate scrolling at the roofline and ten-foot windows, their black metal trim now freshened. The entire outside of the building had been tweaked and polished and turned into an attractive, welcoming structure.

Near the wide front door, a bronze plaque announced the restaurant's name:

LA BANQUE
A Fine Eating Establishment

"Wow, Izzy said. "It's eye-catching for sure."

She walked closer to one of the large windows and looked inside at a blur of movement. Workmen. A painter, carrying a ladder and buckets, walked by and spotted Sam. He gave a wave in recognition, then walked inside through an open door.

"Hey, where's Abby?" Sam said suddenly.

Izzy swiveled around. "Abby," she called out, wondering why five-year-olds found hiding from parents such a fun game, one that paralyzed parents. Thankfully, Abby never went far. She didn't like it if she couldn't see her parents.

A knocking on the tall window brought her attention back

to it, where Abby's small face was flattened against the glass, a distorted grin looking out at her mother.

Izzy rushed to keep up with Sam as he hurried through the open door and scooped up his daughter.

"Okay," Izzy said, catching her breath. "Let's not do that again, Abigail Kathleen Perry."

Since no one had seemed to notice the ruckus nor chased them out, Izzy roamed around the space, amazed at the transformation. As if by magic, the old bank was being transformed into an interesting, comfortable restaurant. It was sure to become a favorite, she thought. Even in its unfinished state, it was lovely. Black and white stone tiles were piled up in a corner, ready to cover the floor, and intimate upholstered booths looked nearly ready to welcome diners. The building's history hadn't been neglected, either. She looked at the original teller booths, now with the windows removed, providing a long, polished bar.

She glanced over at Sam and Abby. The painter had joined them, pleasing Abby with a purple lollipop, and showing her old carvings along the bar edges that were tiny people when you looked closely.

Seeing they were occupied, Izzy walked off by herself. She spotted the old bank vault off a wide hallway, its large round door open and polished to a high sheen.

Two workmen stood nearby, leaning against the opposite wall.

They seemed to be deep in conversation, unaware of her presence as she walked closer to the vault, impressed by the floor-to-ceiling wine racks inside the space.

She started to walk inside when a familiar voice stopped her. The two men were still talking, their voices louder now.

Izzy frowned, then walked their way, her footsteps stopping the conversation—or argument—she couldn't be sure.

"Marco Costa?" Izzy said.

He looked up, a surprised look on his face that quickly turned into an embarrassed one, as if he'd been caught stealing cookies. His face turned red, but in the next moment, he puffed out his chest and muttered a hello.

The dark-haired fellow with bushy eyebrows, standing next to him, spoke up. "Hey, can I help you?"

"I know her," Marco muttered to the man.

Sam walked up then, with Abby riding on his shoulders. "Hi, Marco," he said, lifting Abby down to the floor. "I thought I saw you over here."

"So, whatta you guys doing here?" Marco said.

"Puppets," Abby said happily.

Izzy's thought was to send the question back at him. It was strange to find Bobby Palazola's top kitchen helper in someone else's restaurant. Especially since he claimed to have nothing to do with the place, like she thought Gracie said.

"We're looking around," Izzy said, watching his face.

"I came to see a buddy," Marco said, nodding at the man standing next to him, who had a slight smirk on his ruddy face.

Before Marco could say more, his buddy spoke up and thrust a large hand out to shake Sam's, then Izzy's.

"Name's Tony," he said.

Sam introduced Izzy and Abby, who was already pulling away to explore the vault. "I got a tour a few days ago," he said.

"Oh," Tony asked, his voice was suspicious. "Who with?"

"A friend," Sam said.

"Well, okay, I guess. Whatta ya think?" Tony asked. "I'm making sure things go right."

"It looks good. A nice place."

"*Good?*" the man guffawed. "*Nice?* It's fantastic. Seafood prepared in special, unique ways. Where else in this town will you find a place like this? Nowhere, that's where. I've seen a couple of places here that claim to have good food. *Wrong.* They don't know good food from nothing. You'll see."

Izzy's first thought was that the man didn't look or sound like a someone who would be in charge, at least not like the restaurant managers and owners she knew. Tony looked more like he worked down on the dock. For the restaurant's sake, she sincerely hoped he wasn't the chef.

Aloud she said, "It's a beautiful place. And seafood specialties? That sounds good, too."

"Yeah. We picked a good town to get fish in, right?" he said. "My brother's the new chef."

"Oh," Sam said. "So, are you a manager?"

The guy laughed. "Nope, not by a long shot."

Izzy was instantly relieved, and she could see that Sam was, too.

"I asked, because when I was here the other day with—"

But Tony had more to say. "Like I said. My bro's the chef. A great chef. That's how I'm connected to this place. We're an LLC."

Sam's brows lifted at the strange answer.

"Anyway. My brother's working at a posh restaurant in New York right now, but he can't wait to get up here."

Sam paused for a minute, looking at the guy more closely. "Have we met, Tony? You look vaguely familiar. I'm not good at names, but I photograph a lot of faces and usually remember people I've seen."

Tony laughed. "I sure doubt it. Although I've been up here some. Spent a month here recently, looking for a place to live. That's how Marco and I met."

"Where's the New York restaurant?" Sam asked.

"In Manhattan. Why are you asking?"

"Just curious," Sam said. "That's a great place for restaurants."

"Agreed. Much better than where my old man started out. Hated it there. But it all worked out. We're livin' off the hog now."

Izzy frowned, having lost the conversation train.

"Why do you want to move up here?" Sam asked.

"Great opportunity," Tony said quickly.

"Why do you think so?"

"Why? Geez, man. Have you seen what's around here? We're about to change the whole eating scene. We'll come in and take over, maybe close down those no-good little cafés and bring in great food for you folks. You know?"

"No, I guess I don't," Sam said. "We don't have any 'no-good little cafés.'"

Izzy turned to Marco, who seemed to have lost his voice and was looking a little pale. "What about you? Looks like you'll be working in two kitchens?"

Marco made a sound that could have meant, *In your dreams,* or *Yeah,* or *So, what?* Or words she chose not to consider. He seemed agitated.

Finally his mutterings turned into words. "Are you crazy?" he said. "One kitchen's plenty. I could use more money, though. Those guys don't pay what I'm worth." He had regained his composure, even though his buddy was laughing at him now.

"People come in here all the time," Tony said, pulling the attention back to himself. "We're the best attraction in town."

"Hey," he focused on Izzy. "You wanted to know the menu, right? It's going to be a great one. I tell you, this chef's amazing. Wait here a minute."

Tony headed over to the bar and hurried back with a sheaf of papers, pulling one out and thrusting it into Izzy's hands. "Here's a sample. It'll make you hungry just looking at it."

Izzy scanned the menu, smiled, then handed it to Sam.

Sam glanced at it. "You're right, Tony. It looks good." Then he corrected himself before Tony had a chance to. "It's great. We'll give it a try."

"Sure you will." Tony clapped him on the back. "Just make sure you make reservations. The place will be packed to the gills." Then he laughed and looked at Marco. "Get it, Marco? *Gills!*"

Abby came out from examining the bank vault and tugged on the edge of Izzy's sweater. "Mommy? When's our puppet show?"

The puppet show. They'd nearly forgotten it.

"The puppet show. That's right, sweetie. We're headed there right this minute."

She explained their quick good-byes to Tony and thanked him. "May we keep this?" She waved the menu.

Tony not only said yes, but followed them to the door, handing her a few more. "There's so much more to see in our place," he said to their backs, seemingly disappointed that they had to leave so quickly. "Looks like none of you are sticking around."

Izzy looked around for Marco, but he seemed to have disappeared.

Until they got outside.

Marco was halfway down the block, looking like he was in a major hurry to get somewhere, maybe anywhere, where Izzy and Sam were not.

Chapter 9

"How did your afternoon go, Ben?" Nell asked. But her mind wasn't really on what Ben was up to. It was on a mayor passing out cupcakes in a new bakery, and the angry face she'd seen glaring out of the car window. She liked the mayor, even her quirks. But this chameleon of a mayor troubled her.

Nell put the key lime pie in the refrigerator and checked her messages. It had taken her longer than usual to make her way back home from the bakery, but they still had some time before leaving for dinner at Izzy's.

Ben had come out of the den and joined her. He straddled a kitchen stool and checked the wine she'd purchased, picking out a Malbec and uncorking it. He poured two glasses and slid one across the island to Nell.

"How'd your day go?" Nell asked.

"Not much news. The planning committee called a quick meeting because of that new restaurant coming in. The owners are working on various licenses and wanted to touch base with as many people as possible. French seafood dishes, I guess."

"Bouillabaisse in our future. That sounds good. We're becoming a fine-food mecca. Was the meeting with Nick before or after your coffee meeting?"

"Ah, I have no secrets. How did you know Nick and I met?" Then he answered himself. "No secrets around here. I should know that by now." Ben laughed. "I wanted to meet over at the Source Bakery in Gloucester. Way more private and the break-fast biscuit sandwiches are far better than Coffee's donuts. But we both had busy days and not enough time."

"You probably should have gone over there. I hear Beatrice almost hit you with her broom when she saw you two together. She's having a bad day."

"Nick must have told you. Where did you run into him?"

"At the new cake bakery. Unfortunately for him, Beatrice was there, too. Two encounters in one day were too much for her. She's not happy about whatever is going on."

"You mean the far-off election that Beatrice seems to think is tomorrow?" Ben said.

"Yes, that one. How serious is Nick about running? After Beatrice left, he filled me in a little. Not much, though, which I was fine with. But Beatrice made it clear to him how she feels about it. She did the same to us when she made a surprise visit to our knitting night, telling us Nick simply couldn't run against her."

"Not that it's her decision."

"Well, she seems to think it is. And she's upset he might not be compliant. She made it sound like it's very likely Nick will run against her. Do you agree with that?"

"What part?"

Nell chuckled.

"Yes, I think he'll run."

"Why?"

"He's being encouraged by a lot of good people. Many who supported Beatrice when she ran the last couple times. Some are her good friends at city hall. But people think a change would be good for Sea Harbor, and that Nick would make an excellent mayor. You normally don't get someone his age willing to take the mayor's job in a small town."

"Because of the salary, I guess."

"That and age. People Nick's age can't afford it, even though some would be excellent. That's why our mayors are usually older, mostly retired. Younger men and women are busy supporting families, or even just themselves. Nick is that generation, but he doesn't have any financial needs. His company practically runs itself."

"But does he want the job?"

Ben thought about that for a minute before answering. He grabbed a bowl of peanuts and added a pour of wine to his glass. "This is how I see it. Nick is very bright, excellent at business things. Personable. Honest."

"Agree. But does he *want* the job?"

"Yes, I think he does. He knows himself well. Knows he could do the job, and he loves this town. The people encouraging him are doing it for all the right reasons, and he agrees that he'd bring fresh ideas to Sea Harbor management—a new and creative approach to things. He's good at working with people on all sides of an issue. It intrigues him. A good challenge that he feels capable of meeting."

Nell thought about those things. She was fond of Nick, and also saw in him all the qualities Ben had voiced.

"He's a good man, Nell," Ben said. He got up and took his glass over to the sink.

"I agree." She checked her watch. It was almost time to dress and leave for the Perrys'.

"He'd run for the right reasons. Certainly, not for power, which in the size of our town is practically nonexistent, anyway. But because he could contribute something."

"My feelings, too. Nick would be effective, just like his grandfather was. My dad knew the older Nicholas Cabot from summers spent up here. He was a fisherman and a mayor. And a well-loved one, according to my dad."

"So, what do you think? I mean, personally. Would you support him? How do you feel about it all?"

Ben didn't hesitate. "I feel good about it, Nell. I'll support him."

He rinsed out his glass, then turned back and met Nell's eyes, holding her look. He had a glint in his eye, but tried to feign a frown. "But it'll be separate bedrooms for us, Nell Endicott, if you whisper one word of that to Beatrice Scaglia."

Nell chuckled all the way up the back stairs to the shower.

Chapter 10

The sun had nearly disappeared when Ben and Nell pulled into the Perrys' drive. Abby was waiting in the doorway, already in her pajamas, her arms outstretched, and clutching her *Sleep Like a Tiger* book in one hand.

Ben immediately scooped her up, looking back at Nell. "My turn," he said as he and Abby disappeared into her bedroom.

Nell walked into Izzy's white kitchen, explaining where Ben was. "I'm glad you suggested this, Izzy." She put the pie in the refrigerator and walked over to the small island, where Izzy was tossing a salad of spinach and beets.

"Me too. It's been a long time since it was just the four of us."

"I third it," Sam said from his post at a countertop filled with glasses and drink-making tools. "And our deck happens to be a little bit of heaven at this time of year. We need to do it more often."

Ben walked in then, flapping a book in the air. "All right, what did you two do with my buddy? She fell asleep before we barely got the tiger to sleep. It must have been a wild puppet show."

Sam laughed and handed Ben a shaker of martinis for him to do his magic. "We wore her out at the puppet show," he said. "She had a wonderful adventure with Pinocchio and will be having happy dreams of never telling us a lie. Even when she's sixteen. She promised."

"Sometimes adult quiet is good," Izzy said. "Abby tends to change the tempo a little."

"True. But we enjoy absorbing every single word that comes out of her mouth," Nell said.

"And there are a lot," Izzy said.

Nell simply smiled. She adored her grandniece—one of those unexpected life gifts for which she'd be forever grateful.

"The salad looks delicious," Nell said, a catch in her voice. She plucked out a piece of spinach and tasted it, hiding her emotion. "This is good, Iz. Marshall's Farm Stand?"

"Nope. It's from Gracie's garden. She put one in at the Lazy Lobster. Even Abby liked the spinach. Well, sort of. She dipped it in ranch dressing first."

"A garden at the Lazy Lobster? That's smart. Fresh herbs and veggies for the chef's new exotic dishes."

"How's Gracie doing?" Ben asked.

Izzy stopped tossing the greens for a minute, her hands resting on the side of the bowl. Her forehead wrinkled in thought. "Personally or professionally?"

"I'd guess that those two parts of Gracie are tightly tied together right now."

"I thought the same thing after seeing her yesterday. Gracie hides her feelings so well. I think it's because she thinks she needs to put on a welcoming, happy face for customers every single day."

"That sounds like Gracie," Nell said. "But she's proved her mettle. Handling a difficult divorce with grace and good sense can do that for you. She's certainly resilient."

"She's also been getting a lot of attention with all these

changes to her restaurant," Sam said. He lifted a stack of napkins and silverware from cupboard drawers. "That's not Gracie's thing. Especially people commenting in a way they hadn't
done before, being critical. That's tough. But Nell's right—
she's weathered a lot of storms. This'll just be a blip."

"Hopefully," Izzy said. "She managed to turn on her cheer-
ful self yesterday when she showed us her garden. But I don't
know. Cass and I both thought there was something going on
inside her that we were missing. Her uncle drove up as we were
leaving. Maybe that had something to do with it."

"Alphonso has a stake in Gracie's place," Ben said. He
poured chilled gin into a martini shaker. "He's probably keeping tabs on the whole thing. Knowing him, I'm sure he'll handle any difficulties with care."

Sam held out two chilled martini glasses for Ben to fill, then
handed one to Nell and put Izzy's next to the salad bowl.

"You sometimes overthink things, Izzy," Ben said. "That
might be what Gracie is doing, too."

"It's your lawyer's mind, Iz," Sam added. "Always looking
for clues."

Izzy shrugged. Sam knew her so well. While he looked
for angles and light and color in his photography work, she
looked for clues and motives, causes and effects. Things that
had served her well when she briefly practiced law in Boston.
She supposed it also helped in knitting and creating patterns.
But maybe not so much when figuring out if a friend was
happy or sad.

"Was Bobby Palazola there?" Sam asked.

"He was. He mentioned that you two knew each other, way
back in the day."

"I like him—he's a personable guy—and I enjoyed the job.
The guy has—or at least had—a great sense of humor. Although,
his staff mentioned that he wasn't always that jovial. He had a
temper when it involved culinary problems, apparently. Bobby

admitted it was true. Not unusual for a chef, I hear. It can be hectic back in those kitchens."

"What was his restaurant like?" Nell asked.

"It had been a neighborhood deli in an old Bronx neighborhood. Bobby did a decent job fixing up an old space. I think a relative had given it to him for almost nothing. He had friends in the restaurant world who helped him fix it up. The restaurant took off quickly because Bobby created such unique entrees. He catered it to the tastes of the people in the neighborhood and quickly developed a following. He's like an artist with food. But it wasn't without its problems, which he weathered admirably."

"What kind?" Ben said.

"What you'd expect. Competition. It came to a head about the time I was doing that photography work for him. A restaurant nearby catered to the same clientele. It had been there for a while, a father-to-son sort of thing. The father had been loved by the neighborhood, but after he died, the place was turned over to the son. The son was a fine chef, apparently, talented, but had no business sense and made terrible decisions trying to compete with Bobby. He spent money on foolish kinds of advertising, fancy furniture, and things like that. He focused more on driving Bobby out than servicing his diners. His place started to look shabby. Even longtime customers got sick of going there.

"Bobby was smarter. He had hired someone to handle the things he wasn't good at—like managing the place. His staff was friendly, knew the neighborhood, and the food was great."

"So, what happened?" Ben asked.

"The other place closed."

"One of the pitfalls of that kind of work."

"Right. Bobby felt bad about the whole mess. He thinks competition is good for both parties. A challenge to be better. But the other chef was an angry kind of guy. Nasty."

"Nasty how?" Nell asked.

Sam took a drink of his martini, scrunching his forehead as he tried to pull up the memory.

"The guy blamed his failure on Bobby and had trouble controlling his anger. He hated Bobby, tried to smear him, sent letters to vendors that they shouldn't do business with him, that he was a crook. But clearly, it didn't work, and eventually he moved away. Cursing Bobby as he left. He was a mean son of a gun. In fact, the day they left the area, they threw cans of bright orange luminescent paint all over the front of Bobby's place. I was there when it happened and took a photo of it, in case Bobby wanted to sue the guy."

"That's sad," Izzy said.

"It had a decent ending, though. Bobby didn't sue. In fact, he was concerned about the guy and checked up on him. The guy ended up being a chef in a new restaurant. He didn't own it or manage it, so all the guy had to do was cook, which is what he was very good at. That restaurant had good managers and got great reviews, and the guy ended up doing well. Bobby was relieved, I think."

"In the case of the Lazy Lobster and Soup Café, Gracie's managing Bobby. How is that working?" Ben asked.

"Gracie told me that Bobby is great and nice to be around," Nell said. "Fun. Not what we always hear about great chefs."

Izzy listened, holding back her thoughts about Bobby's feelings toward Gracie. She'd tried to scold the thoughts away, reminding herself she'd seen them together for all of fifteen minutes. Not to mention that it was none of her business.

"They've expanded their kitchen staff," she said. "Maybe that will help things."

"Speaking of restaurants," Sam said, "We went through the new one being worked on in the old bank building today. I'd seen it before, but Abby and Izzy had not."

Ben nodded. "I had a walk-through, too. They're doing a good job."

"Speaking of La Banque, guess who we saw over there?" Izzy said. "None other than Marco Costa."

"That's odd," Nell said.

"I thought so, too. And the guy he was meeting with is also odd. A guy named Tony, who's somehow connected to the place. I'm wondering if Marco is working for them, though he said he wasn't. But he's part-time at Gracie's, so she thinks he must be working somewhere else."

"Interesting," Ben said.

"And curious," Izzy said. "Why would he lie about it? I'm with Gracie. She doesn't trust him, and I don't, either." She grabbed a hot pad and opened the oven door, pulling out a pan of cheesy potatoes.

"That's my cue," Sam said. "Coals are hot. Brats will be sizzling in seconds."

Ben picked up the tray of sausages and followed Sam out to the deck.

Nell looked over at her niece. "Izzy, what aren't you saying about Gracie?"

"Nothing, Aunt Nell. Really. She was happy showing off her garden, but before she saw us that morning, she looked kind of sad. Or distressed, not sure which. And then again, when her uncle showed up."

"I assume it's those few unimpressed reviewers?"

"Maybe. Who knows? I mean, it's only been a couple reviews. And town rumors, too, I guess. It seems to be sporadic, though. Ben may be right. Cass and I sometimes read into things." She smiled away her unfounded feelings and picked up the pan of potatoes, nodding toward the door. "Time to join the guys."

Although the Perrys lived in a modest, family-filled neighborhood, their home's location at the top of a hilly road afforded a million-dollar view of the ocean. Sam had made the

most of the small deck, equipping it with a place for his tele-
scope so they'd never miss a full moon or the glorious patterns
of light on the water or, sometimes, views of unsuspecting
beachcombers. In nice weather, the deck was where the Perrys
spent most of their at-home time, even sleeping in warm bags
on starry nights, with Abby cuddled between them.

Tonight the foursome settled into Adirondack chairs with
arms wide enough to hold their plates and drinks. Sam had
heaped each plate high with grilled corn on the cob, potatoes,
and warm buns holding fat, juicy bratwurst blanketed with
sauerkraut and condiments. Izzy passed out extra napkins to
catch the drips of butter and juice.

For a while, the only sounds were those of the gulls and the
crunch of grilled corn. From a small speaker in the corner of
the deck came the soothing lyrical strains of "Avalon."

Eventually, and between bites, they managed to catch up on
family things and relatives—Izzy's brothers and her father and
her mother, Nell's only sister. Ben's heart health issues were
covered quickly, and Sam's next photography show in a Boston gallery was typed into phone calendars.

Finally, when Nell's key lime pie was nothing but a few buttery crumbs in the pan, Sam suggested they take a walk out
back and enjoy the evening breezes.

One of the things that Sam and Izzy loved most about their
house was the gentle incline at the back edge of their yard. It
was filled with sea-twisted and stunted trees and butterfly
bushes, wild grasses, and flowers, a natural shield when strong
nor'easters came in over the water. Every season was a new discovery of wild-growing things that found a home on their
small hill. Somewhere in the thick of it was a short, nearly hidden path that led down to the water's edge.

Izzy ran in and checked on Abby, making sure the monitor
was on. Then she and Nell grabbed windbreakers and followed
Sam and Ben down the deck steps and to the path, pushing

branches out of the way as they made their way to the rocky stretch of shoreline below.

In the distance, the last bit of sunlight was slipping beneath the outline of Sea Harbor. They watched in silence as a brilliant, red-streaked sunset dissolved completely into a deep sky, a faint crescent moon growing brighter as they watched.

Ben and Sam began walking along the narrow shore, passing Sam's binoculars back and forth as they picked out shapes in the constellation-studded sky.

The wind had picked up some, and the soothing sound of waves washing up on the outcropping of boulders held Izzy and Nell in place, listening. "I love that sound," Nell said.

Izzy hooked her arm through her aunt's. "When things seem tangled and tilted, being on the edge of the ocean like this puts the world back on its axis for me."

"Do you feel the world tilted, Izzy?"

"Sometimes. Not often."

Nell nodded. She understood life's tilts well, the vagaries in life that had brought grief and happiness and great joy and great sadness. She thought of Ben's heart attack a few years before, of losing friends to Covid, but somehow, even in the deepest shadows, believing things would be okay. When allowed to simply be, hope moved in.

She shivered, surprised at the emotion that suddenly welled up in her. Turning slightly away from Izzy, she looked in the other direction, where the sky was already dark. An outcropping of granite boulders was ghostly against the starry sky and water, helping her turn off her thoughts.

Izzy followed her look. "That area always seemed private and kind of mysterious to me, like it has its own identity. It's almost as if the boulders are telling one to be still."

"It's beautiful, in an eerie way," Nell said.

Izzy nodded. "It's the dramatic angles of the boulders and all the shadows created in the moonlight. There's a very small patch of rocky beach beyond and between the boulders, and a nearly invisible path that goes up into the next neighborhood."

"Is it a public path?"

"No. There's a privacy sign at the top, but it's mostly ignored. People around here call the area Lovers' Surf. A place for private rendezvous in the rocky coves."

Nell looked more closely at a large boulder that seemed to define the area. "It looks like someone might be proving your point."

Two figures emerged, seemingly out of nowhere. They were standing close together, forming a dark silhouette against the moonlit sea.

"Ah, young love." Izzy smiled.

Izzy and Nell stood there for a moment, watching the strangers. One, clearly a male, stood near the boulder that seemed to grow directly out of the ground. The other was a woman, an outline of her shape visible. They were standing close to each other, their heads leaning in, dark hair nearly touching.

But suddenly what had seemed to be an affectionate togetherness was illuminated by an anchor light on a sailboat moored a short distance offshore. The two figures moved out of the glare.

From where Izzy and Nell stood, most facial features were obscured. The man wore a baseball cap on dark hair, the other's hair was also dark and long. As the woman shifted, moonlight fell on her physically striking profile.

Hidden by the brush and tangled vines, Izzy and Nell started to turn back to the path leading up to the house, slightly embarrassed, as if they were interrupting a romantic tryst. But then the man took a step out of the shadows and the wind caught words being hurled at the woman, who seemed calm and untouched by them. Even smiling, Izzy thought. She lifted a hand to the man's arm. But a sad, male voice seemed to send an unpleasant message and the woman dropped her arm.

For a moment, the man looked tense. Maybe angry. But in the next instant, his body slumped, and he shook his head slowly. He lowered his head, ignoring a cap that fell to the rocky ground, and turned around, moving away from the woman and disappearing between the two boulders and the hill beyond. But not before a stream of light coming from somewhere on the water fell across the man's profile.

Izzy's mouth opened wide. "I think that's . . ." she started to say. Then stopped, frowning, realizing how shadowy her view was. Trying to identify the people was foolish, and somehow unfair. She had no right to even be watching the small seaside drama. And yet, she thought, there was something about their movements that indicated danger.

The woman on the beach stood still and calm. She ran a hand through her hair and turned away from the boulders and toward the water.

But a moment later, the man came back, walking swiftly toward the surprised woman and embracing her. Then, just as abruptly, turning away and moving up the hill.

The woman watched him for a moment, her hand seeming to wipe her eyes.

Then she turned and walked to the water's edge. Calmly, as if she were alone in the universe, she kicked off her shoes. With what looked like a wave to the moon, the woman dove into the ocean, her blouse ballooning around her, diaphanous in the moonlight.

Izzy and Nell gasped. Then breathed again as they watched strong slender arms stretch and slice through the water, swimming toward a dark boat bobbing in the waves a short distance away.

Later that night, after Ben and Nell had gone home, Izzy walked out to the deck to turn off the lights and bring in the blankets. She looked out into the darkness, toward the sea. The tide was beginning its journey toward shore, the moon lighting the frothy waves. She looked again toward the lovers' spot, the narrow, pebbly stretch of beach shadowed by imposing boulders.

She stood for a minute, replaying the mini drama. The man abruptly leaving, coming back for an embrace and leaving again; and then, as if choreographed for a movie, the woman kicking off her shoes and swimming gracefully in the moonlight.

Kicking off her shoes. Izzy reflected on the image. And the tide was coming in. She wondered if the clothing items were still there.

Without further thought, she grabbed a flashlight from the grill shelf and made her way down the path, a trip she'd made many times when Abby left her toys behind after playing at the small beach. Toys that would disappear at high tide—bad for the environment and bad for Abby's decreasing stash of beach toys.

Carefully, with the flashlight guiding her way, Izzy walked toward the boulder area. She spotted the shoes immediately, the moonlight highlighting their bright color among the neutral rocks and sand. The image of the woman slipping out of them and sliding into the sea like a mermaid flashed before her eyes. She looked out into the water, half expecting to see her swimming back to shore with, perhaps, a mermaid fin appearing behind her.

There was no sign of a swimmer.

The woman had probably swum back to the children's beach, a short distance down the shore," Izzy thought. Its soft, low lights were always on for safety reasons.

Enough imagining, Izzy scolded herself. Perhaps it was the almost romance of it all—the woman gliding into the water, her clothes billowing around her, which lingered with Izzy. She smiled, then leaned down and picked up the sandals. Not far away, an already-muddied cap was stuck on the rocks, and she picked that up, too. Her own sneakers were already damp from the tide washing up against the narrow strip of shore. With one last look for anything else left behind, she started back the short distance to the path.

She looked up and spotted a worried Sam standing at the deck rail, waving at her.

Izzy waved back, then quickly sprinted up the path to the deck, her hands holding a flashlight, a damp Red Sox cap—and a fleeing Cinderella's designer shoes.

Chapter 11

Nell had nearly forgotten she had a birthday brunch to go to.

Sundays were usually lazy and relaxing. If she and Ben weren't going to Annabelle Palazola's Sweet Petunia for brunch, they'd happily stay home. Ben would make his Sunday special—poached eggs with goat cheese sauce—and they'd sit in their robes on the comfortable couch, eating and reading the Sunday paper, and happy that the hours were all their own.

But her calendar reminded her that Ben would have to settle for eating alone. It was a women's brunch for Jane Brewster's birthday. A group of Canary Cove artists, all of whom were like family to Jane and her husband, Ham, was hosting it, and they'd thoughtfully included Birdie and Nell, as Jane's oldest Sea Harbor friends.

Nell put on a light jacket, sent a text to Birdie, reminding her that she was picking her up shortly, and left a contented Ben on the couch, his slippered feet on the coffee table and the Sunday *Times* balanced on his lap. His favorite Segovia guitar music played in the background.

Somehow Nell didn't think she'd be missed.

* * *

The Sea Harbor Yacht Club was located in a lush, treed area just north of town. It boasted a beautiful, well-tended beach, boathouses, and plenty of docks for sailboats, yachts, and small dinghies, which kids took out. It also had a restaurant that served a Sunday brunch that could keep one satisfied for at least a day or two.

Nell and Birdie walked through the comfortable lobby, waving at a few friends. Liz Palazola Santos, the club manager, walked over immediately to greet them.

"The perfect people to see on a lovely Sunday," Liz said, her smile wide. She gave them each a hug.

"It looks like you have quite a crowd today," Nell said.

"We do. Lots going on. Even the mayor is having some kind of meeting in one of the private rooms. Beatrice is very wise—she plans her meetings around delicious food, making sure the invitees are sure to come."

"A business meeting on a Sunday?" Birdie asked.

"Yes and no. Beatrice certainly wasn't secretive about it, or I wouldn't say anything. Besides, you'll probably be invited to the same kind of thing down the road. The meeting is mayoral in the sense that she's dining friends in high places that she'd like to be her advisors for the next election. And, of course, her voters."

"She's a planner, isn't she?" Birdie said. "Usually, her campaigns are so, well, so casual. She's gathering a posse for this one."

Liz laughed. She stepped aside for a minute, greeting a group of club members, then turned back. "I didn't mean to delay you two. I'm guessing you're here for Jane Brewster's birthday brunch?"

"And you would be right," Nell said.

"We're looking forward to it," Birdie said. "The mayor will have nothing on us."

Liz laughed. "As long as I'm not in the kitchen, it will be fabulous. And trust me, I won't ever be. I have a wonderful young chef who'll be with us for the summer."

"We're becoming a haven for chefs here in Sea Harbor," Birdie said. "Do you suppose your new chef will be competing with your cousin Bobby for the most coveted brunch? Bobby's become quite the town celebrity."

Liz chuckled. "Well, Bobby's a colorful one, I'll say that. But underneath all that bravado, he's a great guy. I love Bobby. He's one of my favorite cousins. As for the restaurant, competition is always healthy. I worry a little, though. This club has a powerful rumor mill and I hear things. I hope Gracie and Bobby can put things back on track at the Lazy Lobster. They got off to such a great start. Bobby is truly a gifted chef."

"The lobster mac and cheese I had last week was magnificent, as delicious as ever," Birdie said. "Sometimes people are a tad too picky."

Liz smiled. "My girls love that dish, too. But I think that's Gracie's special recipe, not Bobby's. Bobby's are interesting, though. Unusual and delicious. That's why I don't quite understand some of the chatter."

"I don't, either. A month ago, they were praised all over the North Shore," Nell said. "Apparently, the reviews are sporadic."

"It's a mystery," Liz said. "I know for a fact Bobby is a great cook. Even before he turned pro, he used to cook for our Palazola reunions—he even impressed my mom Annabelle—and you know what a great cook she is. Honestly, no matter what the guy made for our family gatherings, it was delicious. Mom always said Bobby would someday make it big in the culinary world and we'd all be saying 'we knew him when.'"

"Is Alphonso concerned about Gracie's place?" Nell asked. Liz's marriage to the wealthy business owner some years before came as a surprise to many people. She was the most sought-after young woman in Sea Harbor, and the age gap between her and Alphonso Santos was significant. But neither age nor money seemed to matter to either of them. Their relationship was the envy of many and was only enhanced when three little girls were born into their lives.

"Well, you know how Alphonso is, Nell. He adores Gracie. He wants his niece to be happy. He was the father she never had."

"You're all linked together so closely," Birdie said. "Bobby's your cousin, working with Alphonso's niece."

"It's all a bit incestuous, isn't it?" Liz laughed. "It gets worse when we get into friends and cousins and growing up together. One of my cousins is my closest friend. For a while in high school, we even exchanged boyfriends back and forth. We Palazolas have a lot of history. It almost scared Alphonso off."

"I doubt that." Birdie chuckled. "But it's true that if you dig deeply enough, nearly everyone, somewhere down the line, has some connection to everyone else."

"One big, happy family," Liz said. "Most of the time, anyway."

In the distance, a waiter waved to get Liz's attention. The manager excused herself, promising to stop by their table later.

Nell and Birdie walked through the wide entrance into the restaurant, a sunny room with large glass doors opening to the veranda and a panoramic view of the beach and ocean beyond. They spotted the table they were looking for immediately: A bouquet of balloons floated in the air next to a pitcher of Bloody Mary drinks and baskets of crisp calamari.

Jane was already seated at the table, looking comfortable and happy as she greeted other diners, who spotted the balloons and stopped by to extend birthday wishes to the well-loved founder of the art colony. Several Canary Cove artists—

including Willow Adams, who had put the birthday celebration together—were seated with her at the round table, happily celebrating.

Nell spotted Elizabeth Hartley sitting on the far side of the table, looking down at her phone. *It's nice she's here,* she thought. She hadn't seen much of her since they'd had dinner together. She had wondered often about those months and months between Elizabeth leaving Sea Harbor and her job as headmistress of the private school, and then coming back these years later.

She followed Birdie over to the table where they claimed the two empty chairs on either side of Elizabeth.

Elizabeth looked up from checking her phone. Then instantly a smile slipped in place. "Hello. I'm happy to see you two. Jane mentioned that you'd be coming."

"And we heard from our fine mayor that you're now taking over the art auction. Thanks for that. Izzy's happy about it. Sometimes those things fall on her, and it's always when the shop is especially busy."

Elizabeth nodded. "Happy to do it." She slipped her phone into a small purse on her lap.

Birdie glanced at the movement. "I'm sorry, Elizabeth. We barged in and interrupted your call."

"Oh, no. It's fine. My head is fuzzy today. Lack of sleep, I guess. Weekends aren't my best time."

A waitress appeared, placing glasses of Bloody Marys in front of Nell and Birdie.

Birdie slid hers over to replace Elizabeth's empty glass.

"Thanks, Birdie. That's what I need." Elizabeth took a sip. "Cell phone texts are annoying when they're not answered. You know it's sitting in someone's pocket, but not being answered." She paused, then added, as if an explanation was needed, "I need to talk to Nick today and we seem to be missing each other. It's frustrating."

"I am the chief offender of missing calls. I simply don't hear it, or even more often, I can't get it out of my pocket in time, or it's in the next room."

The tense expression on Elizabeth's face relaxed slightly. "You're right. Sometimes I am too anxious about things. It's clearly a downfall of mine."

"I haven't seen much of you since you moved back," Birdie said, changing the subject. "Nell and I were concerned after you left town so suddenly after leaving the school. I hope the moving back has been good for you."

Elizabeth nodded, then managed a smile. "I had to leave. I was like Humpty Dumpty. I needed to be put back together. But I always hoped to come back." She finished her drink.

"Well, there's really nowhere else to be," Nell said. "We are blue minds, all of us."

"Nick gave me that book as a homecoming gift. There's truth in it. Some people need to be near water. He's really quite an amazing man, that he would sense that in me. He seems to know me sometimes better than I know myself."

"Nick is a sensitive soul," Birdie said. "And that blue-mind theory is real. Nell's husband is a great example. I swear, being out on his sailboat helped him recover from a heart attack some years ago."

"Nick is like that, too," Elizabeth said.

"Oh yes," Nell agreed. "Ben truly loves that boat of his."

"Do you enjoy sailing?" Birdie asked.

"No," Elizabeth said. "I mean, I wish I did. Nick has invited me to go sailing with him. I think he'd love it if I'd go out with him."

"But it's not your thing?"

Elizabeth looked embarrassed, then said, "As much as I would love to be out on water with him, I can't do it." She paused for a second, then said, "The truth is, I can't swim."

"Oh, my," Birdie said. "Well, that can be changed."

"No. I've tried. My body just doesn't want to stay afloat. I can't tell you how many times I've tried. The last instructor said I was 'negatively buoyant.' I've accepted it. Anyway, enough about me. Birdie, I've been hearing about your granddaughter's dog-walking business. It sounds incredible."

Birdie smiled, pleased to talk about Gabby. Anytime, anywhere. "She loves having her business. Loves dogs. Do you have one? Gabby would probably take on another."

"No. But Nick has told me how wonderful she and her friend are with his dog. One of the girls in his office told me Squid had even spent the night at your house. I offered once, but he probably wanted a pro." She smiled.

"Well, Squid was a most pleasant guest. And we hear he will come to us again soon."

Elizabeth nodded, then turned to Nell. "Nell, I've been wanting to apologize to you for a long time."

"Apologize?"

"You mentioned at dinner a few weeks ago that you'd tried to get in touch with me after I left town."

Nell looked puzzled.

"After the school episode," Elizabeth clarified. She looked at Birdie, too. "Sometimes I try to run away from those times, and we were having such a good time that night—that's what I did. I apologize. When you two were on the board, we did good things. But the new board wanted different things. It was extremely stressful. Nick was on the board then. He--and Laura Danvers, too—supported me, but lost the fight. Stress can do bad things. It played with my head. Sometimes I can't even think over the noise it makes. Anyway, someday, when we've each had a few glasses of wine, I'll share my journey through it all with you. I'd like to do that. You both knew me before that stress controlled my life for a while."

Nell imagined herself in that position—losing a job because

you followed your instincts to help kids make their world a better place, even if it meant getting rid of some of the traditional private-school traditions.

But no matter, Elizabeth looked younger and healthier than when she was a headmistress. The few gray streaks in her curly, dark hair contributed to her fine features, almost as if some fine stylist had put them there. *She's actually quite beautiful,* Nell thought.

Nell looked up and saw that Jane was watching them, a smile on her face. When their eyes made contact, Jane leaned forward and called across the table, "Did Elizabeth mention that I hired her?"

Nell and Birdie looked at Elizabeth, surprised, but not really. Jane had mentioned several times that Nick had asked her to get Elizabeth involved in the art colony.

Elizabeth nodded. "She did."

"Since the mayor had already talked Elizabeth into managing the art auction, I figured she might as well be paid for it," Jane said. "We've been without an association director for months, and Elizabeth has agreed to take it over."

"You're a good fit, Elizabeth. You certainly have had experience managing things," Nell said.

"And they have a wonderful board," Birdie said, laughing. "I'm on it, and Ben. Nick Cabot is, too. Everyone has to pass the 'nice' and 'fun' test before we let them in."

Nell watched the exchange, and the smile that came at the mention of Nick's name. "That's comforting." Her smile dropped then, and she pulled her phone out of her pocket, looked at it, and then looked around, as if suddenly forgetting what she was going to say. She put the phone away, and pressed her fingers into her temples, frowning.

Nell cast a sideways glance at her.

But as several more guests joined the party, the moment passed. Soon the table was filled with laughter and conversation, and anticipation of the yacht club's birthday brunch of clam chowder, freshly baked biscuits, and heaping plates of spinach, beet, and arugula salad.

Finally Jane, her round cheeks flushed from the abundance of wishes and love she was receiving, clinked her glass and gave her own toast—to friends, to art, to life and love—and to people with birthdays everywhere.

And the birthday party began.

Chapter 12

It was after the brunch hour when the guests reluctantly began their good-byes, gathering handbags and bidding Jane a final birthday wish.

Nell spotted Elizabeth heading out and hurried over to say good-bye.

"I'm happy you came, Elizabeth. Let's get together sometime. You and Nick should come for dinner soon."

For a minute, she didn't answer, as if giving the casual invitation more thought than Nell expected. Then Elizabeth nodded, as if making a decision, although Nell wasn't sure it had anything to do with her dinner invitation.

"Yes," Elizabeth said aloud. "I'm sorry about my fuzziness—" She took a quick breath and smiled. "It's just a headache. Sometimes it brings noise."

"Do you need a ride home?"

"No, no. I'll be fine, Nell. If I seemed a bit off-kilter earlier, it was because of too many Bloody Marys. And too many things crowding around in my head." She smiled again.

"That can happen," Nell said, although she wasn't at all sure what Elizabeth was alluding to.

"Anyway," Elizabeth continued, "I'm heading home. My condo is a mess. Some cleaning is required, and then later, I'll take a long walk in the park. It's the best kind of medicine."

"That sounds nice. Where do you walk?"

"I usually go to that little park down near the water. Nick introduced me to it months ago. It has wonderful walking paths."

"I know that park. It's beautiful. Nick Cabot is largely responsible for making it so, I hear. He cares about Fishermen's Village and making sure there're outdoor places."

"Yes, he's a caring man, " Elizabeth said. She smiled again, then impulsively hugged Nell. In the next minute, she turned and walked briskly across the crowded dining room toward the exit.

Nell watched her disappear. Elizabeth's head was high, her back straight, and her walk determined and almost brisk. How strange, Nell thought. But she wasn't sure why it was strange. She shook her head, and walked back to the table, where Birdie was busy collecting Jane's gifts.

"It looks like you two could use something to put all those gifts in," Liz Santos said, handing them a couple of large bags.

Nell looked over at Liz, one of her favorite people in town, and one who knew everyone. "Liz," Nell said, "this may be a totally inappropriate thing to ask you." She took a few steps away from the others.

"Go for it, Nell," Liz said.

"You've met Elizabeth Hartley?"

"Yes. Nick brought her here for dinner a couple times when she moved back. We tease Nick about being Sea Harbor's welcome wagon. But he does a good job. He's mentioned that Elizabeth had a difficult time recovering from all that mess at the day school. He was surprised she came back here. It was brave."

"Birdie and I were on her school board, but right before that all happened, so she knows us. Anyway, I was thinking it'd be nice if she met women here more her own age—"

For a minute, Liz looked puzzled. Then she said, "You mean introducing her around?"

"Well," Nell began, almost instantly regretting her request.

"Actually, Nell, Nick and I have talked about it, and I know Nick and Jane have already both tried to do that, but if—"

At that moment, a waitress came over, needing attention, and Liz excused herself. Nell felt somehow rescued, happy she didn't have to finish whatever it was she was asking.

Birdie came over and said quietly, "You are sometimes too sensitive, my dear friend. I suspect Elizabeth Hartley is the kind of person who would much prefer to pick her own friends."

"You're right. I overstepped. Why did I do that? Besides, look at us, Izzy, and Cass. Could you ask for any closer friends with more remarkable age differences?"

They both started laughing, and when Liz returned to the table, she looked relieved that Nell didn't make an effort to continue the conversation.

"It was truly an amazing meal," Jane said, looking up into Liz's face. "Not that I would have expected less. But I won't eat again for days." Jane patted her girth and chuckled. "It's why I always wear my tie-dyed caftan when I come here."

Nell and Birdie started to join in the thanks, but were interrupted when someone came up behind Liz and wrapped his arms around her, surprising her.

Startled, Liz twisted out of the hug and turned around, grinning up at the tall man. "Oh, Nick, it's you. You surprised me." She hugged him back.

Nick Cabot turned and greeted Birdie and Nell. Then he looked down at Jane, still seated in the guest of honor chair.

"I really came over to see who the balloons were for—and to find out why I wasn't invited to the party."

"It was a major oversight, Mr. Cabot," Jane said.

Nick laughed, leaned down, and kissed Jane on the cheek.

"And then I find out that it's all for you, Jane. My favorite artist, growing gracefully older behind my back. Happy birthday."

"It was a ladies-only affair," Liz said. "No men—not even charmers like you, Cabot—were invited."

"Though some of my artist friends wouldn't have minded at all," Jane said.

"There's always a next time, Jane. You have my number."

"Oh, you bet I have your number," Jane said with a chuckle. "I've known you a long time, Nick Cabot. Don't you ever forget that."

"It looks like a great group of party guests. I saw a bunch of your Canary Cove artists heading out just now. You have a lot of people celebrating you, Jane Brewster."

"Yes, I do. A lot of dear friends, too. And you hold a big space in there, Nick."

Nick gave a courtly bow.

"Speaking of knowing people," Nell said, "you just missed another Elizabeth. She *did* get invited."

"Elizabeth Hartley, I'm guessing? I thought I saw her walking out to the parking lot. Sorry I missed her. I need to touch base with her about something she wanted me to do for her, but we keep missing each other. I'll catch up with her in a couple days, maybe. It's a busy weekend. Busy days ahead, too." He glanced at Liz, who answered his glance with a huge smile.

"Speaking of her, Elizabeth agreed to take that job you thought she might be interested in," Jane said to Nick. "It was a good idea. She'll have plenty to do."

"That's great, Janie," Nick said. "Thanks."

Overhearing the conversation, Birdie joined in. "You both have been a help to her. She was brave moving back here after that mess at the school."

"That she was," Nick said. "I was surprised, frankly. But Sea Harbor is a friendly place, and most of the board members involved in replacing her don't live here, anyway."

"Nevertheless," Nell said, "I can tell she appreciates having you at her side."

Nick shrugged, then laughed. "Well, her name's Elizabeth, after all—" He looked over at Liz. "There must be something in that name that brings people into my world." He turned to the others. "My best buddy, Liz here, for example. And one of my favorite office women is a Beth. Surely, there's a Betsy around I haven't met yet. And from my small sample, I am concluding all Elizabeths are classy people. Way too classy for me sometimes."

"Well, you do seem to be attracted to the name," Jane said. Her smile was teasing, as if there was a private joke passing from her to Nick and Liz and back.

Liz chuckled, then looked at Nell and Birdie. "Jane is showing her age and how long she's been around here. She's subtly referring to a long-ago time when Nick and I were 'an item,' as they said back in those high-school days. Can you all believe it? The two of us?"

"Ah, those were the days," Nick said. He looped an arm around Liz and hugged her close.

"Yes, they were," Liz said. "Good times. My best friend and I were all in the same bunch of high-school buddies. We grew up together—and they're still my closest friends. But anyway, in high school we'd pair off now and then. One week or month, it'd be me and Nick. And the next one, my best bud would be Nick's girl, and I'd be dating Jack Risso's son or someone else. And then a new girl would move to town, someone who needed a welcome, so welcome wagon Nick would take over that job briefly. Sometimes my cousin Bobby Palazola would step in, although not so often."

They were all laughing now, thinking back to the musical chairs of high-school dating.

"Those years were magical ones. A true rom-com time," Liz said. "We could have won an Emmy for our roles in it. Believe it or not, I was truly crazy about this guy here." She gave Nick a sly, sideways glance.

"Ha! Not so you'd notice," Nick countered. "It didn't take long for Alphonso Santos to chase me off."

They laughed at the image of the gentlemanly Alphonso Santos chasing anyone.

Liz put her hands on her hips. "You have nothing to complain about, Nick Cabot. I made you my man of honor at our wedding."

The laughter got even louder, imagining Nick holding a bouquet of peonies.

"Anyway, we were all great friends. And we still are." She looked at Nick with a knowing smile.

"True enough," Nick said. "And just for the record, Liz, I'm counting on you to be my best woman of honor."

Liz looked at him with a huge grin and gave him a giant hug, acting as if he were announcing an engagement right then and there. "I thought you'd never ask. I may have to play a dual role, though—"

A waitress came up and offered to help Nell and Birdie finish packing up the pile of gifts.

Liz thanked her, and she and Nick stepped out of the way.

Nell watched them, their voices muted, but their faces expressive and their smiles full. Hugging again. A nice sight. They seemed so happy, she thought.

Jane was watching, too. She looked over at Nell and Birdie. "I think the two of them are still back in those high-school days, talking in a language we don't understand."

Nick and Liz heard her and laughed. "You are a mind reader, Jane," Liz said. "This has been an old friends' reunion weekend for us, and we're a little crazy. Sometimes when we're together like this, we forget ourselves and think we're eighteen again, instead of fifty. But it's been the best weekend you can possibly imagine."

She turned toward Nick. "Oh, and before I forget, I asked the kitchen to make you some sandwiches to take to the dock. You're fixing, what? A tiny, tiny scratch on the bow? I heard from a good source it's invisible. And what you deserve for a midnight rendezvous." She grinned.

"Hey, tiny scratches can grow. It was wavy out there. But anyway, you're amazing, Liz. You take good care of me."

"It's not you. It's your boat," she said. "I love your boat. It's always about the boat."

"Not always," Nick said, matching her grin.

"Why do I get the feeling you two are full of double-talk today?" Jane teased.

Nick laughed off the comment, then noticed the large sacks Birdie and Nell had packed. "Hey, Jane, how about you pass over your key and I take this birthday loot to your van?"

"Well, they're counted, Nick. So don't try any funny business."

"No worries. I'm not big on lingerie these days."

Nick gave a hearty guffaw, then gave Jane a final birthday hug and took her key fob. He lifted one large bag of gifts over his shoulder and handed the other to Liz. With a wave, the two wove their way through the restaurant, talking and laughing in that way old friends did.

"Talk about good people," Jane said, watching them disappear. "Did you know Nick is single-handedly sponsoring our Canary Cove artist scholarship next fall?"

"That doesn't surprise me," Birdie said. "Supporting the arts seems to also be a top priority for Elizabeth Hartley, too. Those two could be a power couple."

"'A power couple'?" Jane smiled. "I don't know about that, but I do know that Nick has always loved the arts. He told me he'd once thought of becoming an artist, much to his fishing family's surprise. So he took a painting class. But the day his teacher mistook his 'magnificent' painting of fall seagrass for piles of dung, he decided he'd be better at making money and buying art than doing it."

"A wise man," Birdie said, chuckling and imagining the painting.

"Wise and smart and generous. You know, if he signs the papers to run for mayor, he'll give our Madam Mayor a run for her money," Jane said.

"Yes, that buzz is getting louder, isn't it?' Birdie said. "I agree, Jane. He'd bring something fresh and creative to the city."

"Yes, he will. He has all the qualities needed, not to mention being a personable, likable guy. And I don't mean to disparage Beatrice and the work she's done. Goodness, she loves this city and has supported many good things as mayor. But there comes a time—"

"I agree with you both," Nell said. "Except I think the possibility of losing her position is causing her great anguish. I feel for her. I've never seen this side of Beatrice before."

"She's tough," Jane said. "She'll be okay."

"Maybe too tough," Nell said. "She's defiant about Nick running against her. I think she's aware that if he does, he will win. She hasn't had to face that before."

"That's true," Birdie said. "Her previous opponents have run against her on a lark—remember the year Jake Risso ran because he had lost some bet to Harry and Gus McGlucken?"

"And based his campaign on free beers to anyone who would vote against him," Jane said, laughing.

"Well, maybe it'll work out. I hope so."

"It has to," Birdie said. "That kind of defiant ambition isn't good for the soul."

Jane pushed back her chair. "Beatrice is a good woman. At least, I hope so." Jane looked around the table. "And now we should be good women and allow Liz's remarkable staff to clean up our mess."

*   *   *

It took longer than usual to get through the restaurant, be-cause Jane's birthday was now being acknowledged by each table they passed, with happy cheers and many hugs. By the time they had reached the front entrance, Nick and Liz had al-ready gone their separate ways, but Nick had left Jane's car waiting for her at the wide steps.

Jane hugged her friends good-bye. Then she bunched up the flowing skirt of her caftan and pulled herself up into the van. In the next few minutes, she was off, driving too fast around the circle drive. The loud, happy sounds of the Beatles' "Birthday" song blared out her open window.

Nell and Birdie watched for a minute, shaking their heads and smiling at their spirited friend.

"You know, I think I would have made a good hippy," Birdie said, watching the vehicle disappear.

Nell laughed and looped her arm through Birdie's. "What do you mean, 'would have'? I've always thought of you as a hippy."

They walked across the drive and through the parking lot to Nell's CR-V. As she reached for the door handle, she glanced across the parking lot at a tall, attractive woman in frayed jeans and a summery striped sweater, standing beside the bike rack. Her perfect smile and an interesting face held Nell's interest. Nell opened the door, then stood beside it, looking at the woman.

"Look over at that red bike, Birdie. How do I know that woman? She looks so familiar, but I can't place her." The woman was now securing the red bike to the rack. Then she pulled a beach towel from a bike bag and looped it around her well-exercised shoulders.

Birdie squinted to bring the woman into focus. "Oh, my goodness. Yes, we know her. Or I do, and I suspect you've met her over the years." Birdie frowned as she tried to pull up a name. "Oh, phooey. I know her as well as I know anyone. Now where did her name go?"

Nell took off her sunglasses, still watching the woman as she pulled out a cell phone and began tapping into it.

"Except for that gorgeous head of black hair, she could be Liz Santos's twin. Maybe that's why I thought I knew her." Nell found some relief in remembering that much. Remembering details and faces was something she prided herself on, and she refused to let it turn fuzzy on her. Not for the first time, she considered getting that cataract surgery her friends recommended.

The woman was still looking at her phone, a wide smile on her face. Her tall, slender body looked comfortable, as if she knew it well, knew how to stand and walk and be at ease in it, as if she had the whole world in her hands. She looked self-assured, and not uncomfortable with being looked at. Someone used to a stage, Nell thought.

Suddenly Birdie sat forward in the seat and slapped her knee, a triumphant look on her lined face.

"Bella. That's Bobby Palazola's twin sister. Liz and Nick's good friend. She's in that group of friends we were just talking about."

"Another Palazola? They're coming out of the woodwork this week."

"It came to me when you said she looked like Liz Santos. Bella definitely does. Except, of course, for the hair color. It's pretty close to the opposite. Liz's platinum, on one hand, and her cousin's shiny black locks, as beautiful as my Gabby's. Genes are strange critters, aren't they? She's Liz's cousin. The 'best friend' she referred to inside."

"So, which Palazola family is that?"

"Well, most of them are related. Even the ones who spell their names with two z's, thanks to Ellis Island. Let me think about that. I sometimes get them mixed up."

Nell looked again at the woman. She was now slipping her phone into a pocket of her jeans and began walking toward the clubhouse. Nell felt a little embarrassed watching her, but there was something about the woman that made Nell think she didn't mind it, or was even aware of it, because she was used to it.

As Nell watched, the woman tilted her head back, looking up into the trees that bordered the parking lot, smiling at whatever she noticed among the branches and leaves—a wren or warbler, maybe. Then she looked beyond the trees, shielding her eyes against the sunlight as a squabble of gulls flew over, mewing down at her.

When the woman reached the circle drive, she started walking toward the clubhouse entrance. Then she stopped, looking at someone on the other side of the lobby door windows, who seemed to be waving words to her. When the door opened, Nell recognized Liz Santos, gesturing to Bella. Somehow Bella seemed to interpret Liz's gestures and changed directions, heading down the drive toward a sundrenched beach and an inviting line of beach chairs.

"She's lovely, isn't she?" Birdie said. "Good genes. And as nice a person as you'd ever want to meet. Liz's mom, Annabelle, told me once that when Liz and her cousin Bella were in middle school, Liz had dyed her beautiful blond tresses black one day so she and her cousin could confuse their teachers. And it worked, at least for a day, Annabelle said. But it was a horrible chore getting Liz's hair back to its platinum sheen."

"Teenagers." Nell chuckled. "Does Bella live here?"

"No. She went to college in California. I believe she studied something about the atmosphere. Meteorology, yes, that's it. "

"I'm wondering why she looks so familiar to me."

"Probably because she's on television. She's a weather person. My mind isn't totally on vacation. Look at all the things I'm remembering?"

Nell smiled and rested one hand on Birdie's knee. "Oh, Birdie. I love you. Okay, let's test it. Where does Bella live now?"

"She moved up the ladder of television weather forecasting

and when Lillian Palazola—her sweet mother—had to move into an assisted-living home, she wanted to be closer, and ended up getting a plum television job in Boston. But she's up here as often as she can be. She's devoted to her mother."

"I met her mother several times before she became ill," Nell said.

"Yes, she was in Izzy's shop often, and helped us out on the library board for a while. She also helped Annabelle, her sister-in-law, at the Sweet Petunia. I see her at the Ocean View home sometimes when I visit my friend Eunice. Apparently, Bella always brings gifts to the nurses and staff and residents—or 'inmates,' as my old friend Eunice calls herself—although, of course, she doesn't mean it. Eunice is a joker. Anyway, Bella is a celebrity over at Ocean View."

"Good grief. It's impossible to keep track of all this."

"Yes, it can be confusing. But not Bobby and Bella. But how could I have forgotten her name, even for a minute? Oh, my."

"Are she and Bobby close?"

"Oh, I think so. Siblings should keep in touch. And twins? Don't they sometimes have their own language? Bella has close to those old friends here, too. I see Bella and Nick Cabot together often when she's here. You could sense all those old connections when Liz and Nick took us back to their teenage years."

Nell nodded. "They lost me a few times in their memories, but I definitely got the feeling that maybe this weekend was about more than just old friends getting together. Did you sense that?"

"Now that you mention it, I did. And I got the feeling Nick Cabot was in the middle of it somehow."

"Well, let's keep our ears open. Whatever it might be, it sounded like a weekend to remember."

Nell looked over at the clubhouse as they talked, thinking of the deep feelings the friends had clearly expressed for one another. And then her attention went back to the impossible task of fitting those who belonged into the Palazola's family tree.

Liz's mom, Annabelle, was the easiest.

She and Ben both loved the restaurant owner. Her Sweet Petunia was Ben's very favorite brunch place. Now she needed to plug Bobby into that family tree. Cousin to Liz Palazola Santos, so Annabelle's nephew. And now twin brother to this beautiful woman walking across the parking lot. She'd never keep them all straight and wondered briefly what they did for reunions or family get-togethers. A hotel ballroom, perhaps. And, hopefully, nametags.

She looked over at Birdie. "I miss that sometimes. The extended family."

"But you have Izzy right here."

"True. But the others—my sister and her husband, Izzy's brothers, Charlie and Jack. A handful of Kansas cousins. The Midwest seems to have a grip on them, even though Charlie and Jack move around some. Although Lily Virgilio told me she's trying to get Charlie back to help out at her free health clinic, so maybe there's hope."

"That would be wonderful. And you also have sundry Endicotts nearby. Ben's family isn't that big, but there are enough of them around."

Nell laughed. "True. It's as if the North Shore has a special hold on families. All of Ben's relatives have stayed on the east coast."

"There are plenty of extended families around here. It seems to be in the genes. Many people leave and travel around, and then eventually come back.

"But sometimes families prefer warm, wonderful reunions like yours. *Occasional* reunions, not every Sunday. It's okay not to see one another at every curve of the road. It doesn't make the love any less."

Nell started the car and pulled out of the lot. They drove past the yacht club entrance, then down the winding road toward town. She glanced at the small woman at her side, feeling an unexpected and unexplainable rush of gratitude for a friend who was closer to her than family. And one who knew her better than anyone, even Ben, she admitted, surprising herself. Yes, extended family could take all shapes.

"You're in a pensive mood, Nell. Are you bothered by something?"

Nell mulled over the question. There was something else mixed into the rush of emotion she'd felt a second ago. Something Birdie, of course, would sense. But something she couldn't identify. It was a niggling feeling, undefined.

"No," she finally said. "I'm not really bothered about anything. I'm a little anxious, I guess. Which still doesn't make any sense, does it? We just had a great brunch, enjoyable conversation with interesting people. Our beautiful herringbone afghan is coming along. Summer is unfolding nicely."

Nell swerved slightly to avoid a squirrel, then slowed her speed as they approached a more heavily trafficked Harbor Road.

"Things seem slightly askew, perhaps?" Birdie suggested.

"*Askew*. That's a good word."

Birdie chuckled. "My brain often feels that way. I know that word well."

"It's the way I sometimes feel the day before Ben has his annual cardiac checkup. But he just had one, and he's doing fine, so I can check that off."

Birdie's short white bob moved slightly as she thought about that. Things to check off. "I suppose it's often the future—not knowing it—that makes us slightly anxious. And yet that's so silly, isn't it? The unknown, the future, will always be out of reach, and there's not much we can do about it, anyway. We certainly can't live *in* it, even though we sometimes try. Such a waste of energy. Just live the moment."

Birdie leaned over and turned on the radio, stopping her scan when she reached a golden oldies station, with Marvin Gaye and Tammi Terrell assuring them there wasn't any "mountain high enough."

Nell's head began moving to the catchy tune; then Birdie lifted her arms, swinging them back and forth.

"Birds don't worry. They just sing," Birdie sang over the music.

And in the next minute, the still-strong voices of the two friends joined together, and "Ain't no valley low enough" filled the whole car as they drove up the hill to Birdie's home.

Chapter 13

A branch slapped against the open bedroom window, shaking Birdie Favazza out of a deep sleep. She shifted in the wide bed, tugging her lids open. The bedside clock glared at her.

It was two in the morning.

She frowned, her senses more alert, and slipped out of bed, grabbing a robe and wrapping it around her small body. She shuffled across the room to close the window, shaking the sleep away and hoping the racket didn't wake up Gabby, who was sleeping down the hall. She placed her fingers on the top of the window to pull it down, then quickly let go, coughing and staring up into the night sky. The swash of stars was still there, but their light was hazy now.

Birdie squinted to bring things into focus. From her home at the top of Ravenswood Hill, she could look down on the harbor and the darkened, sleeping town. Then she turned her head and looked toward the northeast end of the harbor. On that end of the town, the shoreland curved, shaped and reshaped by years of tides, and it was there she spotted a cloud of smoke, spiraling into the sky. The sound of sirens followed, at first loud, coming from the downtown station, then growing fainter as the trucks moved toward the other part of town.

She realized then that it hadn't been the breeze and branch against the window glass that had awakened her. It was the distant smell of burning wood. She stared through the dark sky, unable to tell exactly where the smoke was coming from. Then she took a breath, forcing calm back into her body. Wherever the smoke was coming from—perhaps the beach—the Sea Harbor Fire Department had lots of experience and was on its way. Of course they would.

She shuffled back to bed.

Across the harbor, in a cozy home above the Canary Cove Art Colony, Cass sat straight up in bed, her senses suddenly alert. It was a practice born of being a fisherman's daughter, alert to the sounds of coast guard sirens or the harbor patrol going out to help a boat in distress. Next to her, Danny snored peacefully, and through the intercom, the sounds of their son Joey's slow breathing said he was sleeping as soundly as his father.

Cass slid out of bed and tiptoed over to the bedroom deck door, which she'd left slightly ajar to bring in the soft breeze. She stepped out on the small deck, shivering as the waves below her deck washed up against the rocky wall below, sending sprays all the way up to her railing. She peered over the trees and down the shoreline toward the sounds. The sirens seemed to be heading toward the beaches not far from an old neighborhood Cass knew well. Fishermen had settled in the area hundreds of years before, helping to establish the trade Cape Ann was known for. Mostly modest homes. Many employees of her Halloran Lobster Company lived in the neighborhood, their small houses passed down from generation to generation. Decent, hardworking men and women. For the most part, anyway.

There was a park nearby. One of her crew said he'd had to

call the police a couple times for bonfires kids lit in the wooded area nearby.

Maybe that was it. Or the beach. There were often bonfires down there.

She coughed as the breeze brought a thick smell of burning wood up to her small house on the hill. Once her eyes adjusted to the night, she saw a streak of red, and then another, flashing up through the spirals of smoke. And the shrill sounds of sirens.

Cass frowned, uncomfortable with the smells and the sky. Finally she walked back inside and crawled back in bed, curling up next to her husband. Eventually, the sounds quieted and she dozed off in the warm comfort of Danny's sleeping body.

Izzy thought her daughter, Abby, was having a nightmare. She rushed into her bedroom, but the sight of the sweet smile on her daughter's face, and her small body wrapped around a well-loved stuffed elephant, stopped her from waking her. Instead, she turned toward the window and a night sky that had been studded with stars when she had fallen asleep that night.

The stars were still there, but hazy and gray, and the sound of a child's nightmare turned out to be sirens, heading, gratefully, away from Izzy's home. She kissed Abby's forehead and went back to her own room, slipping into bed and hooking one arm across Sam's chest. The Sea Harbor Fire Department was fast and brave and efficient. "Help was on the way," she murmured as she drifted off to sleep.

Nell Endicott heard the familiar siren sounds and rolled toward her husband. Ben's eyelids had slowly opened, then closed again. He reached over and rubbed Nell's shoulder. "A wild bonfire party that got out of hand down near Fishermen's Village," he said softly. "Summer visitors." He murmured a few more probable scenarios as to what was happening until, finally, his voice drifted off completely and sleep settled back in.

Nell lay back into the pillows and tried to slow her heartbeat. Ben's words floated around her head. Sensible, logical, and calm. Cape Ann beaches hosted beach parties all summer long. Local kids home from college were simply having fun. That's what Ben's logical mind had zeroed in on.

But Nell didn't find sleep as easy as her husband did. It was a while before she finally slipped into a restless sleep. The echo of sirens and the faint smell of smoke spoke to her of more than burned s'mores and hot dogs and kindling wood.

Chapter 14

It wasn't a convoluted dream of sirens or smoke that woke Birdie up the next morning. It was a loud shout from the kitchen door, a floor below.

"Nonna, please come. I need you!"

Birdie shot up in bed, shaking the fog of sleep from her body. At first, she couldn't breathe, her heart thumping too quickly. Gabby's voice was plaintive.

"Gabby," she called as loudly as her still sleepy voice allowed. Then she pushed herself out of bed, grabbed a robe and slippers, and hurried down the back stairs leading to the kitchen and the sound of Gabby's voice. And hoping she didn't fall on the way. One hand pressed into her chest, calming her heart as she hurried, and allowed a soft prayer to escape her lips: "Please keep my Gabby safe."

In the back kitchen hallway, sitting on one of Mae's hand-hooked rugs, was Gabby. And on her lap, or perhaps Gabby was on his lap, Birdie couldn't be sure, sat a quivering Squid.

The dog flapped his tail vigorously against the wall when he saw Birdie. It wasn't the friendly flap he usually gave her, Birdie thought. It was a desperate one.

"Something's wrong, Nonna," Gabby said. "Squid's acting weird. He's scared and lost. Feel him. He's shaking."

Birdie reached down and petted the dog softly, then straightened up, looking through the small window in the back door, half expecting Nick Cabot to be standing there. "How did he get here?" she asked, then pressed her lips together at the lameness of her question.

Gabby held Squid closer, rubbing her head against his shaggy coat.

"How did you find him?"

"No. I didn't find him. He found us, Nonna."

"How, Gabby? Explain—" She looked down at a sweet dog with sad eyes.

"I had a bad dream last night, and I woke up this morning, feeling kind of awful," Gabby said. "But I couldn't figure out why. I came downstairs to get the last piece of Ella's chocolate pie. I thought it might help. And then—and then I was sitting at the kitchen table, just *eating.*" She said the word with disdain, as if she had somehow betrayed the dog by eating pie when he may have been in danger or lost or hurt. "Then that's when I heard him," she finished.

"Who?"

"Squid, Nonna."

"Of course. Squid. I'm sorry, Gabby. I'm just confused."

"I know, Nonna. I was, too. Squid was scratching at the door, crying and lost. And he smells terrible."

"Well, he isn't lost, sweetheart. He came here." She forced a smile. At that moment, there was a rap on the door behind Gabby and Squid. Ella was peering through the glass pane.

Gabby and Squid moved to let her in.

"I thought I heard a dog howling," Birdie's housekeeper said, the wrinkles in her forehead deepening. "What's going on here?" She looked at Squid, then leaned down and rubbed him on his belly. "Is our Squid okay?"

But before Birdie or Gabby could answer, the back door opened again, and Ella's husband appeared in the frame. At first, Harold didn't seem to notice that they had a canine guest. Instead, he spoke slowly, concern coating his words. "There's been a fire," he said. "A bad one 'cross town."

Squid barked, as if in answer to Harold's news. As if he could tell him more.

Harold stared down at the dog, seemingly noticing him for the first time. "Oh, Squid," he said. He reached down and, with one large hand, scratched the dog's ears.

Birdie looked at her groundsman's weathered face. His slight, always present smile was gone. The furrows lining his forehead were cavern deep. Harold was bringing bad news.

"The radio," he began. Harold rarely went anywhere without his police radio. As technology advanced, making it more difficult for him to listen in to what was happening in Sea Harbor, he simply upgraded his own equipment, boasting that there wasn't an encrypted radio he couldn't decipher. And with his trusty invention, he kept detailed track of what was going on in the town he loved and the one he had lived in for all of his seventy-plus years.

"A fire in the old Fishermen's Village," he said. "At 9 Fishermen Row."

Gabby's eyes flew open.

That was the house she visited nearly every day.

To pick up the dog she loved.

Chapter 15

News of the fire reached the Perry home as Izzy was mixing a playgroup lunch for Abby. Sam had been trying to find out exactly where it was, and all bits of news pointed to the area where local fishermen lived, many of them Cass and Pete's employees.

"Nell and Ben will know more," Sam said. "Ben has that magic network of buddies."

Izzy nodded. She zipped up Abby's lunch box, and with Sam's assurance he'd get Abby to her playgroup on time, she drove to work, with a slight detour for Nell's coffee and information about the fire from people who would know.

Nell was on the phone with Birdie when Izzy walked in. Ben was standing nearby, as if sensing the call was important. He and Izzy both stepped closer to listen. Nell switched her phone to speaker, nodding to them that Gabby was fine, the first thing that they wondered about when seeing Nell's worried face.

Birdie went on to explain about their unexpected canine visitor, then filled in the scant details of what they knew.

"Squid showed up early this morning, carrying with him the clear stench of burning wood," Birdie said.

In answer to Nell's, Ben's, and Izzy's questions, Birdie filled them in on all she knew.

The day before, Sunday, Gabby had taken Squid to his home, just as she did each day. A little earlier than usual, because Nick asked for it.

Nick was there and everything was normal and okay when she left. He'd been in a great mood, and Gabby said she could smell food from the kitchen. Nick looked especially good, too, she said. Like maybe he'd just taken a shower because he had someone coming over that night. Or guests. They'd talked a little, but nothing important, and Gabby made plans to pick up Squid the next morning. All normal things.

But normality disappeared when Squid showed up at their back door that morning.

Gabby immediately called Nick, knowing he'd be worried about Squid. But he didn't answer his phone, she said.

"I'll come over," Nell said. "Maybe Ben, too. Just in case—" She had no idea what "just in case" meant, but from the sound of Birdie's voice, it was a good idea.

Izzy had to go to work, but she asked Nell to call her there when they knew more, and she headed out, her phone plugged into her car as she related to Sam what little she knew.

Nell carried breakfast dishes to the sink, while Ben texted a friend who worked for the city. He heard back immediately.

"Birdie's information is pretty much what the mayor's office knows. The fire is definitely at Cabot's house. They don't have enough information to say more, except that it's a bad one—and they're concerned that there still may be someone in the house."

By the time Ben and Nell arrived at Birdie's home, the smells of bacon, waffles, and scrambled eggs filled the Favazza kitchen.

They gathered around the kitchen table, except for Gabby, who sat on the floor next to Birdie's chair, her long legs twisted like a pretzel, with Squid's head resting in the lap her legs formed. Ella, who also refused to sit down, moved back and forth from sink to table to stove and back. She was far more comfortable refilling coffee cups, or looking out the kitchen windows above the sink, or making more biscuits, than sitting still. And in between each back and forth, she stooped low to give a love pat to Squid, who'd been happily fed before anyone else, but was not one to refuse a tasty muffin or biscuit crumb.

Harold sat next to Ben, his knobby elbows resting on the table; his long, angular face attentive to whatever Ben might know that he hadn't heard over his own radio. Nell and Birdie sat on either side of Ella's empty chair, hoping she'd forget about filling coffee cups, take a deep breath, and sit down with them.

Ben looked down at Gabby and Squid. "Gabby, I am so sorry about this," he began. "I've been in touch with a couple of people, and they filled me in on some things that we need to know. The address Harold gave you is correct. The fire during the night was at Nick's home."

Gabby looked up and nodded. Her blue eyes were thoughtful and sad—and knowing.

"It's not good news. It was a bad fire, and they think there was someone who didn't get out in time."

Nell watched Gabby's face as Ben talked, knowing he was being as gentle as he could be, but he'd never put out false hope. It never helped, but only prolonged the grief. He had softened his comments as much as he felt was fair.

"Someone?" Gabby looked up at Ben, then at Squid. Her body stiffened.

"There hasn't been an official word yet. The fire is still smoldering in places, preventing the firemen from getting to certain areas. They think the fire started late in the evening, maybe sometime between eleven and midnight, but the fire had a good start before the firemen got there." Ben glanced again at the dog, then back to Gabby. "And since Nick lives alone, they need to consider that fact carefully, and that Squid somehow escaped the fire. But maybe Nick didn't."

"No," Gabby said, shaking her head fiercely. "It's not Nick in there. Squid would never have left Nick behind. He was so loyal to him. Maybe there was someone else in the house. A robber, maybe. And somehow Nick and Squid escaped, and were separated." She got up from the floor as she talked, staring at Ben as if to make him retract his words.

"The neighbors agree with you," Ben said. "They told the firemen and police the same thing about Squid's loyalty. He's an amazing dog, Gabby. And so smart. He came to you as a refuge."

Ben's voice was kind, describing the events as gently as he could, and watching Gabby's face carefully. He knew it would be unfair to foster hopes that were unrealistic, almost nonexistent.

"The police don't have any kind of identification yet. There will be one soon, but what we know for sure is what I've said. They don't know yet if he was alone that evening, but they will find out. Firemen are good at that. They will cover every detail. It's still so early. But no one has heard from Nick yet—the police are actively looking for him. They've checked all the hospitals on the North Shore. They've checked friends, but so far we haven't heard. And it's a concern. Nick would have contacted someone."

Gabby was quiet for a moment. Then she said, "No, you're right, Ben. Of course he would. But Nick has to be okay." She crouched down and wrapped her arms around Squid, then looked up at Birdie. "He has to be, Nonna. Squid loved him."

Birdie watched her granddaughter doing exactly what all of them were doing. An instinctive, protective reaction—trying to convince themselves that Nick Cabot was safe. Hoping it was a mistake. That it was someone else in the house, someone they didn't know. A stranger. And except for a burned house, life would go back to normal again. Then, as she watched, Gabby's fine mind kicked in and she put emotions aside briefly, long enough to acknowledge what Ben was saying.

Gabby wiped the fear and disbelief and tears from her eyes and looked again at Ben.

"At first, the fire chief thought Squid might be somewhere in the house," Ben said. "But they couldn't find any trace of him. And now we know why, and that he's safe, thanks to you, Gabby. I let the fire department know that Squid was with you. Safe."

"Squid is a very smart dog," Nell said. "He must have known he'd be safe here."

"Safe and loved," Ella said, leaning down again and handing the dog a strip of bacon.

"Squid loves Nick so much," Gabby said. Her words caught in her throat. "It must have been so awful for him. To see whatever it was he saw. Or . . . or to be unable to help his best friend. What will happen, Ben?"

Nell watched Gabby as she processed the news. She'd been just eight or nine when she'd come into all their lives. A granddaughter Birdie hadn't known she had, and then someone she had fallen in love with almost instantly and deeply. As all of them had.

Now, suddenly, in what felt like minutes, Gabrielle Marietti was dealing with a tragedy. An intelligent, loving teenager, facing life with all its darkness and light. Growing up too quickly.

"There are too many unknowns, Gabby," Ben was saying. "It's just too soon to say for sure. But we know Squid is content here with you, because you're the person he chose to come to. I told the fire and police that you'd keep him here until we know more." He looked over at Birdie, who was already nodding her head.

"Of course he will stay here," Birdie said.

"Good." Ben looked down at Gabby. "I had coffee with

Nick a couple days ago and he was talking about you. He told me how close you and Squid had become. And that he trusted you with Squid's safety. With his dog's life. He must have told Squid that, too."

Gabby teared up, just a little, and burrowed her head into Squid's shaggy coat, hugging him tightly.

"Yes," Birdie said again, "Squid will stay here for now, where he's safe and loved, as Ella has wisely said."

Gabby wiped away the tears with the back of her sleeve. Then she stood up and announced that she and Squid were going out. It was Monday, after all. A workday for the Pawfect Day Dog Walkers. Squid needed exercise. And they had other dogs counting on them.

Squid got up and walked behind Gabby as she gathered up several leashes from a hook hanging beside the kitchen door.

Without looking back, Gabby and Squid were gone on their way to meet Daisy Danvers and embark on a day full of dog walking. And emotion.

And uncertainty.

Chapter 16

Monday was Cass's day off, one she often spent part of in Coffee's, the local coffee place on Harbor Road, drinking lattes and napping, or reading in her reserved corner chair near the fireplace.

But the call from Pete had entirely changed her plans for the day. In fact, it had changed the day. Every minute of it.

Her brother picked her up in his Jeep and drove directly to the neighborhood that housed many of the fishermen families who worked for his and Cass's Halloran Lobster Company.

"Geesh, Cass, it's a bad fire, they're saying," he said, driving around the corner and onto Fishermen Row.

Cass grabbed her seat belt tightly. She nodded, trying to clear her mind. Trying not to think of what they would see. She hated fires. But friends lived in that neighborhood. Employees. Pete was right. They needed to go.

Two fire trucks and an emergency medical vehicle blocked the narrow neighborhood road. Pete pulled over to the curb and parked.

Cass jumped out of the passenger side of the car and stood on the sidewalk, staring at what had been Nick Cabot's house.

Pete got out and stood beside her, his hands shoved into the pockets of his jeans.

The scene in front of them turned Cass's stomach. She could feel the neighborhood's pain. Nick's house was a place most of the neighbors had been in, at one time or another, because that was how Nick wanted it. His house was always open to the families in the neighborhood. The whole neighborhood looked forward to his annual Santa party. And Santa always came holding a fishing pole and looked a lot like Nick Cabot with an overstuffed pillow inside his red suit. The kids had to fish for the gifts that each one of them would receive. New bikes and dollhouses and game sets. In warm weather, there were barbecues and Frisbee contests and beer-and-brat fests. Everyone was welcome. *Always.*

Pete nudged her and pointed to two men just inside the rope blockade the firemen had set up. "What are the police doing here?"

Cass looked over and saw Police Chief Jerry Thompson talking to Alex Arcado, head of the fire department.

"I don't know. Jerry's probably making sure they have all the help they need. It's the kind of thing he does."

"Hmm," Pete said. Then he turned and looked across the street at a group of their Halloran workers' families huddled together, trying to make sense out of what they were seeing. "I'll go talk to our folks, see if they need anything."

Cass nodded, but didn't move, staring beyond the rope barrier. She couldn't take her eyes off what had once been a beautiful home—the home of a man she'd just had lunch with on Friday. But it wasn't the debris, the blackened books and paintings, or the dangling window slats that were now grotesque figures and lumps out of a horror movie.

No, it was what she *couldn't* see.

The man who owned the house. And the dog who would never have left him, fire or no fire. But somehow Squid had.

Izzy had texted her on the way over and told her what she

knew from Ben and Nell. What the firefighters had surmised, but had not confirmed. Someone had died in the house fire. An unidentified someone.

No, Cass thought. *Not unidentified. Unconfirmed. No.*

Pete walked back across the street. "All the neighbors' houses seemed to be okay," he said. "Apparently, the Cabot house has enough land around it that the fire was contained to the property. The neighbors are anxious for updates. They love the guy. He made their neighborhood a better place."

Cass nodded, her eyes still on the house.

"Marco Costa is over there," Pete said.

"Why? He doesn't live here anymore."

"He muttered something about wanting to be sure Elena was okay. I asked why he wasn't in the house with her, instead of staring at the fire."

"And?"

"He cussed me out and moved away."

They watched a policeman walk across the street to the crowd, explaining to them that they wouldn't know anything for a while, and they should all go home.

But no one budged. Their concern was for Nick and Squid. No one had any idea where they were.

Cass and Pete watched Marco take the policeman's advice and disappear, while the others stood for a short while longer, watching the firemen do their job. Imagining that if they stood there looking at the house long enough, Nick and Squid would walk out of the rubble and tell them everything was going to be okay.

Acknowledging that wasn't going to happen, and realizing there was nothing they could do, Cass and Pete climbed back into the Jeep and took one last look at what was left of their friend's house. Across the street from it, the crowd of onlookers had grown larger, with people now backing onto small yards or spilling out into the street.

Pete started the car and was beginning to make a U-turn when Cass put a hand on his arm. "Stop for a second." She stared over at the crowd again.

At the edge of the crowd, nearly hidden by a couple of fishermen she knew, a familiar face stared over at the burned-out house.

"I'm surprised to see him here," Cass said, nudging Pete to look. "He lives on the other side of town, in his mom's house."

Pete followed her look and shrugged. "Who knows? It's what happens. News travels fast. It's weird, but fires bring people out of the woodwork. Grim fascination, I guess." He stepped on the gas and drove down the street.

Cass twisted against the seat belt to look through the back window at the growing, curious crowd. She squinted, then frowned.

Bobby Palazola had disappeared into the throng.

Chapter 17

By late afternoon, Nell felt she'd been up for a week. She was exhausted and sad and worried. Ben had been right when he'd said that by day's end, they'd have confirmation of the person found in the house at 9 Fishermen Row. But it wasn't news. Not in a small town.

Nick Cabot was dead.

His neighbors in Fishermen's Village were already leaving flowers and mementoes near the curb in front of where his beautiful house had stood, despite the firemen trying to keep them at bay.

Later in the afternoon, Chief Jerry Thompson announced that he'd be holding a press conference outside the police department. Alex Arcado, the fire chief, would be there, too, to provide the town with specifics of a fire they had all heard about.

The chief had called Ben earlier and had given him a brief summary of the news the town would have to swallow. Press conferences weren't something normally done in Sea Harbor, and Jerry suspected that many people would show up to hear the details of the fire. He had asked the mayor to come, too.

*   *   *

The police chief, with Alex Arcado standing beside him, started off without much of a preamble, except for the basic fire details: a house being burned, something most of them already knew. A fire, he said, that was still under investigation, but posed no danger to other homes in the neighborhood.

And then he went on with the news of a well-liked Sea Harbor man. A man that some of them thought might be their next mayor.

"Nick Cabot, the homeowner, is dead," the chief announced, his face grave.

The crowd stirred, even though many had already suspected it. Somehow it was different coming from the chief of police. They could no longer hope it had been a horrible mistake.

Once the crowd quieted down, Jerry Thompson went on, giving condolences to friends and family. And assuring those who knew Nick's dog that Squid had escaped the fire, and he was safe and being cared for.

And then the tone of his voice changed from sad to grave.

"Contrary to what we originally thought, and what many of you had also surmised," he said, "Nick did not die in the fire."

Before he could go on, there was a rush of words, with questions tossed out loudly, colliding in the air. Finally Fire Chief Arcado was able to calm people down, and Police Chief Thompson was able to finish the few facts that had been confirmed, at the same time assuring people there would be more news passed to them as soon as additional facts were known.

It was the final piece of news that stunned the crowd into total silence.

"Nick Cabot's death is being investigated as a homicide. Nick died from a gunshot fired before the fire began. It appears he died instantly."

*   *   *

It was the devastating news and the healing powers of a sunset that lured Ben and Nell to put on light jackets and walk hand in hand down to the shore near their house.

"Murdered," Nell said softly, the word catching in her throat. *How could such a perfect night, such unimaginable beauty, allow such tragedy to exist?*

She looked at the large field of boulders, stretching far out into the sea. They looked like they'd grown directly out of it. Crevices in the mounds of granite held small tide pools filled with ocean life. There wasn't a beach along this part of the shore, which made it a treasured place of hers and Ben's, a place they'd walk to when they needed to be away. Sometimes they'd climb out on the boulders, feeling the ocean spray on their faces, then finding a smooth spot to sit and look into the vast nothingness. Alone together. To talk softly or not at all.

"How can they be sure it wasn't an attempted robbery?" Nell said, forcing an explanation into the irrational act. "It wasn't a secret that Nick was a wealthy man."

Police Chief Thompson hadn't specifically told the crowd and reporters that it wasn't a robbery. In fact, he'd ignored the question when it was asked from someone standing on the police department steps.

"We're still investigating," the chief had said firmly.

"If there had been even a slight chance that it had been a robbery, Jerry would have spelled that out. People could get their thoughts around a robbery, as awful as it would have been. But until they have more specifics, he needed to be vague."

Nell shivered. She knew that was what Ben would say before he said it. Ruling out a robbery didn't leave many options, and certainly no semi-rational reason that might bring the case to a close. Or one that would eliminate, at least, the possibility of an intentional murder.

They stood in the quiet of the evening, looking out over the water, where the moonlight painted a path of light from the sky to the water. And back again.

"It was clear that Jerry Thompson wanted to get facts out to the town as soon as possible," Ben said. "Things can get out of hand so quickly and it only helps to let people know as much as he can—facts that won't deter the investigation, but things that people need to know."

"Jerry's a wise man—and good friend. He knows how quickly fear spreads when people don't feel safe."

"He told me that they think whoever shot Nick knew him. I suppose there's some relief in that. At least we know there's no serial killer wandering Sea Harbor."

"If that's true, we may know the person who did this, too." What she wanted to add was a denial. *The kind of people we know don't kill.*

But that was a wish, not a fact. A troubling one.

"It doesn't make sense, Ben. Nick was a good man. And respected. Even by people who didn't know him personally. The entire Cabot family has a tradition of doing good things for the community."

"Which is why he would have been elected mayor."

"But running against Beatrice? Even the thought of it upset her terribly. She wouldn't have allowed it." Nell realized what she had said and attempted to retract it. "I mean, she would have tried hard to defeat him."

"I don't think Nick was expecting Beatrice's reaction," Ben said. "Frankly, I wasn't, either. It was a little bit over the top."

"Maybe. But not unexpected," Nell said.

Ben was quiet. Finally he said, "The chief had asked Beatrice to be there today. As mayor. To offer comfort. Leadership."

Nell frowned, and then thought back to the gathering. There were reporters there, needing details. But also many neighbors and fishermen and shopkeepers looking for comfort from their police chief, their mayor, anyone to help them feel safe.

"Beatrice wasn't there," Ben said quietly.

Nell started to say something, trying to pull up some reason that would explain the mayor's absence. The same mayor who wouldn't pass up a bakery opening, but failed to appear when her town may have needed her most.

But no words came.

Instead of talking, she leaned her head against Ben's shoulder until she felt his comforting arm wrapped around her, holding her close. She closed her eyes, trying to block out the uncomfortable noise in her head.

It was Beatrice Scaglia's voice. Loud and defiant.

Nick Cabot cannot be mayor. I simply won't allow it.

Chapter 18

It was late afternoon the day after the press conference, with a cloud settling over Sea Harbor. People were leaving work. Shopping the Harbor Road stores. Going to meetings and to the grocery store and returning books to the library. Ordinary things.

On a day that wasn't in any way ordinary.

"I'm glad Gracie is still going to go through with this family dinner special tonight. It was a good decision not to cancel," Birdie said.

The decision had been made with some hesitation, Nell knew. She waved to Harry Garozzo, who was standing outside his deli talking to customers. Everyone asking questions and no one answering, although Harry would be trying his best.

"I understand her reluctance," Birdie continued. "But I think it will help everyone."

The idea to have a weekly family dinner night with special prices at the Lazy Lobster and Soup Café had been Nick Cabot's idea just days before he died. It was intended as a kind of goodwill gesture Gracie could put in place to counter the negative reviews. He had suggested it in a quick text message late one night, something he did often when an idea hit him that he thought might help his friend with her recent restaurant woes: **It's a good marketing device. Remind folks that the Lazy Lobster's a friendly place, cozy, a place to see neighbors and friends, and that it has the best lobster mac 'n' cheese in town.**

He'd ended the text with a PS: **Save me a seat. And, Gracie, it's all going to be okay.**

She had forwarded the text to the four knitters, the poignancy of it leaving a mark on all of them.

Birdie took a deep breath. "So," she said, "we'll all put on our best faces, eat a delicious meal—"

"And go home early," Nell said, knowing that many people would want that, too, as they coped with an unexplainable tragedy.

"Gabby's coming. She needs the distraction. Who knows, Pete may even lure her to the mic to sing with the Fractured Fish."

"This certainly isn't the summer she had planned on," Nell said. "It's a lot to deal with. How's she doing?"

"All right, I think. We spent time at the mall this morning, buying dog beds and bowls and other canine necessities. So far, the only bed Squid is comfortable in is Gabby's. They're both sad, but they're finding comfort in one another. In my whole long life, I've never had a dog, but I'm beginning to see what I have missed out on. There's communication and unconditional love there. It's beautiful. As Gabby said last night, 'Dogs don't judge. They just love.'"

Nell thought about that and tucked the thought away. "I suppose it's too early to know what or where Squid's future will be."

"Nick's sister, Nancy, lives in Portugal. She and Nick have always been close."

"Is she coming?"

"The Chief said that he's talked with her. Several times, in fact. He suggested she wait a few days before making plans. And that he'd keep in close touch with her."

Nell slowed her steps, imagining a woman so far away, hearing such devastating news.

"There's the car." Nell pointed ahead to her car, parked in front of MJ's Salon. She pulled out her keys.

"Look," Birdie said, stopping near the salon window. Nell stepped over to the window,

Elizabeth Hartley was sitting alone in the salon's lounge and waiting area. Her body appeared tense, her head low. A magazine sat on her lap, unopened.

"I'd almost forgotten about Elizabeth in all the drama and tragedy," Nell said. "I'm sure she's devastated."

Birdie was already opening the salon door. The soothing sounds of Tori Amos and her piano met them as they stepped inside. They walked past the reception desk and turned into the lounge. The subdued lighting and soft music that MJ preferred encouraged soft voices, too.

Elizabeth looked up as they entered, her magazine dropping to the floor.

At that same moment, MJ, the shop owner, walked in from the salon area. She welcomed them with warm hugs. "How did you know I needed a touch of Nell and Birdie today? I'm sure Elizabeth does, too. I think we *wished* you here. Is that possible?"

MJ Arcado's compassion and caring were topped off with lots of otherworldly practices, and she may have done exactly that.

"I think she lured me in, too," Elizabeth said.

"This is such a sad, ugly happening," MJ said. Her voice was firm, as if the resolve in her tone would somehow get rid of the ugliness. "I told Elizabeth and all my customers that canceling salon appointments doesn't help anything."

"How is your Alex doing with all this, MJ?" Birdie asked.

The fire chief's heart was as big as his beefy body. He embraced every call to his fire station as if it were his own home, his own pet caught in a tree, his own family losing their possessions.

"None of the crew were injured. That's a first concern. But this one, this fire has its own level of awfulness. *The Cabot Fire,*" MJ said slowly. "It's already assuming that kind of reverence and it'll linger for years. Alex is devastated, as if he should have gotten over there sooner—even though in the end, it wouldn't have made a difference."

She looked down at Elizabeth. *It wouldn't have kept Nick alive* was what MJ was telling her.

Nell shivered, thinking of Nick, their exchange at the bakery and seeing him the next day at the yacht club. It somehow brought a sense of closeness to him. Ben had mentioned the same thing. For Elizabeth, that feeling might be even more intense. She looked different today, as if something had been taken out of her, turning the tall, competent woman into a different version of herself. Her face was strained, rigid. As if she might break if someone attempted to talk too loudly to her.

MJ seemed to be seeing the same thing. She caught the attention of her two longtime friends and clients. "Can you two sit for a few minutes? Togetherness often stills the waters."

She motioned to the empty chairs, then walked over to a bookcase that covered one wall of the lounge area. It was filled with photos, audiotapes, magazines, and a cabinet with liquid drinks and chocolate bars. She pulled a bottle of wine from a rack, speaking over her shoulder as she uncorked it.

"Elizabeth, you're my last client of the day. We're in no rush, hon. Take deep breaths. It helps, believe me."

Nell and Birdie sat down, aware that they only had a little time, but that the moment mattered. Birdie glanced at Elizabeth's hand. It was twisted into a fist. She reached over and rubbed it lightly.

"Are you all ri—" Nell began, then stopped, erasing her old words with new ones. "That's a useless phrase, isn't it? You're not all right—of course you're not. None of us are."

Elizabeth managed a thin smile, her fingers relaxing slightly. "It's more than . . ." She stopped talking, frowning, looking perplexed.

MJ placed four glasses of wine on the low coffee table and sat down. "Here. Drink," she said.

Elizabeth picked up her glass, gratefully, and took a drink.

Nell glanced at MJ, then back to Elizabeth, who was slowly emptying her wineglass as she looked out the window, a frown appearing on her forehead.

"MJ, does Alex know anything more about the fire?" Birdie asked, attempting to fill the silence.

"I'm not sure how much you've heard, but they've ruled out arson," she said.

"Not arson?" Elizabeth asked, looking back. "But—"

"I know," MJ said. "It seems more logical that the fire was intentionally set to hide anything that would tell us who or how or why someone did it. Right? That's how it is on TV. But apparently not."

"How did it start?" Elizabeth asked.

"They think it started from some candles."

"Candles?" Birdie asked.

"Nick loved candles," Elizabeth said, lifting her head. "He had a collection."

It was as if she were plucking pieces from the conversation that brought happy memories and ignoring the rest.

"I remember seeing the candle collection in his beautiful home," Birdie said. "And once in the old house, when his mother was still alive. She dusted them constantly. Many of the gorgeous holders had been designed by Canary Cove artists. All different shapes—both the candles and the holders."

"He loved the way candlelight reflected off all the glass in his house," Elizabeth said. "It created such beauty. The table candles couldn't have started that fire, though. There must be a mistake."

"Alex said the ones that started the fire were bigger candles in large artistically creative holders. Some of those holders actually survived the fire. The others were in a cabinet Nick had built especially for them," MJ explained.

"But how?" Elizabeth asked softly, as if she were seeing their light, the warmth of the flames. She looked down at her hands again, her wineglass shaking. The awfulness of the scene seemed to be affecting her whole body, as if she might be getting sick. "They were on the table—"

"Yes. Alex said he's only seen a fire starting that way once before." MJ checked the look on Elizabeth's face and seemed to regret that they'd brought up the fire at all.

"No, MJ, go on. I need to know how that could have happened. A fire . . ."

"Well, I'll make it short. It was an explosion, apparently."

"Explosion?" Birdie said.

"Yes. I'm not a scientist in this sort of thing, but as Alex explained it, if a large amount of hot wax accumulates at the bottom of a holder—and then somehow a gush of water lands on top of it, it can cause an explosion. A gush, Alex said. They think that's what started it, then it sparked some wall hangings and a small rug. And then the fire just took over," MJ said. "They also think the large doors leading to the deck had been left open, and that's how Squid escaped. Or maybe he had wandered out earlier, visiting neighbors. He sometimes did that, one neighbor said. He'd always come back when Nick called."

Elizabeth frowned at the images being created. She was listening intently, as if thinking it might change the outcome.

"But how do they know that?" Nell asked.

"It involves all sorts of things. Fire and arsonist examiners can determine things like wind flow. There had to be enough water to spill into the holders. The back deck doors were already open—that back part of the house wasn't as damaged because of the direction of the wind. But the wind would have been strong enough to tip over a water pitcher on the table."

Nell felt Elizabeth's body stiffen. She tried to think of another, less gruesome topic.

MJ herself stepped in. "Enough about the fire." She refilled Elizabeth's wineglass.

Birdie and Nell explained they were off to dinner soon and refrained.

"Elizabeth, Birdie and I are around these days. Let us know if you need help with anything. Walks? Talks? We're great at following directions, and we always bring sweets to any kind of get-together."

"Or perhaps wine?" MJ interjected with a grin. "Elizabeth and I share a peculiar intolerance. Sweet things. But somehow the sugar in wine doesn't affect either of us one single bit."

"Well, then, my Ella makes a fancy fruit dish with passion fruit. And she insists it's very healthy," Birdie said.

Elizabeth seemed to relax at the change of subjects. "Thanks. I went into the art association office today because . . . Well, I'm not sure why. Maybe because I needed a reason to get out of bed. Having the two of you around would be nice. Thanks. Tomorrow maybe? I'll be in touch."

The rest of the conversation moved along more comfortably, leaning toward topics that felt more like hugs—knitting and friends and an auction that would benefit the children's hospital—things that help heal.

Eventually Nell and Birdie excused themselves, leaving Elizabeth Hartley in the capable hands of MJ Arcado, and knowing that even in the short time it would take to have her hair cut, it would be time used to help soothe Elizabeth's spirit.

Chapter 19

It had been Ben's idea to go to Gracie's first family night at the Lazy Lobster and Soup Café—and to pass the word around. He'd run into Gracie that morning, walking alone to her restaurant, looking like she was carrying the world on her shoulders.

When Ben called to her, she turned, saw who it was, and walked into the hug he was offering. As if Ben had turned on a faucet, Gracie began sobbing into his shoulder, releasing things too heavy to express any other way—restaurant worries, the fire, the death of one of her closest friends.

Finally Gracie pulled away. She wiped her eyes with her sweatshirt sleeve and managed a small, embarrassed laugh. "Well, I'm glad it's you and not the trashman I attacked."

"Hey, Gracie, we're like family. I'm glad it was me, too."

"It's just too much, you know? I was about to burst, and then there you were, as if you knew it." Gracie's voice was husky. "His face is everywhere. He and my uncle are the most important men in my life."

"You picked two good ones," Ben said.

"Remember those early days of the restaurant, Ben? You guys were all there, every night, helping to get it ready."

"I do," Ben answered. "Nick was right there in the middle of us. He was lousy at painting, but great at bringing pizza and beer." He saw a smile coming.

"Right." She gave a small laugh. "And then when we opened, Nick came to eat all the time, tipping my waitresses so outrageously that there was no way any of them would ever think of leaving me for a better job. 'Continuity in help is critical,' he'd say, and then he'd flirt outrageously with whoever was serving his table. They loved him. Everyone loved him."

"Well, I can't promise you about the tips, Gracie," Ben said, straight-faced. "You know what tightwads Danny Brandley and Sam Perry are. But no matter, we'll all be there tonight. And I promise I'll work on the tip issue. I'll shame them."

Gracie hugged him again, tightly. Then she pulled away and hurried into the restaurant, leaving a damp spot on Ben's shirt.

Gabby was already at the restaurant when Birdie, Ben, and Nell arrived. She was sitting with Gracie on a tall barstool, their heads together, talking like two old friends, the age difference irrelevant. There was no need to eavesdrop; they all suspected what they were talking about. Nick was ever present.

The Lazy Lobster had been Gabby Marietti's favorite restaurant since the first time she'd set foot in it, back when she'd help Izzy out by watching Abby now and then. She'd take her into Gracie's for a special cornmeal hot-dog bite, which Gracie'd concocted just for them. Gracie soon became one of Gabby's favorite adults. Always with an ear ready to listen to whatever was on her mind. Tonight, comfortably sitting on the floor between the two women, his head resting on his paws, was Squid.

"Oh, my," Birdie whispered, pointing. "It's Squid."

Squid lifted his head immediately, slapping his tail in welcome. Gracie looked over, seeing Birdie's surprised look. "It's okay, Birdie. I told Gabby to bring Squid. He and I are old friends, and I wanted to give him a special hug tonight. I wanted him here."

The dog was on his way to Birdie, now that he knew he was safe. He sat down in front of her, waiting for a pat. Birdie smiled at him and brushed strands of long, shaggy hair away from his eyes.

"That's intuitive, Nonna," Gabby said. "You do the same thing to me."

Birdie smiled. "The better to see, my dear."

Gracie had saved a long table for them. It was at the far end of the restaurant, next to the wide doors leading out to the deck.

"A quick escape out the back, in case Squid needs a short walk to the grass," she said. "And if anyone needs exercise, our guy Pete and his Fractured Fish band are going to be playing on the deck later."

In minutes, the Perrys and Brandleys arrived and filled the empty chairs, with little Joey Brandley in a booster seat and Abby Perry beside him, begging Squid to sit between them.

No dummy to the amount of food little kids dropped on the floor, Squid already had eyes on the spot.

They'd come early, but several other tables were already filled, and familiar faces crowded the bar.

"It looks like a good crowd," Cass said, looking around. "I'm glad. Hopefully, the rumors will fade away and people will see that Gracie's is still a great place to be, a great place to eat."

"Of course they will," Nell said. "I wonder if Chef Bobby will show himself. I have yet to meet him."

"I'm sure we can get Gracie to pull him out of the oven or wherever she's stashed him," Cass said. "But seriously, he's not a bad guy. You'll like him, Nell."

"You're saying that because my aunt likes everyone," Izzy said.

"Well, there's that."

A young waitress came over, a neighbor of Nell and Ben's, and greeted them warmly. She passed out the family menu, then a short menu with Bobby's special entrees.

"You can get the special family meal or order from the other. But no matter what you get, you'll love it," the waitress promised, then moved to the next table.

Across the room, Nell watched Alphonso and Liz Santos come in with their girls. They hugged Gracie warmly. Then Liz spotted Nell and waved, leaving Alphonso and Gracie to settle the girls, and hurried across the room.

"You finally took a night off, Liz," Nell said. "That's a good thing."

"Alphonso and I wouldn't miss something that supports Gracie. We had to be here. It helps with the sadness and takes our minds off things for an hour or two. Nick loved this place so much." She stood between Nell and Birdie, leaning in as her voice cracked. "I'm so glad you both are here. Life has changed so dramatically since we were together. And it was just two days ago. Time is so tangled up."

Sunday. Jane's birthday brunch. The last time they'd seen Nick. A happy and carefree Nick, joking with Liz, carrying Jane's presents to her car. A happy, exuberant man.

Nell looked up. "We're lucky. That day was a gift."

"And you had the whole weekend together, Liz," Birdie added. Her voice was soft, separating their conversation from the table's louder talk.

Liz nodded. "It was really an amazing weekend. Beyond expectations. Lots of talking and closeness and loving each other. Nick was the happiest I've ever seen him. He's always been fun and personable. But he was especially happy last weekend. We all were. Sometimes being with friends you love, those you've shared a history with, people who know you inside and out, was pure joy. Remember that old Joni Mitchell song about looking at clouds from both sides? We did a lot of that."

"It sounds like a special time," Birdie said.

"And especially so now," Liz said, "in this terrible pool of sadness." Liz's eyes began to fill. "I'm not handling this very well. It's like a part of me is gone."

"Are any of your friends still in town?" Nell asked, hoping her answer was yes. Friends would be comforting.

"No, they all left Sunday afternoon. Except for Bella. Nick convinced her to stay a couple extra hours." The thought brought a smile to Liz's lips. Then she went on. "She left Sunday evening, heading to Switzerland. She called me from the airport, so very happy." Liz took a deep breath, but couldn't control the tears that began to run down her cheeks, now untouched. "We should all still be together. With Nick. Sitting on his deck, teasing him about the scratch on his boat from being out too late the night before, reliving our old lives, loving—"

Just then, a child's cry pulled Liz's attention to the other side of the restaurant. They followed her look to her youngest daughter, trying desperately to get out of her booster seat and find her mommy.

Liz grabbed Nell's napkin and hastily wiped her eyes. "I'm so sorry," she said. Then she forced a smile to her face. "I'm being paged. But please let's talk soon." Liz leaned over and hugged them both with the kind of embrace that speaks louder, sometimes, than words.

Sam ordered the family dinner for everyone—platters of lobster rolls, Gracie's lobster mac and cheese, coleslaw, chicken legs, and then added one extra dish: "Cod," he said. "I've been salivating for Bobby Palazola's Cod Arracanato ever since he bartered with me, trading this very same meal for a photo shoot I did for him a thousand moons ago. The cod was *magnifico* that day. I still taste it in my dreams."

Nell looked over at him. Sam Perry was as transparent as his water glass. He ordered Bobby Palazola's special dish so he could see for himself why there were bad reviews. And then he'd declare it delicious and dampen the irritating reviews that were causing problems for the restaurant. And for their good friend Gracie.

By the time the entrees came, the restaurant was nearly full. Out on the deck, Pete Halloran's band was playing catchy tunes, which were luring small bodies outside to wiggle and giggle and sing while waiting for their mac and cheesy cheese dinners. Abby Perry and toddler Joey led the pack.

Nell looked around the dinner crowd for Gracie and found her circulating the tables and looking pleased that somehow the comfort she had wanted for her diners seemed to be happening. It was as if they'd all gathered in a kindly grandmother's kitchen, being told that everything was going to be okay.

Ben proposed a toast to Gracie's stamina. "She has an intuition for what people need."

"I heard my name," Gracie said, making her way back to the table of her friends.

"Okay, guys, so what do you think?"

She glanced around their tables at the nearly empty plates. Then looked up at the smiles.

"Hated it," Cass said. "Every bite."

Gracie chuckled. She looked over at Sam. "And you?"

His plate was almost empty. He looked up at Gracie with a broad smile. "And me?" He raised one hand, as if taking an oath: "In cod and Gracie and Bobby, we trust."

A while later, sufficiently full, Cass and Izzy looked over at their tired kids and took over, wiping Joey and Abby clean of chocolate sundaes. Ben took care of the bill, while Nell and Danny began packing up the kids' drawing pads that carried them through most of the meal, and then headed for the exit, stopping briefly to speak with friends as they wove their way around tables. Words were shared about the fire on Fishermen Row. And looks of sadness at the tragic loss of a well-liked Sea Harbor man. Many of the diners expressed appreciation for what the restaurant had provided, inviting people to this family dinner night.

It had been a good night for Gracie. Sam and Izzy detoured toward the bar to tell her as much, and to see if Chef Bobby would want to hear some encouraging words as well.

"You're a master at bringing people together, Gracie," Sam said. "The chef has done a great job, too. Any chance of luring that curly-haired culinary genius out of the kitchen so I can give him a congrats?"

"I would love to bring him out, Sam. Bobby needs a pat on the back now and then these days."

She motioned for the bartender to get Bobby. Then she looked at Sam with a concerned frown. "I noticed you ordered one meal from Bobby's special menu. 'His cod with a French twist,' we call it in the kitchen."

Before Sam could answer, the chef appeared, his toque in place and his apron, though slightly wrinkled, clean.

"Hey there, Chef Palazola," Sam said. "You're looking great. Food was great, too."

"Thanks, Sam. It's good to see you still have good taste."

His relieved smile belied the light words. He looked at Izzy. "You got yourself a good man there, Izzy."

Izzy started to respond, but a rubbing against her leg distracted her.

Startled, Izzy looked down. Squid sat at her feet, his shaggy body pressed against her leg. His eyes looked up at her. "Squid! Lordy. What are you doing here? She leaned over and scratched his ears, her head craned as she looked for Gabby in the crowd. But before she found her, Squid had abandoned her legs for those of the chef's, sniffing his pants.

"I guess the dog liked the food," Bobby joked.

Izzy finally spotted Gabby across the room. She was holding a leash in her hand, frantically searching the restaurant for her canine charge. Izzy tried to turn Squid around to lead him over to Gabby, but before her fingers could loop beneath his collar, Squid leaned his head sideways and snapped sharply at Bobby Palazola's pants.

Bobby jumped, and Izzy reached down, scolding Squid and trying to pull him away.

Squid saved her the effort. He abruptly turned away, pulled out of her grasp, and headed back into the crowd of exiting diners.

Izzy watched the dog make his way around the tables, making sure he found Gabby.

But Gabby was no longer looking for the dog.

She was standing near the exit, perfectly still, staring across the room at Bobby Palazola as if seeing a ghost. Squid sat obediently at her side, pressed tightly against her leg.

Later that night, Birdie stood at her bedroom window, looking out over the town. Lights blinked off in windows as the town slowed down and prepared for sleep. A routine as normal as the tide coming in and then going out again. But sleep might not come as easily for some. Not for the firemen who had bravely put their lives at risk, nor the police who were now faced with probing the lives of people in the town, having to ask painful questions. Nor those who had lost a good or loving friend in a grim and tragic way. She knew death altered people's rhythms, their lives. And murder altered a town.

And then there was her very own Gabrielle, who had expanded Birdie's heart until she sometimes thought it might simply split wide open. Birdie shivered. And with it came something she hadn't experienced in her life before. She had loved her husband, Sonny, more than life itself. But it was different with Gabby. Along with the love came an intense need to protect her. And today, this week, that feeling had been accompanied by fear.

She had tried to keep it at bay, hadn't even talked to Nell about it. Talking might have made her fears seem more possible. But it still crept in at night. And when she walked down Harbor Road, into stores, aware that a murderer could be right there, looking back at her. Or across the street, or in Harry's deli, or in Gus's hardware shop. Someone had killed Nick Cabot. Someone who may have seen her Gabby near the house she visited nearly every day. Someone who may have thought she knew something? Saw something? Heard something?

The thoughts twisted together until she couldn't pull them apart, and they grew into a dark shadowy lump of fear.

Birdie pressed a hand against her heart, then took a few deep, calming breaths until the fear lessened and moved back into the shadows.

At least, the evening at Gracie's Lazy Lobster and Soup Café had turned out to be comfortable. It was wonderful to see the smiles that the diners had put on Gracie Santos's face. And she on theirs.

She knew without a doubt that Nick Cabot had been very much present, but somehow the tragic and malicious part of his death had been put aside for a few needed hours, and conversation about Nick was mostly about his person and his charisma, and how loved he was.

Finally Birdie yawned, stretched her arms, and looked up into the deep night. She murmured a silent prayer to the moon—and to those she loved who were up there, somewhere. She closed the window shades and walked toward her bed, her whole body weary. With the help of a small stool, she climbed up and slid between the cool sheets. The comfort of sleep began to close in, and she opened her small body to it, her eyes closing almost before her head had touched the pillows.

The soft flap of bare feet stopped at her door. And then a whisper.

"Nonna . . ."

The voice was so soft that Birdie thought she might have imagined the sound. Or maybe she was already dreaming. She opened her eyes slowly and looked toward her bedroom door. A tall figure stood in the open space, silhouetted against the hallway night-light.

"Gabby?" Birdie pulled herself forward, leaning on one elbow. She peered through the darkness of her room until she could focus on her granddaughter's eyes and on what she had heard in her voice. An urgency.

"Gabby, come closer. What's wrong, dear?" Birdie's heart began to beat faster. She held out her arms for Gabby to come into them.

But Gabby didn't move. She remained in the doorway, her arms folded across her chest—as if protecting herself from some unknown danger.

"Nonna," she said again. "Nonna, I have something I have to tell you."

Chapter 20

"Okay, Sam," Izzy said the next morning. "Truth time."

She'd been too tired to ask him the night before. Getting a sugar-high Abby to bed had required major effort. That, and the emotional cloud hanging over them, had put both her and Sam to sleep shortly after Abby went down.

Sam continued to pour batter into his cast-iron skillet. "I'm all ears," he said. "Truth is good."

"Did you like the cod?"

This time, Sam turned his head, looking away from the stove to their small kitchen table, where Izzy sat in her running clothes, drinking a glass of water.

"What cod?"

"You know. Bobby's special."

"I gave you a bite."

"Yes, you did. I guess it tasted like cod. But I don't like cod, so I'm not much of a judge."

"Me neither," Sam said, turning back to his cooking. He flipped a pancake, trying for a Mickey Mouse look.

"Nice pancakes," Izzy said. "Why does Mickey have three ears?"

"The better to hear you with, my dear."

"About the cod," Izzy said.

"All right, then. The cod was okay. Absolutely okay. Edible."

Izzy listened carefully, not to his words, but to how they sounded. Sam inhaled leftovers and cold pizza, stale sandwiches, and frozen dinners, so Izzy wasn't sure what to make of his comments. On the other hand, he swooned over Nell and Ben's great Friday-night dinners, so she knew he had discriminating taste buds in him somewhere. But then, all that being said, Sam never, as long as she'd known him, which had been almost forever, complained about food. He'd had too many reminders in his childhood about starving children in faraway countries, Izzy had assumed.

Izzy finally decided that Sam's comment to Bobby about the meal was an honest one. He had enjoyed it. He'd all but licked his plate clean and it had satisfied his appetite. But Sam wasn't a restaurant reviewer. If he were, or if he knew much, or anything, about baked cod, he might have said what she herself had thought—that it was well seasoned, but a bit subpar at its core, at least when considering its source: a fairly well-known chef who had even received an award or two.

And that thought made her sad.

Izzy showered and dressed, kissed Abby and Sam good-bye, then headed off to work on her bike. She hoped the brisk morning breeze might help clear her head of family things and prepare her for the madness she'd meet, once the shop opened. A couple of classes, new shipments, customers working on knitting art auction items and designs, would make it a busy Wednesday. And beneath it all, friends and customers would be asking themselves and their neighbors and anyone who would listen why a good man was dead.

And who in Sea Harbor would kill such a man.

Good man. The word echoed in Izzy's head, and she wondered briefly why everyone seemed to assume that being good came with a free pass to a happy life and the privilege of not dying. Or of not being killed.

The thought caused her to barely avoid crashing into a skateboard that had somehow made its way to the bike lane, thankfully without a rider. The breeze wasn't working as well as she had anticipated, either, and as she regained her balance and began pedaling again, she realized how scrambled her thoughts were, twisted together like strands of yarn in a beginner's knitting class. It definitely wasn't her normal lawyer's mind, as her aunt Nell called it. The one that easily put things into charts and Excel sheets and diagrams. She checked her watch.

She had time enough to stop at Aunt Nell's for a decent cup of coffee. Maybe that would help.

But when Nell met her at the door before she'd had a chance to walk in, even her muddled thoughts dimmed.

"You've never met me at the door before, Aunt Nell. Not in the whole time I've lived here. Or before that." Her words were jerky and quick, without a single hello. She stepped into the front hall before Nell could respond and immediately looked toward the back of the house.

"I hear voices. Who's here, Aunt Nell? What's going on?"

"Nothing we can't handle. Come on back, Izzy," Nell said. She motioned for Izzy to follow her. The wide deck doors off the family room were open. Sitting on the chairs around the unlit firepit were Ben, Birdie, and Gabby. Squid lay on the deck floor next to Gabby. Izzy checked her watch again and frowned.

"Just go on out, Izzy. I'm glad you're here. I'm bringing coffee. There are muffins on the patio."

But the faces she looked out on didn't look like they'd been invited to a cheery breakfast on the deck.

Ben looked up and smiled—his serious but soothing smile—and pointed to a chair next to Gabby. "G'morning, Izzy. Join us."

Next to him sat Gabby Marietti, whose smile was more tentative than Uncle Ben's.

"So, what's up?" Izzy asked.

"Birdie and Gabby came over to talk about something that happened last night that might pertain in some way to Nick Cabot's death," Ben said.

"We needed to talk it through," Birdie added. "Isn't that something we always seem to do? Come over to the Endicotts' and talk through things until they make sense to us?"

Izzy gave a nod and a puzzled smile. She walked around a few chairs and stood behind her uncle, wrapping her arms around his neck for a light hug. "Well, yes, I think I get what you're saying. I've done that a million times. It's that Endicott thing Uncle Ben does," she said lightly.

Nell walked in as Izzy was talking and placed a carafe of fresh coffee and mugs on a table. "The more heads we have to straighten this out, the better," Nell said.

Izzy wondered if she should confess that her mind was mush today, and she probably couldn't help anyone sort through anything, not even Abby's shoelaces that morning. But she sensed she wouldn't be expected to, so instead she smiled, then leaned over and gave Gabby a quick hug, then a pat for Squid. And then she sat down.

Izzy glanced sideways at Gabby. Then over at Birdie, who caught her look and smiled back in that peaceful way she had, even when she was worried about those she loved. Which, Izzy thought, seemed to be in spades.

"We've only been here a few minutes, Izzy," Birdie said. "Gabby was about to fill us in on what happened last night."

Last night? Izzy thought. They'd all been together last night. Her thoughts went back to Sam's lukewarm review of the cod.

Then she dismissed it. That didn't—couldn't—have anything to do with Gabby.

Gabby started in before Izzy's thoughts went haywire.

"I guess I should go back to something that happened at Nick Cabot's house a few weeks ago," she said. She looked at the people sitting around the firepit, listening carefully.

"Actually, I started to tell all of you about it that night when Squid and I disrupted your knitting night. It was when you were talking about how great Nick was. And I kind of joked—or started to, anyway—that maybe not everyone was as crazy about him as all of you were. But Daisy showed up then and I left without finishing my story. I was on the clock and had dogs to walk." She managed a smile.

"I remember," Izzy said. "You were in a hurry—"

"Right," Gabby said, as if wanting to get her story out quickly. "So here's what happened." Quickly she told them about the man who had rushed past them as she and Daisy were headed to the Cabot house on their way to pick up Squid. How the guy looked like he had some kind of emergency, so they had stepped back and waited at the curb while he ran up to Nick's front door.

"That's when you heard him yelling at Nick?" Ben asked.

Gabby nodded. "He started in, almost as soon as Nick opened the door. The guy was mad and really loud, shaking his fist, cussing, and telling Nick to leave him and a woman or women alone, that Nick was trying to ruin his life and other people's lives, too, and then he said that he wished Nick were dead. Or something like that. Maybe it wasn't exactly those words."

"Did Daisy hear all of it, too?" Nell asked.

"Not everything. She's been interested in a guy we know who lives down the street from Nick's, and she was watching him mow the lawn, more than listening to the fight. But she heard the loud voices. It would have been hard not to."

They listened as Gabby talked. As she went on, the words came more freely. Soon she had laid out as much as she could remember about the conversation, and how the stranger had finally left in a rush, nearly knocking her and Daisy down.

"Could you tell if Nick knew him?" Ben asked.

Gabby nodded. "I think he did, although I'm not sure. He was surprised to see him. And the guy knew him. At least, it sure sounded like he did."

"What did Nick say when you went in to get Squid?" Nell asked.

"Nothing about the man. It was as if it hadn't happened. He was gracious and charming, as he always is, as if he hadn't just been threatened and screamed at. I don't think the man had frazzled Nick at all. Daisy and I even hung out with him for a while. He showed us a picture of his family. And he had this great collection of candles that his mother used to collect. The holders were made by artists and some of the candles, too. They were beautiful."

Nell handed Gabby a glass of water and refilled coffee cups.

"I guess that's why we forgot about the argument so quickly. Although it wasn't really an argument, since Nick seemed to be so calm and nice, even while the guy continued yelling at him. It seems like it was a century ago. Besides, we weren't a part of the conversation. It clearly wasn't a big deal to Nick. It wasn't until last night that it came back to me."

"Last night?" Izzy asked. "After we all left Gracie's?"

"No. Just before we left. I think the rest were outside or getting into cars. But Squid and I were still inside. You and Sam were, too, talking at the bar. And then Squid wandered away from me. He must have seen you, Izzy, because he went over to the bar, probably wanting you to give him a treat."

Nell and Izzy were both frowning, confused where Gabby was going with this.

"I finally saw Squid there. And that's when it came back to

me, because that's when I saw the man again," Gabby said. "He was there at Gracie's restaurant."

They waited, looking at Gabby's face. Izzy noticed the regret in her eyes. And a sliver of nervousness. As if she knew that what she was about to say might bring more problems into an already-sad week.

Gabby took a deep breath.

"It was the chef. He's the guy who yelled at Nick that day. Gracie's chef," she said. "The man with the dark, curly hair."

There was silence for a minute as they replayed Gabby's conversation in their heads, and then Ben told Gabby what he'd told Birdie the night before.

"It was smart of you to share this with your grandmother. Even though you weren't part of that conversation, the police would be interested in knowing what you'd heard. It's not like you're telling something out of school or anything like that. I know you're aware that in a case like this, the police need to look at the smallest detail. They have a tough job, and it's important that the public helps them in any way they can."

Gabby was nodding along with Ben's words. She clearly had known those things, but hearing them coming from Ben seemed to be giving her more confidence.

"I'd never met the chef," she said, "which is why I didn't think much about the conversation afterward," she said. "It was Nick's business, not mine. But I know now that he's the man who works with Gracie, and that's why this is all hard for me. I love Gracie Santos. I don't know what the police will do with this, and I don't want to do anything that complicates her life."

"Of course, Gabby," Nell said. "Gracie loves you, too. And this won't complicate her life. She'll be proud of you. Gracie is one of the strongest women I know. She may even know more about that argument than any of us do. They work so closely together, and Bobby's her friend."

Ben agreed. "You're not turning anyone in with this information, Gabby. The conversation you heard isn't incriminating anyone. It's simply doing what the police have asked of all of us. To pass along anything, however insignificant, that might help the investigation. What you heard simply tells the police that those two men didn't get along. And that's not a crime. But it is something they'd want to know about."

Gabby nodded. "Sure, I understand that."

"Bobby Palazola might be able to fill in some of the details, like the names of the people they were talking about, which might move the investigation in a new direction. And then you'd both be helpful citizens." Ben smiled.

"Of course," Gabby said, seemingly more relaxed as they talked. "I see that. That's why I told Nonna last night. I knew it was something that I should pass along. I just needed an hour to think it through in my head before I told her last night." She took a bite of a muffin, her face thoughtful as she mulled the whole conversation over in her head.

"You know Chief Thompson, right?" Nell asked.

"Yes. I met him over here once, I think. And I know Detective Porter, too. In fact, I walk the dog he gave his wife Janey for their anniversary. He's a wonderful golden named Dunkin."

Izzy found herself smiling at Gabby's composure. *She could take over being the attorney I left behind,* she thought. She'd known Gabby since that first day she had appeared in Sea Harbor as a child, but she was definitely not that child any longer. Izzy also suspected that even if the head of the Sea Harbor Police Department hadn't been a close friend of her uncle Ben's and a kind, gentle man, Gabby Marietti would be just fine talking to nearly anyone, police chief or garbage collector or president. And she'd do it with aplomb.

As if reading her mind, her aunt Nell looked over at her and gave a slight nod, and then a smile.

Ben got up and excused himself to go inside and make a call, checking on the police's availability to talk with Gabby.

When he returned with the news that someone would be available midmorning, he offered to go along with her, but Gabby half smiled and assured him that she, her nonna, and Squid could handle it.

"We've got this one," she said, her smile confident.

Chapter 21

Bobby Palazola. The name took up Izzy's whole brain. It was so big and uncomfortable that she was getting a headache. The nice guy she'd met so recently, and the man she suspected might be in love with Gracie. He'd threatened a man who was now dead.

She stood outside the Endicott home for a minute, trying to process it. And what it all might mean for people she cared about.

And then she scolded herself fiercely. Good grief. It wasn't like her to assume things, and that's exactly what she was doing. And she knew as well as anyone the need for proof before any ill-founded assumptions were made. Maybe it was because of Gracie that the argument between Bobby and Nick bothered her so. Gracie was her good friend. She wanted her protected, kind of what Gabby herself had expressed.

She put her helmet on and climbed on her bike, trying to turn her mind off. Sometimes she wished she'd never gone to law school.

She pulled up in the small alley beside her store and leaned her bike against the side of the building. *Chin up, Izzy,* she told herself, then walked through the side door of her shop and into what was sure to be a chaotic day.

Hours later, Izzy stepped out of the yarn shop's side door and into the alley. Light clouds hovered over the town, with thin streams of sunlight filtering through. Izzy took a deep breath, held it, then released it slowly.

The shop had been noisy and crowded all morning. She and Mae juggled customer needs, along with training summer helpers and filling cubbies with new yarn. And there were the hugs with friends who shared the pain of Nick Cabot's death.

And beneath all the hugs and talk ran the knowledge of a killing in their small town. It was like a deadly current seeping into all their lives.

Seeing the stress on Izzy's face, Mae finally convinced her to get some fresh air and clear out her head. They'd all be better off for it, she'd said.

The gravel alley dead-ended at a retaining wall that stretched behind all the shops along that side of Harbor Road. Behind and below the four-foot granite structure was the water, which, at high tide, reached halfway up its side.

"It's close enough to jump into," the Realtor had told Izzy when she had purchased the broken-down bait shop and turned it into her welcoming yarn store years before. The water was sparkling today, and Izzy walked back toward it, the salty air feeling like medicine for her body and soul.

She lifted her legs over the wall, and sat on the cool slab of granite, her palms flat on the stone, sorting through the morning. And the recent days and nights. She wished she could go back a week and somehow make the world a safer place. A start-over. That useless thought she always had when bad things happened, and she wasn't sure how to make them good again.

"What's up, Iz?"

Cass came up behind her, startling Izzy, but only for the briefest of seconds. Cass often showed up when Izzy's thoughts, no matter how far away, got too heavy for her.

"We're starting to act like Aunt Nell and Birdie," Izzy said. She pushed a thick band of streaked blonde hair from her face.

"How's that?"

"That thing they do. Feeling the vibe when one is thinking something or needs the other."

Cass lobbed her legs over the wall and sat next to her friend, her feet dangling. "Could be worse. But I cheated the vibe this time. Nell called after all of you left her house this morning. She filled me in. I had a mess of work on my desk, but finally just pushed it aside. Mae said I'd find you out here."

"Gabby was such a trouper. She wished she hadn't heard the argument in the first place, but was smart enough to know she had to tell someone about it."

"Nell was concerned about Gracie when she called me. Wondering if she knew."

Izzy had wondered the same thing. "Have you talked to her this morning?"

"I tried to. She didn't answer."

"What do you think?"

"About what?"

"About anything. The whole mess. This mysterious, awful argument."

"I think I shouldn't have painted Bobby out to be a bad guy. We all know a high-school kid who doesn't obey all the rules, but that doesn't equal a killer. Right?"

"Of course not. And you didn't paint him that way. It's clear that you and Gracie both like him. You probably had a crush on the 'bad boy' when you were fourteen. I liked him, too."

"*Like* him," Cass corrected. "And you're probably right. He added lots of color to my teen years. Gracie and I both like him. One thing's for sure, he isn't a killer." She turned from Izzy and looked out at the water.

Izzy was quiet, too. She *did* like Bobby Palazola—he was friendly and had a good sense of humor. Sam had felt the same when he met him those years ago. His memory was that he had a good feeling about him right off. One of those people you instantly like.

She took a deep breath and tried to sort through her feelings. Could killers look like nice guys? Who knew what went on inside anyone? Even good guys.

And then Izzy shivered, remembering a long-ago time, when she was a young Boston attorney out to prove her worth. She also remembered the day she left it all behind, packed up her small car and moved to Sea Harbor, where her aunt and uncle's love helped make things right again.

She had taken a pro bono armed-robbery case for the firm, a case involving a nice guy, not much older than her younger brother. He'd pretended to have a gun and had held it to a convenience store clerk's back so he'd give him a pack of cigarettes, then pushed him to the floor and ran off. His pastor had come along to the courthouse with him, and said he was a good fellow, polite, churchgoing. Izzy was convincing in her plea, and her client got another chance.

He had tears in his eyes, and hugged Izzy tightly, something an ambitious reporter had recorded and filmed for the evening news.

But two days later, the newly freed nice man had walked into a deli, not far from Izzy's apartment, and shot the owner and his daughter dead. For a ham sandwich.

The memory startled her and saddened her all over again. She pushed it out to sea as she watched the harbor waters starting to rise, the waves beginning to lap against the retaining wall and sending up a spray. The familiar sound was soothing. She took in a deep breath, the salty air tangy.

"Hey, Izzy, are you okay?" Cass asked.

She answered with a question. "Do you know why Bobby didn't like Nick?"

"I don't know that there's a single reason. Bobby simply didn't like him. We probably all have one or two people like that in our lives, people we'd rather stay away from."

"Maybe."

"It was mostly on Bobby's part. Nick seemed to brush it off. More mature, I guess. It had to have been awkward growing up because of the family connections. Nick was so close to Liz and Bella, Bobby's cousin and his twin. It did seem that things came more easily to Nick—girls liked him, hockey star, high grades, awards, including awards Bobby vied for. So jealousy, maybe?"

Izzy thought about that. That was the missing part. *The reason.* It's certainly what the police would care about. "Do you think Gracie might know what was going on with those two?" Izzy asked.

"I don't know. Bobby's sister might be able to shed light on it. They're close."

"I almost forgot about Bella. She comes in the yarn shop sometimes when she's in town."

"This must be really hard for her. She left after their get-together this weekend for Switzerland to give a talk or something. I'm sure she and Liz have been in touch. And maybe Bobby. He's also close to his aunt Annabelle."

"It's good he has people who might be able to help him sort all this out."

"To sort what out? Izzy, it was a simple argument they had. Not a murder."

"I know that, Cass. Calm down. But even so, Bobby will have to go through questioning. That's not fun."

"You're right. Sorry if I snapped. Gracie will—"

"Gracie will what?" a familiar voice asked from behind them.

Izzy and Cass jumped and spun their heads around.

"Sorry to scare you," Gracie said. "I'm glad you didn't fall into the water. I thought you'd hear me coming."

"It doesn't matter. We're glad you're here," Cass said.

"I saw that you called. I was heading to the bank, trying to process my life. I was going to call you back once I figured it out."

"Throw my life in there, too, would you?" Cass said.

"I third it," Izzy said.

Gracie managed a smile. "Anyway, I saw you both back here as I was walking by, and I figured you had forgotten to invite me. I came over to find out why."

"Now you know—we were talking about you."

"I figured as much."

"All the scuttlebutt," Cass said, trying to draw a smile out of Gracie.

"Anyway, in the middle of that *scuttlebutt,* you've probably both heard that Bobby blew up at Nick, and our Gabby overheard it all," Gracie said.

"We heard," Izzy answered.

"Any idea why?" Cass asked. "Have you talked to him about it?"

Gracie took a deep breath. "I haven't seen Bobby to talk about it. I mean, he's been around, doing his thing in the kitchen. But there's always someone else around."

"Is Costa there? I'd forgotten what happened there. Nick wanted him gone," Cass said.

"Right. I had given him the weekend off, but he came in Monday, as usual. And honestly, Cass? I just can't deal with it right now."

"Sure. Of course, Gracie. I get it. But you might share your feelings with Bobby when the time is right."

"He's definitely been avoiding me. He doesn't talk easily about his feelings, you know? I've heard him on the phone a couple times, I think with Bella. The connections are bad, so he talks loudly. Anyway, he's upset. And he feels bad about things at work. That's probably what's on his mind. Not all this other—"

"So he wasn't upset that Nick was murdered?" Cass asked. "They've known each other practically since birth."

"No, no. That's not what I mean. I just meant that he's focused on work problems."

"What problems?" Izzy asked.

"You know, the complaints we've had about the food. He doesn't want me to worry about it, so he doesn't talk about it. Not knowing things means I won't worry, according to Bobby. How wrong men can sometimes be."

"But it's your restaurant," Cass said.

"Exactly. But he wants to take care of it himself. One of the vendors we work with told me Bobby thinks someone is tampering with things in the kitchen. We've hired some new kids. I don't know. Maybe deliveries."

"Like what?"

"I honestly don't know. Something that might affect the taste of his special dishes."

Izzy thought back to the conversation Gabby had heard. Some pieces of it sounded like Bobby was blaming Nick for the problems at work. But that didn't make a lot of sense.

She looked over at Gracie. She looked defeated, and slightly overwhelmed by their questions. It was clear she didn't want to talk about it anymore.

When the tears began to roll down her cheeks, both Izzy and Cass slid off the retaining wall and hugged her close.

Gracie finally pulled away. "Thanks, guys." She tried to wipe the tears away and smile, failing miserably.

"It's a lot, Gracie. But it'll work out somehow. Your uncle is a miracle worker, we all know that. The restaurant will be fine."

Gracie shook her head. "Sure, I know that. It will. All this stuff—menus, reviews. Problems. I mean, who needs reviews. Right? I'm tired of them."

She stopped and took a deep breath. Then, as the tears began again, she said, "It's really about Nick. That's what's wrong with me. With my life. My heart is broken. His dying. His being *gone*. Forever. Like I won't ever see him again. How can that be? He was my friend. I . . . I loved him so much." Her voice choked on her words and stopped for a minute to gulp in some air.

"Gracie," Cass began, but Gracie had started in again.

"I mean, you know how much Nick helped me through all those hard times. He's always been there for me. Always. When I got divorced those years ago. Nick was there—like you two are—holding me up. And when I decided to start a restaurant, Nick showed up all the time, even when Bobby took over the kitchen. Always willing to help, to listen. And even now, I don't know. I *feel* him. Like somehow, if we try hard enough, we can bring him back because he needs to be here. How could . . . I mean, who could . . ." Her words finally stopped coming, and the tears rolled freely.

"I get it, Gracie. You were so close, I was even jealous of him sometimes. I guess I overlooked that awful sadness in the middle of the tragedy. Nick was the best. I miss him, too."

Gracie's head bobbed and she went on. "And then I think of his sister, and I feel selfish, like maybe there's only a certain amount of grief to go around, and I'm trying to hog it all. Imagine what Nancy is going through. There were just the two of them in the family. Now Nancy has no one. Have you called her, Cass?"

"A couple times, but I didn't get through. I left messages. It's got to be hard being so far away."

"Uncle Ben said Chief Thompson has been in close touch with her," Izzy said.

By then, all three women were wiping their eyes, their hearts hurting for things and reasons that had little meaning in words.

When Gracie left a short while later, Cass and Izzy stood at the retaining wall, looking out at the sea, as if the answers were somewhere out there, hidden in the froth of the waves. But even if the answers were out there, at that moment they weren't entirely sure what all the questions were.

Chapter 22

The unusual start to their day, on the Endicott deck hours earlier, had caused memory lapses for both Nell and Birdie. They would have forgotten this late-afternoon Wednesday meeting entirely, if Elizabeth hadn't sent a text reminder on each of their phones.

"Well, whatever it's about, are you sure you're up for this, Birdie? I know you didn't get much sleep last night, and spending an hour in the police department this morning couldn't have been restful, either," Nell asked as she drove toward Canary Cove.

Birdie didn't answer immediately. She was looking out the car window at the stores they were passing, one after one. People going about their day. Horns honking as people vied for parking places. Women pushing strollers.

Finally she turned back. "I'm okay. But I'm going to admit my worries to you, something I haven't wanted to do. But you're my friend. And you're worried about me. We need to share times like this."

She quickly ran through all the scenarios that her imagination had conjured up because of Gabby's unexpected involvement in a murder. Gabby's daily presence in the fishermen neighborhood, in Nick's house, and a terrible murder. Was she safe? Had someone seen her there?

When she finished, she took a deep breath. "Okay, there you have it. I've confessed my fears to my dear friend because she cares about me." She smiled at Nell.

Nell had anticipated all of it. She worried about it, too, but the weight her dear friend carried was so much greater. Gabby's proximity to the murder was closer than simply an overheard conversation from the curb.

Birdie continued talking. "But one thing we both know for sure is that sitting at home isn't going to dismiss any of my anxiety. Only solving this murder will do that."

"So perhaps we owe Elizabeth a thank-you for luring us over to Canary Cove, for reasons we know not. At the least, it will keep us occupied for a bit of time." Nell smiled.

Birdie agreed. "And keeping her company for an hour or so may be a help. We're good at that. Maybe that's all she needs. We should have brought cookies."

"Except MJ said Elizabeth doesn't eat sweets."

"I meant for us."

Nell chuckled. "I do feel for her. She hasn't lived here long enough to have the kind of friends you need at your side through things like this."

"That's surely true. And grief is such an unpredictable thing. Elizabeth may find some kind of solace in working. I was different. When Sonny died, I just wanted to be alone. I spent a lot of time hiking and talking to myself. And to him."

Nell wasn't surprised. She suspected her friend talked to Sonny often, even now, decades after her husband had died.

"Harold told me that he saw Elizabeth coming out of the police station. He stopped and offered her a lift, but she declined."

"I suspect he wanted to find out why she was coming out of the police department," Nell said.

"Of course he did. He could guess why she was there, but not what was said. The interesting part. That's what he'd want to hear."

"Cass said the police have talked to all Nick's neighbors. Nick was so integral to that neighborhood. Hopefully, someone will have seen something that might help."

"Nick seemed especially happy that Sunday," Nell said. "Tommy is a good detective. He'll take it wherever it goes."

"He was professional with Gabby, but kind. He never spoke down to her. That mattered to her, and she responded to him in like manner, answering questions honestly and precisely. I was so proud of her."

"How did Tommy react to what she had overheard?"

"He didn't react. He just listened, taking in everything she said. Then he followed up, asking a few questions, mostly to clarify one word or another in what she had heard. He told her he appreciated her coming in, and that it was helpful information. He said he would talk to Bobby, too, who might be able to provide even more information that might help the police find the person who committed the crime. He worded it nicely, leaving both of us feeling that Gabby wasn't handing anyone over because he might be guilty of a crime."

Nell thought about the young detective's discreet way of accepting Gabby's information. It would take him a long way in his career; hopefully, it wouldn't come from questioning Sea Harbor people about a murder.

"I wonder how Bobby's questioning will go," Nell said.

"He seems to have landed squarely in the middle of everything. Unfortunately, that will draw Gracie into it." Birdie pointed out her window. "Oops, Nell, here's our turn."

Nell slowed, then took a right into the small lot in front of the arts association building, distracted by thoughts of Bobby

Palazola running around in her head. She didn't know the entertaining and likable person as the others did. She knew mostly what the police would be looking at: someone with a temper, whose restaurant work wasn't going well, and who had threatened a man he didn't like who was now dead.

Things that wouldn't be passed over lightly by the Sea Harbor police, no matter how they'd downplayed his role when they talked with Gabby. At least, not until they learned more.

The art association's all-purpose room was located at the back of a long seaside building. Today the spacious room was filled with late-afternoon sunlight that fell on the hardwood floor from tall panes of glass framing a water view.

The talented architect had designed the windows with enough wall space in between to accommodate artwork and sculptures. A sliding door to a smaller meeting room allowed the room to grow as needed for events and large meetings.

Elizabeth was already seated at a small conference table. She looked up immediately and started to stand. "You came," she said, a smile softening her narrow face.

"Oh, sit, sit," Birdie said, walking over. "Of course we came. We're like mailmen. Through sleet or snow or even on a beautiful sunny day." She sat down next to Elizabeth.

Nell wandered around the familiar, light-filled room. "This is such a beautiful room, Elizabeth. It feels like a happy room to me. We had a fiber show in here a few years ago. It turned out to be a perfect place for it."

Elizabeth had a small tablet in front of her. In the center of the table were hand-thrown mugs, napkins, and a coffee carafe. A bowl of plump purple and green grapes, and a small vase of wild hyacinth and purple coneflowers, added color to the ensemble. The whole thing looked enough like the setting for a watercolor class that Nell half expected an instructor to walk in. "This is lovely," she said, sitting down across from Elizabeth. "You have an artistic touch."

"Thank you. This is almost like old times, isn't it?" Elizabeth said. "The three of us sitting at a conference table together, preparing for a board meeting." She attempted a smile, but it didn't have staying power.

"No," Birdie said sternly. "Whatever that was is over. All gone. This is a new life. That's how we live, isn't it? Certainly not in the past."

"Of course," Elizabeth said. "It was an unfortunate comparison."

"Now," Nell said, seeing some confusion on Elizabeth's face, "what can we help you with? I know this is a rough time. I know you haven't had much time to settle in here, but are you feeling comfortable? Do you think this job is going to work out for you?"

"It's grounding. I don't know what I would do otherwise. Any plans I had, I no longer have. Maybe Jane had that in her head when she offered me this job."

"She may have," Nell said. "But she also needs help. And you are graciously filling that void for her."

Elizabeth nodded.

"I am not entirely sure how we can help," Birdie said. "But Nell and I are quite flexible. If it's to help you settle in or simply to talk—anything is fine with us."

Birdie and Nell sipped their coffee, quietly waiting for Elizabeth to begin the discussion. She glanced once or twice at the tablet she'd brought, but her mind seemed to be elsewhere. She looked thinner, Nell thought—more fragile than she had, even a day before.

When she finally looked up, her face was somber.

"The truth is, I have little left in Sea Harbor. I had Nick, and, quite honestly, that was all I needed or wanted. I loved him more than my own life. But I ran away once. I won't do it again."

Birdie and Nell were silent, not entirely sure where Elizabeth was taking the conversation. She looked confused, as if she had lost her anchor when Nick died.

But when she started to talk again, she had shifted into a more professional mode. She put on a pair of glasses attached to a chain around her neck and looked down at the electronic tablet on the table. She picked up the pencil and tapped it on the tablet, making little black dots as she began to talk again.

"I just thought," she said, then stopped, the tapping on the tablet continuing. "Well, maybe what I am saying is, I haven't been very social here. You two are loved by everyone. I'm hoping maybe you can help keep me on course."

Birdie and Nell listened quietly, not at all sure what course Elizabeth was talking about.

"It's difficult, you know . . ."

Her voice had faded by the end of the sentence. She took a drink of coffee, then shifted in her chair, as if looking for something.

"Elizabeth," Birdie said, reaching out and touching her arm. "Are you all right?"

At the sound of Birdie's voice, Elizabeth looked back at her visitors.

"I'm sorry," she said. "I'm distracted. I keep thinking about what I should be doing. What I would be doing if it were a normal day. I did love him, you know. I know this is hard on you, too, but you have others in your life—"

For a moment, there was quiet. And then Birdie spoke. "There's no need to be sorry. Grief gives no warning, Elizabeth. It doesn't care if you're in the grocery store or alone or sitting here with Nell and me. It just sneaks in and takes over your heart and your head. Sometimes even your whole body. How you move or don't move. I do understand, believe me."

Neither Birdie nor Nell could tell if Elizabeth was listening, but then she looked back and forth between the two women and said, "I haven't been honest about why I wanted you to come here. I might need help with the job, that's true, but—" Elizabeth paused, her brows pulled together, her body still, as if trying to pull out the correct words. "But mostly . . ."

Elizabeth focused on something beyond them again, but from the look in Elizabeth's eyes, Nell knew she was only seeing what was inside her own head and not the art on the walls or the view of the sunset through the windows. But she had no idea what that view in her head was.

Finally Elizabeth looked at them again, her face composed now and looking worn, as if she'd been working hard on something and was suddenly worn out. There were lines in her face that Nell hadn't noticed there before.

"I suppose I need people," she said again. "Support. People who know me."

"We're here," Nell reminded her.

"When Nick died, I wanted to run away. He was here, and then in an instant, he was gone. That wasn't supposed to happen. Not what I'd planned when I came back here to live. I wanted to run away and drown that night."

Birdie and Nell listened in silence to the shifting conversation, unsure of how they fit into it.

Elizabeth's face and body were still. Although she was speaking coherently, matter-of-factly almost, her words were coated with an emotion that was difficult to listen to. She looked like she would crack into pieces if someone touched her.

"But then I stopped," Elizabeth continued. "I'd run away before. It was a difficult time, and I didn't care what happened to me. But Nick had cared back then."

"And this time?" Birdie asked gently.

"This time, I won't run. Birdie, I have nowhere to go."

"This is a good place to be," Nell said, and she hoped that it was true. She wondered briefly where Elizabeth had gone after that first incident that had shaken her life. And how she had healed.

"No, I won't run," she said again. "I don't need that kind of help. I just need to survive. Or not."

She took a deep breath that brought a little color to her cheeks. "It will be okay."

Birdie and Nell listened in silence.

Then Birdie said softly, "You need closure, Elizabeth. We all do."

Elizabeth listened, as if trying to understand. Finally she said, "Closure. Yes. I tried to get that."

"We'll help you, Elizabeth," Birdie said. "It's a strong person who will ask for help."

"I'm not really strong, Birdie. I'm wobbling. But this isn't how it should be. This is not how it was supposed to end."

When Birdie and Nell finally left the art association a while later, they were still not sure what Elizabeth wanted from them. She was pale, tired, and rambling. And they both felt a little worn out. Some of her comments didn't connect, though they'd try hard to listen and respond.

"She's so terribly sad," Birdie said.

"Were you in another world for a while after Sonny died?"

"I was," Birdie said. "I saw him everywhere. And I wanted to blame someone. I thought everyone I saw was responsible for him dying. It couldn't have been that magnificent heart of his giving up. But I can't compare it to Elizabeth's. I think our 'other worlds' are very different. I don't know hers. And I don't think I completely understand it. Their relationship, I mean."

Nell had the same wonderings. She had seen Nick and Elizabeth a few times together around town. Everyone had. But the most intimate time she'd seen them together had been at the hotel event when she and Ben had dined with them in the crowded banquet room. She remembered it now with renewed—and curious—clarity. Especially the warmth in Elizabeth's eyes and her touches and expressions when she'd walked out of the hotel with Nick. It had been touching. But something else. *Needy?*

But what they both knew, and what ran through their conversation on the way home, was that whatever the relationship was, Elizabeth Hartley clearly loved Nick Cabot.

Chapter 23

Cass was up early the next day. She stumbled out of bed, her head a mess of dreams that hadn't made much sense. A shower didn't help much, either.

"Cass, go do something," Danny said to his wife as he dished up pancakes for her and their son, Joey. "Sam and I are playing hooky from our jobs today to take Joey and Abby to the train museum in Wenham. And we don't want your long face along. It'd scare the other kids at the museum."

Cass managed a smile, and a reminder to Danny to take water bottles and extra diapers. Then she gave extra hugs to her small family before she walked out the back door.

She glanced at her car, then her bike, and then finally decided a jog would work best. As long as she was playing hooky, too, it might as well be on foot. A jog to the Lazy Lobster might jiggle her body parts back into their proper position and untangle her thoughts.

It was too early for the restaurant to open, but she hoped she'd find Gracie there. Maybe weeding her garden. They'd hug, and she'd make sure her friend was doing okay, and then she'd get back to the Halloran Lobster Company and try to distract herself from things—such as murder—by checking out the month's profits.

She spotted Gracie's truck in the lot, but the café's front door was locked. When she walked around the restaurant, the garden was empty, save for two rabbits enjoying a healthy breakfast of carrot tops.

Then she heard signs of human life coming from the restaurant's back deck area and walked in that direction. Halfway to the deck steps she stopped, realizing that someone was talking on a phone. She started to walk toward the side door, hoping to find Gracie in the kitchen. But the voice from the deck reached her again and she stopped, recognizing Bobby's voice.

His tone was worried. Not the cheery voice he'd greeted her with a few days before.

"No. Please don't," he was saying. "I told you before, it would be bad. It's so messed up."

Cass heard another voice then, though inaudible, and realized the cell phone was on speaker, and she moved away, not wanting to hear. Hearing one side was bad enough. She tried the kitchen door, but it was locked.

Looking back toward the deck, she heard muffled, far away crying.

Then Bobby spoke. "No, I beg you. You can't. It would just make it harder. For both of us. Even the cops agree."

There was total silence. Then Bobby spoke again, his voice much softer.

"I'm sorry. I know you hurt, I know. But it's so messy, all of it."

The speaker connection was faulty, and Cass could only hear fragments on the other end.

There was silence for a minute, and Cass thought he had hung up.

But Bobby spoke once more. His voice soft and almost kind now, with only stray words and phrases falling from the deck to Cass's ears. The word *love*.

The next sound she heard were footsteps walking across the deck. Cass concentrated again on the kitchen door, banging harder and calling out Gracie's name.

She glanced quickly over her shoulder, one fist still on the door.

And then her hand dropped.

Bobby stood on the deck steps, his dark eyes moist. He looked up, his eyes meeting hers, and stared, wiping the moisture away with his sleeve.

He took the short staircase in two steps, and by the time he reached Cass, there was no sign of tears and his familiar smile was back in place, his voice friendly, if a bit off-kilter. Before he had a chance to say anything, the kitchen door finally opened.

"Well, hi," Gracie said, opening the door from the inside. "What's with the hammering, Cass? Couldn't you have just huffed and puffed?" Gracie tried to smile. "Sorry about the door. It automatically locked after one of the kitchen staff came in earlier."

"Sorry if I dented it," Cass said.

"Yes, well, we bill for things like that. Anyway, it looks like we're all here. How about we go in?" She stepped back and held the door, ushering them both inside.

"Ah, the magic morning aroma of Gracie's amazing coffee," Bobby said, a little too loudly, and his grin slightly crooked. "Let's go for it, Halloran."

Cass noticed that he was gripping his phone tightly in one hand, as if afraid she'd grab it from him. She attempted the same nonchalance. "Okay, Bobby," she said. "But here's the thing. I'm married now, with a child. And a husband. It's time you called me Cass. Or Catherine Mary Theresa Halloran Brandley, if we're being formal."

Bobby repeated the names with exaggerated pronunciation, while finally slipping his phone into his pocket.

He repeated the words again, in that way he had, making something ordinary sound hysterically funny and putting people at ease. Cass and Gracie both chuckled.

"What do you think, Cass?" asked Gracie. "You haven't been back here in the kitchen since we spruced it up."

Cass looked around, her mouth hanging open. A spotless stainless-steel counter ran the length of the room's center, with shiny pots and pans hanging from the rafters; and burners, already hard at work, boiling pots of fragrant broth, warming the room.

"Geesh, Gracie, this is amazing. It's not the same kitchen I stole a lobster roll from just last summer. Actually, many of them. What's happened here?"

"Nice, huh?" Gracie said.

"So I know *you* had a role in all this, Bobby." Cass held back the fact that she knew Uncle Alphonso had a big hand in it, too.

Bobby shrugged, but was clearly pleased.

She hoped she wasn't trying too hard to act like she hadn't just heard him having an emotional conversation with someone. But it didn't seem to matter to Bobby. He had fallen in line and was slowly becoming the old Bobby she'd grown up with. Or at least he was trying hard to be.

"One question," Cass asked. "Why is there a TV on the wall over there?" She pointed to a huge television above a built-in desk.

"Why?" Bobby asked, feigning incredulity. "Why? you ask. Isn't it obvious? It's so I can tune in to Rachael Ray or the Barefoot Contessa every morning to learn how to cook that day."

Gracie and Cass both laughed, Cass more robustly than Gracie, but both letting Bobby take center stage. The mood was becoming slightly more normal, more relaxed, and Cass could see that whatever had bothered Bobby seemed to be fading, or was blocked out. Or maybe she had imagined the whole thing. Listening in on other's private calls could make her do that.

"Hey, Cass," Gracie said, pushing the swinging door to the restaurant open, "there're some things at the bar that I need to take care of. Come over when you're done in here and grab a coffee."

Cass noticed the look on Bobby's face as he watched her leave. She had trouble reading it. Apprehension, maybe? She wondered briefly if they'd had some kind of argument.

But he then turned back to Cass. "Okay, Cass, it's tour time."

He looked at the far end of the kitchen, where a couple of guys seemed to be checking shelf ingredients and another was intent on a large book with RECIPES printed across the page in comical-looking letters.

"Hey, guys!" Bobby called out, getting their attention. "Come over here and help me show off our kitchen paradise to our friend, Cass Halloran."

One of the guys, muscular with a scruffy beard, looked up, then quickly lowered his head. With some hesitation, he closed the recipe book and followed the other two, standing slightly behind them. His head was down, looking at the floor, as he shifted on his large feet, from one foot to another.

Cass looked over at him and took a deep breath, standing back a step.

Seeing him startled her, as if she were seeing him at Lucky's Place, eavesdropping on her and her friends all over again. And about to be fired, once Nick got back to them.

Finally she managed a hello. "Are you trying to hide from me, Costa? You're too big to hide behind those guys. Have you put on weight?" She watched his face carefully to catch an expression, something that would indicate he'd eavesdropped on a private conversation. A conversation about him.

He lifted his head just slightly. His voice was low. "Oh, it's you. How're ya doing?"

Guilty as sin, she thought. Aloud she said, "Okay. I heard you were working here." She tried to keep her voice neutral. But Nick's words kept interfering and filling her head. How he was going to gather more information about Marco Costa and then he'd be gone from the Lazy Lobster. Did he know Nick was looking into his background? If she was right that he'd heard them talking, he knew. And unless he had buried his head in the sand, he knew Nick Cabot was dead. And Marco still had a job.

Bobby stepped in. "You know this guy? He's amazing. He knows a lot about fish." He punched a finger in the air, pointed in Marco Costa's direction. "Wish I could have him full-time."

"That's true, he knows a lot about fish," Cass said, hoping her face wasn't telling him anything more.

"That's all you have to say?" Bobby said. "I heard from guys where we buy our fish that he was a great fisherman."

"That's true. They're right about that."

Cass was getting more uncomfortable by the moment.

Marco simply put his head down, shuffling his feet as if bugs were crawling across them.

"Hey, Cass," Bobby said, turning toward her. He leaned his head toward the kitchen proper. "Come on. I want you to see the whole thing. All our tools and gadgets. We do great things around here."

The guys scattered, and she noticed Marco heading outside, a lighter and pack of cigarettes in his hand.

Bobby took his tour seriously, circling the whole room with Cass in tow. When they reached the worktable at one end of the kitchen, she noticed the book with the colorful title that she'd seen from a distance. The one Marco Costa had been looking through.

At closer range, she noticed BIBLE scrolled beneath RECIPES.

"What's this?" she asked. "You keep a Bible in your kitchen?" She picked it up, grimacing. "It weighs a ton."

"A ton of secrets. It's "Bobby's Bible," as you can plainly see."

"So explain it to me, O Exalted Chef."

"I don't use cookbooks. I've read all the how-to masters, from *Larousse Gastronomique* to *Escoffier* and Julia Child's tomes. Made everything, all the classics. But this book is filled with all my own original recipes or my take on the masters."

"That's impressive."

Bobby looked at the book, his face serious. "Thanks. It's who I am. Not to puff myself up, but I look at my recipes like artists look at their original paintings. This is my art. It's me. I keep this thing under lock and key. I was just checking some recipes, some herbs I need Marco to track down."

Cass looked at him and smiled. She couldn't remember Bobby being this sincere. Somehow it eased the tension she felt hearing him on the phone. It was the old Bobby standing with her. "I get that. That's great, Bobby."

Bobby nodded, clearly pleased, and urged her on to check out a new fast-freeze gadget.

Fifteen minutes later, after Cass had been introduced to appliances and equipment that looked lethal, and that she would never in her life consider using, she excused herself, claiming she'd collapse on his shiny kitchen floor if she didn't have a cup of Gracie's coffee, and soon.

She paused at the swinging door, glancing back at Marco Costa, who had finally come back inside.

Their eyes met, and then Marco quickly looked away.

Cass waited for a moment, but he was already at the other end of the kitchen, listening intently to whatever Bobby was saying.

Marco Costa clearly had no desire to renew old acquaintances. And if she had to bet on it, he had heard every word that Nick Cabot had said in the crowded bar.

Cass walked into the restaurant proper and found Gracie sitting at the bar. She poured each of them a cup of coffee in a large mug with a lazy lobster painted on it.

"Gracie, what's he doing here?" Cass asked before Gracie had a chance to speak.

"Who?"

"Costa."

Her shoulders slumped. "I know."

Cass climbed up on a stool next to her. "Oh, I'm sorry, Gracie. I didn't mean to come on so strong. We'll talk about it another time. I just want you safe."

Gracie nodded and got her composure back. "Did you like the kitchen? It's shiny, right?"

"Very." Cass poured cream into her mug. "Gracie, I was worried after seeing you yesterday. We were all in kind of a deep slump. But I was more concerned about you. Now that I'm a mom, I do that kind of weird thing."

Gracie reached over, throwing her arms around Cass and nearly knocking her off the stool. "Oh, you—how did you get to be such a friend? I love you, Cass."

Cass felt Gracie's tears on her cheek, and then air came between them as Gracie pulled away.

"Do you have time for a walk?" Gracie asked. "We can take our mugs with us. Good coffee tastes even better with a little bit of salt air in it." She wiped her eyes on her sleeve.

Cass poured a generous pool of half-and-half in her mug and followed Gracie out the restaurant's front door. They passed Lucky's Place, then walked down to the end of the pier, where the waves crashed like thunder against both sides of the wide granite structure.

With forearms balanced on the wide wooden railing, they sipped their coffee, watching and feeling the rolling swell of the waves against the pier.

Finally Gracie spoke, cupping the mug in between her palms.

"This is one of my favorite places to come," she said, her eyes on the water. "This view makes troubles seem small. There's nothing but wonder out there. Beauty. Peace. The Earth and the moon and gravity doing their thing with the ocean, no matter what we think or say or try to do. The waves come in. The waves go out. Nothing short of miraculous, when you think about it."

Cass nodded. "Those troubles I'm seeing on your face today are something new, Gracie. Something different from the deep sadness of Nick's death. Is it about our favorite chef?"

Gracie took in a deep breath, then released it softly. The salty air had done its job and her voice was stronger. "Yes. And, well, no. It's about what Bobby told the police when they called him in for questioning yesterday morning. About the argument. Bobby's temper getting out of hand."

Cass was quiet as Gracie talked, her coffee mug balanced on the flat guardrail, the brew growing cold and salty.

"Bobby lied," Gracie finally said.

"To the police?"

Gracie nodded, and then she talked some more.

And Cass listened, until Gracie had no talk left.

Chapter 24

The casserole dish was sitting in a box in the car, the sweet smell of garlic and lemon butter wafting up from the edges of the foil wrap and filling her car.

Nell breathed it in, then sat for a minute, her hands balanced against the wheel, trying to collect her thoughts.

It had been a long day, and her whole body was weary. The week's emotions were playing havoc with her thoughts and her body.

Nell had considered dropping the meal off for Izzy, Birdie, and Cass, and then going back home and to bed.

But she knew before the thought completely materialized that she wouldn't do that. Thursday nights were sacred, but tonight they were also necessary.

She'd managed to toss together an easy, comforting pasta dish, which she could warm up in Izzy's microwave in an instant. *Onward,* she thought, turning off the engine and heading inside to the cozy comfort of her niece's yarn shop.

"You're the last one," Izzy said as Nell walked down the short flight of stairs to the knitting room.

"We thought you might be standing us up," Cass added. "I would have tracked you down."

"Forget you all? Not in your lifetime," Nell said. She carried the casserole to the small microwave, closed the door, and pressed a button.

Birdie was putting out plates and napkins and silverware. She filled a basket with rolls.

Nell looked over at her friend, seeing the tired lines in her face. Still worried about Gabby, she could see. And it wouldn't end until the case was closed. It had to be soon.

Izzy was bringing up a playlist trying to brighten all their spirits, although unsure if even Bill Withers singing about lovely days would be convincing enough.

It simply wasn't a lovely day. Or week.

Nell looked at Cass, who, in spite of her cheery welcome, looked like she did when her Joey's amazing nanny had gone off to culinary school. Food would help all of them. And Birdie's wine.

She removed the warm casserole from the microwave and plumped the creamy pasta with two forks, the aroma of garlic and the bright green color of the crisp broccoli creating a stimulating visual. The fragrance floated around the room and seemed to ease Cass's mood, at least a bit.

"Was it just a week ago we were sitting here, enthralled with a shaggy dog?" Izzy asked. She sprinkled grated cheese on the heaping bowls Nell was filling and delivered them to the table.

"Dear Squid," Birdie mused. "Time is fooling us once again. Messing with our mind." She uncorked a bottle of wine and filled the glasses on the coffee table, then sat back in her hearth-side chair.

Nell watched the familiar routine play out, with all four friends finding comfort in a favorite chair, finding comfort in Izzy's music, Nell's food, Birdie's wine.

"To friendship," Birdie said, lifting her glass. "And to a brighter future."

"Soon," Izzy added. "It has to be soon." She looked over at Nell. "Any good news?"

"Not much. At least that was Ben's report as I was leaving. He did say the police put up a fence, in addition to the yellow tape, to keep people away and safe. Although they haven't found the gun, they've determined from the cartridge case that a Glock handgun was used, whatever that is. It's something they don't think Nick Cabot would have had in his house, nor was there any sign of one in the debris. Apparently, Nick wasn't fond of guns."

"Gabby mentioned that once. It seems she and Nick had more chats when she picked up or dropped off Squid than I realized. He seemed to appreciate her curiosity and ability to argue, something I'm also discovering. They had a long discussion once on protecting kids from guns. Gabby had definite opinions about it."

"*Guns,*" Izzy said, frowning and twisting a bite of creamy pasta around her fork. Drips of lemon butter and cheese fell to her plate. "It's almost a foreign word around here. Who owns guns in Sea Harbor?"

"Hunters?" Nell said.

"Probably, but they don't normally use handguns, do they?" Birdie said. "People mostly buy Glocks for home protection."

Izzy looked at her, her brows lifted in surprise. "I didn't know you knew anything about guns, Birdie. I thought you were like me and thought that *Glock* was the sound a duck makes."

Birdie chuckled. "The truth is that Harold Sampson had one once. He even suggested I learn how to use it."

"What?" Nell said, surprised.

"Yes, but I didn't take him up on his offer. However, I think Ella did."

"Why did Harold have a gun?" Izzy asked. "He's . . . well, he's so gentle."

Birdie smiled at the same description she often used for Harold. "He is gentle. And responsible, sometimes to a fault. But a bulldog if he needs to be. I doubt if he would have ever used it. But he said it was part of his job to protect us." She put up her hands to keep them from talking.

"I know what you're thinking. So, yes, I did ask him what he thought he might protect us from."

"And what did he say?" Izzy asked.

Birdie took a drink of her wine. "He didn't, really. Although I know it worried Harold that the property around our house has a zillion trees and goes on forever. Sometimes people wander through. Sometimes by mistake, sometimes looking for a place to sleep near the water. But none of them ever harmed us or the property. I accused him of spending too much time on his police scanner. But anyway, he changed his thinking about having a gun when Gabby started coming for longer visits. And her friends would come around, too. Sometimes they even hung around the carriage house playing Harold's old pinball machine. It seemed there was a rash of reports around that time of kids accidentally finding guns in houses and convinced him that even locking it up wasn't good enough. Even octopuses could pick locks, she said."

Laughter lightened the talk of guns.

"That was the end of that. Harold decided he could come up with other ways of discouraging uninvited campers from our woods.

"Anyway," Birdie said, "that's a long story to explain to Izzy that Glock *isn't* the sound our feathered friends make."

"Thanks, Birdie," Nell said. "Fascinating. Will I ever stop learning about the things you know?"

Cass was soaking up the remains of the lemony sauce in the

bottom of her bowl with a roll, only half listening to the conversation.

"No," Birdie answered, smiling. "Anyway, back to what we know. The police know that the weapon used was a Glock, which is a gun, but they don't know who used it. Is that about right? And they think it was someone who knew Nick."

"That's about it, unfortunately," Nell said. "And right now they have a short list of people they think could have done it. But they don't have the proof they need."

Cass looked up for the first time since she started eating. "Who are the suspects?"

"I think we know, Cass," Izzy said.

"Oh." Cass picked up her bowl and took it over to the small sink near the stairs, then sat back down. She refilled her wineglass and took a long drink.

Birdie collected the rest of the dishes and then walked over to Cass. She rested a small hand on her shoulder.

Cass looked up into Birdie's face, then took a deep breath. "I hate all this, Birdie. People pointing fingers, the uncertainty, the fear. Good people grieving, and other people feeling they're being stared at, talked about, rumored to maybe have had a role in all this awfulness. You know that's happening." Her words fell off, and she stared at her wineglass, twisting it between her fingers.

"Would it help if we talked about it, Catherine?" Birdie said softly.

Nell and Izzy stopped talking and listened. They knew that when Birdie used Cass's full name, she was either concerned about something Cass had done or said, or she was hurting for her, knowing that she was in pain or distress. Cass's face and words told all of them what Birdie had detected.

Cass knew it, too. She managed a small smile.

Nell and Izzy took out their knitting, a calming movement that kept their hands busy and their hearts open. And left an open safe space into which each of them could pour their concerns or worries or emotions.

Birdie sat down next to Cass and pulled out her needles, too.

"It's Gracie that I'm really worried about. Things are a mess over there."

"What kind of mess?" Birdie asked.

"It's complicated. I went to see her. She's having a terrible time dealing with Nick Cabot's death, but there are other things weighing her down, too."

"Bobby?" Izzy asked softly.

"Yes, Bobby," Cass said. "The police, as we knew would happen, contacted him about the argument he'd had with Nick."

Birdie stiffened.

"No, Birdie, it's okay."

"Oh, I know it is. It's just this reaction I have that you mothers know so well. Your heart can flip a bit, unexpectedly, when you want to protect those you love. Sometimes just hearing her name in a serious conversation makes it flip."

"I get it," Cass said. "Although Gracie knew about the argument yesterday from us, she was waiting for him to talk to her about it, not wanting to pressure him. Which was a mistake. He didn't want her to worry, he told her after the fact."

"He must not know the true Gracie," Izzy said. "If anyone could calmly and intelligently deal with that, it would be Gracie."

"You're one hundred percent right. But he didn't. Being the macho guy he is, he talked to the police without her knowing it. But finally, he broke down and told her about it—about the argument, and that the police had questioned him about it. And that he'd told her why he said the things he'd said."

"To the police?" Nell said, finding herself a little lost in the mix of pronouns.

"No. He only told Gracie why he was so upset with Nick.

With the police, he brushed it off. He said it was a personal misunderstanding between two guys who had grown up together and had never been good friends. No big deal. He said that his mouth sometimes got out of control—all his friends knew that, even Nick—but it was nothing, just a guy thing. He told them that if they asked any of Nick's old friends, they'd confirm it. He just happened to be out running that particular day and was in a bad mood and took it out on Nick."

"So he didn't explain why he'd threatened Nick?"

"I guess not."

"And they let him get away with that?" Izzy asked.

"I suppose they wanted to check it out, then call him back in. But when he got back to the restaurant and had had a drink or two, he couldn't handle it any longer. He realized he'd purposely held things back, and that's when he poured it all out to Gracie.

"Gracie started asking questions, trying to get it straight in her own head, because it wasn't adding up for her. And that's when it got tough."

Izzy put her knitting down and leaned in, hearing the concern in Cass's words. "Tough, how?"

"Bobby said he was convinced that Nick Cabot was responsible for the bad reviews the restaurant was getting, and that he—Nick—was trying to sabotage Bobby's success."

"What?" Izzy said. "Nick never wrote reviews."

"No, and Gracie, of course, knew it was a crazy thought. He said he thought Nick was somehow responsible for the food being tampered with or bad fish being delivered, and that was why the quality of some of the specials wasn't so great."

"That's impossible," Nell said.

"I guess Bobby was desperate. It makes no sense to any of us who know Nick," Cass said.

"But somehow it made sense to Bobby," Birdie said. "That's what is important."

"Maybe. Bobby also thought Nick wanted him to fail and leave town because he—Nick—was in love with Gracie."

"What?" Izzy said, surprised. "Bobby doesn't strike me as being a crazy man, but that's crazy."

"And it's not true, of course, at least not in the way Bobby thought. Gracie and Nick were very close, but not that way. I think he knew that. I think the real reason was something else," Cass said.

"And that is?" Izzy asked.

Cass took a deep breath. "It's because of what you, wise and perceptive Izzy, thought the day that you first met Bobby. You said he was in love with Gracie."

Izzy put her wineglass down.

Cass nodded. "He told her he thinks he might be in love with her."

"Geesh, Cass," Izzy said. "That's damning. For Bobby."

There was stunned silence for a minute as they took that in.

And then, when the words settled, they thought about what the possible consequences could be.

Birdie finished a row in her herringbone pattern and put down her needles. "So you're telling me Bobby poured all of that on Gracie? How terribly difficult it must have been for her."

"For both of them," Nell said.

"Yes. It floored Gracie—she had no idea about Bobby's emotions. At first, she didn't know what to do with it. She likes him. A lot, in fact. She's really enjoying getting to know the new, grown-up Bobby. I am, too."

"Oh, my. But from what you've said so far, Cass, I'm assuming that an important piece here is that Bobby didn't share those things with the police?" Birdie said gently.

"That he threatened Nick over a woman?" Cass said. "No. He didn't."

There was a mutual groan that filled the knitting room.

Finally Cass picked up the conversation, filling in the rest.

"Gracie said her feelings were all over the place. First it was guilt, because her grief over the loss of Nick had blinded her to Bobby's feelings."

"How did she manage to handle all that? It has so many parts to it," Nell said.

Birdie spoke up. "I think I know how Gracie would handle it. She would know what all of us thought immediately, hearing your story, Cass. She would put herself aside and think of Bobby. And of how dangerous it was not to have told the police everything."

Cass smiled at Birdie. "That's exactly what she did. She knew why Bobby hadn't gotten into it with the police—it was embarrassing. And in his mind, it was a private thing. He probably didn't even think about the fact that it was incriminating. But Gracie knew. She also knew it would be even worse if the police found out from someone else."

"And they would," Izzy said. "But I'm guessing Gracie took care of that?"

Cass nodded. "She told him what he had to do"

"He went back to the police station on his own," Birdie said.

Cass sat up straighter. "Yep. Gracie insisted on it. He needed to tell them the whole story, and he needed to do it immediately, like Izzy said. If he didn't, it would be bad."

"It must have been so difficult for Gracie," Izzy said. "By telling the police the truth, Bobby was handing them a clear motive for murder. One that fits so perfectly into one of the most common scenarios—a love triangle."

Cass nodded. "Even though it wasn't that at all. And then add that to Bobby's thinking that Nick had been ruining his restaurant? His thinking was messed up."

"That's heavy for both of them," Izzy said.

"They were both being brave," Birdie said. "Love can certainly mess up lives if not tended to carefully."

Cass nodded. "I think it was Tommy Porter who met with

him when Bobby went back in. He was there a long time, Gracie said. Today he came in to work—I saw him at the restaurant
myself—so at least we know he's not in jail."

"And the police? What did they say?" Birdie asked, putting
voice to all their thoughts.

"They recorded everything—"

"And?"

"And then they told him he was not allowed to leave town."

Chapter 25

Izzy and Cass waved good-bye to Nell and Birdie and climbed into Cass's SUV.

"Why does being in the dark, quiet space of your car bring me comfort?" Izzy asked.

"I think it's because we've closed the world out, along with work and worry and stress. It's just you and me, friend. And all the smelly trash my Joey has left in the backseat."

"Right." Izzy leaned her head back and closed her eyes.

Knitting night had come to an early end, and it wasn't only because Nell had closed her eyes during a lull in the conversation and nodded off for a few minutes, losing a dozen stitches in the herringbone row she was knitting.

Their tiredness wasn't just physical, as Birdie had pointed out. Their minds were full of confusing thoughts, and their hearts were heavy. Repeating things over and over again, things that had happened that week, which seemed like it had no end, and things they had learned about that seemed soft, like over-processed cookie dough.

It was time to say good night.

"But," Izzy had said with some optimism as they all agreed to admit defeat, "we managed to make some progress on the afghan. The shades and hues of blues, greens, and golds are coming together miraculously. And beautifully." It had even surprised the knitters themselves.

"This will either be a warm cozy blanket for someone or a spectacular wall hanging," Izzy said.

"Or we can take it apart when we're finished and each have a lovely, long scarf," Nell said.

"Or both," their compromiser-in-residence concluded. Birdie hugged each of them tightly.

Once she and Izzy had buckled up, Cass started the car. She paused before pulling out of the parking lot and looked over at Izzy. "Iz, are you in a hurry to go home?"

"Why? What are you thinking?"

"I don't want to go home. I need to talk to you. Would you be up for getting a drink somewhere before I drop you off? Our hubbies aren't expecting us home this early, anyway. They probably have the kids' bedtime stories all picked out."

Izzy had had the same thought. Gracie was a good friend of hers, but Cass and Gracie had a whole life history together. She could feel the heaviness of Grace's situation weighing on Cass.

She also knew Sam loved his Thursday nights alone with Abby, although rather than reading a story, Abby had probably talked her dad into watching *Willy Wonka & the Chocolate Factory* or *Mary Poppins.*

"Sure," she said to Cass. "Good idea. How about the lounge at the Ocean's Edge? We're less likely to see anyone we know there."

Cass agreed and drove out of the alley, then headed toward the other end of Harbor Road. The restaurant was known for delicious meals and a lovely atmosphere for fine dining. "The special occasion place," Abby called it. Not a place the Perrys or Brandleys would take their young kids for tacos and pizza, possibly leaving a mess on the floor.

Even the restaurant's bar area was more relaxing and subdued than the other bars and grills in town that Cass and Izzy's friends were more likely to go to at this hour.

The night was pleasant enough that Cass and Izzy headed through the lounge and out to the lounge that overlooked the harbor waters. The large firepit in its center still glowed, warming the chilly evening breeze.

They sat in wide comfortable chairs near the fire, not needing the blankets the restaurant provided, and settled in, looking into the fire. For a while, they sat in silence. The dark sky and quiet evening were working its magic, relaxing their bodies, soothing tired minds. The deep night somehow made everything easier, whatever that everything might be.

Cass took a deep, calming breath, more of a sigh, her eyes on a single slight beam from the breakwater lighthouse sliding across the black water.

The waitress came and went, leaving a tray with light signature cocktails and a small bowl of chocolates.

"This was a good idea, Cass." Izzy said, lifting her glass toward Cass. They tapped the rims. "To good friends."

"And solving the world's problems," Cass added.

"Or at least Sea Harbor's," Izzy said. "You were lost in thought when we finally started knitting tonight. This is pretty heavy stuff going on with Gracie and Bobby."

Cass nodded. She took a sip of her drink, then attempted a crooked grin. "I can't believe that I'm calling this drink a cocktail. It has fruit in it. I think it came from a health food place. One of those things you drink in the morning to be healthy."

"Oh, shush. Take another sip. You'll like it."

"I'm sorry I zoned out after I talked about the mess over at Gracie's place. I know I wasn't very communicative. I actually had more to say, but was having trouble thinking straight."

"You drained your brain. I get it."

"Maybe. The surprise and emotion at Gracie's were overwhelming. In fact, it blocked out something else that happened before Gracie shared all the real drama with me."

"What was that?"

"A weird phone call that I'd accidentally overheard. It was before I had talked to Gracie, and probably doesn't mean anything. But somehow everything means something these days. And since Bobby is so messed up right now, I don't know. Maybe it's relevant to finding Nick's murderer."

"Bobby called someone?"

"I don't know who he was talking to or who made the call. But Bobby was upset."

Cass proceeded to fill Izzy in on what she'd heard.

Izzy frowned. "He mentioned trouble? Maybe his trouble with the police?""

"I don't know." Cass took a drink, trying to remember exactly what she'd heard.

"Do you have any idea who it was?"

"None. He didn't call the person by name. But his voice softened at the end of the call, as if he were sorry he got upset. I thought I heard the word *love* at the end."

"Like he was telling someone about Gracie?"

"I don't think so. But I couldn't fit it into the snatches I'd heard, and I didn't hear the whole call, either, so it didn't make much sense. But there was one thing that really got to me. Bobby was sad—even teary."

"Sad?"

"I know. And I forgot all about the call, after later hearing all the other things Gracie was upset about. The call lost its importance.

"Did Bobby see you?"

"Not until he finished the call and started down the steps. I swear he had tears in his eyes. He must have known I had heard him. But then, as he does, he seemed to let go of his emotions as he hit the bottom step. By the time we reached the door, he was the old Bobby, a welcoming grin in place, and the call was never mentioned."

"The old Bobby," Izzy mused. "Which one is that? The high-school Bobby or the one who loves Gracie and recently threatened a now-murdered man he thought might be stealing her away?"

Cass nodded. "Yeah, I know. It's the pits. He has suddenly become more complicated. But here's the thing. I can't get it off my mind. The whole mess. And I don't exactly know where to go with it all. But I know Bobby—"

Izzy just listened, wondering briefly why Cass had to go anywhere. She suddenly seemed so alone.

"When you teased me the other day that I probably had a crush on Bobby when I was a kid, it got me thinking about what he was like back then. I didn't have a crush on him, but we all thought he was cool. And nice. That weird way teens can be about older kids who sometimes seem bigger than life. Someone who isn't really bad, just sort of loud and outrageous and funny. And good-looking. But he was also like Nick Cabot in other ways. He was the guy who, unexpectedly, would stand up for the unpopular kid or invite a girl who never got invited to a dance, to be his date. And then, even when he'd tease someone by giving them a funny nickname and you'd make a face at him, inside you're pleased in a weird sort of way. It almost becomes a compliment. And you know he meant it as a nice kind of sweet teasing, not an insult."

"Sure. I remember the type. A part of being a teenager, I guess."

"What those memories reminded me of, and again when he moved back to town, is that Bobby Palazola isn't a bad guy at all. Not bad in the actual sense."

"It sounds like you're becoming his protector, Cass."

Cass thought about that. "No," she finally said. "I'm not that. I don't know exactly where I am. It's Gracie I want to protect. But, in a way, Bobby too. She said Bobby was almost embarrassed when he said he thought he might be in love with her. It was hard for her and hard for him. And never would even have been an issue if a man hadn't been murdered. That made me wish he were gone. But yet—" Her words fell off.

"It does sound like a bad movie, Cass. Do you think Bobby is on something?"

"Gracie said no. It wasn't like that. But when he told her how Nick Cabot had always been a thorn in his side—not exactly the words he used—Gracie said he sounded sad. Lost. Not the Chef Bobby that she knew and worked with and trusted to run her restaurant kitchen.

"He admitted to Gracie that Nick always bested him when they were younger—awards, sports, and even girls. And as for the threat he'd made to Nick that day? He said it didn't mean the way it looked. Even Nick knew that. His temper just got the better of him. He was afraid Nick was beating him again. And that he might lose the restaurant job and lose Gracie, too."

"Yet he never 'had' Gracie," Izzy said.

"Right," Cass said. "But you saw him, Izzy. You met him. You liked him. He's a good guy."

"And good guys don't kill people," Izzy said.

Cass nodded. "Right. That's what I believe."

"Do good guys kill for a woman they love?"

Cass grabbed a blanket and wrapped it around her, looking as sad as Izzy could ever remember.

Chapter 26

Mae had pulled her hair back into a tight bun. Izzy noticed it immediately when she walked into the shop on Friday morning. It should have put her on high alert. That hairdo usually meant Mae had overslept without time for a shower and she was hiding bed hair. Or she might have had a bad mahjong game the night before and wasn't happy. On those days, Mae liked to be alone in the shop.

After a restless sleep, Izzy wasn't in the best of moods, either. That fact didn't slip by Mae, as Izzy had hoped it might.

Mae approached Izzy in her cramped office in the back of the shop, blocking the door so Izzy wouldn't run off to greet someone or help a customer or make a phone call.

"Izzy," she said, her hands on her nonexistent hips and her voice with an edge to it. "I have everything under control here in the shop. We have classes in the knitting room for the next three hours, traffic will be thin, and you will be a better person if you go somewhere for an hour or two, or three. And so will I. Get some lunch. Go for a walk. Take deep breaths. But leave. You'll feel better. Thank you."

Izzy thought briefly about reminding Mae that it was her yarn shop, but she'd never do that, of course. She loved her shop manager. The shop would fall apart without her, not to mention that sometimes Mae read Izzy better than she read herself and had an uncanny ability to save her from herself.

She knew she'd been less than useful the last couple hours. She'd already mislabeled a shipment of new yarn and was unable to effectively help a new knitter who had handed her a horribly knit scarf. But it was when she realized the same customer was more interested in knowing if Izzy knew the man who had been murdered than she was in getting help that she retreated to her office. Where Mae had found her and given her an out. *Literally.* Izzy was grateful.

She grabbed a cable-knit sweater from her office and threw it around her shoulders, flipped the arms into a loose knot and headed out. For a minute, she stood on the steps of her shop and looked around, having no idea where to go, then headed down Harbor Road.

She looked up at a disappearing sun, now shadowed by voluminous dark clouds that seemed to be following her down the Sea Harbor's main street.

But it wasn't the clouds as much as people who were following her. People in her head. She'd been concerned about Cass and how she'd been pulled into Gracie's troubles. But during the night, Gracie, Bobby, Beatrice Scaglia, and even a dead man had played havoc with her sleep. They were there in her head, as if battling it out in a boxing ring, battling over their lives. And over a terrible death.

Izzy spotted an empty bench across from Garozzo's Deli and sat down, the smooth bench cool beneath her jeans. Without thought or reason, she pulled out her phone and checked it, then scolded herself, and slipped it back into her pocket. What she didn't need right now was news about anything. There was no room in her head.

She closed her eyes and breathed in the scent of the flowers. She wasn't sure how long she sat like that, her eyes closed and her mind trying hard to remain quiet, before she felt a shadow on her lids, interrupting her quiet. She opened her eyes and looked into warm brown eyes.

"Hello, sleeping beauty."

Izzy smiled. "Birdie. My guardian angel."

"And what am I guarding you from?"

"Myself. My thoughts."

"Well, now, that deserves a soup or sandwich at Harry's. Come, my dear." Birdie held out her small hand and Izzy took it. They walked across the street, hand in hand, to Garozzo's Deli.

Harry's place wasn't strictly a deli. Harry's grandfather Enrico had started the deli, then later on added a restaurant on the deli's back side, one Harry had remodeled and made popular and inviting. Enrico had raised his family of nine in the rooms above it, an elaborate story most diners at the deli had heard at least once. The building itself was now a town historic landmark, complete with a small brass plaque beside its door, although no one was quite sure how that came about. Some suspected one of the Garozzos, somewhere along the way, had found someone to cast the plaque and adhere it to the building in honor of Enrico.

The line to the deli counter was already backed up when Izzy and Birdie walked in. Customers were waiting patiently for their fat slices of mortadella, salami, prosciutto, or a take-out pastrami sandwich as big as one's face.

Birdie and Izzy skirted the crowd and walked into the restaurant area. Shannon Platt, a young waitress they knew well, greeted them with hugs and steered them to a table on the room's far side.

"I thought when you graduated, you were putting waitressing behind you, Shannon," Birdie said to her back.

Shannon turned her head, nodding. "Mostly, I am. But Harry talks me into coming in now and then. And who can say no to Harry?"

Birdie chuckled as they reached their table, one with a view of the harbor and the family of gulls who sat on the wide ledge outside, looking longingly at the parade of dishes that came and went from the table. "Besides, I'd miss seeing people like you guys."

"So, how's the boyfriend?" Izzy asked. "I like him."

"He's great, Iz. He finally got the job of his dreams. Coaching freshmen and teaching health education. He's happy. So, what can I get for you?"

Before they had a chance to answer, Shannon glanced over her shoulder toward the kitchen. Then she looked back. "Well, it may not matter what you want. Harry spotted you, and he'll insist your day will be ruined if you don't try the special. Or whatever he thinks your moods need today. You know how he is. And I don't fight with him anymore. He always wins."

"That'll be fine, Shannon," Birdie said, then looked around the crowded room. "It's a busy day, I see."

Shannon nodded. "I don't know what it is. Maybe it's being in a warm, familiar place that makes people feel safe, and where they can laugh if they want to and it's not inappropriate. We need to do that, you know? Be in a place where no one bad would ever enter—a place that allows happy moments when we need them."

Shannon didn't sound very happy.

Izzy looked up at her, reading her face. "You knew Nick, didn't you, Shannon? I've seen you two in here chatting."

Shannon wrinkled her forehead, as if Izzy's question was somehow bringing up something she'd been trying hard not to think about, but was clearly failing. "We were buddies. Nick came in here often, usually when it wasn't too busy. And he always acted like talking to me was interesting—go figure—so we got to know each other. We had things in common—sailing, crossword puzzles—but we talked about anything that we'd been thinking about. Sometimes he had something to eat while he was here, but mostly he ordered takeout. He loved Harry's Ribollita soup. Harry promised him that someday he'd teach him how to make it, but not for a while, he said, because he needed Nick's business. It kept him in cigars."

"That's our Harry," Birdie said. "And I imagine he was able to get plenty of those Cuban ones he liked."

Shannon nodded, looking better. "Sometimes Harry'd ask me to deliver a takeout to Nick's house. Nick would tip me like I'd brought the meal all the way from Italy. I'd have done it for nothing, because, like I said, I loved talking with him. I mean, he wasn't a saint or anything, but he was a terrific guy. Even my boyfriend, Cole, liked him. He helped Nick paint his boat last summer."

Shannon paused for a minute, as if tugging up memories. "You know what I think I loved best about him? It was how he respected people without considering their sex or their job or what they looked like or anything else about them. Like I could have had a green face or four arms and he would've been okay with it. Does that sound silly?"

"It's a beautiful tribute," Birdie said, patting the hand that Shannon had placed on the table.

"I noticed those things about him that night. I don't know why. I just remember it."

"What night was that?" Izzy asked.

Shannon sighed. "The night of the fire."

They still could barely say the words out loud. The night Nick died . . . The night Nick was murdered. They might think it, but none of them could say it.

"Yeah," Shannon went on. "Nick had ordered a big dinner from us that da . . ." Her voice cracked and she stopped for a second, taking a deep breath and then speaking more softly.

"That's crazy, isn't it? It was Sunday. *Sunday.* Not even a whole week ago. And it seems like a whole lifetime ago."

"Time doesn't exist when you've lost someone you care about," Birdie said.

"So you delivered food to him last Sunday night?" Izzy asked, trying to keep her voice as calm and kind as Birdie's.

"Well, not night, exactly. It was late afternoon, early for dinner, but it was what he wanted. It was a lot of food. Several different kinds of pasta, and as always, the soup. He sometimes did that so he'd have food for all week. Harry was going to deliver, but he was busy, so I offered."

"Did you talk with Nick?" Birdie asked.

"Yes. But not for very long. He was busy. Arranging some candles or something. His house looked really nice. I put the boxes of food in the kitchen with instructions on heating it all up. And then . . . then I just left."

Shannon's voice dropped, as if talking to herself—or maybe wondering if she could have changed the outcome if she had only stayed a little longer.

"Was Squid there when you stopped by?"

She thought for a minute. "Yes. But I didn't see him. Nick said Gabby had brought him back early from dog walking. He'd let Squid outside for a while. Squid liked to greet the neighbors when he got home. Eventually he'd come back. It'd give him time to get his Garozzo dinner planned so it looked like he had cooked it himself. He was kidding, though—he said his friend had known him since they were kids, and she knew he had trouble making peanut butter and jelly sandwiches. I offered to help, but he said no, that he'd be fine."

Birdie's thoughts were still on a dog roaming the neighborhood. "Squid went outside without a leash?" She wondered if that was how Squid had escaped the fire. And she also thought about how insanely careful she was about protecting this same dog, now a frequent guest in her home.

"Oh, sure, Birdie. Squid never went off the block. He was safe. My dog's like that, too. Harriet knows not to talk to strangers." Shannon managed a half smile.

"Our dog, Red, does the same thing," Izzy joined in. "He likes the leash because it means we're going off our block for a walk, but otherwise he's happy playing outside with Abby and her friends."

Shannon nodded, her thoughts no longer in Harry's deli, but across town, in a special home on Fishermen Row.

"Nick thought highly of you, Shannon," Birdie said. "We all do."

"I hope so. Thank you. Nick was just . . . just so generous, and smart, an all-around nice guy, you know? So, why?" She shook her head back and forth, until one long blond ponytail batted her cheek. Her voice dropped, her next words almost inaudible, and her eyes pleading for someone to turn back the clock.

"So, why?" she asked again. "Why do bad things happen to the really good guys?"

The emotion came back then, her cheeks flushed and great sadness filling her eyes. Shannon turned away quickly, wiping her eyes with the cuff of her blouse as she hurried over to the kitchen to place their non-order.

Izzy took a drink of water. "The perennial question, right? Why the good guys? And does that mean it was a bad guy who did it?"

Birdie was quiet.

Izzy answered herself. "No, it doesn't. That doesn't follow logically. Maybe it was a good guy doing a bad thing to a good guy."

But why?

Chapter 27

Birdie stood next to Izzy at the Endicott kitchen sink, suds climbing halfway up her arms as she washed a large pan. She rinsed it off and handed it to Izzy, then turned her head sideways so Nell and Cass, wiping off the counter, could hear her.

"It's fortuitous that most of the regulars didn't come tonight. It's a sign," she said.

"You don't think it's because people think we smell?" Cass asked. She scratched at a glob of caramel that had dropped from the warm flan they'd had for dessert. It stuck to the countertop stubbornly, like gum. She mumbled a few inaudible words at the hard blob.

"Well, maybe that, too," Birdie said with a sweet smile, one that she knew would pull Cass, at least slightly, out of her mood.

Cass looked up, her cheeks flushed. "Yeah. Sorry. You're right. It's nice to just be us. You are my people, the ones who don't mind if I'm a pill."

"Birdie didn't exactly say that, Cass," Izzy said, trying to get a rise out of her friend.

The group was, in fact, a mere skeleton of the usual Endicott Friday-night dinners, when the gathering usually numbered a dozen or more.

It was but a brief interlude, Nell knew. The Friday-night group would expand greatly once the warm weather was here for good.

But for tonight, for right now, she was thinking the same thing as Birdie and Cass. Not about the smell, but that it was a small group that had gathered tonight for Ben's perfectly grilled herb-marinated tenderloin. And that it was somehow fortuitous. Or opportune, at least. They'd been going in different directions all week. Wearing themselves out in their heads, if not their hearts. The week had seemed eons long. Uncertainty and stress and grieving were awful combinations.

Nell looked around the kitchen. Their Friday dinner group had shrunk to an even smaller number when Sam asked Ben and Danny to go over to the yacht club dock with him. A new computer had come in for the *Dream Weaver,* Sam and Ben's freshly painted and prized forty-two-foot Hinckley sailboat. It was begging to be looked at, Sam said. And they were gone.

Nell put down her dishtowel. "Why don't we forget about whatever is left to do and go outside? Maybe the moon will soothe our souls."

"Does that work?" Cass asked, putting down her cleaning rag. "I thought it made people crazy."

"Shush," Birdie said, draining the sink and wiping soap off her arms. "Never doubt the power of the moon. It can ground us, make us think deeper."

"I read that it can even improve moods," Izzy said, looking at Cass.

Cass ignored her and made one last attempt to get up the caramel blob.

In minutes, the kitchen light was dimmed, and the four women walked out to the deck. The night wrapped around them like a soft blanket, creating a safe place. They moved chairs closer to the firepit. Nell placed a tray of mugs, along with water, coffee, and wine, on the wide lip around the firepit. Birdie passed out blankets, then sank down into a soft deck chair, sighing with contentment.

"Mmm," Izzy said, settling into one of the chaise lounges. In the distance, waves pounded against the shore, providing a bass background for the musical rustling of new leaves coming out on the trees.

Cass was the last to sit down. She took the glass of wine Nell offered. Then, she turned her face up to the moon and closed her eyes.

For a few minutes, the deck was comfortably quiet, the moon taking center stage and the night sounds, like white noise, shielding them from the world.

Nell glanced over at Cass. She hoped Cass, too, was sinking into the peaceful mood, and that the agitation she'd sensed in her the last couple days was giving way to the warmth of the glowing embers and the deep sky. Cass looked like she might be falling asleep. A good sign.

But before Nell's thoughts completely registered, Cass's eyes opened and she leaned forward in the chair, as if coming out of a bad dream. "Bobby's going down," she said.

Her words seemed to scatter the moon's soothing vibes into a million slivers.

"What?" Birdie asked, suddenly alert. "He's 'going down'? That's a frightening thing to say, Cass." Birdie's small face, lit by glowing embers, was a map of worry—with a tinge of pique.

Izzy was also staring at Cass. "Birdie's right. That's awful. It sounds like a line from a bad movie." Izzy leaned forward and refilled wine glasses, as if fortification was needed. "And it's a scary one."

All their eyes were wide open now. It was as if Cass's statement had ripped the tape off the confusing thoughts they were hiding in their own heads. Bringing them to the surface and hoping the moon would step in and live up to its promise.

"I know I'm disturbing all of this, this nice scene"—Cass waved a hand in the air as if pushing their few moments of tranquility aside—"but we all love Gracie and she's a mess, and we somehow need to figure all this out and help her. And Bobby, too."

At first, they were quiet, trying to process Cass's worry.

"The restaurant . . ." Nell began.

"No. I don't think that's even on Gracie's mind right now. She figures it will work out, or it won't. She doesn't seem to care which way it goes. It's Bobby she's worried about and it's tearing her up. Part of it is guilt, I think. She says it's her fault that Bobby is in this mess. She was so torn apart by Nick's passing that she ignored what he may have been going through the last few days."

"But, Cass," Nell said, reaching for a simple explanation, "Apparently Gracie didn't even know about Bobby's now-famous argument with Nick, or even that he'd been called in for questioning. He hadn't told her about that. Do I have that right? So she couldn't have been responsible for anything."

"Sure, that's true. And it's a rational conclusion. But when he finally told her, it crushed her. She realizes how it looks for Bobby. And she thinks if she'd been more aware, she could have helped him so he didn't come across as being so . . ." Cass paused, as if unwilling to complete her thought. But the word *guilty* hung heavy in the air.

"I understand what you're saying," Birdie said. "We've all been in that position one time or another, wanting desperately to help someone we care about. What one feels or wishes she could have done doesn't always connect to the reality of the situation. All that Gracie knows is that someone she cares about is now in a precarious position. And she wishes she could have prevented it."

"I can relate to that." Izzy nodded. "Like why I let Abby go to kindergarten the day she fell off the swing and broke her leg. I should have kept her home that day. It was all my fault she had to trick-or-treat in a cast that year."

The memory took them all back to that day, one that had traumatized Izzy. But she had made her point.

Birdie brought them back to the topic, her voice calm, but with concern showing on her face. "Cass, is there something you aren't telling us?"

"I'm sorry, Birdie. I don't mean to be weird," Cass said. "And no. All I know is what I've told you. But that's clearly enough, right?"

"Enough?" Nell said. She knew exactly what Cass was thinking and feeling, but she needed her to say it, so they were all on the same page.

"Enough to make Bobby Palazola the number one suspect in the murder of Nick Cabot."

"Mae hears his name passed around the yarn shop," Izzy admitted. "In a hushed way, but it's out there. It's because of all the uncertainty. People need to be able to point to someone so they're not afraid."

"Yesterday a few of the restaurant diners asked Gracie if she was afraid to have Bobby in her kitchen. They wondered why she hadn't fired him," Cass said. "How awful is that?"

That took them all by surprise.

The evening had taken a turn Nell hadn't expected. What she hoped would happen was what she'd hoped for every day since Nick died: that the news would break suddenly announcing that they'd arrested Nick Cabot's killer. And it was someone none of them new, and that the town could then shift back into its summer mode.

All would be well.

She pushed her Pollyanna thoughts aside, and admitted the topic wasn't going to go away. Not tonight. She glanced at

Cass again, knowing that her concern wasn't only about Gracie, wanting to be supportive, but about Bobby, too. Gracie would eventually be fine; none of them were so sure about Bobby.

"Cass, you're forgetting something in all this," she said aloud. "We don't really know that Bobby is a prime suspect. He hasn't been arrested. Clearly, the police don't have proof of anything. Bobby says he's innocent. So whatever we're hearing is rumor. The police are looking at everyone, everything, every detail they can find."

"Nell's right," Izzy said. "And if we're going to talk about this in a constructive way, we need to accept that. We also should face the fact that we already know of at least one other person who has made it clear in recent weeks that she'd like nothing better than to get Nick Cabot out of her life. Someone I can't imagine being involved in a crime. But then I can't imagine anyone I know well committing murder. Beatrice Scaglia had made her feelings about Nick Cabot known to lots of people. Most of the town, probably. And we can't slide that under a rug while trying to prove Bobby's innocent."

The room was silent. Not because the comment was a surprise; they'd all seen a sign of the mayor's discomfort—or actual anger—in the past weeks. She hadn't tried to hide it. It was a true fear of the mayor's—a fear that Nick Cabot might actually uproot her in her cherished role as mayor, a role that was truly her life.

The thought of that leading to murder was difficult to swallow. But then, nothing surrounding a murder was easy to think about.

"It's hard to even say Beatrice's name in connection with a murder," Birdie said. "She's been in our lives for so many years. And she's someone who, in spite of her eccentricities, has a heart big enough to make sure there are extra crossing guards at the school and that the sheets get cleaned at the homeless shelter."

"It will be an awkward interview when the police question her, if they haven't already," Izzy said.

In spite of the seriousness of the topic, the thought of Beatrice submitting to questioning by *her* police department, in *her* town, had a comical edge to it.

"The police could probably make money selling tickets to that," Cass suggested.

They all smiled at the incongruity of it all, but the mood turned serious when Birdie brought them back to murder suspects.

"If Beatrice and Bobby each had serious beefs with Nick, it seems likely there are others," Birdie said.

"There have to be others," Izzy said.

"Yes," Nell said. "And one of them murdered Nick."

"And we know it wasn't Bobby Palazola," Cass said. "So, why aren't we focusing on Marco Costa?"

The others looked at her, waiting to see if she could make the comment more substantial, something more than a wish.

"Bobby swore to Gracie that he's inno—" Cass put up her hands to keep them from talking. "Okay, wait. I know what you're all thinking. That's not proof. I know that. But Gracie is absolutely sure of his innocence. And I am, too. As tough as Bobby likes to pretend he is, he wouldn't hurt a fly. Bobby and murder just don't fit together. He has a temper, sure. But it disappears quickly. I saw it myself just a couple days ago."

"He was angry with you?" Nell asked.

"Well, no. Not me. I accidentally overheard him on a phone call, scolding someone." Cass filled Birdie and Nell in on what she'd heard. "The point is, he was angry, but in the next breath, I could hear tears. I think anger is an instinctive reaction for him. He gets mad, then *poof*, the anger's gone. And that's probably how that argument with Nick started and ended."

Nell heard the sincerity in Cass's voice. He simply had to be innocent.

She also read the minds of the others sitting on the deck, not knowing Bobby as well. They wanted Cass to be right, but they also knew that serious actions could take place during even a very short-lived anger. That moment when the brain triggers one to fight or flight.

"We need music," Izzy said suddenly. "Too many dark thoughts." She grabbed her phone and in minutes Dua Lipa's upbeat voice was filling the deck.

Nell caught the name Houdini somewhere in the music and decided it was a fitting choice.

"Here's another thing," Cass said, her voice a little louder as she spoke above the lyrics, not quite ready to move on. "Bobby is doing fine. If he were guilty, he wouldn't be fine. He's all about protecting Gracie, working like crazy to keep the restaurant going. Not complaining about the situation. Even telling jokes. He says he's innocent, and not accused of anything. So he's not worried."

"So we have two people we want to get out of the suspicion limelight," Izzy said, her voice pulling them all back to what was in front of them. "I think we have to be methodical about this, and maybe we can dig into places the police can't go. On one hand, we need to figure out things about Bobby that will prove he didn't do it."

"What kind of things?" Cass asked.

"Well, things that are more substantial than him proclaiming he's innocent," Izzy said. "And we also need to learn more about Nick Cabot. Like Birdie always says—we need to walk in his shoes—"

"And that may lead to why someone killed him," Birdie added.

"Everyone in this town seems to know Nick and to like him. In that kind of an environment, how does one go about finding a murderer?" Nell asked.

"We're assuming someone killed him because they didn't

like him," Izzy said. "But that isn't necessarily true. It could be that Nick knew something, something that could incriminate someone, and however they felt about Nick, they couldn't let that be revealed."

"Marco Costa," Cass said. Her voice was enough to bring all eyes on her.

For a minute, no one spoke. Then Cass repeated the name and added, "Nick knew Marco Costa. And was about to find out more. He didn't like him working with Gracie. And Marco knew that he was about to be fired,"

"Is being fired from a kitchen job worth killing someone for?" Birdie asked.

"There was more to it, I think," Cass said.

But whatever the "more" was, was now a major unknown.

"Nell's right," Birdie said. "Everyone likes Nick. But what did Nick like? I've known him a long time, but I never felt I really got to know Nick as well as I'd wished. He always seemed to make the conversation about the other person. Cass, you've known him a long time, too, and you're much closer in age. But do you know where he went? Who or what he saw? What he liked and disliked? What compelled him to help people out the way he did?"

The others nodded as Birdie talked, seeing the wisdom in her words.

"Nick needs to help us out here," Nell said. "It wasn't a stranger who killed him. We need to get to know Nick better so he can tell us who that was. Or at least give us hints that we can pass along to Jerry Thompson."

"The chief made it clear that he needs the public's help. It's sometimes the most mundane sighting that can reveal something critical," Izzy said.

"So we're back to those shoes," Cass said.

Birdie smiled. "Exactly. Maybe we can use them to walk backward in his life?"

"So backward from Sunday," Izzy said, nodding. "We know Gabby saw him the day he died. Liz Santos. And the two of you—" She looked at Birdie and Nell.

"And Shannon Platt," Birdie added.

Izzy filled in what she and Birdie had learned at Harry's deli when they talked with the waitress. She looked over at Birdie. "Shannon said it was a large take-out order. Why? Maybe he had a guest?"

"Gabby had thought that, too," Birdie said. "The table was set."

"Elizabeth?" Cass asked.

Nell thought back, then said no. "Unless he surprised her, but she told us she had plans to go for a walk and then an early bedtime."

Birdie agreed. "Besides, Nick was spending time with old friends that weekend. We saw two of them at the yacht club."

"Nick did mention that afternoon that he needed to tell Elizabeth something," Nell said. But . . ."

The others waited. "But?"

"Well, it sounded like he might see or call her that next week, so nothing important. Yet Elizabeth kept checking her phone, as if expecting—and that's my assumption—to hear from someone. Nick, maybe?"

"Who was Nick with at the club?" Cass asked.

"Liz and her cousin Bella."

"Bella? That's right. I forgot," Cass said. She frowned. "I thought they all left that day."

"Shannon said Nick needed the Sunday takeout late afternoon that day, not evening. Maybe one or two were leaving late, so he was having them come over before they left town," Birdie suggested.

"They were just here for the weekend," Birdie said. "The police possibly checked all that out, but it would be good to know who left when."

More ideas flowed, with tired minds trying to grab them, filing them away to be pulled apart in the light of day. Thoughts and suppositions were finally scattered by noise from the front of the house, reminding them that the hour was late and their husbands were back. In minutes, glasses were gathered up and returned to the kitchen. Good nights were uttered in tired voices.

But resolve followed the four women.

Nick Cabot certainly had big shoes, but they were willing to try them on.

Chapter 28

The early Saturday morning phone call startled Cass. She was sitting at the breakfast table and stared at her cell phone, as if scolding it for disturbing her first coffee of the day.

Danny and Joey were in the bedroom above her, banging on a drum Izzy had wickedly given Joey for his birthday. The beat helped to blot out the ring. Slightly. It was probably a crank call. Or Luna, her next-door neighbor, needing Danny to chase a mouse away.

Cass finally picked up her phone.

The phone call was none of those. It was long-distance. A very long distance. And one she was relieved not to have missed.

"Oh, Nancy," Cass murmured, her heart immediately melting at the sound of her friend's voice. Her own voice cracked and tears began to build, flowing down Cass's cheeks. "I'm so, so sorry about Nick."

Nancy Sheridan's voice was also thick with tears. "I know, Cass. I got your messages. Thank you." Finally she cleared her throat. "I couldn't talk to anyone at first, so I didn't take calls. It's pretty awful. Jerry Thompson has been in touch with me.

And my hubby, Jake, is more compassionate than I ever thought possible. But this minute, I needed to talk with a friend. I hope . . . I hope I haven't taken you away from anything."

"Are you kidding?" Cass said, feeling sixteen again, sitting on her bed with Nancy and Gracie, crying and laughing and wishing their parents would leave them alone.

They talked briefly about ordinary things—Nancy's kids, her husband's job, her life in Portugal—as if somehow ordinary things needed to be gotten out of the way. But the mundane conversation was short and difficult to sustain.

In the next breath, Nancy said, "I need you to talk to me about my brother, Cass. I've gotten calls from a few friends. Everyone feels awful. But it's like they're afraid to mention his name. I need to hear his name, Cass."

"I know, Nancy. Me, too. Talking about him brings Nick into the room with us. Or are we going into his room? How many times did we sneak into his bedroom, searching for proof of things? Cigarettes? Girlie magazines?" Cass heard Nancy sniffle on the other end of the line.

"And we found them," Nancy said. "Remember that one . . . ?"

Cass pictured her friend, wiping her nose, a sad smile on her oval face, but with her brother standing right in front of her, telling her not to tell their mom.

"The missing him is heavy," Nancy said. "Like it's hard to breathe. My heart is in a million pieces. It's a horrible bad movie that won't end. My brother is gone. I wasn't there. And I'm desperate that I can't find him."

Nancy's thoughts had turned into words, coming in starts and stops. Cass filled in where she could, but there was little to say. Except that she was here for her. But she wasn't there for her—not physically. And neither was Nick.

"When are you planning on coming home?" Cass finally asked. "If my lobster boat could make it, I'd come pick you up tonight." Cass felt a small smile coming across the phone waves.

"Oh, I know you would. I wanted to come right away. But Chief Thompson suggested I wait a few days while they try to settle things. Whatever the hell that means, Cass. Settle up things? Nick is gone. What's there to settle? But the chief talked to my husband, too, and Jake agreed that it'd be better to wait a few days. We had to think of the kids."

Finding who did this, Cass thought. *That's what needs to be settled.*

"I know the chief was thinking it'd be easier for me. But I don't know, Cass . . . Could it be any harder, no matter where I was?"

Cass was thinking the same thing. What she'd like right now would be to have her friend right in front of her so she could hug her. And cry with her.

But she also figured Jerry Thompson was right, as he often was. There wasn't a thing Nancy could do right now, and it would be so hard to be hearing every single day about a murderer still lurking somewhere in their town. Or not lurking. Maybe standing right out in front of them. And no one seeing him or her.

"Jerry's a good guy," Cass said, not sure where to take the conversation.

"He's very caring," Nancy said. "He or Tommy Porter calls me every day, sometimes with a question or two, like about Nick's love life, which was kind of funny. As if I would know. I think mostly they call just to let me know I'm not forgotten and they are trying to put this all to rest."

"Well, old friend, you aren't forgotten. Not for an instant. And Gracie and I will be here when you do come, with arms open, hugs ready. Kleenex too. And perfect old-fashioneds waiting for all of us at Lucky's Place."

"I know you will. I wish I could turn my mind off until then. Nick and I talked last weekend. He was so upbeat. So happy. He'd just come home from fixing a part on his boat. He'd seen

Nell and Birdie at some birthday thing, he said. And he told me about the scuttlebutt about him running for mayor. Can you believe that, Cass? He would be perfect—Mayor Cabot. My dad and mom would have been unspeakably proud of him."

"They'd be proud of him, anyway," Cass said, her voice sounding different in her own ears. "Did you and Nick talk at all about his social life recently?"

"Like friends, you mean? He told me that Bella, Andy Risso, and a couple others were in town and they were having an amazing weekend together. He was happy to have the old gang together. Liz was, too."

"Anything else?"

"As for romance? I used to bring up his unmarried state, but I gave up on that a while ago. But last weekend, I don't know, Cass. I got the feeling there might be someone special. Did you see that? I mean, was he dating anyone?"

"Dating? I'm not even sure what that means these days."

"But recently?" Nancy went on. "Someone who might have put that nice sound in his voice that I heard last weekend? I guess it could have been just being with his old friends. He mentioned some dinner he was having that night. When I asked why, he said because he was hungry. A typical Nick answer when he thought I wanted to learn more about his life."

"Well, it's what sisters do, right? Nick's been helping a woman he knows get settled in Sea Harbor. People have seen them together. Her name's Elizabeth Hartley. Does that name sound familiar?"

"I met her when we were in town for the holidays. Nick and my kids had gone to the yacht club for dinner and she was there. She saw us and came over. She seemed nice. Really good with my kids. That's sort of my barometer."

"Yes, she would be. She used to be headmistress at that private day school."

"I forgot about that. Nick was on the school board that fired her, right?"

"Right. Some board members were not as fair or nice as Nick."

"I remember that. We had just moved to Porto, but Nick had told me about the problems at the school and how stressful it had been for her. The firing nearly ruined her, he said."

"Ruined her? How?"

"I can't remember. I think it was medical. Nick felt guilty about it because he was on the board and couldn't help. But I remember that when I met her over the holidays, she seemed fine. She's attractive and sociable. I didn't get the romantic vibe, though."

"From her or Nick?"

"Good question. Nick didn't talk to me much about things like that. But like I said, he sounded especially happy when we talked last weekend. And the 'romantic me' always thinks that has to do with love. Anyway, the conversation was a good one, and for that, I'm grateful. At the end, he demanded, like he always did, that I hand over the phone to my kids, because that was really why he had called in the first place. And then he'd listen intently to each one of them, asking them questions, things that would bring him into their lives and them into his, until our next visit to see him or his visit here. My kids love him so. He's the very best uncle in the world."

There was a long pause. Nancy's use of the present tense jarred them both, but they both ignored it and let it be. Nick had been gone less than a week. He was surely hovering around Sea Harbor still, wondering why his friends weren't getting the whole thing solved so his sister, Nancy, would have some closure. Some peace. So life could go on for all of them, despite missing a part of it.

Cass broke the silence, sensing Nancy would need to get off soon. She could hear Nick's nephews and nieces in the background. But there was one thing she needed to ask before they hung up. A practical matter that she promised Birdie she would check into.

"Nancy, one more thing. Did Jerry Thompson mention anything to you about Squid?"

"Oh, my—sweet Squid. Yes, we talked about him. Jerry said someone is taking care of him for now."

"Yes. Birdie Favazza's granddaughter, Gabby. She's great, and she loves Squid. She was one of Nick's dog walkers."

"The Pawfect Day Dog Walkers, right? Nick talked about them. I loved the name. I remember Gabby, now that I think about it. I met her on the beach last summer when we were home. And I adore Birdie. Are you sure they're okay keeping Squid until we come over?"

Cass assured her they were both fine caring for Squid. She held back the fact that Gabby Marietti had completely fallen in love with Squid. And that Squid was caring for Gabby as much as the other way around.

The noise on the other end of the connection got louder, and Nancy raised her voice and talked faster. "Oh, Cass, I don't want to hang up, but the kids are rambunctious. You know how that is. Hugs to you and Gracie . . ." Her voice quavered a little, but she talked fast, as if she needed to get her thought out while she still could.

"Cass, I need to know who took my brother from me. I need to know so I can let him rest in peace. And so I can breathe again."

Her voice cracked, and the phone went dead.

Chapter 29

Harold dropped Birdie off at the city hall.

"Are you sure you don't want me to go in with you?"

Birdie frowned, then scolded him lightly. "Harold, what in heaven's name are you thinking? Beatrice is my friend. You're acting like she might harm me."

"We don't know what's going on, Birdie. Sometimes you're just too darn trusting. Ella and I personally heard that woman yell at Nick one day on the street. She was vicious. Scared Ella half to death. I didn't vote for her, you know."

Birdie held back a smile at both the confession and the thought of Ella being scared of anything. She lightened Harold's mood by teasing him. "Don't worry about me. I've been practicing my jujutsu a bit. Now go on and pick up that order Ella needs from the market. I will text you when I'm finished."

Birdie walked slowly into the empty courthouse lobby, thinking of what Harold had said and wondering how many others in the town were thinking the same thing. But it was ridiculous. Beatrice was in the same boat they all were, grieving the loss of someone they'd known since he was a child. Dealing with a terrible loss. And in need of someone with whom she could share the sad time. And in the middle of everything, the mayor also had the embarrassment of having to be questioned by the police because of her angry remarks. It would be difficult for anyone, especially someone like Beatrice. And that was the whole reason for her visit. Since it was Saturday, she expected Beatrice to be at home, but no, she was at the office. So many things to do, she'd said when Birdie called. But she'd love to see her at the office.

Beatrice's secretary's office was empty, and Beatrice had told her to just walk in when she arrived. She liked working on Saturdays, she'd said. Fewer interruptions.

Birdie knocked lightly on the door, but before she could open it, it opened from the other side. Beatrice stood in the doorway, greeting Birdie with a warm embrace.

Birdie wished she had thought to bring tissues, thinking they might both need them shortly.

Finally Beatrice pulled away, her smile bright and her makeup in place.

Beatrice was dressed to perfection, with every hair in place, her eyes clear. It was so like Beatrice, Birdie thought. Even in a time of grieving, she was the mayor. And she'd need that presence, no matter how she might be feeling inside.

"I'm so happy you are here, dear Birdie. Please come sit." She ushered Birdie to a chair near her desk and sat down herself.

"I thought you might need a friend," Birdie began. "This is such a sad time—"

Beatrice sat still in a wingback chair behind her desk, her hands folded on the polished top, composed and collected, listening carefully.

For a moment, Birdie was confused at Beatrice's calm demeanor and lack of response. It was almost as if the mayor were listening to a citizen telling her that a stoplight was broken, rather than a friend coming to share sadness, coming with comfort.

Uncomfortable, Birdie went on. "This is such a terribly sad time for all of us. I thought you might need a hug. I've been needing them a lot lately—"

Beatrice nodded. "Of course. I wasn't thinking. This is a difficult time for you. I'm sorry for your loss, Birdie. You and Nick Cabot were friends. Ben and Nell, too. Please pass along my condolences."

Birdie frowned, not able to respond, and wondering for a brief moment who she was talking with. Or about.

For a moment, there was silence in the office, with Beatrice's composed demeanor holding strong. Finally the mayor said, "It's a difficult time for the town. I've been trying to help the police as much as I can. They need my help, I know, but as you know, there are a million other things I have on my plate."

"So they have questions for you?" It somehow sounded better than asking her if she'd been taken in for questioning.

"What do you mean? We've been in touch, of course. This is my town, and there's been a murder. When the chief called, I encouraged him to solve this mess as soon as possible. My town needs a resolution. Then I graciously told them my door was open to them if they thought I might be able to assist with the investigation, but they needed to know how busy I was."

"So they came over to you?"

"Yes, Tommy Porter and Chief Thompson. They know I have my pulse on the town, and had a million questions, but I let them know there was only so much time I could give to help them. Finally, the third time they showed up, I told them they needed to be better at their jobs and to solve this quickly. I reminded them that it is their job to solve this, and they certainly couldn't expect me to find the murderer for them. Although I'm beginning to think I may have to try." She smiled at Birdie.

"You understand that, don't you, Birdie? I can't do everything. I even had to remind them that they worked for me."

Birdie was silent, wondering who on earth she was listening to. This wasn't the smart, caring mayor she'd known for years.

A half hour later, Birdie finally interrupted Beatrice, explaining politely that Harold was picking her up, and she didn't want to take up too much of Beatrice's time. She got up and headed for the door. Beatrice followed her.

"One more thing, Birdie, just a reminder before you leave." And then she reminded Birdie of something that had nothing— or maybe everything—to do with a murder.

Chapter 30

The Sweet Petunia, a small, out-of-the-way café, was a favorite Sea Harbor place for breakfast and lunch, and especially for Annabelle Palazola's Sunday-morning brunch. The restaurant was perched on a hill above the artists' galleries on Canary Cove. Birch and maple trees grew to the top of the hill, all the way up to the restaurant's deck, hiding it naturally from those who hadn't heard of it. Or perhaps hadn't known that Annabelle Palazola made the most delicious, moist, and cheesy omelets on the North Shore.

And its regulars weren't about to tell any of those people about their treasure.

Ben and Nell counted themselves among those regulars—and good friends of the owner, too. And as the owner often did, she met them at the front door with a hug. Today they suspected it was accompanied by a need to connect.

"It's been a while, Annabelle," Ben said to the restaurant owner.

"Yes, it has. Please don't do that again, or I'll be tempted to give your table away. I've missed you both."

"Order received," Ben said. "We've missed you, too."

"It's been a week of thinking about people you care about," Nell said.

Annabelle nodded. Then she looked around, checking the indoor tables to see that each held a vase of fresh wildflowers and that napkins were folded, water glasses sparkling and diners happy. There was nothing fancy about Annabelle's Sweet Petunia. It was all about comfort with good friends and wonderful food. And always flowers.

Satisfied that all was going well, she ushered Ben and Nell into a small hallway that led to the kitchen and another doorway that opened out to the dining deck.

Nell saw the sadness in Annabelle's eyes. "How are you, dear friend?" she asked.

As soon as she spoke, Nell took back her own question. "It's a meaningless thing to ask. You're not okay. None of us are fine."

Annabelle patted Nell's arm. "That's right. We're not okay. Not you, not me, not the town. The second worst time in my life. Nick was a close family friend," she said. "You know how it is here for us natives. Nick and I, our families, have a history together. He and my Liz grew up together, but it was more than that."

"We saw Nick and Liz together just last week at the yacht club. Their affection for one another was contagious," Nell said.

Annabelle's smile appeared. "Nick's father, Nicholas, and my Joe were close fishermen friends. Did you know that?"

But Annabelle didn't wait for an answer. She knew they probably did, but she needed to talk.

"It's a tight bond we fishing families have. When my husband and his crew died in that horrible storm, Nick and Nicholas both showed up at our house immediately. Like, that very night. They knew, they understood. They ached with us. And they both, father and young Nicky, stayed here all night long, sleeping on the floor. Just so the kids and I weren't alone. That's the Cabot family in a nutshell. Nick's mother would have come, too, if little Nancy hadn't been sick with a cold. But from that night on, Liz and Nicky were friends forever after."

Nell was moved at the image. Although she didn't live in Sea Harbor when Joe Palazola died, she'd often heard the story of that stormy day when he and his fishing crew were buried in the sea. She knew how Annabelle pulled herself up and, with the help of friends and relatives, opened up a restaurant and supported her five children by making cinnamon rolls and the best omelets in all New England. The story was told often at bridge clubs and hair salons, taverns, churches, and probably in every small home in the Fishermen's Village.

Ben wrapped an arm around Annabelle's shoulders. "Nick was a good man."

Annabelle nodded. "It's hard to absorb it all. It was like that when Joe passed. I'd kissed him good-bye that morning before they left the shore, gave him his lunch box, and then by nighttime, he was gone from this earth. The same with Nick. I had seen him that very afternoon."

"You saw Nick last Sunday?" Nell asked.

"Yes. But just briefly. He, Liz, Bella, and other friends ran by for a brief peck-on-the-cheek kind of visit. Nick didn't stay long. He had a to-do list and not enough hours, he said. Gabby was bringing Squid home, Garozzo's Deli was bringing food, and he needed a shower. He was smelly from checking something on that boat. It's strange that those nonimportant items will now remain in my head for a long time."

Nell nodded. It was like watching a movie of Nick. Her own memories of that Sunday, spliced in with Annabelle's.

"He was happy," Annabelle went on. "Even kind of excited. No, not excited, just wonderfully satisfied. He took me aside and said he'd have a surprise for me if I behaved. But it certainly wasn't the heartbreaking surprise I got."

Annabelle turned toward Ben, her voice turning serious.

"Ben, I don't know if I'm putting you in an awkward position. If so, I know you'll tell me. Is there any progress being made in finding the person who did this?"

Ben paused, but only briefly. "I honestly don't know, Annabelle. You probably know most of what I do. The police are still questioning people and gathering evidence, looking for proof, not just reasons why someone might want to harm Nick. But facts. Something they might find in the rubble from the fire. Maybe a neighbor seeing something. Jerry isn't sleeping much. He's a good man, Annabelle, and he won't stop until he finds the person who did this."

Nell listened, aware of what Ben was doing. Bobby Palazola was Annabelle's nephew and she loved him dearly. She would have heard the rumors about the angry argument. Ben also knew sugarcoating things didn't, in the end, help anyone.

Annabelle nodded. "Rumors are like a pandora's box," she said. "Once you open it up, they fly all over the place."

"That's true," Nell said. "It must make the investigation even more difficult. People start looking at each other, trying to find some way to feel safe."

"It's suffocating," Annabelle said. She looked away for a minute, then took a deep breath.

"You both know that Lillian, or Ma Pal, as all the kids call her, is my sister-in-law, as well as Bobby and Bella Palazola's mother. Lil and I are closer than blood sisters. Especially after Joe died. Our families simply merged together. My five and her two. Sometimes the bunch of them weren't sure who was whose mother. Lil isn't doing well. And though Ocean View is a lovely, caring place, it's not immune to rumors."

"Birdie said the same thing," Nell said.

"I see Birdie there sometimes, visiting friends. I was there yesterday, and I heard someone in the hallway talking about Bobby and the argument he'd had. Bella had popped in to see her mother before she left town and she heard it, too. We both froze. We knew it was just Bobby blowing off steam. I've heard Bobby yell at Nick and other people, too, my whole life, and not once did it lead to murder. Lil and I could never figure out why, but those two were never good friends. Liz and Bella were befuddled, too. Especially Bella. She loves her brother. But those things sometimes happen in families—and we considered Nick family. We usually ignored it. Bobby's dad had a temper, too. I think Bobby was jealous of Nick. But who knows? Moms and aunts and friends don't know everything, unfortunately."

A waitress pushed open the kitchen door, carrying baskets filled with homemade miniature cinnamon rolls. Annabelle stopped talking and reached out automatically, her open palm hovering over the baskets to check that the rolls were warm. She smiled an okay to the waitress, then went on talking, her voice stronger now.

"I love those kids. Bobby probably cooked his first meal right here in my kitchen. Bella and my Liz were inseparable. And Nick? He was practically a member of our family, too. So trying to connect Bobby to his murder is wrong. No matter if they liked each other or not. It's rubbish. They are family."

Her strong words belied the sadness on her face.

"Annabelle," Nell said, touching her arm. But she didn't know what to follow that with. Not without resorting to empty words, like *it'll be okay* or *everything will work out.*

Because it might not.

Bobby had told the police he was home in bed that night. Alone. Essentially, he had no alibi, and he had lots of heavy baggage. None of them knew how it would work out, not if they were being honest.

Annabelle looked into the kitchen through the small glass windows in the door, then nodded to someone inside that she'd be there shortly.

She opened the service door to the deck and ushered them

outside to their table. Her welcoming smile was back. She waved to diners seated along the deck.

The table she always saved for Ben and Nell was at the end of the deck, close to the kitchen service door and the narrow deck steps that led down to the parking lot. It was the most private table and the one shaded by their favorite maple tree and a towering river birch. And the one they could sit at for an inordinate amount of time and not feel rushed.

Annabelle turned to go back to the kitchen, then turned around and returned to the table. She placed her palms on the table and leaned in.

"Thank you, both of you. For listening and for understanding. For being my dear friends." She looked down the deck out of habit, waved a welcome as the hostess seated a family of four at the far end of the deck.

When she turned back, her eyes were moist, but no tears fell. She lifted one hand to her cheek as if to catch any that might escape.

"I hate the rumors. I don't ache for Bobby. He's tough. And Bella is, too. She will be Bobby's biggest advocate." She paused again, and then she said, her voice unsteady, "But if rumors about him being connected in any way to Nick's death reach his mom, my dear Lillian, it will kill her."

Chapter 31

"Izzy, what's this?" Sam called out from the mudroom. He continued his work, digging around in a tall wicker basket that held everything from mismatched winter gloves to flip-flops and sunglasses.

Early-morning sunlight filled the small area, highlighting a pile of things Sam thought should all be thrown away, all except for his hat, which he was sure was in the pile somewhere.

"What's *what*?" Izzy called from the kitchen sink. Not getting an answer, she wiped her hands and walked to the mudroom, just off the kitchen. The small back-door entryway had cubbies and hooks holding jackets and coats and most other things, Izzy explained, that came inside from outside and didn't have an immediate home.

Izzy stared at the pile of things on the floor. Then she massaged her forehead, trying to rub away a restless night's headache. "This is a mess, that's what it is," she said. "What are you doing, Sam?"

"I'm looking for that great old hat that I wear on the boat. Ben and I are going over to the dock today."

"You're taking the *Dream Weaver* out?"

"Hope to. But Liz asked us to do a few things on Nick's boat first."

"Where is his boat? It's nice of Liz to handle things like that."

Sam nodded. "She said Nick had used it a couple of times over the weekend. He took it out at night and anchored it somewhere and it got scuffed up a bit."

Izzy frowned. "What night?" She vaguely remembered Nell mentioning something about his boat.

"What night? Why? Probably that Saturday. Liz doesn't know what'll happen to it, but she's keeping it safe until Nick's sister, Nancy, comes back."

Izzy tucked the thought away. "Okay. But why do you need that old hat? Wear your Celtics or Patriots or KU hat. You have a million in your closet."

"Can't do. I love that sailing hat. It's good luck to sail with it. But look at what I found instead. This thing. It's not mine. Nor will it ever be. What is it?"

He held up a Red Sox hat with a smiley face on the back of it. The bill of the hat was caked with dried mud. "It's awful in so many ways."

Izzy laughed. "What? You have a thing about smiley faces on Red Sox hats? Maybe they need a smile now and then?"

Suddenly she remembered. Not only seeing a sailboat that night, but the hat. She took it from him and looked at it more closely. "I know where this came from." She shook off some of the dirt. "I tossed it in there and then totally forgot about it. Is there anything else in there that looks odd?"

"Define 'odd.'"

"Not yours, not mine, not Abby's."

"Got that." He rummaged around, then pulled out a pair of sandals. "Do you have red sandals? These don't look familiar." He stood up and handed them to her.

Izzy brushed some sand off the sandals. "Oh, my," she murmured.

"What? Not odd enough?"

"Actually, they're very nice. And they're not red, they're
fuchsia. I hadn't noticed that when I picked them up. I've seen
them in a catalogue. But they're not mine. So, yes, I guess
they're odd."

She looked at them more closely, brushing off some sand.

"Where'd they come from?" Sam asked. "Cass?"

Izzy laughed. "No, they're definitely not Cass's. These are
expensive. Cass gets her sandals from the drugstore. These are
designer sandals. I dropped them in here one night."

"What night?"

"The night my aunt and uncle were here. It was . . . what?
Just last week? Oh, Sam, I am losing it."

She dropped the items and wrapped her arms around Sam's
neck. "I need a hug."

"Me too." He pulled her close.

"We need to do this more," she murmured into his ear,
breathing in the smell of his aftershave. She wanted to stay there
forever. Or for an hour or two, at least.

They stood there, absorbing the comfort of the other, until a
loud yell obliterated Izzy's wish and pulled them apart.

"Back in a minute," Izzy said, heading toward Abby's bedroom. "She's supposed to be getting dressed. A neighbor is taking her to the park."

When she returned from helping Abby find a pair of shorts,
she found Sam at the kitchen table. He had poured two cups of
coffee and sat, looking proud with his now-found sailing hat on
his head.

Izzy cocked her head to one side, assessing the muddy
brown hat, its frayed brim slightly lopsided. A white spot on it
showed her efforts to bleach out a gull's droppings from a few

years before. "I'm happy you found it, Sam. You look like Indiana Jones after a bad day—sexy in a roughshod way."

Sam smiled broadly. "I didn't know he sailed. But thanks for the compliment, Iz."

Izzy pulled out a chair and sat across from him. She looked at the items Sam had found and now displayed in the middle of the table, looking as if he intended to auction them off to the highest bidder.

"Okay, Izzy, fess up. Tell me again where these came from?"

"It wasn't a secret, I just forgot about it." She then filled Sam in on her late-night rescue of the items the night her aunt and uncle had been over. "We were both tired that night and I didn't want to get into it, so I just tossed them in the mudroom and forgot about them. Besides, I thought you'd accuse Aunt Nell and me of being voyeurs."

"Well, you were right about that. It's an interesting story, though."

"And here's another interesting thing." She picked up the hat. "I am ninety percent sure this hat belongs to Bobby Palazola. He had it on—or one like it—one day when Cass and I were over at Gracie's. And when Aunt Nell and I saw the couple down near the rocks that night, for a second I even thought the guy looked a little like Bobby. I pushed the thought away, though, since I had only just met the guy. And it was dark out."

Sam looked at the baseball hat again. "I'd say you're probably right that it's Bobby's. There can't be a lot of Red Sox smiley hats around."

"Oh?" Izzy looked at the hat and smirked. "You don't like it? I was thinking about getting you one."

"Ha! Bobby Palazola could get away with a hat like this. He's got a great sense of humor. People seeing it on his head would smile or laugh. On someone else's head, it would make them think the person was weird."

"You're right. I didn't think he was weird when I saw this ridiculous hat on his head."

"Okay, so now we have these items." Sam picked up the sandals that Izzy wished were her own.

She hadn't noticed the deep fuchsia color that night. And the beautiful way they were made—simple, but classy.

"See this?" she asked, leaning across the table and using one finger to trace a cutout design on the sandal. "Look. It's a *D* and *G*—Dolce and Gabbana."

"Hmm," Sam said. "Don't think I know him."

Izzy groaned.

"Whatever they are, it looks like you rescued them just in time," Sam said. "They still look wearable."

"They are definitely wearable. And probably would have floated. They're made of rubber. I can wash them off in the sink." Izzy pressed down on the sole. "They're expensive—for sandals, anyway. Even more than your Air Jordans. Whoever owns these has good taste."

"Hmm," said Sam, looking at the items again. "So we should probably return them."

"Return them?" Izzy looked from Sam to the shoes. Then back to Sam. "You're right, I guess we should. But I have no idea who owns them. I'm not sure an ad in the paper is appropriate. It could have been a lady of the night."

Izzy thought about the shoes, and of the graceful woman who had slid into the ocean like a mermaid.

Returning Cinderella's shoes required a knight.

And she was quite sure that Bobby Palazola wasn't a knight.

She wondered again about her instant impression that Bobby was in love with his boss. But Gracie was not the woman with the fuchsia sandals standing with him in Lovers' Surf's cozy cove.

Then she reached for her phone and texted her aunt.

Chapter 32

Ben and Nell had nearly finished their vegetable omelets, with Ben's special crisp bacon on the side, when a shadow fell across their table, followed by a person.

Izzy greeted them both with hugs, then sat down and looked into the basket. She pulled out the last mini cinnamon roll.

"Thank you for saving me one." She took a bite. "And you, Aunt Nell, thanks for responding to my weird text."

"Almost nothing you do is weird, Izzy," Nell said, then looked up and thanked Sophia, who was already pouring a cup of coffee for Izzy and clearing Ben and Nell's plates.

"Working on your knitting project at Annabelle's might qualify," Ben said. "If that *is* the reason you're meeting here?"

"Yes, well, no, maybe. Anyway, I have a message for you, Uncle Ben. Sam found his cherished sailing hat, without which he isn't safe to go near the water. He's heading out in a few minutes and will pick you up here."

"Good timing," Ben said. He pushed back his chair and leaned across the table, giving Izzy and Nell each a kiss on their cheeks. "I presume the other two are on their way? Sophia, our nice waitress, is going to be thoroughly confused when she comes back and sees I've turned into three attractive women."

"We'll set her straight," Nell said. "I hope the boat is easy to fix. And have a good day on the *Dream Weaver.*"

"Aye, aye," Ben said, headed down the deck steps to the parking lot, the thought of boats and sailing hurrying his steps.

"What's this about knitting?" Izzy asked.

"Oh, that's what I told Ben. There's always a stash in my tote, and it was easier than explaining anything else we might be thinking of. He understands knitting better than the four of us trying to figure out a murder."

"Well, sometimes knitting helps focus." Izzy took a drink of water. "I suppose we could have met somewhere else, but Cass was starving, so I hope you don't mind our hanging out here."

"No, this works fine. It's nice that Annabelle has left the deck tables farther apart, like she had spaced them during all those Covid months. It makes it private. I like it."

Izzy twisted around to look at the narrow wooden flower boxes Annabelle had made to ensure distance between each table. Just a few inches wide, the boxes, planted today with multicolored pansies, stood on chair-height legs, and separated one table from the next along the entire length of the restaurant deck.

"They're so pretty," Izzy said.

"Who's pretty?" Cass said, appearing at the top of the parking-lot steps.

Birdie was several steps behind her. "I hope Annabelle doesn't mind us sneaking up the back steps." The words came out in puffs as she tried to catch her breath. "But, oh, my, those steps have grown taller and more numerous since last I climbed them. Perhaps Annabelle will put an escalator out here for us."

Nell laughed. "Some customers actually do use the front door, though. Only two low steps there. It might be a cheaper option."

"Oh, shush," Birdie said, greeting Nell and Izzy with breathless hugs.

"I'm starving, you all know that, right?" Cass said, sitting down.

"Food is necessary for thought," Nell said, looking around for their waitress.

"I should have pocketed one of Sam's Donald Duck pancakes to take the edge off, Cass. He's trying to bring the whole Disney entourage into our kitchen."

"Annabelle's special omelet will do just fine," Cass said with feigned sweetness.

Sophia walked up, carrying a tray. "Got it, Cass," she said, setting down extra coffee mugs, a carafe, and a basket of rolls on the table.

"So, anybody else?" Once assured that the others were fine with coffee and rolls, Sophia disappeared through the kitchen service door.

"All right now," Birdie said. "Here we are." She looked over at Izzy with the wisdom of many decades of life in her eyes. "Izzy?"

"You're wondering why I had the nerve to disturb your morning?" Izzy asked. "A reasonable question."

Birdie chuckled. "Actually, it's quite possible that any one of us might have rounded us up today, had you not gotten there first. We're not comfortable these days. Nor is the town. No one is willing to let Nick Cabot's name slip into a file somewhere with an Unsolved sticker on it."

"Thanks, Birdie. My head's spinning. It's like a blender, mixing everything up until it's one mushy mess. Anyway, robbing you of your Sunday morning is a selfish thing. Basically, I want to sleep better so I'm not crabby in the morning."

They all chuckled, the mood lighter. Nell resisted giving her niece a hug. And then she didn't resist.

"We'll figure it out," Birdie said. "We'll do something, find something, that relieves our friends who are living under storm clouds. Ourselves included."

Cass, uncomfortable with the emotion floating around her, said, "Okay, let's get moving then. Let's figure this out." She nearly drooled at the cheesy omelet Sophia set down in front of her. She scooped up a forkful and looked around the table, waiting.

"Is there any news on the investigation?" Birdie asked Nell.

"Not much," Nell said. "They've looked into Nick's company over in Ipswich. Essentially, they've found nothing of interest. But the staff is missing him terribly."

"I wonder what they had hoped to find there," Izzy said.

"Financial things, I suppose. But it was an expertly run company. Employees were paid well. The manager, an older man, had been there since Nick started the company. He loved Nick like a son. Nick had people in place so that they didn't need him around all the time, Ben said. Another reason he could consider the mayoral race. No disgruntled employees. In fact, he'd set it up so employees owned stock in the company."

"My neighbor's daughter—Kyra Hanson—works there," Birdie said. "I can't remember what she does, but apparently Nick gave her the job. She's an assistant of some sort and she loves it."

Izzy looked at Birdie. "That's our old mayor's daughter, right? She babysat for us a couple times. Could you talk to her, Birdie? Office staff know everything. And even if they loved Nick, somebody didn't. The case gets colder every day."

"It would be a pleasure, and something I need to do, anyway." She pulled out her phone and typed in a note.

"The case is colder and the rumors are louder," Cass said.

"Have they found the gun?" asked Izzy. She made a distasteful sound. "It's so difficult to even say the word."

"No," Nell said. "Jerry doesn't think they will. Even if they do find it, if it's not registered or the serial number has been removed, it won't necessarily help them find out who owns it, or, more importantly, who used it."

"I still can't get my arms around it," Izzy said. "The fact that someone we know used a gun to kill someone we knew. Someone we liked very much. I don't think I know anyone who has a gun."

"Well, you probably do. You're just not aware of it. None of you knew that Harold had a gun," Birdie said quietly. "Let's accept the fact that someone we know who had a gun, and in a moment of terrible anger, when the brain isn't working right—" Birdie didn't finish.

That stilled their voices, but their minds were in overdrive, sorting through invisible lists, neighborhoods, motives. Who? And why?

Izzy sat back in her chair. "I agree that an angry person, losing control, is a possible scenario. And easier to digest, maybe. But it also could have been someone who went to Nick's house to kill him. That's blunt, but a possibility."

The rolls were passed around again and coffee refreshed.

Nell finally pushed her coffee mug away, realizing she had had enough caffeine that morning to last a week. She took a breath, then said, "So maybe we need to be more methodical about this and try to step away from our own emotions, as hard as that may be."

"Aunt Nell's right," Izzy said. "Here's what we have: two people who have motives to kill Nick, and their alibis hold about as much water as a colander. I think we need to at least talk about them first. To consider what we know, what we've heard."

She looked at Cass. "No matter how we feel about Bobby's innocence, Cass, it will help us out. Sometimes probing into suspects' lives a little bit can be like a shower, washing away any chance they could be guilty, and remove that awful cloud that's following them around."

"And the same goes for the mayor," Nell said. "It must be a difficult time for her. I'm feeling sorry I haven't gone by. Has anyone talked to her?"

For a minute, Birdie didn't say anything.

Nell looked over at her. "Birdie?"

"Yes," she said. "I went to see her. I was worried about her. We four have each other and others we're close to, but I don't know who Beatrice has to mourn with, to talk with. So I went, thinking maybe I could be that person. I was concerned about her and how she'd be handling all this. Being questioned, having to explain herself, her comments, her actions. It would be embarrassing, I thought. And not the kind of thing Beatrice would get through easily."

"And?" Cass asked.

"Well, she didn't really need me at all, although she was happy to see me."

"What do you mean?" Cass asked.

"I haven't quite processed it. But I will try to explain."

She took a long drink of water, and then laid out before them what she called a truly unusual experience with their esteemed mayor. She explained that their mayor was doing just fine. And then she filled in, as best she could, how their conversation went. Although, she added, it was not quite a conversation. More like a monologue, perhaps.

When Birdie finished, all were silent.

Izzy spoke first. "That's downright crazy," she said.

Nell put her hand over her mouth to hide an unwelcome smile at the ridiculous scene Birdie had described. Beatrice scolding the police?

But Cass and Izzy couldn't restrain laughter, causing a couple sitting at the table on the other side of the flower dividers to look over the flower box. They looked puzzled, then quickly went back to eating their omelets.

"I'm sorry," Cass apologized. "I know this is a serious discussion we're having, but that's so bizarre that it almost seems like proof of her innocence. I mean, what murderer could be that outrageously confident?"

Izzy took a deep breath. "A delusional one," she said, her smile gone.

They were all quiet for a minute, Izzy's comment bringing them back to the mayor. And to a murder.

"This is the hard part of all this," Izzy said. "Looking at friends and acquaintances as murderers is almost impossible. It's so hard to get past the part we see and like. The nice person who comes into my yarn shop and pretends to knit. The mayor whose been known to take an ill crossing guard's place when there's a need. But how do we know what any 'nice' person might do if pushed to the edge, whatever or wherever that edge might be? Beatrice is an intelligent woman. That behavior is crazy. Or else brilliant."

They were quiet for a moment, letting the thought settle and trying to envision their mayor, and their friend, as having other qualities that she kept well hidden.

Finally Cass spoke up. "I don't think Beatrice is crazy. I think that's who she is. And I also think she meant everything that she was heard saying all over town about Nick Cabot. That he absolutely should not be mayor, and that she would see to it that he didn't run. Or whatever her threats were. And she was true to her word."

Her comment stunned the others. Birdie slowly sipped her coffee, while Izzy stared at her iPad, as if telling it not to write Cass's comment down. Not yet, anyway.

Nell turned to Cass and asked, "Does that mean you think Beatrice killed Nick?"

"I don't know, Nell. But like Izzy said, we don't know what it takes to push someone over that edge. And we all agree that being mayor is who Beatrice is. Not mother, not someone who plays bridge with friends, not a woman who goes out to eat with friends. What does she do? She does *mayoring*."

"But being obsessive about one's job doesn't make that person a murderer," Nell said.

"I know that," Cass said. "But I think she truly meant that she would not permit Nick to run against her. How was she going to accomplish that? Well, that I don't know."

"Did she say anything else?" Nell asked, looking at Birdie and hoping she'd come up with a plausible explanation for Beatrice's attitude.

"Nothing of consequence, although there was one thing that surprised me, considering everything. And I hesitate to say it." She looked at Cass.

"It might be better if you did, Birdie," Nell said. "Just so everything's on the table."

"She told me that she was counting on all of us being on her election committee. She'd be having the first meeting soon, and she would be in touch."

"Oh, my," Nell said. She shook her head. She'd known Beatrice for years. But what didn't she know about her friend?

A sinking feeling was pulling her deep into the chair. She looked around the table at her dear friends. They all had the same weary demeanor, as if they'd exhausted one another. And that they were letting murder take over their lives.

It was time to knit.

Chapter 33

"There you all are," Annabelle said, coming over to their table, which was now filled with skeins of yarn, needles, and colorful knit panels, which were awaiting more rows. Without a word to one another, each of them had stashed in their bags the herringbone afghan project, still portable before knit together into a whole.

Izzy had asked Sophia to remove everything edible and drinkable from their table, including crumbs, coffee, and the basket of rolls.

Annabelle took in the soft knit rows, the colors of the sea melding together. "This is a first for the Sweet Petunia," she said. "And absolutely beautiful."

"Perhaps it shouldn't be," Izzy laughed. "Our brains died, Annabelle. The magic of knitting is pulling us and our thoughts back together. Better than paying a therapist, right?"

"Seeing you back here makes me smile. I love all four of you. It reminds me of the days when my own kids would gather out here and play Parcheesi or Clue."

"That's a great memory," Birdie said. "This deck holds many memories for all of us."

"That's my hope," Annabelle said.

Cass leaned in. "Not to change the subject, but in addition to letting us take over part of your dining corner, you have, somehow, someway, absolutely outdone yourself with the omelet I just ate."

Annabelle chuckled and picked up a napkin, then leaned over, wiping a bit of egg from the tip of Cass's chin.

"This is most definitely a full-service restaurant." Cass grinned. "It reminds me of when I begged my mother to let me live with you, Annabelle. In fact, come to think of it, I thought you *were* my mother sometimes. We all did. 'She had so many children, she didn't know what to do,'" Cass chanted.

"I remember that well. You and Gracie were often mixed in with my own mob and the cousins. And Nick's sister. Sweet Nancy was often here, too."

"Yes, she was. I noticed that Gracie and I didn't get the 'sweet' put before our names?"

Annabelle chuckled. "So, how is the big art auction coming along? I'm going to fool you all and donate something I've made this year. You didn't know I was artistic, did you?"

"Annabelle, nothing you do surprises me," Birdie said. "Elizabeth Hartley is coordinating it. She'll be pleased. A Palazola original could bring in big money."

"How is Elizabeth doing? Jane Brewster told me she's working at the association office now."

"She is. I think it'll be a good thing for her right now. Or we all hope so."

"I don't know her well, but she seems nice. I know she was fond of Nick. He brought her in for breakfast a while ago. She had recently moved back to town. Nick was single-handedly introducing her to everyone he knew, which, of course, is a cast of thousands."

"I don't think Elizabeth had much time to make friends when she was headmistress," Birdie said. "Nick was wonderful to do that."

"I never knew much about the Sea Harbor Day School thing. But I remember that Nick was upset over how some of the board members treated Elizabeth."

She paused, then looked at Birdie and Nell. "But I'm telling you things you know. You were on that board for a short while."

"We'd left the board before that happened. It's nice Elizabeth gave our town a second chance," Nell said.

"Nick was surprised she came back after she recovered. He had lingering guilt over how she'd been treated. He was determined that she be welcomed back appropriately."

Nell watched Annabelle's face as she talked. She was moving herself into a comfortable zone, a place where she could say Nick's name more naturally. Bringing him into their lives, no matter what amount of grief was carried in her words. Speaking his name was a healing thing.

"Anyway, that's how he and Elizabeth became friends," Annabelle said, finishing her thought. "I'm sure this is hard for her."

"For many people," Birdie said. "Including your Liz. We talked with her and Nick at the club last week. Liz mentioned that the weekend was a friends' mini reunion. A lovely one."

"Yes, it was. It was good to have them here." Her motherly demeanor returned. "Bella's been coming into town more frequently these last couple months. I don't always see her, but Liz does. She sometimes stays with her in that big house she and Alphonso have near you, Birdie. My grandchildren adore her. She'll be a good mom someday."

"Oh?" Cass asked. "Is there something you're not telling us, Annabelle?"

Annabelle smiled. "No prodding, Cass Halloran. Secrets are

hard to keep around this town. But she does have a special look about her."

"Have you ever counted how many Palazola relatives you have in this town?" Izzy asked. "I'm not a native, as Cass has told me a million times, but sometimes it's difficult keeping your very extended family straight. We don't have that in Kansas, where I'm from."

Annabelle laughed. "Sometimes I forget you didn't grow up here with all these kids, Izzy. Be assured you'd have been one of my favorites if you had."

"That's good to know, Annabelle. I'll remember to get here sooner in my next life."

Annabelle chuckled. "My sister-in-law did good with my niece and nephew, don't you think? One a television star and the other an amazing chef."

"She sure did. She must be very proud," Izzy said. "Bella is a star. She's finally explained to me on her weather show what atmospheric pressure is."

"Well, Izzy, since you brought Bella up, I'll brag a bit about her. She flew to Switzerland Sunday night to give a paper at an international meteorology conference. I think her real interest lies in climate and environmental research."

"Wow," Cass said. "That's great. Is she still there?"

Annabelle was quiet for a minute. "She is. She wanted to come back immediately, but Liz and Bobby both encouraged her to fulfill her obligation there. Jerry Thompson has talked to her, too, and gave the same advice. There's nothing she can do here. She'll be back in a couple days."

"Jerry called her?" Nell said. "That was gracious of him."

"Well, there was that. But Bella was with Nick all weekend. He has been in touch with all of them. Especially Bella and Liz."

She pinched a brown leaf off a marigold in the narrow flower box between two tables, then wiped her hands on her apron. "And Bobby, of course," she said, almost to herself.

Annabelle's eyes were thoughtful when she turned back to the four women sitting at the table. "It has been comforting having you all here today. You may make my deck your office any day you like."

"Are the rolls and coffee included?" asked Cass.

"Of course. And frankly, if I had my druthers, I'd pull up a chair, have Sophia bring me a cup of coffee, and sit quietly with you. You're all a comfort to me. Thank you for being here today."

Annabelle's eyes were moist as she looked at each of them, nodding, as if she might actually pull a chair over.

Instead, she threw them a group kiss and disappeared down the deck, meeting and greeting, before heading back into her kitchen.

"A good lady," Izzy said.

"And a very sad one," Birdie added. "Bobby is very special to her. And Nick was like a second son. What a difficult place for her—grieving for one man—with worry pressing down on her heart for another."

"She's always been the center of the Palazola family—all sides of it. And the Cabots, too. She mothered all of them," Cass said.

Birdie looked over at Izzy. She was pulling an iPad out of her tote bag. "I hope that means you're going to get us organized, Izzy. Our conversations this morning have been going in many different directions, and I'm not sure that's what you had in mind."

"Thanks, Birdie. I didn't really have anything concrete in mind. Frankly, I just needed to be with you. I haven't slept much the last couple nights. And last night, when I finally did fall asleep, I had a nightmare in which I was taking a law school exam and I didn't know the meaning of a pile of parts that were scattered on a table. Every single piece was a different shape. Straight, fat, crooked, narrow. Kind of like the way my thoughts are." She laughed at herself, then went on.

"The parts all looked familiar, like somehow I had met them before, but I had no idea where or how they fit together. Which family they belonged to. And the argument for the court case we were studying wouldn't make sense if I couldn't fit them together. And someone could die if I didn't.

"Then the parts started shrinking. So I frantically tried to shuffle them around, but every time I touched one, it wiggled away. There was a clock somewhere, ticking. I had to complete the puzzle before the bell rang or I'd flunk and I wouldn't graduate."

"Wow," Cass said. "And then?"

"Then I woke up with a terrible headache and a real need to talk to the three of you. I needed grounding. I needed you three."

Izzy looked around the table. They were leaning in, listening. And somehow they understood her, even though the dream made no sense.

"So. Thanks for coming and for not thinking I'm crazy."

"Well, we didn't exactly say that," Cass said. "But seriously, I'm guessing we all have the same headache. Different dreams, maybe. I almost never have law school dreams."

That lightened the mood a little.

"Oh, and there's something else." Izzy took a quick drink of water. "This morning, after I took a couple aspirin and drank a cup of coffee, this happened."

Izzy rummaged in her tote again and tugged out a cap and sandals. She dropped them on the table.

Birdie, Cass, and Nell stared at the bright fuchsia sandals and the slightly battered Red Sox cap. Then they looked at Izzy, curiously, as if she'd lost far more sleep than they had thought.

"Garage sale?" Cass asked.

Nell was frowning, staring at the table. "Izzy, are these what I think they are?" She picked up the cap and turned it around, revealing the smiley face. It seemed to be moving its mouth, grinning at them.

Cass took it from Nell. "Why do you have Bobby Palazola's cap?" she asked.

Izzy's brows lifted. "Ah, so you agree it's his."

"Sure it is. I mean, who else would have a baseball cap with a smiley face on it?"

"Sam's words, exactly," Izzy said.

"So, where did you get it?"

Izzy looked at her aunt. "You were there, too. Maybe you can explain it better."

Nell put the cap down. "I don't know how these got in Izzy's mudroom, but I do know where they were before the mudroom."

In a few sentences, Nell described what she and Izzy had seen near the so-called Lovers' Surf spot near the Perrys' house. She included the bit of drama—what looked like an argument between a man and a woman, the man stalking back up the hill, and the woman slipping out of her shoes and diving into the ocean, clothes and all.

"Have I forgotten anything?" Nell asked her niece.

"Just one thing. When we first spotted the couple, I thought the man looked a little like Bobby. But then I realized I had only recently met him. And that was for all of fifteen minutes. But maybe I was right."

"Was Gracie the swimmer?" asked Birdie.

"No. Even in the dark, we knew it wasn't Gracie."

"None of that scene speaks of Gracie in the slightest," Cass said. "Never in a million years would she swim in the ocean at night. She doesn't even like to do it in the daytime. And she doesn't need a beach to argue with Bobby. They can do it right there in the restaurant."

"That's logically true," Birdie said.

"Oh, and another thing," Cass went on. "There's no way Gracie would go down to that spot. It's been there forever, but it wasn't just for lovers. It's where all of us—Gracie included—

used to go to smoke when we were young and foolish and needed a hideout where our parents would never find us."

"If it wasn't Gracie, who was with Bobby?" Birdie asked.

"We couldn't tell," Nell said.

"She didn't remind you of anyone?" Cass asked.

Izzy shook her head. "Not really. She was a beautiful swimmer. Graceful as a dancer. And her left-behind sandals are not your drugstore specials." She picked them up and looked at them again, then dropped both items back in her tote.

Cass was drumming her fingers on the table, thinking. Finally she said, "I'm trying to figure out who might have been with Bobby. I can't put it together. Bobby being there. Arguing? What night was that?"

Izzy thought back. "It's weird how distorted time is. It seems a lifetime ago, but it was last week. Saturday night. The day before Nick died."

"Why wouldn't Bobby have been at Gracie's restaurant?"

"It was late," Izzy said. "Are you sure it couldn't have been an old girlfriend? Maybe someone who was trying to catch up with Bobby, seeing if the old flame was still there?"

"The woman probably wouldn't have turned into a mermaid if she was hoping to rekindle anything with Bobby," Nell said. "Although I'm not much of a judge at how things are done these days." She smiled.

Izzy laughed. "Also, it didn't seem to be that kind of argument, anyway, although I can't explain to you exactly what I mean by that. After stalking away, Bobby came back to the woman and hugged her."

Birdie shifted in the chair and looked at Cass. "Catherine, you look worried."

Cass ran her fingers through her thick hair. She'd had it cut shorter when Joey was born, but it still went a little wild when the wind blew, or she forked through it to calm herself down. She pushed it back in place. "I don't know, Birdie. I'm so sure that Bobby is innocent that anything strange like this worries me. I'm not sure which way it will fall if we try to find out more about it. Why was Bobby upset—if, in fact, he was? Why did she swim away? All those things. Will the answers help prove who killed Nick and, therefore, prove Bobby didn't? Or, maybe, will digging into this make it look worse for Bobby? The whole thing is strange."

"Well, Bobby could clear it up," Nell suggested.

"Probably not," Cass said. "Bobby isn't one for letting people into his head. Especially these days. And knowing you were watching him wouldn't sit well, either."

"We don't know if it has anything to do with Nick Cabot's death, Cass. It probably doesn't—"

"Right. I guess that's the thing. We don't know."

"It's like one of those strange parts in Izzy's dream," Nell said. "Some straight lines, some crooked or wavy. We just don't know which ones will fit. Or how."

Izzy looked over at Cass. "What do you think, Cass?"

"I guess we should consider it. Try to figure out who the woman is and if it amounts to anything, without Bobby thinking we're spying on him. Gracie might know. But"—Cass shrugged—"if not, and if we look like we're butting in where we shouldn't be, it will all come out in the wash, as my mother says. I don't quite know what that means, but it's what she would say."

Birdie watched Cass as she sorted through the thoughts in her head It was more difficult for her than the others when they talked about Bobby. They didn't have the history with him that she did.

"Izzy, maybe you should start typing things down in your tablet so we don't forget things," Nell suggested. "It's all so tangled. We might be able to eventually put some order to things. Hopefully."

"And it will be nice to cross it off when it turns out to be nothing," Cass said.

Izzy did as she was asked and typed in the little drama that took place below her deck.

"So one weird happenstance fully recorded," she said, looking up.

"Did you see the woman swim back to shore?" Birdie asked.

"No," Nell answered. "The ocean was calm that night. There was a sailboat, anchored not far out, and the moon was bright."

"Night swimmers usually head for the children's beach when they're coming in. It's well lit," Izzy added.

"Well, that's good, then," Birdie said. "One would otherwise be concerned."

But Izzy was thinking back to that night and to the graceful woman Bobby Palazola had walked away from. The woman had left expensive sandals behind and slipped into the vast ocean—alone. And she was a good swimmer.

Izzy wondered if they were missing a big part of the picture of why Nick Cabot was killed.

Chapter 34

The time had gone too fast, but the restaurant, in retrospect, hadn't been the best choice of places to try to work through their tangled thoughts.

It hadn't even been very good for knitting.

They headed down the deck steps to the parking lot.

"I think it's because our brains are trained to tell us that the Sweet Petunia is for eating wonderful omelets and laughing and seeing friends," Birdie said.

"You nailed it, Birdie," Cass said. "And if we'd stayed any longer, I would have gotten another one. Not at all good for the cholesterol."

"But it was worth it," Nell said. "It meant something to Annabelle to have us there. She also gave us some insight into the Palazolas. I think we learned more than we realize. We just need to pull it together."

"We got to know the Cabots better, too," Izzy said. "I agree with Aunt Nell. We talked about walking in Nick's shoes, and we did some of that today. I'm just not sure we walked far enough."

"So, what do we know now that we didn't know before?" Cass asked.

Izzy was standing next to Nell's car and she pulled out her iPad, resting it on the hood and flipping it open. "Hmm," she said. "Okay. Here are a few things. And maybe, at the least, it will help us sort out the mess in our heads."

"We wanted to learn more about Nick," Nell said.

Cass looked up immediately. "That reminds me of something I nearly forgot to tell you about. I talked to Nick's sister yesterday. I was so hungry and involved with the omelet I almost forgot to tell you I talked to Nancy. But she thought that Nick's personal life was going well. Like maybe in a romantic way?"

"Was she more specific?"

"Not really. She said Nick is private about things like that, but something was different. And she thought it had to do with that weekend."

"Annabelle said Nick mentioned a surprise for her, too. Maybe that was it?" Birdie suggested.

Still typing, Izzy said, "A surprise. That's curious. For Annabelle?"

"Well, that would be nice. We could all use a happy surprise these days," Birdie said.

Izzy nodded and kept tapping on her laptop. "We know he hung out with friends that last weekend."

"And many of us saw him that day. We know he was at the club, that he fixed his boat, that he went over to Annabelle's—" Nell began.

"Slow down, Aunt Nell," Izzy said as she clicked the keys rapidly.

"Gabby and Shannon saw Nick, too."

"Right," Cass said. "He'd ordered a meal from Harry's."

"Big enough for two?" Izzy looked up again. "Why? Who?"

"Elizabeth?" Birdie said. "But no. She would have mentioned

it. In fact, she said something about going for a walk in the park." She looked at Nell. "Do you remember what she said?"

Nell thought a little more. "Nick mentioned he needed to talk to her." She thought back, then said, "No, whatever it was, he was putting it off until his friends were gone. I don't think Elizabeth had a part to play in the weekend."

"We don't even know for sure he was having a guest. Shannon said he sometimes ordered a big meal so he'd have food for a few days. I don't think Nick liked to cook," Birdie said.

"But Shannon also talked about the table being set, the candles?"

"Well, I often light candles at my dinner table," Birdie said.

"You do?" Izzy said.

"Yes," Birdie said. "I mean, when it's just me, in the small dining area where Sonny and I used to eat. I have candles that I light, and I turn on music that both Sonny and I loved—classical guitar is a favorite, a little Segovia, Julian Bream. I sit at the table in the candlelight, looking out at the darkening sky. It's a special time."

Izzy, Nell, and Cass were silent, allowing Birdie some space. She seemed alone in the parking lot, her thoughts with the love of her life. And Sonny Favazza seemed as present as the iPad sitting on the hood of Nell's car.

They were all quiet for a moment, imagining Birdie alone in her intimate dining room.

Birdie looked up at the trees surrounding the parking lot. A mourning dove appeared on one of the branches. She smiled at it, then turned and looked at her friends.

"Now, why are you all just standing there?" she asked. "Where were we?"

They moved back to the iPad, their temporary office offering a slight breeze that rustled the leaves as it came through the trees.

"So we know Nick was with friends during the day Sunday,

he was at the yacht club, he stopped by Annabelle's, and he went home for an early dinner provided by Harry's deli."

"For himself and a guest. Or not," Birdie said.

Izzy glanced up once, then returned to her tablet, typing it in.

"And then?" Cass said. And then she stopped talking, her face in a grimace. "Oh, geesh," she said.

"What's the matter?" Izzy asked. "Are you okay?"

"No. Here's something I hadn't mentioned because it didn't seem relevant to what we're trying to figure out. But now I'm not so sure. Gracie and I had lunch with Nick a couple days before he died. Gracie wanted to talk about Marco Costa."

"Elena's husband?" Nell asked.

Cass nodded. "Right. He's been weird, Gracie said, and she's uncomfortable around him. He's kind of secretive, he'll only work part-time, although Gracie thinks he has another job that seems to be paying him very well. He was secretive about it. And she just has this bad feeling about him, but Bobby really appreciates the guy's help. And I know from working with him that he probably is a big help. He does know a lot about fish and fishing. Nick knew him, too."

"How?"

"Fishermen's Village. I gathered from what Nick *didn't* say that Marco may have been in trouble a few times. Pete and I had heard rumors about him, too. It was clear that Nick took Gracie's concerns about Costa seriously and wanted to check into something. He couldn't get to it until the first of the week because his weekend was full, but he wanted to get some more information for Gracie. And he wanted Marco out of Gracie's kitchen."

"He was going to talk with Gracie the day after he died," Nell said, giving voice to what they were all thinking. The timing of Marco's hypothetical involvement was clear.

"Why didn't Gracie just fire him right away?" Izzy asked.

"Because the guy seems to be a big help to Bobby—he does

know a lot about fish. And Nick was aware that Bobby can be difficult. He didn't want an instant firing to create more problems for Gracie. But bringing in some clear reasons for firing him, and showing Bobby that he'd be better off without him, would make it easier for Bobby to let him go."

Izzy sighed. "And you think Marco heard all this."

Cass nodded. "I didn't connect it to Nick's death until now. I've been worried about Gracie's restaurant problems, and that's where my thoughts have gone. I haven't been connecting all the dots, or any dots, I guess."

"I have that problem sometimes, too, dear," Birdie said softly. "Tangled thoughts. But saying them out loud sometimes does the untangling for you."

They were all tired of thinking and talking, but Birdie's voice sometimes brought a soothing clarity to situations. No matter what she was saying.

"You're right, Birdie," Cass said, giving Birdie a grateful nod. "I have a mess of thoughts in my head. Here's why I think there might—or might not—be a connection."

The image came back to her immediately, and she related in vivid detail the man who had been standing behind the ficus trees in Lucky's Place listening to Nick's possible plans for his future.

Chapter 35

Cass pulled out of Annabelle's parking lot, with Izzy in the passenger seat.

Izzy looked over at her. "Cass, I have an idea. Instead of dropping me at home, would you mind making a detour? It's this Marco thing. It's bothering me. Do you really think he heard the whole conversation? Maybe he just didn't like Nick and that was the look you saw. It didn't sound like Nick was crazy about him."

"That's true, but no, I'm sure he heard. I could hear the conversation going on in the booth on the other side of us. And he was closer."

"Does he know you saw him listening?"

"I don't think so."

"Could you read his expression?"

"It was like, *if looks could kill.* He was upset."

"It doesn't make much sense to me. Who would kill someone to prevent him from possibly being fired from a part-time job in a small restaurant kitchen?"

"By itself, that doesn't make sense," Cass agreed. "Nick

chose his words carefully, but I got the feeling that he knew more about Marco than he was saying. He wanted to double-check some facts before he disrupted things at Gracie's."

"What kinds of facts?"

"It might have had something to do with whatever else Marco was doing while working part-time for Gracie and Bobby. But whatever it was, he wanted Marco gone from the Lazy Lobster," Cass answered.

"Here's another possibility. What if there's a reason he needs to stay in that job at Gracie's? It's kind of strange he keeps the job at Gracie's, anyway, if his goal is to get rich," Izzy added.

"It is definitely strange. For some strange reason, he seems to be making decent money from somewhere else."

"*Somewhere,*" Izzy repeated.

Cass was silent, putting pieces in place. Then she stopped at a stoplight and looked over at her passenger. "Izzy, where in the heck are we going?"

"Sorry. I don't know if this will shed light on anything, or end up as nothing. But a few of us now have seen Marco at that old bank building. I'd like to run by there again. It's Sunday, so it might be all locked up, but maybe not."

"Let's go for it," Cass said, not sure of how the dots were being connected, but willing to try. She took a couple of turns and pulled into a parking space in front of the old bank. Izzy sat still for a minute.

"Was Marco just hanging out when Nick saw him?" she asked Cass.

"He was outside. Smoking."

They sat in the car another minute, looking at the now-attractive building and how the sunlight reflected off the polished LA BANQUE sign.

A couple of trucks were parked in the wide drive next to the restaurant—the space that had once allowed customers to access the old bank's drive-through window. A painter was carrying some tarps through the door, held open by a brick, while another man was rummaging around in the truck's cargo bed, pulling out a ladder.

"If one of these guys is the same painter who was here before, we're in luck. He was friendly. Want to go inside?"

"Of course."

The painter met them at the door. He stepped aside and balanced his ladder against the door. He smiled and motioned for them to go on in.

"Nice to see you again," he said. "It's Izzy, right?"

Izzy laughed. "Yes. Izzy Perry. You must think I'm casing the place."

"It's a mighty nice place to look at, I admit. Go on in. They don't mind. I'm the supervisor today, anyway. Name's Murray, by the way."

The place was busier than when she'd visited with Sam on Saturday afternoon, before the puppet show. More painting was going on, sanding, pounding, measuring, and lights being added above the bar.

"I can see you fellows don't rest on Sunday," Izzy said.

"Right," Murray said. "It always happens at this point in a project. I like it."

"So it's all workmen today?"

"Mostly. The head contractor isn't here, so I'm sort of keeping track of things. There're a couple of other guys here—"

Izzy followed his look toward a hallway, where she spotted two men walking toward the back part of the restaurant.

"Are they the guys we talked to the other day?"

"These men? No. One of them is part of the group that owns this place. He's dropping off some things the contractor asked for. Business cards and contact information. We've had people come in with questions about the place—reporters and others.

This makes it easier for us to get our work done. They can contact the right people."

"That makes good sense."

"When you were here a few days ago, you talked to Tony, right?"

"Right. What's his job here, anyway?"

The painter laughed. "Tony? Well, he's kind of a blowhard, but he does have a connection to the place. His brother's the new chef—but he probably told you that."

"How did you know?" Izzy laughed.

"Tony checks on kitchen things for his brother. The chef comes in sometimes, too—he's a very particular guy, I suspect. But I hear he's won awards, that sort of thing."

"Have you met him?" Cass asked.

"Just in passing. He doesn't talk much. Rumor has it the guy gets paid megabucks, so he'd better be good, right? Anyway, he works in another restaurant run by the same folks who invested in this one. Tony's his errand runner, far as I can tell."

"Tony was with another guy the other day. Marco Costa?" Izzy asked.

"Yeah. He's in here often, too."

"He used to be on my fishing crew," Cass said.

Murray looked at Cass. His eyes widened. "Halloran Lobster, right?"

Cass laughed. "You got it."

"I knew I'd seen you before. I painted your office when you and Pete remodeled it, when, five years ago?"

"That's right," Cass said, smiling. "I remember you now. Great to see you again, Murray. You did a great job."

"It's Cass, right? I enjoyed working with you guys." Murray grinned as he talked, as if he'd just met a long-lost friend. "Okay, so what can I help you with?"

"We were talking about Marco Costa?" Cass said.

"That guy, yeah," Murray said.

"From what he said the other day, I wasn't sure if he worked here or not?" said Izzy.

"Work here? I don't know about that. But he comes around when the head chef is here. And he's often here with Tony. But now that you mention him, he was here earlier today waiting, when I unlocked."

"On a Sunday? Why?"

"He said Tony was supposed to be here. He ended up dropping something off in the kitchen for him, then left."

"So maybe he and Tony work together?" Cass asked.

"I don't think so. But that's all above my pay grade. Maybe he's been hired for something that I wouldn't know about." He laughed. "As painters, we're around a lot, so I do know some of the ins and outs. But hiring? Don't know anything about that."

The painter was scratching his head, as if he realized the whole thing was a little odd, and he suddenly wasn't sure how Marco fit into the big picture. Or why he was hanging around so much.

Izzy looked again toward the wide hallway. "You mentioned that one of the owners was here. Do you know where they went? It'd be nice to meet him."

"There's a temporary office off that hallway. That's where they were headed."

He looked around, saw that things were getting done, and waved for the women to follow him. "Come on, I'll show you."

As the trio turned and started down toward the long hallway, the two men were walking out the back door to the restaurant parking lot. Izzy hurried back, but was too late. She watched them through the door window as the car drove off.

"Well, I guess that wasn't meant to be," Murray said. "Sorry."

"No problem. But you mentioned that they were dropping off some contact information?"

Murray glanced into the open office door, then walked on in. Izzy and Cass followed.

The room looked more like a storeroom than an office, with boxes piled against two walls and a stack of smaller packages on a makeshift desk.

Murray followed her look. "Yep, they left it all here, just like they said. Mr. Riley, the one who's a part owner, was dropping off business cards for people just like you." Murray looked as pleased as if he'd made the cards himself.

"I was told to give these to people who had questions. You two fit the bill." Murray chuckled and walked to the table, opening one of the cardboard boxes. He pulled up several stacks of business cards. "Here, take a few."

He handed a couple to each of them, looking down at the cards as he did. "There are phone numbers and emails on there if you need them. It looks like there are several different ones — the LLC folks' numbers and names. Addresses. A general one for the restaurant. And the chef even got his own card. I guess that makes sense. Mary Pisano was already in here saying she wanted to do a piece on him for her column."

They laughed, knowing that the energetic columnist for the Sea Harbor paper would get the interview before any of the reporters — and whatever she wrote would be colorful.

Murray started walking away, then turned around and pointed to a double door across the hall. "Hey, that's a side door to the kitchen. Don't know if you saw it the other day or even if you care about it. But you're welcome to take a peek if you want."

"Thanks, Murray," Cass said. "It's been great seeing you again, and I'll be calling you for a fresh paint job soon. The office is looking a little dull."

Murray chuckled. "About time, Cass. Ring me anytime." He disappeared back into the main restaurant room.

Izzy pushed open one of the wide swinging doors, looking into the cavernous kitchen.

Cass followed slowly.

Izzy glanced back at her. "I know. It feels weird, doesn't it? I wonder if we should be in here."

"Well, there's probably nothing we can walk off with." Cass looked at the enormous stoves and ovens and stainless-steel sinks big enough to bathe in. It was so shiny, it was blinding as sunlight poured in through several large windows.

"It's not that different from Gracie's. Except for being twice as big. And not as welcoming. But you've seen one fancy restaurant kitchen, you've seen them all, don't you think?"

Izzy laughed. "I agree."

"Let's go," Cass said. She spotted a door near the back of the room. "That probably leads outside to the trash cans. Let's sneak out and leave Murray to his painting. I remember when he painted our place. He was a great painter, but he loved to chat."

The door opened readily, but instead of facing the garbage cans, they found themselves in what looked like a chef's office. Roomy, with a couple of leather chairs, still wrapped in plastic, which formed a small sitting area. Opposite were floor-to-ceiling bookcases holding boxes of cookbooks and several framed awards. A skylight filled the office with light, cascading down on a mahogany desk.

"Now, this is something Gracie's kitchen doesn't have," Cass said, looking around. "It's nice."

Izzy checked out the desk. It was the only thing in the room free of dust, with pencils and scratch pads, envelopes, an empty water bottle, and stacks of papers scattered on top. Someone had been working at it.

Izzy frowned, then walked closer. She picked up a sheet of paper from the top of the stack and looked at it, then another. She tried to open the desk drawer, but it was locked. "Hey, Cass, look at these. I think they're recipes."

Cass looked over her shoulder. Then she walked around

Izzy and picked up several sheets of paper. "Yes, they are most certainly recipes." She took a deep breath and looked at Izzy. "But they are someone else's recipes, not La Banque's."

They left soon after, hoping they wouldn't run into anyone, and feeling like a detective duo in a crime show, and headed over to Gracie's Lazy Lobster and Soup Café.

Chapter 36

The deck at the Ocean's Edge Restaurant was quiet when Nell and Birdie walked out. Two wide deck chairs facing the water welcomed them.

"That short walk through Ravenswood was exactly what we needed," Nell said. "My body feels like it belongs to me again."

Birdie felt the same way. The two slightly sweaty women had the deck almost to themselves, save for a few tables of early-dinner or late-lunch guests, and several couples standing at the railing, enjoying the view.

No sooner had they settled into a couple of deck chairs than a waitress appeared with two glasses of iced tea.

"Compliments of the boss man," the waitress said with a grin. "He saw you come in and thought you looked like you needed it. Enjoy," she said, and disappeared inside.

Nell sat back, sipping her tea and looking out over the water. "If we look carefully, we may see Sam and Ben out there." She shaded her eyes against the late-afternoon sun. The breeze was gentle but with enough heft to satisfy sailors who were regaining their sea legs after the long winter.

"Sailing is such great therapy for those two," Birdie said. She reached down and pulled out a half-finished sock she was knitting for Gabby. "It's like what knitting is for us."

Nell looked over at the bright orange and green balls of yarn that Birdie's quickly moving fingers were turning into a sock. It was magic. And therapeutic. As she reached over to feel the soft yarn, another waitress, this one with bright purple accents in her silky blonde hair, and her apron looped over one arm, rushed over to their chairs.

"Oh, Birdie. I was so glad to get your call. It's been such a long time. I hope it was okay to meet here."

Birdie smiled and, reached, hugging her young friend enthusiastically. "And this is a perfect place to visit. Your text response to mine was so quick, and now here you are. You look wonderful. You know Nell Endicott, don't you?"

"Of course I do." She greeted Nell warmly and sat down in the empty chair. "My dad and Ben love to sail together. And Sam Perry, too. It's like this secret club those sailors have."

"You're absolutely right about that, Kyra. In fact, Sam and Ben are out there right now," said Nell.

"I'm so glad this worked out. Especially today, when we needed a cool breeze and a cold iced tea. But most especially, a chance to see you, Kyra. But when did you get a second job?" Birdie asked.

"I only come in on weekends when Don is short staffed. He's an old friend of my dad's, too. I like coming in here if I have a free night."

"Haven't I also seen you working at the yacht club?" Nell asked.

"Right. Not often, but I sometimes waitress there on weekends, too, if Liz needs extra help. She's so great. I'd scrub the toilets for her if she needed me to."

"Liz is lovely," Birdie said. "And going through a hard time these days, as I'm sure you are, too."

"*Nick,*" Kyra said, the single word carrying on deep sadness. "She and Nick were so close."

Birdie nodded.

"That kind of friendship is almost sacred," Kyra said. "I haven't seen Liz this week. My mind's not been working at full throttle, but I know she's devastated. And Bella Palazola . . ." Her voice fell off and her eyes immediately filled with tears.

Birdie reached out and touched her hand.

Kyra nodded. "It's hard on my dad, too."

"It's difficult for many of us," Birdie agreed.

"Nick was my boss. My friend, too. I loved him. We all did. Our whole company did. It's . . . it's . . ." She wiped the moisture away with a tissue Birdie handed her. "I'm sorry to react like this. It's still so raw. Nick was amazing, and this whole thing—I can't even give it a name—it's just not real. No one would kill Nick. They say someone did, but it doesn't make any sense. This was such a great time in Nick's life. He was really happy. Not that he was unhappy before, but I don't know. Something was different about him the last couple weeks. And in a wonderful way. It was contagious. We felt it in the office."

"How was he different?" Nell asked.

"It's hard to explain because Nick was a good-natured guy most of the time. But recently he seemed happy in a more settled way. Like a mixture of contentment and joy, mixed up together. Like his life was coming together for him. Does that make sense?"

"It does," Nell said. "You're insightful, Kyra. That's such a nice description."

"It was the talk of the office. You know, watercooler talk. We even teased him about it, which, I suppose, was our subtle way of trying to pry into his private life."

Birdie chuckled. "And I'm guessing you didn't get far. Nick didn't seem to be the sort that talked about himself much."

"Right. He was private for sure. But he could take a joke, too, and he didn't seem to mind our teasing. In fact, recently he even seemed to enjoy it." Kyra smiled, seeming to be thinking of the happy Nick.

"Could he have been opening a new store?"

"It wasn't that kind of happiness. New stores put him in a good business mood, not this other kind. I don't know, we could have made it all up, our imaginations going crazy, but we had the feeling he was unusually happy about his personal life. And in a really nice, happy way."

"Had you heard that Nick was considering running for mayor?" Birdie asked. "Could that have affected his mood at work?"

"Hmm. I'd heard that. And I knew Nick was talking to my dad about it."

Nell and Birdie were quiet, remembering back to when Kyra's father had been mayor of Sea Harbor. Stan Hanson had been a well-loved and respected town official before he re-signed, passing his position to Beatrice Scaglia.

"My dad liked Nick a lot," Kyra said. "He didn't tell me what advice he had given him, but my dad loved being mayor, so I suppose he passed that along to Nick. It could have af-fected his mood. We—meaning the talkative office crew—would never have considered that being mayor would make anyone excited."

"You don't sound convinced."

"No, I'm not. But I admit that it's partially because in all our ripe, romantic minds, his mood was something far more fun. We had him getting married to a gorgeous woman and having beautiful kids."

"Nick?" Nell smiled.

"I know. That wasn't exactly his reputation. But I think that was changing, and we loved seeing that new smile he brought into work with him recently. And we also clung to our fanciful dream of why there was that lightness in his step, which matched his mood far better than running for mayor."

"Had you picked anyone out for him?" Birdie asked, happy to see a hint of a smile on Kyra's face.

"Yes." Kyra responded with a whole grin. "*Me*. But barring that, I have my thoughts . . ."

"I understand Nick had plenty of women friends," Birdie said.

"He sure did. We used to kid him about some of his friends, trying to convince him they would be nice 'long-term' friends. We all thought it was a shame Liz Santos got married. We told him that."

"What did Nick think about that?" Birdie chuckled.

"He laughed. And he knew why we thought that way. He teased that if he and Liz hadn't been able to remain such great friends after she got married, he'd probably have gone to the priesthood."

Nell chuckled, remembering Nick's comment at the yacht club. He had been Liz's best man at that wedding.

"I can't quite imagine that," Birdie said.

"Right? We all laughed pretty hard. And then he told us that he was working on having Liz Santos cloned. And he said something interesting, that, of course, we all mulled over. He said he was happy he hadn't gone the priesthood route because sometimes 'one can suddenly become aware of what has been right in front of you all along.'"

"I imagine that gave way to plenty of talk," Birdie said, tucking the comment away.

Kyra nodded. "It did. And we all believed that might be exactly what had happened. Or at least what we hoped for."

They were all quiet for a few moments, content to imagine a happy Nick.

Then Kyra spoke again, a concerned look on her face. "Speaking about Nick's friends made me think of a woman I'd nearly forgotten about. I just this minute realized that we were all so caught up in our own feelings at work that none of us thought of her, and I know she must be very sad about all this. Nick was a good friend to her when she came to town."

"Elizabeth Hartley?" Nell asked.

"Yes. Do you know her?"

"We do," Birdie said.

"We liked her," Kyra said. "She dropped into the office often, and she always surprised us with donuts or candy or something special. A nice lady. She'd surprise Nick with little goodies, too. I know she's feeling bad about Nick. I don't think she knows a whole lot of people around here. I should have called her—"

"I think she would like a call from you. It would be a connection to Nick. And that's comforting."

"Thanks, Birdie. I'll do that. I have her contact info at the office. She was crazy about Nick."

She tapped a reminder into her phone.

"What exactly do you do at the Cabot Company?" Birdie asked. "I suspect you are very good at whatever it is."

"Thanks. It's an easy company to be a part of. We're a tight-knit group. We all have stock in the company, which helps the closeness, I think. But what do I actually do there? Well, that's hard to describe. There wasn't an open position when Nick hired me. I think it was a mercy hiring." Kyra smiled. "Anyway, he made up a title for me. I was the IA—indispensable assistant, definitely not to be confused with AI, he joked. I do a lot of different things—arranging business trips, making reservations, plenty of computer work. Research, which I love. Phone calls. Every day is different and almost always interesting."

"Are you working on any interesting things now?" Nell asked.

Talking about her job seemed to be soothing for Kyra, relaxing her.

"Well, Nick asked me a couple weeks ago to check his calendar for the summer. He wanted to be here when his sister came for her family vacation. And also when he'd have time to go to Porto, where she lives. He might've taken a friend with him later in the summer or early fall."

"Was that unusual?"

"Going abroad? No. He visited his sister regularly. But taking someone with him was. And he threw into the research some additional places, like Paris, that he might add on to the trip. But it was in the research stage, he reminded me. Just in case I had nothing else to do.

"But that got me thinking romantic thoughts again. And last week, all of us at work went back to imagining who would be sitting in that other airplane seat. Or strolling along the Seine with him.

"'Marriage in the future?' I teased him. And he only laughed, not giving me the usual 'Ha, who'd have me?' comment."

"Do you think you knew whoever the person might be?" Birdie asked.

Kyra shrugged. Then smiled.

They both held back from asking more questions. But Kyra, as if sensing the unasked questions, or maybe just needing to talk about her boss, continued speaking.

"It was that Friday, I remember. He wasn't working that day—he was getting together with friends for the weekend— but he thought he should check in. He said he'd be in on Monday.

"*Monday,*" she repeated. Kyra took a deep breath and let it out slowly. "And then that day never came."

Her eyes filled again. She turned away and looked out at the water.

Finally she turned back. "I went in that Monday and sat at my desk, just wanting to feel close to him. I picked up the mail, tearing open envelopes, just out of habit. There was one . . ."

She stopped for a minute, as if holding back something personal she found, then seemed to be unable to hold it back. "He'd had a ring made, Birdie. A beautiful artistic ring from an artist he knew. I didn't tell anyone else. But it just came out today. Like I had to share it with someone or I'd burst. I'm so sorry."

Her tears were flowing freely, and Nell pulled tissues from her bag, handing them over.

"I'm so sorry for ruining your peaceful Sunday," Kyra apologized.

"Maybe you've saved it, my dear," Birdie said. "It helps Nell and me, too. Losing a friend is hard. And in a manner like this, it's unfathomable. We need each other."

"See, Birdie?" Kyra said, shaking her head back and forth. "You're doing it again. Just like those skinned knees you helped heal when I was a kid Rollerblading on your driveway. You hugged me and wiped away tears. And now you've helped my damaged spirit. At least for a minute or two. I love you."

Kyra looked away, across the water, wiping her eyes. Finally she stood, looking back at Birdie and Nell. "You two have saved my Sunday, too. Thank you."

Nell and Birdie watched her disappear across the deck. Silent for a long time as they thought about yet another life Nick had touched. And about another part of Nick's life that had been shared with them.

Chapter 37

The restaurant was dark when Izzy and Cass walked up to the front door. Then they noticed the sign. *Sunday.* The restaurant was closed.

"Geesh, Iz. Where are our minds?"

"It's been a long day."

Cass *humphed,* and when she couldn't get ahold of Gracie, she left her a text.

"Our minds are messed up," she said again. "We may have created an elaborate diversion here, just to get away from the fact that there's a murderer wandering around Sea Harbor, probably smiling at people, maybe bagging their groceries, or babysitting for someone. It's making me crazy. Thinking about a restaurant's problems is more tolerable than thinking about a murderer."

"Who knows that they're not connected?" Izzy reached into the pocket of her jeans to be sure she still had the business cards Murray had given them.

Quiet followed Izzy's remark as they climbed back into Cass's car.

Finally Cass asked, "Where are we going now? If there's somewhere else on your list, please don't let it send us to jail."

"Are you free?"

"As a bird. Danny and Joey are at his parents' being spoiled for the day."

Izzy checked her watch. "Let's see if Nell's home. She mentioned earlier that Gabby was having friends over, and Birdie was going to go to her house to give the kids some freedom to be loud. Even Ella thought it'd be good if she left."

"That's probably because Ella wants to be right in there with them, doing whatever they do. Gads, I feel old."

"It's the day."

"No, it's the years." Cass looked up and saw that they were pulling up in front of the Endicott house.

They found Nell in the backyard, a bucket of mulch beside her.

"I wanted to get this weeding done before it gets dark," Nell said, looking up and smiling. She was kneeling beside a dappled willow hedge that surrounded her guesthouse, at the back of the property. The rich red stems of the willows were showing new growth.

"We thought maybe you were preparing for guests." Izzy looked at the guesthouse, a cozy cabin that had been hers many times when she spent her college breaks with her aunt and uncle.

Nell smiled. "Well, summer is coming. I think there's a silent law here that says when you have an empty guesthouse and live a block from the water, the cottage needs to be filled. Maybe by one of your brothers, Iz. Or your parents. I've sent out the yearly reminder that they are welcome."

"I hope they come. That would be great."

"Enough about the future. Tell me what you two have been up to since leaving Annabelle's? Birdie and I took a walk and had a very interesting talk with Kyra Hanson. Birdie is coming over shortly."

Nell pushed herself up from the ground and brushed the dirt off her knees without waiting for an answer. "You two look thirsty," she said. "Let's go inside."

They walked the flagstone path up the long backyard to the deck, talking mostly to Nell's back as they gave a brief account of where they'd been that afternoon. And that they'd learned something new about Marco Costa.

Nell paused as she started to open the deck door. "Elena's husband?"

"Yes," Cass said. "He also works in Gracie's kitchen."

"Yes, I heard that." Nell knew from the tone in their voices that whatever they wanted to talk about wasn't anything her mind could take in at that minute. Not until she had a moment alone in the shower to wash off the troubling thoughts crowding her head.

She pulled off her gardening gloves and dropped them on the counter. "I need a quick shower. But not a word about Marco until I come back." She hurried up the back stairs, stripped off her muddy jeans and tee, and jumped in the shower.

When Nell came down to the kitchen a short time later, her hair damp and cheeks flushed, Izzy had taken some Brie out of the fridge and put it on the island with a basket of crackers. Then she'd used the den printer to print some photos from her phone. Cass had done her part, uncorking a bottle of cabernet she'd found on Ben's wine rack and bringing it, along with several wineglasses, to the kitchen island.

Nell looked at each of them. "You two look concerned about something. Or sad. Or tired."

"All of the above," Cass said, sitting up on a stool near the island. Izzy stood beside her, looking down at the copies she'd just made. "They're a little blurry," she murmured to herself.

"The whole town is blurry," Nell said, pouring three glasses of wine and sliding two across the island. She glanced over at the papers Izzy was looking at.

"What are those?" She put on her readers and reached over for one, holding it up to the light. "Is this a recipe?"

In a few words, Izzy explained their trip and conversation with their painter friend.

"He insisted, sort of, that we check out the kitchen," Cass said. "So we did."

"It looked like any other new restaurant kitchen," Izzy said, "not that we've seen that many, but we did find the small kitchen office interesting."

Nell opened her mouth, but before she could say anything, Izzy went on. "We thought the door would take us outside, not into an office, so we weren't trying to snoop."

"But sitting in full sight on a desk was a homemade recipe book," Cass said quickly. "Not a book exactly, but photocopies of Bobby Palazola's recipes. Dozens of them."

"We didn't take them," Izzy said. "You're looking at photos I took."

Nell looked at the photos again. "Are you sure these are Bobby's? And why would they be over there?"

"That's the question," Cass said. "I've seen Bobby's recipe book. These are photos of the cover and a couple pages." She pointed to something in the photo. "See the doodles? And this one?" Cass pulled out another photo, this one of the handmade cover with Bobby's unmistakable scribble beneath the word *menu*. "Bobby keeps this locked in the desk drawer. He calls it his gold bar. Marco Costa would know where the key is, because he needs access to it sometimes. In fact, I saw him looking at the book the other day. All the recipes are Bobby's own creations, along with some that are his remake of the classics. The uniqueness is what makes his recipes so special. These are the ones he's won awards for."

"We think Marco copied them and gave them to his buddy Tony at the La Banque restaurant."

"Why would he do that?"

"We're not sure. Tony's brother is the chef."

"But—" Nell looked at the printout again.

A ruckus at the front door announced that Ben and Sam were back. Birdie, following them, was the surprise.

All of them carried small white boxes with metal handles and THAI ORCHID printed on the side.

Izzy slid her photocopied sheets out of the way as they put the boxes on the table. In minutes, the aromas of fresh ginger, garlic, lime, and curry filled the kitchen.

"You're sunburned, Sam," Izzy said.

"It's the 'first time out burn,'" he said, walking around the island and planting a kiss on her cheek. "But well worth it. It felt liberating being out there, engine off, letting the wind have her way with the sails. Energizing and peaceful all at once. Freeing the spirit."

They all seemed to be listening to Sam as if he were a preacher and they were his flock. Izzy leaned over and returned the kiss.

"That sounds just about right, Sam," Nell said. " 'Freeing the spirit.' I like that."

Even though nothing had been planned to bring them all together in the Endicott kitchen, no one seemed surprised that they'd become a gathering, or that there were more take-out cartons than there were people.

Ben pulled cold beers from the fridge and handed one to Sam. "Should we eat first or confess?"

No one was quite sure who Ben was looking at.

"What?" Izzy asked. "Confess what?"

"Confess whatever is making you look frustrated. Or upset. All of you. Or maybe it's something else? I can't quite read the looks."

"Things," Izzy said.

"Would food help?"

"It's not even dark. It's too early to eat," Nell said.

"Well, I'm starving," Cass said.

Cass's decision seemed to go down more easily with the group, except for Nell, who looked back at the photos of the recipes with a frown and a dozen questions.

In minutes, plates were placed on the long table near the windows, along with napkins, silverware, serving spoons, and a long line of white take-out boxes.

They sat around the table, passing boxes of pad Thai and vegetable tempura, steamed dumplings and crab Rangoon, and several sweet-smelling unidentified entrees, all eagerly spooned up onto plates, until the last box had made the rounds.

"There's enough food here for the next month," Nell said.

"Sailing makes one hungry," Sam managed to say around bites of a steamed dumpling.

For a while, the only sounds were slurps and crunches and the click of chopsticks.

"This goes down so fast," Sam said, passing the small buckets around for seconds. But in no time, chairs were already being pushed back. Wine poured and napkins scrunched up next to plates.

Talk resumed, but in lighthearted tones. As if the talk of "something else" that Ben had alluded to might end the Thai dinner.

And eventually it did.

A slight noise from the front door went nearly unnoticed, until light footsteps in the hallway announced another visitor.

"Anyone home?" Gracie Santos called out.

Immediately chairs were pushed back, and Izzy began collecting empty plates.

"Gracie, hi," Nell said, piling up the empty boxes. "Come in."

"Oh, shoot," Gracie said, looking at the table. "I'm sorry. Am I interrupting dinner?"

"Absolutely not. It was impromptu and it's finished." Nell walked across the family room, wrapping an arm around Gracie's back and walking with her into the kitchen. "You're just in time for brownies. Or a drink. Or both."

"There's still a bit of pad Thai left over, too," Birdie said, waving a dishrag at Gracie from her post at the kitchen sink. "Though you may have to fight Cass for it."

"I'd definitely lose," she said, looking over at Cass.

"Yes, you would," Cass said. She motioned Gracie over to the stool next to her.

Ben had uncorked another bottle of wine and poured Gracie a glass.

Cass held hers up for a refill. "So, Gracie, what's up?"

"I saw your car parked outside and remembered that you'd texted me hours ago. Knowing the Endicotts have an open-door policy, I thought I'd answer it in person. Liz and I took her littles to the Fishermen Park's playground so I didn't see the text until we left."

"The playground Nick built for the neighborhood," Nell said, bringing over a plate of brownies.

"Right. Actually, Nick was responsible for that park," Cass said. "He took good care of his 'villagers.'"

Gracie nodded. "He sure did. It's a great place. Walking paths, a great playground. Basketball court. Gardens everywhere. And it seemed even more glorious today as I watched my little cousins running around, squealing for more pushes on the swings. Simple and ordinary. An amazing tonic for Liz and me, proof that life goes on."

"That's a wise and beautiful way to spend time, Gracie," Birdie said. She wiped her hands off and joined them at the island.

"I'm glad you mentioned the park," Izzy said. "It reminds me that the Fishermen Festival is coming up, right?" Izzy started looking at her phone calendar.

"It's tomorrow," Gracie said. "They were getting things ready while we were over there."

"Tomorrow?" Izzy looked over at Cass. "Geesh, I forgot—"

"It's some kind of postal holiday," Cass said. "A free day for kids."

"Right," Gracie said. "Anyway, that's why I didn't see your text right away."

"Good," Cass said. "This is easier to explain in person, anyway."

Gracie frowned. "That sounds cryptic."

"Cryptic goes down better with sweets," Nell said, placing napkins and a plate of buttermilk brownies on the island.

Cass gave Nell a grateful smile.

"Okay, first the background." Cass took a brownie from the plate. "While you were pushing little girls on swings, Iz and I were pulling a Rizzoli and Isles."

Hearing Cass's comment, Ben and Sam abandoned their side conversation and moved closer to hear.

Quickly, with Izzy's help, Cass replayed their visit to the old bank building.

"What are you talking about? Recipes?" Gracie said, not sure she had heard correctly.

Izzy pulled over the copies she had printed out. "Here they are. I only photographed a few. It was a tall stack. The copy is blurry, but you can see enough. They're Bobby's recipes."

"What we found were copies, not originals," added Cass. "Hopefully, those are still in Bobby's book. Someone photographed the recipes and those copies are now in the chef's office at the new restaurant."

Gracie took a sip of wine, frowning, and looking like she was waiting for the punch line.

Izzy gave a few more details, and when she finished, the others all spoke at once, questions colliding above the island.

"Stop," Nell said, her expertise at handling boisterous board meetings coming in handy.

"Thanks, Nell," Gracie said.

Gracie seemed calm, but there was an edge to her voice, something those who knew her well didn't often hear.

"Are you saying Marco Costa stole Bobby's recipes and gave them to another chef? That sounds crazy to me. And stupid, right? Why would the new chef even want another chef's recipes? And why would Marco do that? Surely, they wouldn't pay for them."

"Or would they, Gracie?" Cass said. "I've known Marco a long time, and I've never known him to be the gift-giving type. He had to be getting something out of this."

"That only makes sense if they were paying a lot of money for them, don't you think?" Sam asked. "And would a chef or restaurant owner do that? Especially since the chef they've hired is supposed to be talented."

"Yet it looks like that's what Marco did," Cass said. "The recipes didn't fly over there. And no one else had access to them. Or even cared about them."

"Bobby will kill him," Gracie said, bowing her head, her voice low.

Nell heard. "I hope not," she said. "There has to be an explanation."

"Maybe. But no matter why he did it, it's a crime. Marco stole them," Izzy said. "*Presumably,* he stole them," she added quickly.

They all agreed, even though in the light of other concerns, the theft of Bobby's recipes took a backseat.

"Wait," Izzy said suddenly. "I just remembered something that may help." She reached into her back jeans pocket and pulled out a handful of business cards. "Murray, the painter, gave these to us."

She spread them out on the island. The cards were official-looking, blue and gold, and printed on thick, shiny stock. They were all similar with the restaurant name, logo, and phone number on them. However, some also had names of people at the bottom, with other contact information.

Sam picked up one of those and held it beneath the island's pendant lights. Then he looked at it again. "This is Jack Riley's card. Nick's friend. He's part owner in the restaurant. I'm guessing he's the person Nick was going to call about Marco."

"We may have just missed him today," Izzy said. "A nice-looking guy about Nick's age?"

Sam nodded.

"He's the one who brought those cards over," she added.

"So you know him, Sam?" Nell asked.

"I met him the day Nick took me over to see the place."

Nell riffled through the other cards. Most were identical, with a name or number different on some.

"What's that one?" Birdie asked, watching Nell go through the cards. Nell handed it to her.

Birdie put her glasses on and smiled at the card. "This is clever. It must be the chef's calling card. There's a toque in the background." She passed the card around.

Cass looked at it. Then at Nell. "May I use your computer for a sec?"

Nell reached over to the countertop and grabbed her laptop, noticing as she turned back that Ben and Sam had disappeared. In the distance, she heard the den television being turned on. She handed her laptop to Cass.

Nell looked over at Gracie. She'd grown quiet, sitting with her elbows on the table, her chin balanced on one fist, and looking as if her mind had gone somewhere else. "Are you okay, Gracie?"

She sat back and looked over at Nell. "Not really. I'm think-ing about Bobby, and his hiring Marco Costa. He was overworked and Marco seemed the answer. He knew fish." She looked at Cass.

Cass looked up from the computer. "That part is true. But are you thinking that maybe Marco was messing with Bobby's kitchen for some reason?"

"Maybe," Gracie said. "Or it could be me he was messing with. It's my restaurant and it's clear he doesn't like me. I'm not crazy about him, either."

"But there's something more, I hear it in your voice, Gracie," Birdie said.

Gracie managed to smile a thanks to Birdie. "I don't know how you know thoughts and feelings before they're revealed, Birdie. It's like you have another sense."

"She does." Nell confirmed.

"I was thinking how messy and mismatched this whole picture is. Bobby was convinced that Nick was doing something to hurt him and the restaurant. Messing with the food. Doing *something,* even if he couldn't figure out what it was. It was crazy to think that Nick would do that. *Ridiculous.* And most of us—well, me, maybe—wondered if it was Bobby himself who hadn't quite reached his stride here, causing the reviews. Nothing nefarious at all. And now . . . and now maybe Bobby was right. Maybe someone has been messing with the food. Maybe there is someone who wants Bobby to fail."

No one spoke.

Eventually Birdie cut through their thoughts. "And that someone could be Marco, I'm thinking, from what's been said."

"I don't know, Birdie, but Bobby had trusted Marco with a lot while he was trying to get things back on track. No one else, except me, had the kind of access Marco had."

She looked at Cass. "You know Marco better than any of us, Cass. Could he have done something with the fish, or herbs, or something else, that might have made the food taste bad?"

"Well, he could have been buying inferior fish, and presenting them as more valuable ones. Intentionally doing the opposite of what he was hired to do." Cass grimaced at the unpleasant thought. "It happens more frequently than you'd think. Diners don't always get what's listed on the menu. But usually, the sauce covers it up and the ordinary diner doesn't know the difference, so she or he doesn't complain. The restaurant paid less for the fish, so it comes out ahead."

"Bobby's specialties are his sauces," Gracie said. "He's won awards for them."

"Would it be possible for someone to alter the taste of the sauce *after* Bobby approved it?" Izzy asked.

Gracie thought about that, then said, "Bobby samples his sauces often, making sure of the taste, the temperature, the consistency. Sometimes the staff gets impatient. He's a little neurotic about it."

"What if something was added just before the entree left the kitchen?" Izzy said. "When Bobby was on to the next thing."

Gracie paused, considering. "I think it might be possible."

"Marco only worked part-time," Izzy said. "If he's responsible for this, that could explain why the reviews and the diner complaints were sporadic."

"It would," Gracie said, her voice lifting, as if something finally sounded plausible to her.

Nell shifted on the kitchen stool, looking out the window at an old apple tree that Ben climbed when he was a child. A gentler world, she thought. Kinder, perhaps.

Gracie went on. "Despite Bobby's rants at Nick, Nick was on his way to helping me figure this out. He knew Marco from the neighborhood, and he didn't like it when I told him that Marco was working in our kitchen. I'm sure he thought Marco had a part to play in it." She looked over at Cass.

"I agree, Gracie. As soon as he heard Marco's name, he looked worried."

"And he was going to check on it—"

Nell was watching Gracie's face change when she spoke about Nick. Her narrow shoulders seemed not wide enough to carry her sadness. Nick's death had affected so many. And somehow it was now a part of the mess involving Bobby and Gracie's kitchen.

But like in Izzy's dream, when she tried to touch the puzzle pieces to pull them together, they wriggled away, leaving only stolen recipes, tampered food, and three men.

Two who had never met one another until Marco walked into the Lazy Lobster and Soup Café's kitchen, asking the chef for a job.

And a third, who was dead.

Chapter 38

Ben and Sam walked out of the den a short time later. Ben was yawning, and Sam announced that their sitter would turn into a pumpkin if they didn't relieve her soon.

The others were talking quietly, except for Cass, who had gone back to Nell's computer.

Izzy stood and nodded. She was fading, too. "It's been a very long day."

"Right," Sam said. "Even Rizzoli and Isles get tired."

"Gracie," Ben said. "I think Izzy mentioned earlier that if Marco had stolen those recipes, that's a crime. If Bobby is up to it, or thinks it's worth it, he can file a police report."

"I don't know, Ben. Everything seems so fragmented right now. Maybe we need to wait a few days?"

"That might be wise. I'm just putting it out there."

Nell watched the exchange, wondering how Bobby would take all of this. She suspected Gracie was thinking the same thing. Bobby's anger had been an issue.

At that moment, Cass looked up from her computer, scattering Nell's thoughts. "Fumagalli," she said. "I found it."

They all looked at her.

"It sounds like a pest control company, Cass." Sam said.

"Nope. A name. Chef Maurice Fumagalli. Does anyone recognize it?" She was looking at Gracie.

They all tried to repeat the name and dig it out of their memories.

"If I had heard that name before, I think even I would remember it." Birdie said. "*Fumagalli.* Such an interesting name."

"Wait," Sam said suddenly. "I think I've heard it before. At least, it's familiar. Birdie, you're right. It's the kind of name you don't forget. Or make up. Where did you find it, Cass?"

Cass held up the small business card. "It's on the card. He's the chef at the new restaurant here. I also googled it, wondering if it was a mistake or a misspelling."

"What did you find?" Sam asked. He repeated the name to himself, walking around the island to where Cass sat. He leaned in to see the page she had brought up.

"It's a New York restaurant review," Cass said.

Sam leaned in and looked at the picture beside the article; then he read the review.

"It's a great review," Cass said. "It says the chef is top-notch. It makes you wonder why he's leaving there."

"Did you find anything else about him?" Nell asked.

"He's won some awards. And once owned a restaurant."

"I guess that's when he got the title of chef," Gracie said. "Bobby told me some people say you need to own a restaurant to be called chef."

"Well, he's using it on his business card."

"I wonder if he has family here," Birdie said. "Maybe that's why he's coming to Sea Harbor. Although I don't think I've ever heard that name up here."

"Maybe he's coming for the same reason the Endicotts and we Perrys are here," Izzy said. "It's a slice of paradise."

"There's that," Nell said. "Whoever this chef is, he has good taste in places to live."

Sam was still leaning in, reading. Finally he stood up and stretched out his back, rotating his shoulders.

They all looked at him.

"Okay," he said. His face showing both surprise and disbelief. "I now remember how I know Chef Fumagalli. And I'll leave it to someone smarter than I am to decide if it's a coincidence he's coming here, or some conspiracy theory, or something else."

It took Sam's brief explanation of the photo gig he'd done for Bobby years earlier to explain how he knew the chef, and how Bobby Palazola knew the chef, too. Much better, much better than he in fact.

"Chef Fumagalli blamed Bobby for having to close his badly run restaurant. He hated Bobby, according to the close-knit neighborhood."

"He hated Bobby?" Gracie said.

Sam was still holding Jack Riley's business card, the part owner of La Banque. He typed the number into his phone.

Cass continued to search the Internet. "I found something else," Cass said. "It's interesting. One of those 'breaking news' kind of rumor posts that sometimes show up on a foodie sites. Chef Fumagalli had a visit from the police." She squinted and tried to check the date. "It's not clear, but it looks like it was put up yesterday."

Gracie's phone vibrated. She looked at the caller's name and answered. "Hi." Her eyes opened wide as she listened, finally managing to say, "Wait for me. I'm at the Endicotts'." There was a short pause. Then Gracie said, "No. I'm coming." And she hung up.

Still holding her phone, she stood up. "Bobby got a call from Tommy Porter. There's been a break-in or a fight or something at the old bank building. That restaurant. Marco's involved and he gave Bobby's name as place of employment. He's headed over there. I am, too."

"Not alone. I'm going with you, Gracie. In case you need help calming Bobby," Cass said.

Ben was pulling out his car keys and Sam had headed for the door.

And then they were gone.

A half hour later, Izzy, Birdie, and Nell had cleaned the kitchen until it looked like no one had ever used it.

"Enough," Nell finally said, waving them to the far end of the open living area.

"Nervous energy, I guess," Izzy said. She pulled out her phone and pulled up a playlist of Grammy-winning songs. Soon Billie Eilish's sweet, soft voice began smoothing out the tension in the room.

They settled into the comfortable couches and cushy chairs that surrounded the fireplace, pulling knitting needles and whatever was attached to them from their bags.

Izzy had checked with the sitter, and all was well at the Perry home. Birdie gave in and called Ella, only to be chastised for checking in. The teenagers were having a fine time. "Good grief," Ella said. "I was married at that age." All was well at the Favazza estate.

But, apparently, not at La Banque.

Cass walked in first, but was followed closely by Ben and Sam. Bobby and Gracie came in last.

"Well," Bobby said, looking around. "That was fun."

Sam shook his head. "I never much liked boxing. Or maybe it was wrestling?"

"Which one has the most blood and cussing?" Bobby said. "I didn't know half the words coming out of those guys."

"Guys?" Izzy said.

Ben pulled cold beers out of the fridge and set them on the coffee table near the hearth. "Make yourselves comfortable."

Birdie looked up from her knitting and said quietly, "Talk to us, dear people. Now."

There was a round of soft laughter.

"I'll start," Sam said. "First, though, the most interesting thing tonight is that the amazing women in this room pretty much figured out all the whys and wherefores before the fight at the restaurant ever happened. Congratulations."

Bobby Palazola laughed—a relieved laugh—and reached for a beer. "That doesn't surprise me at all. I know Halloran— oops, sorry—Catherine Mary Theresa has always had my back." He grinned at Cass in that way that used to make her blush when she was fourteen.

"Shush Palazola," Cass growled. Then looked back at Sam. "On with it, Sam."

Sam took the cold beer that Ben put in his hand and sat on one of the overstuffed chairs.

"Here's the long and short of it. Marco Costa and his buddy Tony Fumagalli, drunk as skunks, had an argument and then pulled out the fists inside La Banque. They not only damaged each other and the place, but created enough noise that the museum security guards around the corner heard the ruckus and called the police. Tommy Porter answered the alarm and brought a posse.

"That's when it got interesting. The two guys were tearing into each other, yelling and cursing, blaming each other for the cockeyed and awful things they'd been up to, throwing accusations and blame back and forth so no one could hear anything. After a couple of officers finally pulled them apart, they continued to hurl insults and blame at each other. The police finally took the guys off to the police station. Tommy stayed behind. Here's what was pulled out of it all, most of which you already know.

"Chef Fumagalli and his brother had hired Costa to help them achieve their goal, which was to destroy Bobby Palazola's career. The chef had nurtured that hate for years, according to his brother, Tony, who got scared and started blaming his chef brother, as well as Marco. They'd kept track of Bobby over the years so the chef could get revenge someday. When the owners of the New York restaurant started talking about opening a place up here, Chef Fumagalli thought he'd died and gone to heaven. He and Tony hired Marco to get a job in Bobby's kitchen, steal recipes, and manipulate Bobby's recipes to make the food taste bad. And I guess when La Banque opened, they'd add other things to screw Bobby, if more was needed. And they'd use Bobby's original recipes as their own.

"Marco, in turn, blamed everything on the Fumagallis. He didn't know anything about anything. It was just a job."

Sam stopped and took a drink.

"Your throat's dry, Sam. Let me take a stab at it," Bobby said.

Nell couldn't help but smile as Bobby talked. He looked like he'd just been given a new life.

"I didn't know the guy hated me like that. Geesh. What a burden on the guy. Hate's a heavy thing. Anyway, we learned something new about the chef. The accountant for the LLCs that owns both restaurants just discovered that the chef was embezzling from the restaurant. Maybe to pay Marco? Who knows? Things aren't looking good for him."

They were quiet for a moment, digesting it all.

"And you guys had figured it all out yourselves," Bobby said.

Cass laughed. "Maybe, in theory. But nothing has the power of proving the truth of our guesses like two thugs battling it out and screaming at each other. But there's one more thing that needs to be fit into this picture. The bigger picture."

Everyone looked at her.

"Nick Cabot was about to find out what Marco was up to. Something that would end Marco's nice cash flow. He was expecting the information on Monday, the day after he died. And Marco knew it."

Images of Marco standing behind a rubber tree plant flashed across Cass's mind.

There was silence.

Then a phone *pinged* and everyone who had a cell phone nearby pulled it out.

It was Bobby's phone.

He frowned, looked over at Gracie, as if she'd be the only one calling him. Then he held it to his ear and listened.

"I'll be there. Text the information. Yes. I'm glad. It's time. I love you." He put his phone down and looked up to see all eyes on him. Then he turned and looked at Gracie.

"Hey, boss, I'm going to need a few hours off this week," he said. "My sister, Bella, is flying back from Switzerland. I'm picking her up at the airport."

Chapter 39

Izzy walked into the yarn shop on Monday morning, her head still hurting from trying to keep too many facts and emotions and suppositions in the air at the same time. And there were still too many unanswered questions.

Some of the links refused to connect, even though they were all grateful that at least Gracie's restaurant woes would soon be put to rest.

Yet, she was anything but restful. There was still a murderer out there.

And she suspected that in the back of their heads, they were all leaning closely toward the same person. One who was only an inch away. But which way?

Mae pulled Izzy aside as she walked in, nodding toward the stairs. "Guess who's here?"

Izzy rolled her eyes. She walked over and glanced down into the knitting room. But she knew before she looked what she'd see.

Beatrice Scaglia turned and waved at her as their eyes met. It was a knitting morning and Izzy could see the room was full.

Beatrice would get a lot of news about her town from the many conversations going on.

"I'm not eavesdropping, this is research," she'd proudly say to anyone who questioned the silent knitting needles in her lap.

Or maybe she was there today for a different reason. Maybe she came to show a roomful of good people how interested and loyal—and innocent—their mayor was.

Izzy started back to her office when she heard her name called out. She turned quickly, almost into the arms of Laura Danvers. Since they were that close, her old friend completed it with a warm hug.

"Oh, Izzy," she said, stepping back. "The girls are so brave. Is Birdie okay? I know they're taking care of Nick's dog. Daisy has been spending more time over there with Gabby than at home. But that's good. I'm so glad Gabby is here this summer. They need each other. And they need this dog-walking busi-ness, I—"

"Breathe, Laura," Izzy said. She held her friend's shoulders.

Laura Danvers was a confident and well-respected philan-thropic young leader in Sea Harbor. But she moved so fast that sometimes Izzy worried she wouldn't have enough oxygen in her body to stay upright.

Somehow, though, she always did, and managed her busy life in a way others envied. She and Laura were as different as day and night, and it all equaled out to an unusual, but valued, friendship.

"Do you think the girls are okay, Laura? This has been a dif-ficult start to their summer."

"I think they're good. They're smart and resourceful, and learned things from Nick, I think. Daisy told me she wanted to be him when she grew up. I knew what she meant. He was kind and good. A mom couldn't ask for a better role model, right?"

"Right. Some days, I feel he's out there trying to point us in the right direction. To make the fear and disruption of lives stop," Izzy said.

"I feel that, too. We all thought Nick hung the moon. But there's someone in our town who didn't think that way. It's creepy and awful. When do kindness and generosity and enjoying life—all that Nick Cabot was very good at doing—twist another's mind enough to kill?"

Izzy listened to Laura and realized, not for the first time, that in addition to being talkative and a leader and a friend, Laura was wise.

This time, Izzy hugged Laura. "Okay, now why are you here?"

"To buy yarn. But you're even better than yarn." Laura took out a piece of paper and read off her needs. "Two of my daughters are working on something for the art auction. I guess Gabby and Daisy are doing their own thing."

"I didn't know that. That's great." Izzy looked at the list and pulled out skeins of yarn in seconds.

"And as usual, I'm short on time," Laura said.

"Which board meeting are you headed to today?" Izzy asked.

Laura laughed. "You sound like my husband. You're right, both you and Elliott. Too many boards. Here's what happened. It's a middle-child thing. Cecelia wanted to go to the Sea Harbor Community Day School because big sister Daisy had gone there with Gabby that school year she stayed here with Birdie. Elliott and I decided it was a fair request. Cecelia feels we give Daisy more. Anyway, I agreed to stay on the board— this was after Nell and Birdie went off the board. Nick Cabot was on the board then, and that made it more palatable. He and I also bonded when the board decided that Elizabeth Hartley should go. We were the dissenters, supporting Elizabeth. It was definitely a learning experience for me."

"I didn't realize you were there then. Ugh." Izzy wondered how far to pursue the conversation without asking Laura things she shouldn't. But she had some questions about Nell and Birdie's time there. And things they had said.

"Her firing wasn't all it seemed to be from the outside," Laura said. "But most complicated things aren't. Sometimes even simple ones."

While Mae processed Laura's purchase, Izzy stood against the far wall with her friend and listened intently as Laura quietly and discreetly told Izzy about the board members, and the firing of a woman who had done good things for Sea Harbor Community Day School, and the town of Sea Harbor as well. And all that swirled around it.

She finally finished, pulling out her phone and checking some numbers. Then she looked up. "I just sent a phone number to your phone. It's a place the school was connected to. Another lens to look through," she said.

Izzy stayed where she was for a minute, leaning against the yarn shop wall and watching Laura hurry out the door. She thought again about how wise her friend was. And how sometimes the right thing was unexpectedly spoken aloud at exactly the right time.

Yes, Izzy thought. Sometimes things can look very different, depending on your lens.

It was almost noon, after a reminder text from Cass, that Izzy realized she had less than an hour to get Abby ready for the Fishermen Festival. She grabbed her bag and was about to walk out the door when Mae called her over.

"You got a call on the shop line. I took a message." She handed a piece of paper to Izzy: *Please call at your convenience. You left something at the café.*

Annabelle Palazola's number was at the bottom.

Izzy walked out to her car and punched in Annabelle's number, trying to balance her cell phone, her bag, and the car door.

"Annabelle?"

"Izzy, thanks for returning my call. I've been meaning to call you, but you know how that goes. Anyway, I think you left something here the other day. It was under your chair."

"What's that?"

Izzy frowned as Annabelle talked. She sat down in the driver's seat and put her phone on speaker. With her feet still on the ground, she pulled open her bag, digging through the deep tote, pushing aside a deodorant container, some of Abby's breakfast bar wrappers, old grocery lists, makeup, a hairbrush. Sam swore she could fit the microwave in the bag. Or maybe their daughter. She was beginning to think he was right.

She rummaged around some more, and there at the very bottom, she found the delinquent pieces of clothing. Bobby's cap. And a sandal. One sandal.

"Is it fuchsia?" she asked.

Annabelle said she thought it was red, but acknowledged it could be fuchsia. She wasn't sure what fuchsia looked like.

"Is it yours?"

"Well, yes and no. Yes, both sandals were in my tote, and one is still there. But no, it's not mine."

There was a pause on the other end. Finally Annabelle asked, "Whose is it? Where did you get it?"

"I spotted it from my deck one night when the tide was coming in so I rescued it. I'd like to find the owner, because I know they're expensive. But how do you go about that?"

Annabelle was chuckling when she answered.

Then Izzy's mouth dropped open. "Wow! What a surprise. You found my Cinderella."

Izzy listened some more, feeling Annabelle's smile as she talked.

"Was she a good swimmer?" Izzy asked.

Now Izzy was smiling, too, listening to the rest of Annabelle Palazola's story.

It was enormously comforting when even a few border pieces of a puzzle fit together.

There were simply too many unknowns crowding around her. How nice to erase one, albeit a small one, leaving her with an intense desire to move on.

Chapter 40

Cass picked up Izzy and Abby, and together, with Cass's Joey in his car seat, they drove the short distance to Fishermen's Village, pretending not to listen to Abby's nonstop one-sided conversation with Joey Brandley, who was three years younger and willing to do anything and everything for six year old Abigail Perry, his favorite person on earth. But at this moment, Joseph Archibald Brandley was sound asleep, his head leaning to one side and long eyelashes resting on his cheeks. Something that didn't seem to deter Abby's one-sided conversation.

"Sam and Danny will show up shortly," Cass said. "Something about a phone call?"

"Yes. Sam wants to call Nick's friend to fill him in on the restaurant episode. This whole thing with Marco is unsettling. What else is this guy responsible for?"

"Costa knew Nick was going to turn him in."

Izzy nodded. "It's so ugly. And I think of Elena, too. Even though she's not involved, she'll suffer for this."

Cass agreed, imagining her Joey having anyone but Danny for a father. Danny was perfect. Marco Costa was not. Speaking aloud, she went to easier topics.

306 Sally Goldenbaum

"Danny needed a little more writing time, too, so it worked out for him to come with Sam. He's frantic about this book. Someone's in danger and he's trying to get them out of it."

Izzy laughed. "If only he could write an ending to the mess in Sea Harbor right now, preferably a happy one."

"We wish."

"Cass, I won't go into this whole thing right now, but Annabelle called me today because I'd left that lost sandal at the restaurant, and the mystery is solved. It makes perfect sense. In fact, a lot of things are starting to. Cass, I think we're looking at all of this the wrong way."

"Tell me before I have to wake Joey up. We're almost at the park."

"The woman arguing with Bobby wasn't just any woman, and it wasn't a romantic tryst gone bad. Bobby was having an argument with his sister."

The car came to a stop sign and Cass stared at Izzy, her eyes wide. "Of course it was! I should have guessed it, Iz. The way you described her—the expensive sandals, the way she walked and swam—she won so many swimming medals in high school they wanted to take some back. And then, the most telling thing of all—arguing with her brother. Perfect." Cass chuckled, shaking her head. "Did Annabelle have any idea what the argument was about?"

"I think she did, but she wouldn't say. She acted like it was an argument they should never have been having, and she didn't want to get into it. I think it was one of those family things that you keep private."

"Did she mention that Bella's coming home?"

Izzy shook her head no, then wondered briefly why she hadn't. But maybe that's why Annabelle was so happy. She loved the twins. Both of them.

An excited crowd of families was already filing into the park when Cass and Izzy walked through the garden entrance. Hundreds of colorful balloons were attached to the gaslights along the walking paths, serpentine pathways lined with trees and flowers and the colorful balloons waving a welcome. More balloons were handed to the kids as they walked into the park, and a number had already escaped from tightly closed fists. They floated up against the deep blue sky, creating magical patterns until they disappeared from sight. Tents with hot dogs, pizza, cotton candy, and drinks were scattered around the treed park, and other tents were filled with friends cheering on friends at fishing-themed games. Dry fishponds were full of stuffed sea creatures—lobsters and sharks and dolphins—easy to catch and cuddle and take home. It was a magical place. Magicians strolled the pathways and swarms of children already sported fanciful marine animals painted on their cheeks.

On the far side of the park, with the ocean as their backdrop, Pete Halloran and his Fractured Fish band were set up on a small stage. Pete tuning up his guitar, Andy Risso behind his drums, and Merry Jackson testing the mic, getting ready for a full-throated version of "We Don't Talk About Bruno," her bevy of clapping and jiggling children on alert.

"Pete is having the time of his life," Izzy said, looking up at the stage.

She saw Abby taking Joey's hand and running ahead.

"How could he not? With that adoring crowd," Cass said.

Izzy looked over heads and saw that Joey and Abby were now settled happily on the stage, with Uncle Pete and the other members of the Fractured Fish embracing them.

In the distance, Danny, Sam, and Ben approached the kids on the stage. Earlier than expected.

"Izzy! Cass!" A familiar voice behind them turned them around, happy their children's fathers were now in charge.

"Oh, my!" Izzy yelped. "Elena."

In the next minute, Elena had wrapped them both tightly in her arms.

"I'm so happy to see you two."

"Wow, you've been working out, Elena," Cass said. "Great biceps."

Elena laughed, but there were tears in her eyes.

At first, Cass and Izzy were silent. They'd almost forgotten that Elena's husband was across town, sitting in a jail cell.

"I miss him," Elena said.

"Marco won't be—" Cass started, but stopped when Elena shook her head.

"No, not Marco. Nick," Elena said. "I loved Nick, and this is all about him today. I am happy and sad at once. Even my little James senses a loss."

Izzy crouched down in front of a dark-haired toddler pressed against Elena's side. "Hello, James," she said, handing him a furry whale a volunteer had slipped into her hands when they walked in.

James took the whale and rubbed it against his cheek. "Dank you," he said with a small smile.

James looked over at Cass then and waved. She responded with a crazy face that made James laugh with more force than his small body looked able to handle.

"Okay. Now I know the way to his heart," Izzy said to Cass. "Crazy faces top fuzzy whales."

They walked on, Izzy focused on Elena as she and Cass talked about toddler music classes and appetites and potty training. She looks good, Izzy thought. Content, and she had barely mentioned Marco. She wondered if she knew where he was. There was something about her, though—maybe lots of yoga? But Izzy suspected it was also due to her strength of spirit. Whatever happened with her husband, she could see that Elena would be okay. And she'd thrive.

As if reading her thoughts, Elena said, "I don't want to talk about Marco right now. Tommy called and told me he was going to be in jail for a few days. I said that was good. It might keep him out of trouble and give him some time to think. Even if you know more, either of you, I don't want to know about it today. Today is Nick's festival day."

As the pathway curved around a small fountain, Elena stepped off the path and called out to a woman standing near the edge of the fountain. She was holding a large camera. But it was the woman next to the photographer that Elena was pointing to. Elizabeth Hartley turned, smiling broadly at the group, and quickly walked over to them.

"What a surprise," Elizabeth said. "Three of my favorite people all in one spot." She looked down at James, who was also grinning at her. "Excuse me, Sir James. I meant *four* of my favorite people."

James giggled.

"You guys know Elizabeth?" Elena asked.

"We do," Cass said. "It's good to see you here, Elizabeth."

"I'm partially here for my new job," Elizabeth said. "We're taking some photographs for an exhibit at the art colony." She nodded toward the photographer, now capturing a group of little girls dancing with their balloons, their faces alive with joy. "But I'd be here, anyway. It's Nick's park, Nick's festival," she said.

"I remember the first one he held here," Cass said. "It's meant a lot to the families who live here."

"Oh, that's for sure," Elena said. "And for others, too." She looked at Elizabeth and smiled.

Izzy watched, marveling at how the lives of two people with very different experiences and lives might cross paths. "How do you two know each other?" she asked.

"Through my neighbor, Nick," Elena said. "Nick came over here often to shoot baskets with a group of teens. A lot of them don't see too much of their dads. Sometimes Elizabeth came with him."

Izzy watched Elizabeth, who was standing quietly, listening, smiling as Elena told her story.

A six-foot duck was waddling down the path playing a kazoo, with dozens of kids following him and catching the candy he tossed. Elena's voice was drowned out as they waved good-bye to Elizabeth who was being summoned by the photographer.

Elena scooped James up and steered them down a quieter path, still talking. "So, yes, it was Nick who introduced us. In his park, which I dearly love. I planted a lot of these gardens, and I think Nick thought Elizabeth might take to the gardening, like I do. He was always trying to suggest things, wanting her to get engaged in things around town. But she didn't seem to care about that. It was Nick she loved. I am so very sad for her."

As she talked, Elena waved to neighborhood friends and kept James happy, bouncing him on her hip.

"I come here to walk whenever I can. It helps me not to worry about Marco. And seeing other kids here is so good for James. He's shy, maybe because he has his mom's genes and is so small. But the kids are bringing him out of his shyness. And it's such a beautiful spot.

"Anyway, so that's how I know Elizabeth," Elena finished. "She's a thoughtful lady."

"That's nice," Cass said, waving to the wife of one of the men on her lobster crew.

"She loved Nick like crazy," Elena said. "And he was important to me, too. That can bring people together, I think."

They walked for a few more minutes, getting closer to the band and the dancing kids.

Cass seemed to be half listening to Elena as they talked, looking around the park. She stopped at a grassy spot, glancing down a side street across from the park. Small houses lined both sides of the narrow street, except for a garish and blackened lot midway down. On the other side of the street, she recognized Elena's small, neat home.

"You live so close to Nick's," Cass said suddenly. "I never realized that."

Elena followed her look. She nodded. "That's how Nick and I became friends. We saw each other nearly every day. And at night, when James and I would walk down to the park, he'd see us and wave. And I know he kept an eye out for us, especially after Marco left."

"You come down here at night?" Izzy asked.

Elena nodded. "James has trouble going to sleep. So I put him in the stroller and walk him down here. It's like a magic tonic. He goes to sleep so quickly."

"And you feel safe?" Cass asked.

"Oh yes. I always feel safe here. We all do. The gaslights along the pathways give enough light. The basketball court is lit for a couple hours. People watch out for one another. It's not scary. It's peaceful. Elizabeth sometimes walks with me here, keeping me company. I almost always find a friend to sit with. But being alone is good, too."

At that moment, Danny stood on the stage step and waved over the crowd, looking for Cass. He spotted her just as she looked over to check on him. His wave was the kind of emergency wave that meant he needed her.

"Uh-oh," Cass said, taking off toward the stage.

"Bathrooms are behind the stage," Elena called out after her.

Izzy looked over at Elena and noticed that James was now asleep on her shoulder. "Elena, let's find a bench. You look terribly uncomfortable."

"An excellent idea." Elena followed Izzy to a pair of park benches on the edge of the festival crowd. Izzy sat down, then glanced down the street. The yellow tapes and fence were a glaring sight in the midst of the small, neatly kept gardens.

Elena sighed as she sat down. "This feels so good. Thank you, Izzy. But see? This is what I was saying. This park is magic—it puts James to sleep almost immediately, even in the middle of all the festivities."

Izzy looked at the sleeping little boy. She rubbed his back lightly, feeling his body warmth. "There's something so wondrous about watching children sleep. It's soothing. It makes the whole world seem calm again."

"Yes, that's exactly it, Izzy," Elena said.

They both fell silent, content to watch a sleeping James, his small lips moving, with music and children's laughter playing behind them.

Cass soon returned, sensing their mood, and sat down beside Izzy, looking up at the sky.

"That peace you mentioned," Elena said, looking over at Izzy. "That's what I felt *that* night. The peace."

They could tell from the sound of Elena's voice what night she was talking about. *That* night. The night Nick died.

Her voice was soft. "James couldn't sleep that night, so I put him in the stroller, and we headed down the block to the park. There was an airport taxi in his driveway. Nick was standing next to it, paying the driver, I guess."

"He was going somewhere?"

"No. His friend who had come for dinner was leaving. He looked so good that night, like he was feeling peace, too. He looked beautiful, if I'm allowed to say that about a man. When the taxi drove off, I yelled that over to him and he laughed. A funny word for a guy, but he did. He looked beautiful.

"Music was coming from his open windows and doors, and I could see through the big windows that he had his mother's special candles lit on that great wooden table. I teased him about them, and he just smiled, then chuckled a little. He'd blow them out before going to bed, he promised me, and he waved me off. He'd keep an eye on the two of us until we got home, he said.

"When I got to the park, I found a half dozen friends strolling around, just like I told you. We all like to walk about here. And that night, I think every one of us wanted a piece of the beautiful night. I joined a friend, and we walked along the paths for a long time, with the moon shining down on us. We could almost feel its power, you know? So amazing. It was a perfect night."

Elena looked up at the sky as she talked, as if seeing it all again.

"We talked softly, watching as James's eyelids began to droop, and soon he was dreaming of stars and moonlight and boats or whatever little boys dream of. And we just kept walking.

"I can't explain it. But both my friend and I were so happy that night. Truly happy. Like everything in our lives was going to be okay. It was the moon, I guess."

"It sounds nice," Izzy said.

"It was perfect." Her voice dropped off. When it came back, it was stronger, but immensely sad.

"But then that night, that absolutely perfect night, was shattered. It fell apart."

Elena stopped talking and looked over at Izzy, her head moving back and forth, her face sad.

"If it hadn't been for Marco Costa, my friend and I might have been able to save Nick Cabot's life that night."

Chapter 41

"Do you know where Birdie and Nell are?" Cass asked Izzy as they sat in silence in her car, still parked in the Fishermen's Park lot. Sam and Ben had suggested Izzy and Cass take advantage of the rest of the day. "Go for a walk. Or better yet, go over to the Beauport in Gloucester and have a sunset cocktail on their deck," Ben had said.

He had added that he and Sam were taking Abby out on the *Dream Weaver* to watch the sunset from the inner harbor. Danny was taking an exhausted three-year-old home for an early bedtime, which would give his dad a few more hours to figure out the problems with his novel.

Maybe they'd all meet up for a late dinner?

The dinner sounded nice, but somehow neither Izzy nor Cass thought a sunset cocktail was what they needed today.

What they needed, they both agreed, was to talk with Nell and Birdie and together get their four heads around Elena Costa's words. Thefts and jealousies and anger. And murder.

"Things are making more sense now. We were headed in the wrong direction," Cass said, drumming her fingers on the steering wheel.

"Maybe. But maybe that's where we had to start. Motives are a logical place to begin. But it takes other things to make a good stew. I think we were getting closer, inch by inch."

Izzy pulled out her phone and called Birdie, figuring that they might be at her house. Maybe finishing up the neglected afghan. Before she could send off a message, she noticed she'd missed an earlier message from Nell. She read it, then looked over at Cass.

"They're at the yarn shop," she said to Cass.

"Isn't it closed?" Cass checked the time on the dashboard.

"It is. Except for the two of them. They wanted to work on the afghan. Mae waited for them and asked them to lock up when they left."

"Hmm," Cass said.

"Right," Izzy said, reading her mind. "They want to talk."

"Good," Cass said. She turned the car around and headed toward Harbor Road.

"Mind if I make another phone call while you drive?" She'd completely forgotten the number that Laura had sent to her phone, probably because she hadn't intended to use it. But Laura seemed to think it would explain some things.

The phone number was answered by a machine message from a pleasant-voiced woman who identified herself as a social worker. Izzy left her name and number, and a short message that Laura Danvers had suggested she call. The fact that she wasn't sure *why* she had called would most likely not escape the social worker, so Izzy hung up, certain she would never hear back.

Which was why a nearly immediate callback startled her. The pleasant social worker explained that Laura Danvers had told her Izzy might be calling. And then, after explaining quickly that she wouldn't normally provide information to a stranger, she believed that it could possibly prevent another death in Sea Harbor. And that made it worthwhile.

* * *

Nell and Birdie were waiting for them, yarn and needles mixing with yellow pads on the old library table in the middle of the knitting room.

Several bottles of water sat at one end of the table, alongside a plate of Ella's oatmeal cookies. Long knit columns of the herringbone afghan created an eye-catching attraction at the other end.

Cass filled them in on the Fishermen Festival highlights. "But I know that's not why you wanted us here—."

"It's good to know the festival was successful," said Birdie. "But you're right. We need to do some serious thinking."

"Laura Danvers said something to me this morning about how different things can look, depending on your lens," Izzy said. She looked at Birdie. "It's like walking in another's shoes, which you always tell us to do."

"We've all come around to that in our own ways, I think," Birdie said. "It's a fine dance. So, if I may use my age advantage here, why don't I begin with some thoughts?"

They all agreed, and Birdie started in, slowly, methodically opening the floodgates. It was a great relief to go off the beaten path.

After sharing pieces of conversations they'd had, Birdie pointed to a dry-erase board on which she and Nell had attempted to write things down, including observations they'd had over the past days:

Nick's mood, his behavior.
Bobby Palazola's notable revelation.
Nick's affinity for helping people.

Izzy slipped in another extraordinary revelation that she just received from a stranger who lived miles away. A social worker she didn't know, and one she would likely never meet.

They were quiet for a few minutes, looking at the dry-erase

board, which already was painting a far clearer picture than they'd expected when they had begun.

"Nick knew himself so well," Birdie said. "He was confident and self-assured—"

Izzy broke in. "Yes. Which is why he was able to be there for others, helping them, listening to them. All those things. People with low self-esteem can't do that."

"But sometimes, like you said, Iz, his actions needed to be seen through a different lens. That's what we hadn't been doing at first. And that's why we missed some things that were sitting in plain sight."

Nell looked over at Izzy and Cass. "When Birdie and I got in touch with Kyra Hanson yesterday afternoon, as someone had suggested, Kyra had a remarkable sense of who Nick was. And how he was with others. How he loved people. But in different ways. It was revealing to see him through her eyes."

They went silent, then, mulling over the many ways kindness can be misinterpreted.

"We had completely missed that there can be motives behind kindness," Birdie said. She looked over at Izzy. "But that phone call explained so much to us."

"It's slightly overwhelming," Izzy said. "I almost didn't make the call. It seemed somehow inappropriate."

They talked for a while longer, pulling it all together as tightly as they could.

Finally Izzy repeated their conversation with Elena Costa, how lovingly she had told them about a perfect Sunday night, sitting quietly in Nick's park. With her friend. And how it had been shattered.

The night, she said, Marco Costa had prevented her from saving Nick's life. But in a manner they hadn't expected.

"Everyone is exhausted," Izzy said a short while later, again looking at the whiteboard. "Deflated balloons, that's us."

"It's my brain that's exhausted," Cass said. "But my body is starving."

Izzy checked her messages.

"Okay," she said, looking up. "Here's a report from Sam. They had a great time sailing and are back at your house, Aunt Nell. They picked up some steaks and chicken, and Uncle Ben is all hyped to start up the grill. He suggested we come over and they'll do all the work." She looked at the message again.

Birdie looked out the shop window, noticing the streetlights were on. "That's a nice offer from Sam and Ben. You have special husbands, you know."

Izzy looked over at her. She looked tired, and sad, and relieved. And thankful for the extended family they'd formed together.

Nell agreed with Sam's plan. "It'd be helpful to run our thoughts by Sam and Ben, anyway. There's not much we can do tonight—"

She stopped when a cell phone rang. Not a message *ping,* but an actual call. They all reached in their pockets, suddenly alert.

"It's mine," Cass said, looking at the caller's name. "Elena," she said, frowning and putting her cell phone on speaker.

Without a hello, Elena began talking, her words urgent.

"I've been watching Nick's place," she said. "Something's really wrong over there. I saw someone walking through what's left of the house. And then . . . Oh, just please, you need to come right away. James is sick and crying and I can't leave him. I'm going to call the police."

They piled in Cass's car, unsure of Elena's message, and whether she was calling the police to help her with James or for something going on at a burned-out house. She had sounded frantic, either way.

Birdie sat shotgun, with Izzy and Nell in the back. Izzy immediately called Sam and told him what little she knew, and that they were on their way over to check on Elena.

The streets were nearly empty, and they made it to Fishermen's Village in record time. Elena was out on her front porch, holding a crying James.

Cass pulled her car to the curb.

Elena pointed over to the Cabot place, still ringed with yellow tape, and urged them to go.

"The backyard!" she shouted.

In seconds they were out of the car, racing across the street and around the fence, toward the back of the property, not sure at all what they were looking for. It was quiet in the back. The dock's lights had somehow escaped damage, and were shimmering off the water. It wasn't until they got to the sloping yard that they realized they weren't alone.

A figure, standing on Nick's dock, was silhouetted against the moonlight. She stood still, looking much as she had when Izzy and Cass had seen her just hours before. And then she began to walk slowly down the long dock that ended in the harbor's deep waters.

As they approached, Cass heard another car drive up.

While the others continued toward the dock, she turned back, walking around the debris, and nearly falling into Bobby Palazola.

"What's going on?" he said, looking beyond Cass to the water. "Bella insisted on coming here from the airport. She needed to see it. Why are you here?"

"I'm not sure." Cass spotted Bella a few steps behind Bobby and ran to her, hugging her close.

"Oh, Bella, I'm so sorry," she murmured into their hug, tears immediately springing to her eyes. Then she turned to Bobby and urged them both to follow her, not sure yet what was going on.

"The police are on the way," she said as they hurried down toward the water.

"The police? Why?" Bella asked. "What's going on?"

"Vandals?" Bobby asked.

Cass didn't answer, because she didn't really know. But she suspected help might be needed. She went around the debris and headed toward the back of what was left of Nick's house, with Bobby and Bella close behind.

She looked down at the long dock—Nick's proud tribute to his father. It was completely intact. Sturdy and welcoming, with the low lights shining, lining the wide dock all the way to the end.

Nell was walking slowly and silently along the dock. Izzy was tapping into her phone. And Birdie stood a few yards away, her eyes on Nell, praying she wouldn't fall. Or worse.

Nell walked slowly toward the tall figure, who was almost statuesque in her still posture. Nell's voice was soft and calm, reassuring, as if speaking to a hurt child. "Let me help you. The tide is starting to come in. Neither of us wants to be out here." The words held a message, but they came out of Nell sounding like a soothing song.

Elizabeth Hartley was now almost to the end of the long dock. She stopped walking and turned her head.

"Please don't come any closer, Nell. I'm going to be fine. Honest, I am. It wasn't supposed to end like this. Nick wasn't supposed to die. Please believe me. I found the ring in his house one day when he wasn't home—he doesn't lock his door, you know. And I knew it wasn't for me. You know how you simply know things like that? So I went over that night to tell him it was fine, it would be okay. The gun was for me, not for him. It was my time. But he was stubborn. Kind. He tried to get the gun away from me . . . to stop me . . ." She turned her head and looked down, staring at the dark water, now lapping against the end of the swaying dock.

"Nick forgives you, Elizabeth. He doesn't want you in the water. That's what he would say. It's deep down there, Elizabeth," Nell said, her voice still calm and ordinary.

Elizabeth went on, talking into the night air, as if she were alone, but also somehow with Nick, talking to him. "I waited there at the park. Looking at your house. I'd seen the candlelight earlier, knowing it was somehow a special night. I saw her leave, you know. And the loving way you kissed her.

"Then sweet Elena came, and we walked for awhile, and then sat on the bench. Right there at the park. Looking down at your house. I couldn't come to you while Elena was there, but then her husband finally came and he took her away, leaving me alone on the bench. At last. So I went over to see you. To say good-bye."

Elizabeth stopped talking suddenly, as if unsure of where she was. She turned and saw Nell standing a few feet away and frowned. "I told him—Nick—I told him I was going to take care of myself now."

She moved closer to the edge of the pier, the toes of her tennis shoes at the very edge.

"Elizabeth, it's dark and cold down there. You can't swim . . ."

Nell immediately regretted her last remark. It sounded ridiculous when it came back to her own ears. Elizabeth knew exactly how deep it was. And she knew better than anyone that she couldn't swim.

"This is what I should have done, Nell, what I meant to do in the first place." Her words were eerily pleasant and matter-of-fact. Calm and comfortable.

Bobby and Bella stood near the deck, watching and listening.

Bella wasn't moving, her eyes glued to the tall woman at the end of the dock.

Finally she murmured, leaning into Bobby's side, "Oh, my . . . my darling Nick."

The words came out in a moan as Bella realized in that moment that she was looking at Nick's murderer.

Bella took a step onto the dock. Birdie saw her and moved quickly to her side, hugging her close.

"Oh, Birdie, it's a nightmare," Bella said, tears in her eyes.

Then she pulled away from the older woman, glanced over at Bobby, and then looked at the woman at the end of the dock. She began walking silently along the planks.

"She can't swim," Birdie said softly to Bella's back.

In the distance, sirens filled the quiet night.

Nell continued to talk, her voice still gentle, still soothing. She took a few steps closer, but hearing her footsteps, Elizabeth turned her head slightly and lifted her hand. "No, Nell. Please don't. This is how it has to be."

She turned back to the water, her eyes down, as if examining her reflection. Then, with a single cry, she threw her body into the dark, the water opening as if to receive her, and she disappeared.

Before Nell could think, Bella Palazola rushed past her, kicked off her shoes, and dove effortlessly into the water.

In what seemed like an eternity to those watching, Bella finally reappeared and began kicking her way back to shore on her back, her arms wrapped around Elizabeth's limp torso. The police were waiting with blankets, pulling both women out of the water.

In seconds, they had Elizabeth's still body on a blanket and began administering CPR. Finally a series of coughs brought a spray of water from her lungs. A sputtering, her eyes finally opening, staring up at the crowd around her.

Chapter 42

They'd all followed Tommy to the police station where he'd taken down all the details he deemed necessary for the moment. And then he told them all to go home. They'd talk more in the morning, he said, hopefully after they'd had a good night's sleep.

Elizabeth would be in the hospital for a few days—that was all he could say about her. She'd confessed to killing Nick, having gone into his house that evening with a gun, but the details were sketchy. She had wanted to kill herself, she kept saying. But Nick tried to get the gun away. She said other things, which weren't coherent. But she'd be treated well, evaluated. And they'd know more in the days to come.

In the end, though, it might be something a jury would have to decide.

Izzy had texted Sam from the station, telling him and Ben not to come, but to cook.

They were all starving. There was a chance Bobby might show up, too. He and Bella had showed up at Nick's house on their way back from the airport because Bella had insisted on seeing the destruction.

Both men had honored their request, so when the four women arrived at the Endicotts' home, bedraggled and hungry and sad, the smell of the grill lured them directly to the deck. Sam was already filling wineglasses and bringing a pitcher of water to the deck's side table.

Izzy sank into the soft swing hanging from the oak tree growing through a hole in the deck. Cass sat down beside her.

Ben was spearing chunks of tender steak and chicken wings onto plates. Sam brought out a tray with some sliced vegetables and a dip, which he'd found in the refrigerator—his idea of a salad—and a warm loaf of garlic bread.

Sounds coming from the front of the house brought Nell out of her deck chair. Before she reached the deck doors, Bobby Palazola and Gracie Santos both appeared. Nell gave Gracie a hug, then turned to Bobby, a man she barely knew, and hugged him. "A difficult day," she murmured, then motioned them to sit, while Sam took drink orders.

"I'm so happy you are here," Birdie said, looking over at the weary pair. "It's another one of those nights when it's not good to be alone. Bobby, tell me how Bella is doing."

"She's trying to process it all," Bobby said. "But she's with Liz tonight, and they'll help each other through it. She had insisted we go directly to Nick's house on our way back from the airport. She had to see it, she said. And then—"

"And then she saved Elizabeth Hartley's life," Izzy said.

Bobby nodded. "Ironic, right? It's really hard. She loved that guy so much. He proposed to her right before she left for Switzerland."

"It was you and Bella that I saw from my deck that night," Izzy said, more to herself.

But Bobby heard her and tried to lighten the heaviness they

all felt. "The night you stole my special cap, Izzy? Yeah. And you still haven't given it back."

Izzy leaned over and gave him a slight punch. And then she smiled at him. Cass was right. Bobby Palazola was a likable guy, and one who must be greatly relieved of the shadow no longer hanging over him.

Bobby drained his beer and set it down. " She told me that night that Nick was going to give her a ring on Sunday. I guess Liz had told her ahead of time—Bella's never been one for surprises. Those guys are so close that even if Liz hadn't told her, she'd have read Liz's mind. But anyway, she wanted me to know. And she wanted me to know how much she loved him. She wanted me to be happy for her. At first I wasn't great. And then suddenly it hit me how awful that was. Bella and I were close. So I told her I loved her. That was the best I could do. She gave me a smooch. That's when she took off and swam out to his boat. It was just a little too much, kind of like the last straw that day.

" I wasn't sure if I'd lose her, you know? My cooking was a mess, Gracie's restaurant was losing business. My mom was getting worse. And then my sister announces she's going to marry Nick Cabot? I was a jerk. But Bella knew I'd come around. She still loves me. Even though I don't love myself a whole lot. I should have been happy for her. Those two have loved each other forever. They just misread the feeling."

Gracie was sitting beside Bobby on a chaise. She put a hand on his arm. "You'll be okay, Bobby. You're not always a jerk."

"Did Elizabeth Hartley know about Bella?" Sam asked.

"She said she found the ring," Birdie said.

"She must have suspected there was someone. Nick was a private person, but he never pretended to be something he wasn't," Nell said.

"A lot of us were puzzled by their relationship," Birdie said. "It clouded her thinking."

Ben frowned. "I didn't see that in her. She seemed like a savvy woman to me."

"I didn't see it at first, either," Nell said. "But there was something in the way she talked about Nick that didn't match how he talked about her. Nick was a helper. His friends all knew that. And he was kind. Too kind, maybe."

Izzy listened, and then said, "Elizabeth's emotions were complex, I think. There's a reason Nick was attentive."

"What do you mean?" Gracie asked.

"Laura Danvers told me some things about Elizabeth that Nick hadn't told anyone, out of respect for her. When she was forced to leave her job, the stress was so heavy that she had to go to a hospital in New Hampshire for treatment. Nick was on the school's board then, and he drove her to the hospital."

Izzy took a drink of water, then went on. "Laura also connected me to a friend who had worked with Elizabeth, and who shared additional information, because she thought it might help us to help her. A few days after Nick left her at the hospital, she tried to hurt herself."

The group grew silent.

"That poor woman," Gracie said.

"Apparently, it hadn't been the first time," Nell added. "Elizabeth was fragile, but she hid it well. She had a strange combination of demons in her, I think."

"Both Laura and Nick were surprised when she came back here," Izzy said.

"So that's why Nick was so solicitous," Sam said.

"Exactly," Izzy said. "It makes sense now. It was why he tried so hard to help her get settled, getting her involved in projects. Even getting her a job with Jane Brewster. He bent over backward to be sure she had a purpose here. A role to play."

"But she misinterpreted that for love," Gracie said. "That's terribly sad."

"Even Nick's office staff was aware of the platonic kind of friendship it was," Birdie said. "They knew Nick had a lot of friends like that. The staff had analyzed them all, apparently. They are a young vibrant group of women, and yet know far more about relationships than Elizabeth Hartley did."

"So, how did it happen that she went to Nick's that Sunday night?" Ben asked. "You were with her that day. Was that planned?"

"She mentioned at the brunch that she was going for a walk," Nell said. "But she didn't say much else."

Birdie remembered that, too. "She was distracted that day, a little out of sorts. Thinking back, I wonder now what she was thinking about while we were celebrating Jane Brewster's birthday."

It was a sobering thought.

"The timing fits with what Elena told us," Cass said. "Elizabeth could have gone to the park to watch Nick's house. To know when Bella left? But when Elena joined her in the park, it delayed her going over to Nick's."

"Elena said they sat on the bench together for a while," Izzy said. "Elizabeth must have had the gun with her while she was sitting there with Elena and James." Her voice lowered as she imagined the scene.

"Then later, Marco showed up," Cass said. "He told Elena they needed to talk in private, and Elena agreed to go back to their house with him and talk."

"That's why Elena said that if Marco hadn't come along, she and her friend—who happened to be Elizabeth—might have seen something happening and been able to save Nick."

"Talk about irony," Sam said.

"Here's another irony," Cass said. "What Marco had done that night, though unintentionally, was provide an alibi for himself. He couldn't have killed Nick. He'd fallen asleep on Elena's couch, Elena said. She woke him up when the sirens filled the air, which they think was probably a couple hours after Nick was killed."

Nell sat back and took a deep breath, releasing it slowly as she looked around the deck at people she loved. Ben was back at the grill, filling and refilling plates with his grilled chicken and tender beef. Wine was refreshed and cookies brought out.

The peace they'd been yearning for hovered over them. Not quite touching them yet.

That would take time. And thought. And tears.

And dear friends.

Chapter 43

It had taken a couple weeks, but finally the decision was made to move the art auction outside. And it wouldn't dare rain on a day designed to honor an old friend, a day to bring people together and benefit a worthy organization.

Elena Costa had come up with the brilliant idea. And also organized much of it, calling on her park-walking moms to pitch in and help. Elena had found a new calling for herself and she was loving it, discovering skills she didn't know she had. Everything was Nick's doing, she proudly told anyone who complimented her on her new leadership role.

Nick's Fishermen Park was a great choice. Fresh air, a blue sky, and Pete's Fractured Fish up on a stage pulling people together.

It was perfect.

Small auction items—such as Annabelle Palazola's clay petunias; plenty of decorated T-shirts and caps; vases; small, framed watercolors and the like—filled tables beneath a gigantic tent with open sides and bidding cards attached to each item. Live auction items—afghans, hand-hooked rugs, hanging fiber art, paintings, and sculptures—were displayed on easels and special stands that Alex Arcado and his crew of firemen had constructed around the stage.

Crowds filled the park for the second time in a month, recognizing a noble man who would be missed for a very long time.

Cass and Gracie stood near the edge of the tent, watching the happy auction crowd jotting figures and names on white cards.

"So, Gracie, now that the restaurant's back on track, how're you going to handle all this?"

"What's 'all this'?"

"You know. Bobby. His feelings."

Gracie chuckled, then looked out at the festivities. "Oh, we've figured it all out," she said airily.

Cass waited while Lucky Bianchi's deep voice echoed through the park, announcing the bidding on another live auction item to oohs and aahs and cheering.

"Don't be coy. Tell me," Cass said when they could hear again.

"A therapist," Gracie said.

"*What?*" Cass laughed. Then she stopped chuckling, realizing Gracie was serious, at least to a degree.

"It was Bobby's idea. And it's brilliant. She's been a terrific help. I even went with him."

"But, Gracie, you're not a couple. You know that, right? Why would you go to therapy with him?"

"Okay, here's the thing. Bobby's my dear friend." She gave Cass a stare, daring her to say something.

"Seriously, Gracie—don't play games with him. Or me."

"You know me better, Cass. I don't know if we will be dear friends forever or if it will someday be something more. It happens. Look at Bella and Nick. But here's what's going on. I love being in business with Bobby. So the therapist is helping us figure out how to make that relationship as healthy and effective as it can be. And still be good friends. Or whatever."

"Oh?" Cass said, her brows lifting.

"Shush, Cass. Let life happen. Anyway, what Bobby is working on with her are his emotions. How they are sometimes misplaced. Even the troublesome relationship he had with Nick. And his anger. He says his sessions are very helpful on all fronts. He told me last night that maybe it wasn't me he was in love with, anyway. Instead it could be my kitchen. My restaurant. My customers, and my friends."

"In that order?"

She grinned. "Oh, he also added Squid and Gabby to that list, now that Nick's sister has decided that Squid needs to stay with Birdie and Gabby. He's determined to get the dog to like him. Nancy said it wasn't fair to the poor dog to cart him across the ocean. And she could see how happy Squid was with them.

"Gabby's in heaven," Cass said. "But I think Birdie is just as happy. She loves Squid, and it will be even more incentive for Gabby to make frequent trips back to Sea Harbor."

Cass laughed and wrapped an arm around Gracie. Squid staying with Birdie and Gabby was wonderful news to all of them.

They wandered over to a crowd of their friends standing near the auction activities. Ben, Sam, and Danny were up on the stage, helping the auctioneer.

Bobby was there, with Bella and Liz and Nancy Cabot. They were standing in front of the stage, near Nell and Izzy, all of them looking up at a completed herringbone afghan, with streams of sunlight highlighting the colors of the sea crisscrossing across the pattern. A soft breeze made it look alive.

And even more alive was Mayor Beatrice Scaglia, standing right below the edge of the stage, her white auction number waving wildly in the air. It was an auction item that she would *win*, she'd made them all aware of beforehand. A beautiful work of art, she said happily, that she would donate to the children's hospital in Nick Cabot's name.

Once Beatrice had successfully silenced her competitors and hurried off to complete her purchase, the auctioneer brought a new painting to the easel.

It was a large painting, needing a loving home.

Framed simply, Nick Cabot and his dog, Squid, in all his shaggy glory, looked down from the framed painting at the crowd looking up at them.

And at the signatures at the bottom of the painting: *Gabby Marietti and Daisy Danvers.*

Also looking at the painting was a small gray-haired woman, with a lovely smile on her face. Birdie was barely as tall as the stage, but the auctioneer was well aware of her presence as she waved her card with each successive bid on the painting—again and again and again.

Until finally the crowd broke into applause.

She turned and hugged Nick's sister and her three children standing beside her. After a long trip across the ocean, the painting would soon find itself on a white wall in a small family home in Porto, Portugal.

Where it would be much loved.

Acknowledgments

The village that helped me bring *The Herringbone Harbor Mystery* to life is a large and kind and generous one. I am grateful and indebted beyond thanks to each of them.

To my most incredible agents, Christina Hogrebe and Andrea Cirillo, whose patience and understanding and caring make this whole writing journey possible, and to the entire JRA family, who have been with me for longer than I can remember.

To my editor, Wendy McCurdy, and the newest member of the team, Sarah Selim, whose thoughtful comments on *The Herringbone Harbor Mystery* have given it a finishing touch. Also, my thanks to Stephanie Finnegan, whose copyediting and suggestions were thoughtful and very helpful. And to the entire Kensington family, an amazing group of professionals who nurture the Seaside Knitters mysteries from copyediting and marketing to publication, and, on the way, make them shine. And to Mary Ann Lasher for her beautiful jacket illustration, and who captured Squid beautifully!

To my dear Fairway and Prairie Village forever friends, whose encouragement and understanding never fail to make me feel like the luckiest person alive, most especially during these past many months when writing would have been impossible without your friendship and support (and food and notes and calls and visits). I can't begin to list your multiple thoughtful and loving gestures. And I dearly miss each of you and our face-to-face group dinners.

To my longtime friend, Adrienne Staff, for being with me

from the start. And for planning our reenergizing Boston get-aways during the writing of this book, making many and all things possible.

A special thank-you to Kenya Stanford, who created the wonderful herringbone afghan pattern for the seaside knitters.

To Kristen Fredrickson, who once again supplied the seaside knitters with a delicious recipe to enhance their Thursday-night knitting time. And also for her continued friendship and support coming to me from across the pond.

To Mary Alice Partee, my safe harbor along this journey in many ways.

To Nancy Pickard, who once again came, then stayed, and helped me conquer and find my way back into the writing of this book.

To Mary Bednarowski, whose comforting photo of moon-light on water also made its way into comforting a seaside knit-ter in this book. And to Sister Rosemary Flanigan, who not only RE-reads the Seaside Knitters mysteries, but who also reads them aloud to others. You are my inspiration in so many ways—and always my friend.

To Memory Lane, for her expert way of keeping me close to my readers.

To the world's best siblings, Jane, Bob, and Mary Sue. I love you three so very much.

To my wonderful readers everywhere, who always seem to send the perfect, encouraging note at just the right time. I am so grateful for each one of you.

And my forever love and thanks and so much more to my amazing family—Aria and John, Todd, Danny and Claudia, and six incredible grandchildren—without whose support, encour-agement, and love this book most definitely would not exist.

Finally, to Don Goldenbaum, my husband, who encouraged me to be a writer, and who inspired every single Seaside Knitters mystery, but, most especially, this one, which he brainstormed with me and was adamant I write, no matter what. Don died in the middle of the book's writing, leaving our lives diminished and hearts heavy, but with his spirit ever present as he watches us from somewhere up there, hopefully with a viola or a guitar in one hand and a glass of wine in the other.

THE HERRINGBONE SCARF AND BLANKET KNITTING PATTERN

The Herringbone Harbor Scarf & Blanket pattern was designed by Kenya Stanford for, and featured in, *The Herringbone Harbor Mystery.*

The scarf is knit in the round, so is double thick. In the mystery, the knitters are creating an afghan, so additional instructions are given to seam multiple scarves together to create a teamwork throw or blanket. Happy knitting!

Sizes: One Size
   Scarf: 8 in/20 cm width, 50 in/127 cm length
   Blanket: 50 in/127 cm width, 64 in/163 cm length

Suggested Yarn
   The sample was knit using Kenya's Knits Marshmallow DK Select in the colorways Rambi (A) and Everstorm (B). This base is 100% Superwash Wool 21.5 MIC.

Yardage
   Color A: 413 yds/378 m
   Color B: 413 yds/378 m

Gauge
   24 sts x 24 rounds = 4 x 4 in/10 x10 cm pattern, worked in the round and blocked.

Suggested Needles
   US 6/4.0 mm circular needles with a 14 in/36 cm or smaller cable for working in the round, a longer cable if working in magic loop, or DPNs or needles needed to obtain gauge.

Materials
    Stitch markers and tapestry needle

Techniques
    How to knit, knit in the round, work stranded colorwork, cast on, graft, and mattress stitch

Abbreviations
    BOR: Beginning of round
    CO: Cast on
    DPNs: Double pointed needles
    K: Knit
    st/sts: Stitch/stitches

Section 1: Scarf
    In color A, CO 100 sts using Turkish cast on or your preferred seamless cast on method.
    Place a marker to mark the BOR.
    Begin working the Herringbone Repeat Rounds 1–6 written directions or chart, making sure not to carry your floats too tightly on the inside of the work.

    When working Round 1 of the Herringbone Repeat for the first time, you may find it helpful to place markers after each 10 stitch repeat.

Herringbone Repeat
    Round 1: (K3 with A, k2 with B, k2 with A, k3 with B) to end
    Round 2: (K1 with B, k3 with A, k1 with B, k1 with A, k3 with B, k1 with A) to end
    Round 3: (K2 with B, k3 with A, k3 with B, k2 with A) to end

Round 4: (K3 with B, k2 with A, k2 with B, k3 with A) to end

Round 5: (K1 with A, k3 with B, k1 with A, k1 with B, k3 with A, k1 with B) to end

Round 6: (K2 with A, k3 with B, k3 with A, k2 with B) to end

Herringbone Repeat Chart
  Knit in Color A
  Knit in Color B

Continue working the Herringbone Repeat until your scarf measures 50 in/127 cm or your desired length. Cut Color B. Then knit two rounds with Color A to match the cast on beginning.

Weave in any ends you have and graft sts using kitchener stitch or your preferred grafting method. When finished, poke the final end through to the inside of the scarf and skim it through a few sts, leaving the tail on the inside of the work.

Section 2: Blanket
  *Note on choosing colors: As this blanket is made using several scarves, you can go all out with color, you can choose all the same colors, or you can have a bit of both. I would suggest using the same color A throughout and different color B yarns in each scarf for a blended, cohesive, and individual look.

To ensure that your scarves are all the same length, place them side by side, matching the start of the herringbone pattern on one scarf with the end of the pattern on the next scarf. Seam your scarves together using Mattress Stitch, or your preferred seaming method, using Color A.

To get the length listed in the size section of this pattern, you will need to seam eight scarves together, but you can customize this to your desired length.

Finishing

Weave in ends, block, and enjoy!

Share your projects on Instagram with #herringboneharbor scarf

#herringboneharborblanket and #kenyasknits

For a photograph of the completed Herringbone Pattern Scarf, please visit: https://www.ravelry.com/patterns/library/herringbone-harbor-scarf—blanket

Please visit Kenya at: kenyasknits.com

CREAMY BROCCOLI WITH PASTA

By Kristen Frederickson, author of *Tonight at 7.30: One Family's Life at the Table* and *second helpings: more tonight at 7.30*

Kristen Frederickson graciously gave this delicious recipe to Nell to make and take to knitting night in *The Herringbone Harbor Mystery.*

(Serves 6)

1 lb/400 g short pasta (farfalle, orecchiette, conchiglie, penne, or even macaroni)
1 tbsp butter
1 tbsp olive oil
5 cloves garlic, finely chopped
1 white onion, finely chopped
1 tbsp Italian seasoning
1 tsp sea salt
1 tsp fresh black pepper
1 tsp chili flakes (optional)
1 cup/250 g Boursin or goat cheese
6 tbsp/168 g pine nuts or cashews
1 15-ounce/400 g can whole plum tomatoes
1 lb/400 g broccoli, cut into florets and stems
½ cup/50 g grated Parmesan
1 fresh mozzarella, shredded by hand

Put water on to boil, then cook the pasta according to package instructions. When ready, drain and set aside.

Heat butter and olive oil in a large frying pan, then cook the garlic and onion gently until softened. Add Italian seasoning, salt, pepper, and chili flakes, if using, and mix well. Take off the heat. In a blender or food processor, mix the Boursin or goat cheese, the nuts, and the tomatoes. Blend until completely smooth, then pour mixture into the frying pan. Heat until bubbling gently.

Meanwhile, boil or steam the broccoli until tender. Add the broccoli to the sauce, mix well, and then turn the mixture into a baking dish. Cover with Parmesan and mozzarella, and bake at 350°F/180°C for 25 minutes.

Bon Appetit!